D0003834

BRIMSTONE KISS

"Filled with kisses and kick-ass action. . . . Douglas's dishy style complements the twisty plot."

—*Publishers Weekly* (starred review)

"All of the dark, dangerous, and unique paranormal elements readers seek, along with the passion, love and exciting temptations that add spice to the mix."

—Darque Reviews

"A wonderful second Street urban fantasy . . . *Brimstone Kiss* is a magical mystery fantasy tour."

—Alternative Worlds

"Douglas has populated her Post-Millennium Las Vegas with the most outrageous and outlandish cast of supporting characters this side of *The Wizard of Oz.* . . ."

—SciFiGuy

"A brilliant follow-up to Ms. Douglas's first novel."

—Romance Junkies

"The world and the characters are rich and easy to believe in. . . . The plot thickens and the tension builds and you find yourself carried along for the ride. . . . Douglas has a way of drawing you in and keeping you entertained."

—SFRevu

"Another fabulous job of drawing the reader into the story, making them feel as if they are a part of it."

—Bitten By Books

DANCING WITH WEREWOLVES

"A wonderfully written story with a unique take on the paranormal."

—*New York Times* bestselling author Kelley Armstrong

Don't miss any of Delilah Street's adventures!

Dancing with Werewolves
Brimstone Kiss
Vampire Sunrise

Available now from Pocket Books/Juno Books

CAROLE NELSON DOUGLAS

SILVER ZOMBIE

DELILAH STREET:
PARANORMAL INVESTIGATOR

POCKET BOOKS

New York   London   Toronto   Sydney

Pocket Books
A Division of Simon & Schuster, Inc.
1230 Avenue of the Americas
New York, NY 10020

This book is a work of fiction. Names, characters, places, and incidents either are products of the author's imagination or are used fictitiously. Any resemblance to actual events or locales or persons, living or dead, is entirely coincidental.

First Juno Books/Pocket Books paperback edition December 2010

JUNO BOOKS and colophon are trademarks of Wildside Press LLC used under license by Simon & Schuster, Inc., the publisher of this work.

POCKET and colophon are registered trademarks of Simon & Schuster, Inc.

For information about special discounts for bulk purchases, please contact Simon & Schuster Special Sales at 1-866-506-1949 or business@simonandschuster.com.

The Simon & Schuster Speakers Bureau can bring authors to your live event. For more information or to book an event, contact the Simon & Schuster Speakers Bureau at 1-866-248-3049 or visit our website at www.simonspeakers.com.

Cover design by Lisa Litwack, art by Gordon Crabb

Manufactured in the United States of America

10   9   8   7   6   5   4   3   2   1

ISBN 978-1-4391-6781-6
ISBN 978-1-4391-6783-0 (ebook)

For Racie Rhyne,
my super-supportive, artistic sister-in-law
and Delilah's best friend

Meet Me, Delilah Street

EVERYONE HAS FAMILY issues, but my issues are that I don't *have* any family. My new business card reads *Delilah Street, Paranormal Investigator,* but my old personal card could have read *Delilah Street, Unadoptable Orphan.*

I was supposedly named after the street where I was found abandoned as an infant in Wichita, Kansas. (I guess I should just thank God and DC Comics it wasn't Lois Lane.) I've googled and groggled (the drinking person's search engine) the World Wide Web for Delilah Streets and not a single bloody one of them shows up in Kansas.

Whoever my forebears were, they gave me the Black Irish, Snow White coloring that is catnip to vampires: corpse-pale skin and dead-of-night-black hair. By age twelve I was fighting off aspiring juvie rapists with retractable fangs and body odor that mixed blood, sweat, and semen. Really made me enjoy being a girl.

My growing-up years of group homes in Wichita are history now that I'm twenty-four and on my own. I had a good job reporting the paranormal beat for WTCH-TV in Kansas—until the station's jealous weather witch forecaster forced me out.

Now I'm a freelance investigator in wicked, mysterious post–Millennium Revelation Las Vegas. Vegas was wicked, of course, long before the turn of the twenty-first century brought all the bogeymen and women of myth and legends out of the closet and into human lives and society. Now, in 2013, Vegas is crawling with vamps and half-weres and all-werewolf mobs and celebrity zombies and who-knows-what-else.

My ambitions are simple.

One, staying alive. (Being turned into an immortal vampire doesn't count.)

Two, being able to make love on my back without having panic attacks. (Whoever thought someone would *aim* for the missionary position?) Position hadn't been an issue until recently and neither had sex, until I finally found a man I *want* to make love with, ex-FBI guy Ricardo Montoya—aka the Cadaver Kid. He's tall, dark, handsome, Hispanic, and my brand-new horizontal ambition. He has my back—and my front—at every opportunity.

And, three, tracking down Lilith Quince—my spitting image—to find out if she is a twin, double, clone, or simulacrum. Or if she is even still alive. It's rumored some *CSI V* bodies are real . . . corpses. Seeing her/me being autopsied on *Crime Scene Instincts V: Las Vegas* one rerun-TV night in Wichita brought me to Sin City in the first place.

Lucky me, Lilith became the most desirable corpse ever featured on the internationally franchised show. Millennium Revelation pop culture and taste tend toward the dark—now I know *how* dark. When Hector's *CSI* show made Lilith Quince into a macabre worldwide sex symbol, he inadvertently made me, Delilah Street, a wanted woman. Not for myself alone, mind you, but for the naked and dead image of another woman.

The *CSI* cameras showed a discreet maggot camping out in a nostril that held a tiny blue topaz stud like my very own, so Lilith in filmed corpse form was dubbed Maggie and became the It Girl of 2013: Maggie dolls and merchandise are hot and so are bootleg Maggie films, outtakes, and my hide, if anyone could snag it—dead or alive. One werewolf mobster almost did already.

At least ambition number four is now a done deal: Identifying the embracing skeletons Ric and I discovered in Vegas's Sunset Park just after I hit town and just before the town hit me back, hard.

I discovered more than Ric and corpses in Sunset Park. I found an ally who has heavenly blue eyes and is seriously gray and hairy. That's my dog, Quicksilver. He's a wolfhound-wolf cross I saved from death at the pound. He returns the favor with fang, claw, and warm, paranormally talented tongue.

(I have a soft spot for dogs—especially since Achilles, my valiant little Lhasa apso in Wichita, died from blood poisoning after biting a vampire who was trying to bite me. Achilles' ashes rest in a dragon-decorated jar on my mantel, but I haven't given up the ghost on him.)

Oh, the location of that mantel might be of interest. It's in the Enchanted Cottage on the Hector Nightwine estate. Hector rents the place to me cheap because, as the *CSI* franchise producer, he's presumably guilty of offing my possible twin on national TV. Hector doesn't really have a conscience, just a profit motive. He's banking on my finding Lilith or becoming her for his enduring financial benefit.

The only thing Hector and I share is a love of old black-and-white films. The Enchanted Cottage duplicates a setting from a 1945 movie. A shy-to-the-point-of-invisible staff of who-knows-what supernaturals run the place, and I suspect it's supplied with the wicked stepmother's mirror from *Snow White*. Although it's been mum with me so far, I do see dead people in it.

The most complicated beings in my brave new world are the CinSims. Cinema Simulacrums are created by blending fresh zombie bodies illegally imported from Mexico with classic black-and-white film characters. The resulting "live" personas are wholly owned entertainment entities leased to various Vegas enterprises.

Hector and Ric blame the Immortality Mob for the brisk business in zombie CinSims, but can't prove it. Hector wants to wrest the CinSims from the mob's control into his. Ric aches to stop the traffic in illegally imported zombies. It's personal—he was forced to work in the trade as a child.

I'd like to help them both out, and not just because I'm a former investigative reporter crusading against human and unhuman exploitation. My own freedom is threatened by various merciless and sometimes downright repellent factions bent on making life after the Millennium Revelation literal Hell.

Luckily, I have some new, off-the-chart abilities simmering myself, most involving silver—from the silver nitrate in black-and-white films to sterling silver to mirrors and reflective surfaces in general.

Which reminds me of one more sorta sidekick: a freaky shape-changing lock of hair from the albino rock star who owns the Inferno Hotel. The guy goes by three names: Christophe for business; Cocaine, when fronting his Seven Deadly Sins rock band, and Snow to his intimates. He seems to consider me one of them, but no way do I want to be.

While thinking of my lost Achilles, I made the mistake of touching one long white lock of Snow's hair he'd sent me as a mocking gift. The damn thing became a sterling silver familiar no jeweler's saw or torch can remove from my body. Since it transforms into different pieces of often-protective jewelry, it's handy at times. I consider it a variety of talisman-cum-leech.

That attitude sums up my issues with the rock star–hotelier, who enslaves groupies with a onetime mosh-pit "Brimstone Kiss."

Then I discovered *why* those post-concert kisses are so bloody irresistible . . . and Snow forced me to submit to his soul-stealing smooch in exchange for his help in saving Ric from being vamped to death. This kiss-off standoff between us is *not* over.

I've been called a "silver medium," but I don't aim to be medium at anything. I won't do things halfway. I intend to expose every dirty supernatural secret in Las Vegas, if necessary, to find out who I really am, and who's being bad and who's being good in my new Millennium Revelation neighborhood.

Chapter One

A COYOTE YIPPED in the desert night surrounding Las Vegas.

Its sharp introductory barks escalated into a full, soulful howl at the moon.

I straightened from my feral crouch to listen.

Then I smiled.

That lonesome coyote might be the only natural critter within hearing tonight.

Even the glowing yellow moon, half full, looked pretty unnatural. Its blade-straight inner edge reminded me of a giant casino chip split down the middle.

I wasn't used to working under moonglow. Usually Sin City's gigantic bouquet of neon lights backlit my night-crawling expeditions.

Tonight, though, my beat was a raw desert landscape of distant mountains that made the flat valley floor into a huge, empty, open maw surrounded by massive saw teeth. I stood at its center, the moonlight reflecting from the steel studs embedding the arms, legs, and torso of my form-adapting black catsuit.

"Bite me," I whispered at the jaundiced half-werewolf moon, "and you'll get a jawful of broken fangs."

Something came barreling out of the darkness right for me, as if answering my invitation. Fast and furred, the yellow-beige flowing blur grew ears, hackles, and hulking shoulders as it neared—like a panting locomotive with a boar's-head cowcatcher.

I turned sideways as it charged by, kicking up sand chest-high. Then it wheeled and leaped for my throat.

"Quick," I shouted, using the word as a name, not a command. A huge pink tongue swiped my jaw and slimed my costly, FBI-approved night vision goggles. Only borrowed, alas.

I couldn't wipe the wet lenses clean on my steel-studded outfit. Scuff City. So I swept off the goggles and shook my head at the grinning wolfish face now at standing height. My waist.

"Quicksilver, you're supposed to find *prey,* not me," I told him.

I fished in the secondhand cop utility belt swagging my hips for a microfiber cloth, then glanced around. All around. The new bone-reading night vision lenses had tinted everything a Beatles-submarine yellow. I pushed them, cleaned, atop my head like sunglasses.

It was pleasant to see the true moonshine-silvered landscape, cool and serene. Silver is my talisman, including this silver-gray dog who's half wolfhound, half wolf, and all partner. Quicksilver is more lupine than K-9, and just what a girl needs for a bodyguard and buddy after the Millennium Revelation.

Hmm. A hummock of Joshua tree–tall cactus was edging into sharper focus. I snapped the lens strap back around my head and the lenses down over my eyes. Several hummocks of cacti were shuffling toward me. Quicksilver had accomplished his Australian sheep dog act, after all.

I drew the police baton at my hip. The idea was to serve and protect, not to hurt.

And not to *be* hurt.

The closer they came, the bigger they got. Human figures, three of them. These were professionally big guys, the kind who walk with beefed-up arms out from their sides at acute angles, with thigh-heavy legs pushing their feet apart so they make a waddle into a threat.

Muscle, in the classic PI term.

And you just a slip of a girl, Irma commented sardonically.

Shut up, I told my inboard invisible friend since orphanage days. I'm on the tall and solid side. Quick and I can handle these Three Stooges.

Sadly, that's about all they were. As much as twentieth-century zombie movies celebrated a dogged will to ambulate, the New Millennium's feral zombies share the same lack of social graces, not to mention coordination.

Quicksilver immediately trotted to circle behind them and nip at their shambling heels or backsides if necessary.

The three were still shod and wore "rent"ed suits . . . not the hired kind, but the tattered variety rent apart by werewolf fangs and claws. Their dim memories of being torn to death by Cesar Cicereau's werewolf mob didn't make them want to gnaw brains yet, but somewhere deep down they must still be plenty pissed.

Nor were they visibly rotting on the hoof. In fact, their pre-chewed condition put them in more danger from predators than the other way around. Those mortal wounds had never healed, but remained blood-crusted scars of their last stand some twenty to seventy years ago. Werewolf chieftain Cicereau had been offing competition since Vegas began in the 1940s. The Millennium Revelation had unfolded a lot of mysteries along with all the variations of supernatural underworld creatures it had coughed up.

Still, three guys heading for a lone woman was never a safe situation, even if she had a hundred-and-fifty-pound dog in attendance.

"Okay, fellas," I told them, brandishing my club, "welcome to Rancho Second Chance-o."

That stopped them dead in their tracks.

Or perhaps what had stopped them was sighting the low bunkhouse and corral behind me, where a horse lifted its head to nicker. Home, sweet, home on the range. Don't ask me why, but horses have a soothing effect on feral zombies.

I stepped aside to let the trio stumble into the ranch's safety zone surrounded by silver barbed wire fencing. That's when a pack of shadows rushed me from the surrounding sagebrush, from every last bush.

A coyote pack!

No time to play zombie tourists.

My night stick prodded all three Zobo butts hard to keep them moving, and I raised my right arm just as the lead coyote leaped for my throat. With my leather-gloved palms at both ends, I managed to wedge the police baton between its fangs, then twist my upper body. That threw the alpha male off to the side in time for me to knee the next coyote in the leaping chest, so it fell back.

Quicksilver, snarling and snapping up a storm, was harrying ears and tails and flanks to drive back the middle of the pack of five. Coyotes don't weigh much, maybe thirty pounds, and neither Quick nor I wanted to kill them. These were just desert dogs, doing what comes naturally. It's actually harder to fight off opponents you only want to discourage.

From the grunting sounds behind me, the zombies had

roused to kick away coyotes trying to slip through the barbed wire isolating the corral, protecting the nervous horses that had bunched and whinnied.

Quick raced over to add the discouragement of his big bad wolf teeth, while I shouted and flailed with my baton, trying not to break any animal's delicate leg.

Between the kick-dancing zombies, Quicksilver's slashing speed and teeth, and my shouts and hard knocks, the coyote pack was retreating, snarling, with ears down.

The oncoming dirt-bike roar of a Ranger RZR utility vehicle spitting up twin funnels of sand and snapped-off brush finished the job. The coyotes vanished into the moonlight-dappled sand as if made of it.

The ATV ground its noisy way to the enclave's open gate. I followed, dusting off my supple yet rhino-hide-tough Inferno Hotel catsuit. The driver doffed his helmet and goggles. My Vegas-based, designer suit–wearing ex-FBI guy was looking provocatively off-*Road and Track*.

Oooh, chica, Irma purred in my mind. *Our Ricardo is flaunting his* muy macho *mode. My motor is revving.*

Yup, my uninvited alter ego is the Queen of Shallow.

"Coyotes?" Ric greeted me. "Are they okay?"

Quicksilver circled the Ranger to sniff its huge tire footprint, hackles raised.

"A bit bruised and cut," I said. "We pick a time werewolves aren't out and then run into their innocent little brothers on a tear."

"They must be hungry to pack in fives," he said. "Coyotes generally stick to mated sets or run in threes."

"Like zombies?" I asked, nodding at the stolid waiting trio.

"Just more stragglers from that lot I resurrected at Cicereau's Starlight Lodge."

"What are you going to do with them?"

"Keep them out of the zombie trade, at least. You bring something back from the dead, in whatever state, you're kinda responsible for it."

His words left me speechless. My tough FBI guy didn't know it, but I may have done exactly that with him.

"I really understand," I said in a serious tone that slipped past him. His mind was still on the wandering zombies.

"The rest have scattered pretty far," he said, "but I won't need you and Quicksilver for roundups after this. Didn't know if Cayuse here"—he slapped the Ranger's sand-blasted engine cover—"would work to round up stray Zobos. It sure does. They shy like horses at unnatural sounds."

"Jeez, Ric. A man and his wheels. You've *named* that mobile mechanical monster of overbearing tires and sheer ruckus?"

"You've got Dolly."

He nodded at the barely visible black bulk of my '56 Caddy convertible. Her full name was Dolly Parton, and she had the awesome chrome "bumper bullets" to prove it. She was parked on the dirt road that was way too far from the highway asphalt for my taste and her black-satin finish.

"Come inside." Ric dismounted easily in his spandex race driver jumpsuit. "I'll show you the setup. We need to get these Zobos tucked away for the night and the next few weeks. Now that they've got horses to tend and guard—and are safe behind silver wire—they're ready for rehab."

"Rehabilitation for what? Basket weaving?"

"I don't know yet. I just can't leave any known dead wandering around to be meat for the Immortality Mob."

I followed him inside the rambling barbed wire, shaking my head and muttering "Cayuse?"

Quicksilver couldn't trot away from the parked Ranger fast enough. We were two of a kind, urban creatures, especially when that citified outpost was Las Vegas, the capital city of all things spectacular and supernatural in 2013.

Inside the fence I saw the usual barn, horse corral, and bunkhouse.

The three rag-suited Zobos were being tended by four of their ilk, this set wearing Lee jeans, work boots, and plaid cotton shirts with pearlized buttons.

Quicksilver whined behind me, whether from confusion or outraged fashion sense, I couldn't tell.

The brown leathery look of the Zobos' visible skin evoked human cowhands who worked outdoors in the desert. Ric could even open a dude ranch with these guys. The Lazy Z.

"This place looks like the *Louisiana Hayride* TV show set," I commented. "What do feral zombies eat? I suppose these guys haven't worked their way up to brains."

"That's a bad rap. They eat nothing . . . yet. Right now they just feed and water the horses. These are the sleep-walking dead. Since drops of my blood animated them, they have to obey me. I don't know if the Immortality Mob exists, but I do know *somebody*'s learned to exploit zombies."

"We need a word out of earshot, Montoya," I told him. How sharp were Zobo senses, or brains, anyway?

We moved to lean against the crossbars of the corral fence, watching the half-moon reflected in the darks of large equine eyes. As a coyote howled in the distance, the horses did an uneasy soft-shoe over the desert floor.

"Other than your obsession to leave no zombie wandering unclaimed," I told Ric, "what's the point of collecting the ones you raised at the werewolf mob's Starlight Lodge? They were all likely other gangsters who got in Cesar Cicereau's hair."

"To *find* dead bodies, I simply have to dowse for them with a forked piece of wood or wire, like dowsers do for water. To *raise* them, drops of my blood have to 'baptize' the dowsing rod. In a sense, those zombies are my blood brothers now."

"Despite being hoodlums and criminals in life?"

"The werewolf mob also ran down and killed a lot of unlucky innocent bystanders over the decades. Even you were on their menu just a couple months ago."

"True. I guess whoever the Zobos were, they're blank slates now."

"Right," Ric said. "And anybody can round them up . . . to use and abuse them."

"Especially the mysterious Immortality Mob you and Hector Nightwine obsess over."

"People talk about the Immortality Mob, but nobody knows what or who they really are. That's worth an obsessive interest."

"Somebody has to handle leasing the CinSims to the Vegas attractions."

"Human lawyers," Ric said. "And technicians go public to service the CinSims' location chips if any wander off their prescribed territory, but they're mere hirees. Whoever masterminded the process of overlaying the Hollywood personas on zombie bodies remains a mystery. No one knows if it's weird science, or magic, or the intervention of some as-yet-unknown paranormal entity."

"Brrr," I said, as the night wind riffled the horses' manes and chilled my spine. "I doubt Vegas or me can

stand any more 'unknown paranormal entities.' The Kar-nak Hotel's ancient vampire empire is evil enough under the ground. Don't you have a way to de-raise these Zobos?"

"Doesn't work like that, Delilah." Ric watched a palo-mino colt side-dance toward us. "There's no easy way to kill a zombie. The reanimated dead can't die again. That's what is so evil about raising them in the first place."

"Then why were you born with that gift?"

"Because it's a curse? Every paranormal 'gift' is a power waiting to be corrupted."

"My mirror-walking too?"

"Look what it's brought you. You're afraid to use mir-rors now that you've imprisoned Cicereau's ghostly daugh-ter in that mirror-world."

"Point taken."

Mirror-world seemed to work like a fey origami box. It could stretch in all directions or take a quirky left turn and have you suddenly facing your worst enemy. I wasn't going there again—unless forced—until I figured out its rules and regulations.

"Where did the bodies you raised years ago end up," I asked Ric, "with the Immortality Mob?"

"There wasn't one yet. They went where the live ille-gal aliens went. They were smuggled across the border as cheap labor on ranches and in factories. CinSims came later."

"Why raise only Mexicans for CinSims?"

"Maybe because border crossings are myriad, and expected. My native country is full of people yearning for a better life in the U.S."

"*Los desperados y los desaparecidos,*" I said in his native Spanish. "The outlaws and the disappeared."

I'd been studying my English-Spanish dictionary since

meeting Ric, particularly the slanguage edition for any naughty words he might use in the heat of lovemaking. Of course, Spanish is a Romance language. Its musical lilt to an Anglo ear can make even a whispered obscenity sound sweet, not that I'd caught Ric using anything but impassioned prose on the flattering level of, oh, the Song of Solomon, say.

His Latin blood made him *muy* expressive. A night with him was a better self-esteem enhancer for a girl than winning the Miss Universe contest.

Um-mm, Irma seconded me. Although I'd always locked her down during the main event, she still had a front-row seat for the warm-up rounds, like now.

"Excellent pronunciation, *paloma*." Ric nuzzled my cheek as the palomino whinnied approval. His lips whispered against mine between a string of soft kisses interspersed with nips. "You know your mouth drives me *loco* when it speaks my native tongue."

That one sentence had taken a full minute to articulate between the lip-lock action, and it drove any sense of night chill from my bones. Ric's mouth pulled back to let me speak against the caressing pad of his thumb, which only prolonged the dizzy desire.

I was melted Velveeta cheese in deep need of a . . . breadstick. Men love to prove they can drive every thought out of even the most coolheaded woman. They had a point.

Get a room, Irma moaned in my vacant mind. *Please!*

"Amor," I whispered to Ric over her mental whimpering, "a Zobo roundup isn't my idea of a rendezvous. Have mercy and tell me more about the current social and political situation in your native land."

He laughed, easing off the romantic pressure to answer my grad school question. "You're a hard woman to shake off an inquiry. I hesitate because I don't enjoy acknowledging the brutal state of lawlessness in the land that birthed me."

"You care, even though you were enslaved there as a child?"

"Especially because of that. Think. Mexican soil near the U.S. border is a no-man's-land thick with unclaimed corpses. Thousands perished trying to cross the border and were left in shallow graves. Others were undiscovered victims of the drug cartel wars or, like the hundreds of murdered women in Juarez, the white slave trade. The dry desert landscape preserves corpses. Look at the Egyptian mummies."

"No more mummies for quite a while, please," I said with a shudder. The dry desert landscape also cooled off plenty at night.

Ric absently put an arm around my shoulders to warm me. "The desirable CinSim zombies only come from the Mojave and Sonora deserts that reach into California, Nevada, Arizona, and New Mexico, not the Chihuahuan that straddles the Tex-Mex border. Something in the Mojave and Sonora sand is a prime natural preservative. Perhaps that's why the Egyptian vampires immigrated here via their underground River Nile centuries ago. You got a good look at these latest guys from Cicereau's Murder Inc. lodge?"

"Yeah, they appear pretty whole for having been werewolf pack bait. With some plastic surgery on their death wounds, they could pass as live."

"How do you think the Immortality Mob, whoever they are, get such clean canvases for their Cinema Simulacrums? You can't show a fine film on a scratched movie screen."

"I don't like to think of my CinSim friends in Vegas as hitchhiking on gussied-up corpses."

"Why not? They probably had cosmetic procedures when alive and acting."

"So your Zobos can be rehabbed?"

"That's the idea. If they can be used by the baddies, why can't they be employed for their own good, at least?"

"And you own this . . . arid land."

"I own a thousand acres of it."

"I didn't know the FBI paid that well or that you were with them that long."

"Consulting pays a lot better. These acres are too far from everything, even Area 51, to cost much."

"Don't remind me of 'alien' issues," I complained as a joke.

Ric grinned. "California isn't the freakiest state in the nation anymore, Nevada is."

"You haven't seen Kansas yet."

"I will soon," he said, brushing a kiss across my temple. "I can't wait to start our road trip back to where you grew up. It'll be a change of scene and a chance to put *your* ghosts to rest."

I agreed. Ric needed a change of scene after what Vegas had dished out to us recently. I wasn't sure my past was any place to find R & R, but I kept quiet.

He reached over to pat a white-blazed horse forehead farewell. "Seven Zobos corralled tonight is a good start," Ric said. "They'll probably attract their former in-ground buddies. We need to get back to civilization, get a shower, some sleep."

A horse whinnied agreement. We must reek if the livestock wanted us washed.

"Most girls are horse-crazy at some stage." Ric nodded

at the restless half-dozen mustangs and purebreds, bracing a motorcycle boot heel on the lower crossbar. Somehow that didn't do the trick of turning him into Clint Eastwood.

"Not me. I was fighting off vamp boys at that age."

He grinned. "You make me wish I was a vamp boy. You look tasty in the moonlight—mother-of-pearl skin, sapphire eyes, ebony hair."

Okay, I was about to blush. What girl believes she's good enough looking, deep down? And I'd had a head start at self-loathing nobody around me had bothered to head off or even see, except Ric.

But I was a piker.

Ric had been through hell and back, maybe even the literal one, since childhood, and recently he'd been vamp-drained of almost every last drop of blood. My Snow-assisted kiss of life had restored his heartbeat, and the docs had declared him fine, but I'd regarded making love as therapy ever since. I was tiring of playing therapist and ready to pronounce him normal again, relax, lose my protective instincts, and enjoy the ride.

So if me in the moonlight brought it on, I was willing to stand there gooey-eyed and sop it up. Looking at Ricardo Montoya had never been a chore for me, either. Girls aren't supposed to wax verbally enthusiastic about how guys look—unless they're Dan Brown's wife describing the dimple in Robert Langdon's chin—but Ric was the disgustingly tall, dark, and handsome Hispanic edition, only he now had one silver iris to add an exotic air. An eye patch would look dashing too.

I stared into that silver eye, unguarded by a brown contact lens for this night-work, and saw my face reflected, tiny and shiny, exactly as he'd described it. His left iris was a reflective silvery surface, a miniature mirror, but I doubted I could dive into and through it with anything but my mind's eye.

"You never got this mushy before your eye turned," I said more throatily than I'd expected. "Maybe I just look better through it now."

There you go, Irma objected. *Putting us down again.*

Ric mock-growled back and kissed me like yesterday, today, and tomorrow rolled into one mega-moment. His lips slipped along my cheek and under my ear, nibbling.

"Back to my place, then, for all that jazz."

By then Quicksilver had finished checking out the perimeter and even he was growling. His tolerance for sloppy sentiments was lower than mine.

"We *do* leave the motorized critter behind?" I asked.

Ric glanced over his shoulder at the ATV. "'Fraid so. You're gonna be my only ride tonight."

Um, frisky. Irma approved. *Quit worrying, girlfriend. The man had a blood count of zero for a couple days there. Even vampires need a fresh feed to get it up.*

I do so not want to think about that, I told her. *You* are getting a time-out, *girlfriend,* starting now.

Chapter Two

"WHY THE SMIRK?" Ric asked, swinging an arm over my shoulder. Navigating the shifting sands made us swagger toward the road, bumping hips and weapons systems.

I was not about to convey Irma's saucy thoughts to *my* guy.

"Look at Quicksilver," I told him instead.

As usual, Dolly had her top down, and Quick had raced ahead to jump into her backseat. "He's ready to roll."

The wolf-spitz family dominated the wolfhound in Quicksilver's looks, so he was a "smiley" dog, with the perked ears and grinning face that looked ever so friendly. It was hard to tell when he was just happy to see you, or ready to attack. His paler beige face showed a gray lupine widow's peak, but his eyes were a lovely "spacious skies" shade of blue, a trait that came from a rare wolfhound gene.

"Do zombies make him nervous?" Ric asked. "Any ordinary dog wouldn't know whether to attack or bury 'em like a bone. These Zobos rambling out here like Xanax addicts must really confuse the issue."

I patted Quick between the ears before working the car keys out of my duty belt and going around to Dolly's driver's seat while Ric stowed my night vision goggles in the trunk.

Ric imitated Quick and bounded over the convertible's closed front door into the passenger seat, just to prove he was fully recovered from the Karnak Hotel mob vampire attack.

I was hoping he was out to prove something else tonight.

"When we go to Wichita, we share the driving," Ric said, glancing at the luminous dial of his seriously multi-function watch. As a former FBI agent, he knew where to get all the latest paramilitary gizmos.

I'd never let anyone else drive Dolly before. Well, except for the Inferno and Karnak Hotel demon parking valets, and those occasions had been emergencies. Dolly had been my BFF since I bought her at a Kansas farm sale five years ago, when I'd been nineteen. Her looks were electric. Licorice-black body paint, channel-stitched red leather interior, and white convertible top. I didn't lightly let other hands curl around her extra-large pizza-size steering wheel.

"Sure," I told Ric, meaning our road trip. "We go halves all the way to yellow-brick-road country. I don't know why you're so keen to leave Vegas for the boonies right away."

By then I had Dolly's three hundred and sixty-five vintage horses kicked in and we—slowly—moved through the abrasive sand-drifted road toward the highway.

"You *do* let her stretch out all her horses on the freeway, right?" Ric asked.

"Actually, I don't like state highway patrol stops."

"No problem. You just gotta know where they typically lie in wait."

"You do?"

"First thing you figure out in the FBI. We didn't like local cop stops, either."

I heaved a dramatic sigh. "I'm installing a fuzz buster before we go anywhere, speed demon."

Ric's grin in the moonlight was as white as Quicksilver's. "What a waste of money when you've got an inboard one riding shotgun."

His hand stroked my nearest inner thigh. "Any Navy Seal would salivate to have this Inferno Hotel battle suit. As impenetrable as Teflon, you say, yet the surface feels as smooth as velveteen." His strokes became longer and Dolly swerved a bit. "No steel studs here, *chica*? You'd think Snow of all . . . people would know how much vamps like femoral arteries and would have ordered the fang-repellent studding everywhere."

By now I was *mucho* glad the suit was also waterproof. Did I even remember the naïve virgin who'd thought she was getting her period the first time she'd met Mr. ex-FBI smoothie in Vegas's Sunset Park a mere couple of months ago? I kept my eyes on the rough road and parted my totally armored thighs a teasing bit more. Sex in a high-tech wet suit was suddenly looking really hot.

Too bad Ric didn't realize this was just necessary physical therapy.

Yowsa! Irma managed to get in as she broke out of solitary for a weak moment—mine.

"This is going to be quite a road trip, Montoya," I muttered.

Behind us, Quicksilver stopped the heavy doggy panting and gave a sharp yip, like a basso coyote alert. Was he jealous of me getting all the petting or . . .

"Holy smoke!" I yelled, choking my grip on the steering wheel.

As we neared the lonesome gray of the interstate, a black hedge of fog had materialized from the concrete pavement, rolling toward Dolly's chrome front bumper like a solid wave of storm cloud.

"Flash flood?" I murmured uncertainly.

"That's no flash flood," Ric shouted, grabbing the fifteen-shot automatic from the very visible shoulder holster over his racing suit.

I looked hard. Yes, the wave was more solid than water . . . and sported moonlit fangs.

I accelerated. Dolly's bumper bullets plowed through a fender-high onslaught of furred shoulders and snarling, snapping maws.

"Quicksilver, no!" I shouted as the gray tide flowed around Dolly's red taillights into the desert beyond.

The dog was already over the rear door and on the desert floor, giving chase.

"Quicksilver, no!" I shouted again. I'd recognized the pack's breed, and mere werewolves would have been an improvement.

"Quicksilver, *come back*." Yeah, like a locomotive would spin on a dime and jump its tracks.

"Quicksilver, leave kitty!" I screamed at the top of my lungs in as deep and commanding a voice as my female vocal cords could manage.

I squealed Dolly into a too-rapid right onto the empty highway to look for results.

Ric regarded me as if I was insane.

By then I'd roughed up Dolly's brake shoes, but had avoided a fishtail as the car stopped. To my surprise, I saw Quicksilver's form lofting into a long leap over the trunk and into the backseat.

"*Good* dog, *good* boy," I said in that exaggerated praising tone deluded dog "owners" use.

Ric was still watching me as if I was nuts. "'Leave *kitty*'?"

"It's the one command he'll obey for our walks in Sunset Park." I shrugged apology. "If it's late and deserted I let him off leash. Of course that's when the cats come out."

"So the only way you can call back Killer Dog is to scream 'Leave kitty' for all the world to hear?"

"It did work. And it's not easy to turn a hundred-and-fifty-pound half-wolfhound from prey."

"Nor a hundred-and-eighty-pound man," Ric added with a mock ogle. "Did you have to call out the hounds on me? Where'd they all go?"

I turned with Ric to eye Quicksilver's "aren't-I-really-good-to-listen-to-you?" smiling mug and the desert beyond.

A bright flash of gold was moving across the valley floor, the darker mountains looming behind it.

"What on earth?" I asked. "Some moonlight phenomenon, like the purported green flash at sunset?"

"What *under* the earth," Ric said, stretching out of his seat to see. "Holy smoke is right. Picture a tomb painting writ large."

"My God. It's not—" I looked again.

Now I saw the smoky flowing cloud that had rushed us was racing to meet the flash of moving moonlit gold that led an army of shadows over the sere ground. A solid-gold royal chariot. Behind that spectacular artifact came the Karnak Hotel's hidden horde of ancient Egyptian vampires taking a run behind their desert steeds, with hyenas serving as their pack of hounds.

"I never noticed these mountains looked like pyramids, from a distance," I breathed. "The royal hyenas just flowed right through us."

Ric nodded as we watched the distant spectacle.

"I never saw the critters personally, but from your description and what we've just seen, the hyenas may have a spirit or ghostly existence as well as a way-too-physical one. They'll sic the Karnak royal vampire chariot corps on us now that we've had a close encounter. Better floor it."

"And Quicksilver just chased them! That dog would tackle Godzilla."

Not to mention a six-hundred-pound white tiger. No way was I telling Ric that Quick had faced off Snow's security shape-shifter, Grizelle, while I was busy erasing Ric's childhood whip scars in the Inferno bridal suite.

Long story, for both of us. Ric hadn't totally recalled his ordeal as mass vampire bait and I was still acting as his lover-cum–private nurse, protecting him as he thought he protected me. Maybe that was love, or maybe it was fooling yourself.

Whatever, I'd discovered even natural hyenas are really ugly customers, more weirdly related to felines than canines, with jaws that can snap and grind bones like the cannibal giant lurking up Jack's fairy-tale beanstalk. The thought of even their spectral forms cozying up to Dolly's paint job . . . *ick*. Hyena ectoplasm must resemble the wet cheesecloth fake mediums spit up in séances.

I was still shaking my head as I revved Dolly down the blessed ribbon of smooth concrete that would take us away from this prickly desert of cacti and khaki-colored carnivores, live and undead.

Ric frowned at my speedometer until I pushed the needle up to ninety. Then he tuned the radio full up on a Spanish-language station, so that trumpets and five-string guitars hailed our return to civilization.

Ric caught me eyeing his profile. "No traffic cops lying in wait until we approach Salt Cedar."

"That's right. Ex-FBI guy likes to take lawless midnight spins out into the desert dark."

"You've learned way too much about my deepest darkest secrets since I was unconscious in Christophe's bridal suite mainlining other people's blood." He smiled his promised revenge. "I'll have to show you some new tricks, then."

"We're heading straight to your home ground."

I checked the rearview mirror, pleased to see only the distant headlights of a semi. "Why were the Karnak vampire armies out for a run?"

"Our scouting expedition to their secret underworld did destroy the centuries-kept herd of human cattle they bred to feed on."

"Only after we released those poor souls to their long-delayed Afterlife," I said. "Howard Hughes is hoping his work with the wine-god we freed will get them all on brewed blood substitute."

"Howard Hughes was a demented genius of a human being and now he's a vampire, Del, not your Big Daddy. You can't trust him."

For a wild moment, I speculated that maybe he *could be* . . . my daddy, that is. Anybody could be, from Hector Nightwine to coroner Grisly Bahr to, hey . . . Donald Trump. That's the catch when you're an abandoned baby. You could be anybody. Or anything.

Ric was still in warning mode.

"And don't let the big, loin-clothed lug you freed from two thousand years of pillar duty under the Karnak lull your defensive instincts. That wine-loving Shezmou dude had a double role in ancient Egyptian mythology. His other specialty was Lord of the Slaughter. So, before everybody in the Vegas vampire empire can get nicely-nicely civilized via some Hughes invention, they still have to seek prey."

"What's out here to prey on?"

"Isolated ranches. I imagine the worker vamps can subsist on herd animals without killing them, if they have to, and the twin Pharaohs would get first dibs on any human herders."

"What about the Zobos and your horses?"

"The silver barbed wire will repel them."

"Vampires? I thought it was werewolves that silver bullets can hurt."

"Silver is one of the oldest vampire repellents. It fell out of favor in the days of the cross and holy water, but ancient Egyptians wouldn't be subject to Christian symbols. Silver recovered much of its mojo after the Millennium Revelation."

I touched my hip. My own silver familiar often went undercover as a slim chain.

"Your newly silver eye?" I asked.

"Yet to be seen," he answered, "but promising."

"Silver barbed wire. Where'd you get that stuff?"

"Custom-made. I have contacts in the Mexican jewelry trade on both sides of the border."

"Sterling silver? Isn't that metal too soft to make effective barbed wire?"

"I gave it the evil eye after it was nailed down around the compound."

"So you've . . . used . . . your silver iris?"

"Sure. If you got it, use it. My concentrated stare produced a cool blue aura around the wire. Then it hardened like your silver familiar did when you touched Cocaine's albino lovelock and it morphed into a solid form. My amped-up wire proved diamond jeweler's saw- and torch-resistant, just like Snow's pretty-pretty white hair. I'm betting this wire now has some supernatural power that makes predators of the paranormal sort back off."

"And how do you know this wire is impenetrable?"

Ric grinned as widely as Quicksilver. "First, my Taxco *amigos* tested it with saw and torch. Second, I have a feeling silver is *our* lucky charm. Even your super-dog has those changeable silver circles on his collar. Time I shared the bounty, babe."

"You know I *hate* to be called that."

"Yeah, but you're hogging the driving and you can't do anything about it now. Or this."

His hand returned to my inner thigh and didn't look to be leaving until we hit Vegas. Gotta say the bouncy road feel wasn't hurting anything, either. Dolly's vintage shocks were set to velvet vibrate. That Ric. From comatose to cocky after just two dangerous missions. Delilah the secret sex therapist was very happy.

"Where does your silver body jewelry thingy go, anyway?" Rick asked, "when you wear that skintight supersuit?"

This was the man who so memorably removed my new werewolf salsa club duds and twenty-four-year-old virginity in front of his bathroom mirror (before I started seeing dead people in looking glasses) asking. I blushed anyway, but only the half-man in the moon could see that with us zipping down the deserted straight-pin road at almost a hundred miles an hour.

"When you got cozy with what would be my bikini wax job—if I had one—eight miles back," I admitted, "the silver familiar, ah, migrated to a less active erotic zone. Sometimes it doesn't like crowds."

Ric's rhythmic caresses stopped. "Living up to its name, I see. But I *don't* see. Where?"

While he examined me for a clue, I watched the speedometer. It took a mile, less than a minute, for him to get it.

Ric sounded smug. "Elementary, my dear Watson. I detect two new symmetrically placed oversize silver studs on the chest of your catsuit. *Hmm,* spiked studs. *Muy* provocative. Your familiar isn't being shy, Del, it's upping the erotic ante. However or wherever that outfit opens and shuts, I'm going to take my time finding out."

Behind us a huge sigh and agitation on the leather upholstery indicated that Quicksilver was settling down on the backseat for a resigned doggy snooze before he spent the night on outside patrol. He'd always been an ultrasmart and sensitive dog.

Chapter Three

ONCE THE GOLDEN glow of the Las Vegas Strip was unfolding like a fan on the horizon, I checked in with my landlord on my hands-free cell phone.

Actually, I checked in with his butler. He was the one who'd fret about my whereabouts.

I didn't even need to worry about waking him up, because he was one of the celebrity zombies known as a CinSims. You really can't wake up William Powell from *The Thin Man* and *My Man Godfrey* films, among other classics, since the actor has been dead for decades and his various acting personas have been grafted onto contemporary zombie bodies at select Las Vegas entertainment locations.

What does it say when the only person who worries about your well-being like a father you can always count on isn't actually a real person?

Quicksilver and Ric listened hard to my end of the conversation.

"Godfrey? Yes, we've stayed out really late, but we're safe and sound." . . .

"Master Quicksilver will be fine. Ric has a smart house but Quick is smarter, so we can always use the extra security." . . .

"Yes, we're heading to Ric's place. Master Quicksilver and I are doing an overnight. Tell your boss I'll check in with him in the morning." . . .

"*After* breakfast, Godfrey, yes." . . .

"Indeed. We *are* being 'deliciously scandalous' and will 'enjoy ourselves.' Yes, maybe even champagne, but certainly Brimstone Kisses."

I winked at Ric as the phone's ultraviolet glow faded with my conversation.

"Brimstone Kiss." Ric mused. "That's the Inferno Bar cocktail you whipped up for the Humphrey Bogart *Casablanca* CinSim when you were trying to ply him with booze to save my hide. Is my liquor cabinet likely to stock the right ingredients?"

"If you have OJ in the fridge and orange brandy on hand, I can mix up a Brimstone Kiss."

"Brandy? Nope. You'll just have to rely on my home-made brews and kisses."

By then we'd arrived and Ric's garage door was opening at Dolly's approach as its interior light went on. Luckily, Ric's Vette was a space saver. Dolly could glide her three thousand-plus pounds right in. She's a big girl and proud of it.

Ric and I were entering the connecting courtyard before the system could close the garage door after us, so Quicksilver lingered behind to ensure nothing even as low and slender as a rattlesnake had slipped in unnoticed.

I loved the moonlit courtyard and the soothing splash of its copper fountain recycling water to the lush foliage. It felt so Old Mexico. Ric loved the stucco wall niches between climbing vines dripping blossoms and rich scent, where he could back me into the dark for butterfly and brimstone kisses.

Quicksilver whined impatiently and then lapped noisily at the fountain pool. He was big enough to sound like a herd of thirty water buffalo.

"I bet he's jealous," Ric said, turning to stare at the wolfish lapper.

Quick stared back and stopped drinking, wearing his innocent-dog look.

"Why don't we leave him on guard duty out here?" Ric suggested.

I walked over to Quick, who promptly sat and gazed at me with his limpid baby blues. My hand brushed his head and neck, fingering the silver medallions on his collar, now all sliced in half, like the moon.

"Okay?" I asked.

Could a dog roll his eyes? Mine did. I took that as a yes.

Ric and I walked through the heavy hacienda-style wooden front door as it opened for us. Ric's house might not contain the Enchanted Cottage's invisible helpers, but he had high tech.

"I don't see any ritzy liquor cabinets," I mentioned as Ric took my hand and hustled me through the dim living room.

"We don't need liquor. We're running on liquid silver."

"You actually like sharing a bit of my silver magic. Concealing your one silver iris most of the time isn't a drag?"

In the dark living room Ric stopped to grasp my upper arms, even then his palms unable to stop caressing my velvety, metal-studded suit.

"I like us sharing everything. What's not to like about you saving my life if the only side effect is a cool silver eye I can cover with a contact lens?"

"Maybe your eye doesn't reflect an aspect of my silver talents. Maybe the color was leached from your eye, rather than added. I didn't even know I had any silver mojo until I came to Vegas."

"Delilah, *querida*. I really don't care about the why and wherefore of my quirky eye right now. What I don't know is how Christophe's rescue party kept their hands off you in this thing. *Mmm*, that warm velvety black stretchy stuff embedded with all those silver metal mega-goose bumps except here. . . . What's the matter? You're holding back."

I felt like such a fraud for not telling Ric I might have brought him back from the dead with the leftovers of Snow's Brimstone Kiss, not my own determined CPR.

"I'm . . . not used to such blatant booty calls."

Ric laughed, a rich and wonderful sound I thought I'd never hear again only a few days ago. "Shy Delilah," he crooned. "Don't you know that's even more seductive? Yeah, this is a booty call. We're going into the lighted bathroom and you're going to strip me naked, shy girl, but then we'll go into the dark bedroom and I'm going to make love to you in that suit like you've never had it before."

"But Ric, I've only *ever* . . . had . . . *you* before."

"Maybe not like this. We've both got the silver mojo now, and I've figured out how to use it some. There's no telling what we can do together."

"Who knows what the silver eye will do for, or against, you. I don't think sex is going to prove anything."

"Aw, Del, sex proves everything. Our connection was white-hot from the first, with our finding those not-so-dead embracing skeletons in Sunset Park. . . . What should I call that co-ed dowsing moment? A sensual shudder?"

"Nicely put," I admitted. He was right. We'd had it all from the first. Sex and death and dark delight.

I swallowed. "This could be dangerous. My silver talents, your quicksilver eye. We could . . . spontaneously combust."

"Yeah, baby."

"You're killing the mood with that word."

"*Sí, Señorita Paloma.*" His kisses avoided my mouth, tracing my temple and cheekbone, along my jawline down to the side of my neck to the drumming pulse there.

The sweet spot for teenage boys and vampires.

I twisted my shoulder away from his lover's grip. I didn't want to play vampire games. It wasn't safe sex.

Allowing myself to tease the site of the vampire bat bite that had introduced Ric to puberty in the Mexican desert had made it an instant highway for the real Millennium Revelation vampires to nearly suck him dry and kill him. I wanted no more neck-nibbling, even if it had been a basic foreplay move since cave days.

"I'm back now, Delilah," Ric reminded me. "Better than ever."

"Your ego never went missing, for sure," I teased. "You really want *me* to strip *you*?"

It wasn't like I'd never been there before, but I'd never been the doer, mostly the do-ee. Convent school and a squeamish fetish for avoiding vampire hickeys will do that to a girl.

I knew once we hit the bathroom spotlights I was going to blush. Pale skin is made for baring every hang-up, but this was what I'd wanted so desperately, Ric alive and vital again. Why did I always find it easier to make war than love? Why was Ric hell-bent on taking me over every hurdle in my once-sheltered life? Why did sex have to be so revealing?

No wonder Quicksilver had wanted to get lost, fast. For the first time, I wondered about his doggy sex life, maybe the reason for all those solo midnight runs of his. TMS. Too much speculation.

Actually, undressing Ric was a good ice-breaker. The

racing-style suit Velcroed open at the extremities and then down from the mandarin-collared neck to the, um, crotch. He stood there like Vitruvian Man with his legs braced and arms out while I went to work high, low, and center. Men can be so out there.

I smiled as he turned his muscular, desert-dusky back to me, the bright lights revealing no trace of the ugly whip welts my tear-salted kisses had smoothed into faint silver scars. My forefinger traced the Catherine's wheel of strokes thinner than barbed wire, each touch evoking his audible purrs of pleasure.

I'd done this.

My silver talents and whatever remnant of Snow's Brimstone Kiss that had lingered on my lips had made the site of untold old pain into a new erotic zone.

Even as my fingers explored the wonder of what my lips had wrought, I winced.

How could I anticipate that Snow would absorb every slash the child Ric had borne as fresh wounds while I healed the old sites? What weird connection had been going on?

Ric was right again. In a paranormal world, every gift seems mated with a curse.

Now, as I played Ric's faded scars like a harpist, I couldn't help thinking of Snow. Could my pleasure-giving here slowly undo the damage done days and miles away at the Inferno Hotel? How much, over how many times? Or would the exchange of damage last forever?

I recalled Snow, fatalistic and as supernaturally cool as ever when we'd last met . . . the first time after Grizelle had told me what I'd done. My knees had been knocking, but the impervious rock-star persona Snow flaunted for the world had shown no signs of craving vengeance.

Why would he? He now had a greater power over me than any werewolf mob boss or undead Karnak pharaoh or vampire Howard Hughes . . . or even Ric.

My guilt. I'd deliberately chosen to undo the last seven lashes of Ric's pain even after I knew each healing touch was scourging Snow. My punishment, so far, was cringing at the memory of Snow every time I made love with Ric. I suspected there was far worse to come.

"You need to stop," Ric told me.

Startled, I assumed he'd eavesdropped on my distracted thoughts. But . . . no.

"Your sensual back massage is making me too happy. I trust we have something joint in mind," he went on.

I stepped back, dropping my hands. Still the amateur, I scolded myself, either avoiding or pushing too far too fast. I didn't know my own powers on any front . . . physical, emotional, or paranormal.

Ric picked me up in a bride-over-the-threshold carry and brought me into the dim bedroom. He settled me on the bed to a rhythm of kisses and caresses that made making love with one person in a wet suit seem perfectly logical, and my suit's silver studs flashed tiny lightning strikes from all the room's mirrored or metal surfaces.

"Electric," Ric murmured, as he rolled onto his back beside me. Of course, I had to remain on my side. My phobia against lying on my back kept me with my head braced on my crooked arm, gazing down into his beloved face. Ric turned his head away from me, so I couldn't see the silver iris. "Delilah, I need your mouth on me."

I ran my hand down his muscled, slightly furry thigh. *"No problemo, amor."*

His hand on my wrist stopped me.

"No. Here." He turned his head farther, his brunet profile etched against the blue satin pillowcase the color of my eyes. I consumed the sight of his dark, thick hair, slanting forehead, slightly aquiline nose, deeply arched lips . . . the image as breathtaking as one of Michelangelo's ultramasculine sculpted angels.

His motion had brought my focus to the strong, exposed column of his neck with the new knot of scar tissue resembling a miniature star gone nova.

"No," I said.

I couldn't miss how shallow, excited breaths lifted his bare chest up and down even as he kept his face and throat immobile for my view. The provocative contrast was playing crazy with my libido.

"No, *amor*," I coaxed. "This isn't a game anymore. That Sonoran desert bat bite left two tiny marks on your neck. I could play ferocious vampiress and leave you unchanged before. Now, real vampires have used that same spot as a spigot. They sucked your blood out. I can't 'pretend' to do that anymore."

"It was a *vampire bat* bite, Delilah, on the neck, a natural site for the tiny beast. I can't help that undead beasts favor the spot too, or what I feel. Your mouth has made the welts on my back into a road map of pleasure points. Think what your lips could do for the new scar here."

Help me, Irma! I couldn't plead that I didn't do oral sex. I couldn't deny that we all had idiosyncratic turn-ons and turn-offs. I'd overcome my distaste of early attacks from predatory half-vamps to feed Ric's harmless thirst for a bat bite rerun. He'd led me to overcome a lot of my hang-ups. How could I deny his one little long-standing kink?

"Por favor," he whispered. "I can beg . . ."

I studied his beautiful, beloved features. Like I shouldn't be begging him to let me touch him, love him.

I launched the most passionate kiss of my being at the damned vampire scar, pouring love and tears on the wound, as I had before when I had healed, sensing the pleasure shivering through his entire body and mind and soul, breathless at the power I had to shake him . . . and at his power to make me abandon myself and my fears.

IT WAS ONE of those paralyzing nightmares, where you know you need to move, change the scene, wake up . . . *and you can't.*

Yes, I was reliving my old alien abduction scenario. Me pinned on my back to an examining table, or an autopsy table, like Lilith. Me in the glare of a sinister overhead light hovering like a pale manta ray. A trio of vampire nurses fencing me in along each side of the table.

Vampire nurses? Howard Hughes's various Vegas venues had finally crept into my old Wichita nightmares.

An alien figure still stood at the foot of the table, ready to inject me with . . . some giant needle device. Yes, the alien was the black-and-white CinSim of Dr. Frankenstein, who wore far too much gel on his thick black hair.

And then he became the gold-glimmering black figure of Anubis, the Egyptian god of the underworld . . .

Really, I had too many alien entities to worry about to stay frozen in this dream . . . and so I awoke. I couldn't move for several seconds, my heart beating as if the captive-on-my-back abduction experience had been real.

And then I remembered that . . . it had been. I'd actually lived through scenarios like this since hitting Vegas. I'd already experienced this in real life, surreal as Vegas was.

Was I finally outgrowing my childhood phobias by living through them?

Beside me, I noticed Ric thrashing on his black satin

sheets. I softly stroked his upper arm. Where I feared to lie on my back, he'd made a habit of doing it to hide the whip scars of his childhood. Now he lay on his stomach, his exposed back and hips twitching with the phantom lashes of his deepest memories and nightmares.

"Ric," I whispered into his ear whenever his head thrashed my way. I ran my fingertips over the pale scars, each stroke quieting his shudders.

He awoke groggy and purring at last.

"You can't leave a man alone, Delilah," he murmured. "Magic Fingers. Put in a quarter."

I smiled, recognizing a reference to massage beds in cheap motels.

"Are we really going to stay in motels on our road trip?" I asked.

He turned over onto his side. Revealing his back had been a big achievement. Someday we'd make love in the missionary position, my own phobias no more too. Who'd believe a modern woman would *want* to be on the bottom. Oh, yes.

"God, I had a horrible nightmare, Del," he said, blinking as the memories flooded back.

"Tell me."

"Unlike you, I haven't dreamed like this in years. Mama Burnside pretty much reprogrammed me."

"I wish I'd had someone like her in the group homes of Wichita."

"We'll get back there and look them all up, *paloma*. And give 'em heck."

"What did you dream?"

He laid his head on my shoulder. "I saw El Demonio, the chief slave-labor smuggler south of the border. He was using his bullwhip on me again—"

I clutched his head to my breast.

"Del, you're gonna hook me on bad dreams."

I unclutched.

"But, Del . . . in the dream, he turned into . . . you."

"No!"

"Yeah, and your crazy silver familiar had taken the form of twin silver whips and then became tendrils of your silky dark hair and they were slashing like black-satin ribbons all over my body and I was really into it . . ."

"Oh, shut up. You just want a pity fuck."

He laughed.

"Any time. No, honestly and truly. I dreamed that old dark dream and then you appeared and drove it back down into the deepest corner of Nightmareland. The day you dream your alien abduction scenario and I'm the one menacing you with the phallic implement from the foot of the table, we'll know we've got both our kiddie nightmares deep-sixed."

"You think that this trip back to Wichita will do that for me? Turn the bogeyman at the alien abduction table into Prince Charming with a hard-on?"

He turned sober.

"I believe that digging to the bottom of our nightmares always pulls up the truth, Delilah. And the truth will set you free."

"That's the reporter's credo, but not an original thought, Ric."

"That's why it's so true, *mi amor*," he said, pulling my face down to his in a deep, soothing goodnight kiss.

Chapter Four

"FAR BE IT from me," said my landlord, Hector Night-wine, the next morning while I squirmed on the carved wooden chair opposite his office desk, "to insert myself into the course of true love, but you and the Cadaver Kid have been absent from the Strip for too long."

He sat in an even more massive chair that cupped him like King Kong's palm would surround a giant prune Danish. For once, I didn't know what to say.

The mental picture of Hector Nightwine inserting himself between Ric and me was physically impossible and emotionally repulsive.

Hector was a mini-me of *Star Wars'* Jabba the Hutt in an Orson Welles smoking jacket. If he knew I had a metal bikini top from the first film of *Cleopatra* in my cottage quarters on his Sunset Road estate, I'd be kept in chains on the set of his *CSI V* TV series forever.

The "Cadaver Kid" nickname was from Ric's few years in the FBI, where his "gift" for finding buried dead bodies was considered gee-whiz great profiling, not an inborn paranormal ability.

As for true love, I doubted Nightwine would ever know it unless it came wearing a bottom line, and I was even more superstitious now about calling what Ric and I had anything that resembled a clichéd happy ending.

So I addressed the only possible part of his comment I could.

"The Strip, Hector? Some new mega-billion behemoth going up there? Where on dry Nevada earth is there room?"

Hector's chubby, hairy hand stroked the black beard that concealed his multiple chin collection.

"No, this is a modest . . . shop, I'd call it. It's sprung up on one of the odd bits of untaken Strip land housing one-story enterprises."

I made a face and crossed my legs to distract his attention to my Betty Grable pin-up shoes: forties platform-sole spikes in VE-Day red. Better to have him leering at my ankles than my bustline. At least I thought so.

"You mean," I asked, just to be clear, "among the cheapie tourist shops, scalped show-ticket booths, palm readers, and naughty lingerie hucksters?"

Something had to occupy and pay rent on the odd Las Vegas Strip corners not commandeered by hotel-casino frontage. What I couldn't figure out was why international media mogul Hector Nightwine cared about a dinky new shop.

He couldn't wait to tell me.

"Some of your old friends," he said, waggling his coarse eyebrows, "are busy vying for this spanking new enterprise. I'd think you'd want to visit, since a *new* friend of yours is the merchant in question."

"Merchant? I don't know any 'merchants' except for a certain ghoulish TV mayhem huckster in my twenty-twenty sights at this moment."

Nightwine's plump hand dipped into a wooden salad bowl filled with crunchy little nothings from the lower orders of planet life. Dead now, I hoped.

"Flattery will get you everywhere, dear Delilah. I confess. You are such a modest little thing." He wagged a forefinger that dangled something black and slimy and boneless. "Does Mr. Montoya know you've set up a bare-chested hunk in a commercial hot spot?"

I straightened my spine, imagining myself standing at my immodest full five-eight, though seated, and glowered to encourage him to go on. Which he did.

"Two major Strip forces you know, Delilah, are fighting wolf-fang and tiger-claw to acquire the business for their hotels, and no doubt franchise it."

Now I got it. "Cesar Cicereau's Gehenna Hotel were-wolf mob versus Christophe's rock-star Inferno Hotel?" I asked.

"*Mais oui, ma petite.* I'm considering entering the fray. The concept is genius, my dear Delilah. You did sign Mr. Shezmou to a personal contract, did you not?"

"Ah . . ." I was so shocked I descended into mob-speak. "He owes me."

"Very wise. Well, trot yourself and your canine companion over there and prepare to protect your interests. And not only from bigwigs. The showgirls and tourist ladies are lining up for blocks in the hot sun in designer heels you would kill for."

I stood. "I don't have to, Hector. I have my own collection."

"Ah, yes, the Enchanted Cottage's new Bottomless Closet. How did you manage to convert the old-fashioned and invisible brownie and pixie helpers that came with the place into a host of personal Red Carpet stylists?"

"Your estate spy cameras are worthy of *Excess Hollywood.*"

"I am always the *auteur,* my dear, the director who writes his own scripts. But, sometimes, I admit, you write yourself into the most delightful corners, far beyond my humble powers to manipulate. Beware, Delilah. Powers less benign than I have also realized your potential."

"Great." I turned on my heel, or Betty's. "Don't forget that I protect my interests, to the hilt."

"And to the last man. Yes, I know."

NIGHTWINE'S MAN GODFREY was waiting outside the door, as usual.

His pencil-thin mustache surmounted a slightly receding chin and he had a slightly receding dark hairline. Still, his white tie and tails were always a swooningly crisp black and white. If you'd ever wanted to glide across the dance floor with a larger, wryer Fred Astaire, Godfrey was your man.

"The master is right," Godfrey told me. "You've been undertaking dangerous duty in the dark lately."

"Godfrey, you eavesdrop?"

"Religiously."

I followed him and his button-down black tails down the Sunset Road mansion's back stairs to the kitchen, our steps clattering on the uncarpeted wood.

In a moment the click of nails joined our percussive procession. The back stairs were narrow and turned like a ballerina on a music box. At the bottom, Quicksilver had come to heel at my side, not that I ever commanded him to do anything.

We faced Godfrey.

"Quick was with me on those missions," I told him. "And Ric knows what he's doing out there on the desert."

"Of course," Godfrey said. "My . . . cousin at the Inferno Bar, Nick Charles, well knows the combined power of man, woman, and dog. Who am I, a humble butler-in-disguise, to argue with that magic? But we CinSims are all merely motion picture phantasms in a way, Miss Delilah and Master Quicksilver. We are dancing with the dead, the resurrected bodies that serve as our sturdy immortal canvas, ever so much more resilient than film. We are not as fragile as living flesh, either."

"But you are as dear," I said, brushing my hand against his black sleeve. CinSims were solid, but I hesitated to touch a phantasm.

Since almost losing Ric to the Karnak vampires, I'd become a real softie.

"Part of the service," Godfrey said, a pre-Technicolor twinkle in his gray eyes. "I was not a matinee idol for nothing."

Well, William Powell had been a starring character actor, really, but I'd always had a weakness for character over flash.

"Sometimes, Godfrey," I told him, "you make me feel like Dorothy on a road trip with one of her trio of cool dudes."

He shrugged modestly. "You'd better follow the yellow brick road to the Strip, Miss Delilah, as the Wizard of Sunset Road suggested. Mr. Nightwine has an infallible eye for the main chance. And take your big dog too."

I curtsied and almost skipped my way out the back door and down the flagstone path to the Enchanted Cottage, so very glad I wasn't in Kansas anymore.

Chapter Five

I'M NOT FAMOUS for following instructions. I left Quick-silver at home in the cottage, chewing on an Awesome Gnawsome stick.

I didn't want to get known around Vegas as a dog and his girl. It was too easy in post–Millennium Revelation days, and especially here, to get tagged by the company you keep.

Besides, I had more than a clue about who the new "in" entrepreneur in town was . . . and who had helped set him up in business, besides the marketing genius of me.

Even a low-end Strip address takes cash money.

The moon's intensity may wax and wane, but the sun is pretty much always on full power during the southern Nevada daylight hours, spreading warm vibes and skin cancer as the tourists soak it up from under funny hats, their white-creamed noses topped by very dark sunglasses.

My Black Irish–pale complexion had made high-SPF sunscreen a constant companion even in a come-and-go sunshine state like Kansas. Sunglasses were my constant accessory too, partly to hide the fabled baby-blues I share with my elusive double, Lilith Quince, but I put Lilith out of my mind before she drove me out of it instead.

Hector's description of sleazy businesses took my Strip walk toward downtown and the last surviving, non-imploded hotel-casinos of the town's fifties and sixties heyday, when the Rat Pack of Frank Sinatra, Dean Martin, and Sammy Davis, Jr., ran wild in Vegas instead of were-wolf mobsters.

After weaving almost to the streetlamps to miss a steamy tourist array of sun-baked Goth and punk leather, I spotted a stunning gold-and-ebony sign above a shop frontage.

CHEZ SHEZ, the gilt letters read, just as I'd recommended.

"Chez"—pronounced as in "the wonderful one-horse shay"—was French for "house of." "Shez" was short for "Shezmou," the ancient Egyptian name for "vengeful, beheading demon under-god who's got great hands for neck-twisting as well as wine-pouring and massage."

The line of women wasn't blocks long, but they did almost kick me to the curb, literally. I'd been dodging ill-intentioned Jimmy Choos since Sheena, the weather witch at WTCH-TV in Kansas, so I simply hopped and skipped around them to the front door, which was manned by . . . a woman.

Of my acquaintance.

She was also one don't-cross tiger of a female, Grizelle, Snow's shape-shifting security chief at the Inferno Hotel.

Right now she was all woman, six-foot-three of ridiculously high-priced and small-sized designer suit and stiletto heels on a velvet-black frame. Her skin was moiré black taffeta, subtly marked with the shadow of tiger stripes. Little-known fact: all spotted and striped cats have skin to match. Grizelle in human form was almost as formidable as her six-hundred-pound white-tiger self. Her eyes were jungle green and her manicure was vampire red.

I'd worn my air-sole sneakers for my Strip stroll—the silver familiar was so ashamed of my unfashionable look it was hiding out as a toe-ring—so I was more pipsqueak than usual measuring up to her. But height is attitude, not altitude.

So I showed some.

"New job as a shop doorman, Grizelle? Was Snow so miffed by your last foiled attempt to stop my Inferno comings and goings that he fired you?" I taunted. "Naughty, naughty kitty. Maybe I can put in a good word for you with Nightwine Productions, Inc."

"I don't do door duty anywhere," she answered. "I was just leaving after I saw the low-rent party hanging around inside. Seeing as *you're* entering, I'll *stick* around awhile longer." She fanned the taloned fingers of her right hand.

"Delilah," said a deep male voice from within.

I promptly did a do-si-do around Grizelle's statuesque presence and doffed my sunglasses. I still had to blink for several seconds to see in the comparatively dim interior.

What I saw was tall, dark-haired, and not unhandsome, but unfortunately, it was not my indebted demigod, Shezmou.

"Sansouci," I said with surprise. "Fancy finding you here. Needing a manicure? Or just a good chiropractic neck adjustment?"

I'm no squirt, but most men of my acquaintance flirt with six-foot-something. Now—between the head muscle for both the werewolf mob and Snow's hellish Inferno operation—I was feeling distinctly outgunned.

Yet intrigued.

"I didn't know you two knew each other," I commented, switching my gaze from Sansouci to Grizelle like a nervous, well, gazelle. She scared me a lot more than he did, perhaps because I'd done her boss wrong in a very big way.

The pause became what you could call pregnant.

Grizelle tossed her mane of spangled dreadlocks that

much resembled an Egyptian wig. I wondered if Shez-mou had seen her yet. They'd make an awesome power couple.

"The doors are barred for now," Grizelle told me. "You can gawk a bit and then you should leave. I'm here for a private business conference with the owner."

"Me too." Sansouci's wolfish grin looked really rakish on a closeted vampire, trust me. "I represent the Gehenna werewolves," he continued, "but I have time to show you and the little lady around."

He had a gift for irritating in stereo.

"Oh?" I said. "You'll want to include me. I can show *you* around. Shez and I are business partners. Where is he?"

"Shez is male?" Grizelle sounded both surprised and condescending.

She eyed the polished chrome, copper, and gold metal-lic walls and shelves of semiprecious stone jars. A similar display of gilded wine bottles topped an ebony-and-tur-quoise bar on another wall.

"I should have guessed," she added.

"I wouldn't call Shez a 'girly man' to his face," I warned her.

Looking around without engaging my reflections too much, I saw a surprisingly modest space, part bar and part boutique, just as I'd envisioned, but unattended. I smelled the pine, sesame, and almond oils used in Shez-mou's potions, though not the castor oil, thank goodness. Methought Chez Shez needed a more fashion-forward sig-nature scent. Time for that later.

Then a glass-beaded curtain behind the counter shim-mied and remained swaying like a belly dancer's skirt at the entrance of a slight young woman wearing nothing more than a mahogany spray tan, a tissue-thin strapless white-linen sheath, and an Urban Decay "smoky eye" to die for.

The curtains' colored beads echoed the red, blue, and green glass on wide ancient Egyptian collars. Their gentle clicking reminded me of the waist-circling, oversize rosaries the older nuns at Our Lady of the Lake convent school had worn . . . and the sound of the millions of flesh-eating beetles occupying the Karnak underworld.

"Are you Mr. Mou's one p.m. appointments?" the girl asked. Her eye-whites dazzled as her focus darted between all three of us.

Mr. Mou? Irma interjected. *The quick start-up forced our foreign friend Shezmou to employ one of the dimmer bulbs on the marquee.*

I was inclined to cut the young woman slack. She was barely twenty, not a ripe old lady of twenty-four like me.

"Mr. Souci?" she inquired hopefully, nailing the only man in the room.

"At your service," he said smoothly. He knew no other way to deliver a line to a female. "You can call me 'San.'"

Oh, please! Irma was hopping annoyed, and so was I. The girl was going into standing swoon mode at one glimpse of Sansouci's deep-set green eyes and one sentence from his even deeper hypnotic voice. Vampire, dearie, and the kind that feeds on women.

"Ms. . . . Gray Zelle?" She next fastened a hopeful hazel eye on me, since I looked a lot less dangerous than Grizelle.

I stepped politely aside.

The young woman took one look at Grizelle's haughty carnivore expression and fastened her gaze on me again for dear life. "And *you* are?"

"Ms. Street, but you can call me Delilah. What's your name?"

"Fawn Schwartz."

"Well, Fawn, I am Mr. Mou's silent partner."

"You're, uh, talking."

"'Silent partner' is a business expression. Shez wants to see me first. Alone. Trust me."

Sansouci raised an eyebrow. Grizelle lifted a sneering upper lip to showcase her carnivore canines. I was glad to ditch the pair when Fawn parted the clicking curtains and I ducked through. Irma and I.

The shop front looks promising but could use some hipper upgrades, she told me.

At this point, merchandising was hardly my main concern. If Christophe, aka Snow, and Cicereau were battling for an interest in Chez Shez, I wanted to make sure they had to deal with *me,* which both would loathe. I had a feeling the *real* silent partner in this setup would like that just fine.

The fluorescent-lit manufacturing area was much bigger than the storefront. Shezmou was working his grape press, the sinewy arm and back muscles of his cinnamon-hued torso gleaming with enough sweat to put him in a well-oiled Mr. Universe contest. Given the new female option of women ogling men these twenty-first-century days, as a product front man he was a Name Brand born.

At the click of the bead curtains his bewigged head turned. He gave the huge cheesecloth wad of grapes one last wring and wiped his reddened hands on a piece of white linen. One would be reminded of an ancient housewife, if one wished to commit suicide and say so.

"You are welcome," he addressed me, "O Deliverer of Shezmou, to my house of fine wines and oils. Thus Delilah has wrought, and I, Shezmou, deliver, reversing our roles as my own nature must also move from wine to balm, and eternal death to eternal life."

Gods require lots of wordy preamble, so I just smiled and nodded.

If I hadn't noticed that Shezmou's twenty-foot incised image on a Karnak Hotel subterranean pillar included actual wrist and ankle chains to keep him inanimate, Shez wouldn't have been freed from millennia of bondage. His captivity had ensured that the Egyptian vampires could rampage without facing any Afterlife music.

Egyptian vampires?

Yup, they were the only ancient culture to have no bloodsucker mythology. Yet, sometime between 5000 and 3000 B.C., the problem had become severe enough that even the royal line was tainted. Many high-ranking mummy heads, including King Tut's, had been severed before wrapping to ensure no awkward resurrections here on earth.

Almost all world religions offer a "separate and save" option for the Afterlife. Not the Egyptians under secret vampire rule. Once infested with vampires, Egyptian culture froze in time, feasting on their own in perpetuity and occasionally sampling stray latter-day humans.

Shezmou had been the demigod, or demon, who twisted off the heads of the damned and cast them into Egyptian Hell. With him in chains, vampires had centuries to create and re-create their own thirsty breed unchallenged.

All those deathless big bad vampires were still ruling the Underworld beneath the Karnak Hotel and Casino. I knew something they didn't, not even their twin brother-sister pharaohs. A big bad modern vampire secretly owned the Karnak and pulled Vegas strings from atop the Strip hotel, and he had twenty-first-century ambitions. Luckily, he and I had an uneasy but mutual understanding. So I had an unseen ally here.

"I was not expecting to receive the mighty Delilah," Shezmou said.

Ric had adroitly impressed the ancient godling with my namesake's Biblical exploit of cutting off Samson's hair to sap his strength. I'm sure Shez didn't want me snipping off any of his wig strands.

"I thought two others of the Upperworld also sought audience?" Shezmou asked me.

"They await without, mighty Shezmou." Okay. Being suddenly thrown into an ancient surviving culture, vampire or not, brought out my high-school Shakespeare play dialogue.

Shez grinned at me. "I owe my liberator a great debt. It is good that you are wise enough to pour sweet oil on my godhead."

Oh, my lord! Irma said. *Did that sound tacky. And hot.*

"Now I practice a modern profession," Shezmou's Darth Vader baritone continued. "I must seem . . . ordinary to conduct commerce. So speak as if I were your . . . equal. Just between us."

"Sure, Shez."

His grinned widened. "You enjoy that, Delilah."

"Sure do, Shez."

"I observe that small women enjoy ordering large men around."

"Your human avatar is only six-feet-five, Shez. And I am tall for my gender."

"Do not I know it."

"If I may suggest, to get along in the Upperworld, cultivate contractions."

"I am not a woman in childbirth," he said, frowning. "Dealing with such matters is my little brother Bez's profession."

Bes, rechristened "Bez" by Ric and me just because it went better with Shez, was the dwarfish god of randy sex and . . . subsequent childbirth. Logical, these Vulcans and Egyptians.

"Don't you know it," I repeated Shez's earlier phrase in a more casual way. "And I'm not a woman in childbirth, either."

"No, you are . . . ah, *you're* slim and limber, although high for your sex."

"You're shortly going to meet a female almost as tall as you, Shez."

"Am I?"

"Yes. Before that, I want to make sure you're properly represented. I assume your boss . . . er, overlord, has a link to the storefront."

"Yes. A link, as in a chain, only this chain is embedded in a fine glass box lid. See."

Shez gestured to a twenty-five-inch flat-screen monitor on an ivory-inlaid table of exquisite Egyptian workmanship.

I sat on the zebra skin X-bench (sorry about that, ancient zebra) and awakened the computer link with a touch.

"Aren't *you* looking Stripside sloppy today, my dear Delilah?" Howard Hughes's shrunken face mouthed into a fish-eye webcam lens. "What do you think of my new shop concept?"

"That it's mine."

Hughes shrugged. He'd had himself made into a vampire at almost his last breath to retain his financial kingdom. With his long beard and hair and gaunt look of pained disappointment, he alarmingly resembled a plastic Jesus figure.

"She who *thinks* is clever," Hughes chanted. "He who *does* owns the world."

"Come on, Howard. You know this concept—and Shez's enthusiasm for it—is my idea."

"Do you have a contract in writing?"

"I expect you to provide one."

"Forty percent for Hughes Tools and Tchotchkes."

"So like you to overreach, Mr. Hughes. Ten percent."

"Thirty."

"Twenty," I said.

"Twenty-*five* to me. Oh, twenty-four. Your age, nicely symbolic," he cackled. "And only fair. I am an old, old man."

"And ever were and always will be."

Hughes's blasted face wrinkled with a rather charming smile. "Give me credit, and I will give you the world."

"'*I'll.*' We're teaching Shez speech with contractions today. Better for the future talk shows."

"Always on top of things, Delilah. Speaking of which, you walked off with my priceless film artifact, the first cinematic Cleopatra's coiled brass serpent bra."

"Yours and welcome to it back. I'd rather wear the push-up bra you invented for Jane Russell. All that heavy metal is cold."

"Like your cold heart, perhaps? Oh, all right. Twenty percent to me and my mammary artifact back."

Hughes's webcam revealed a buxom vampire nurse behind him rattling his IV pole to hang a fresh bag of sterilized blood before the image faded.

"He is a strange creature," Shez noted, "and by rights I should have twisted his fanged head from his stringy neck, but he is not of my people and has been most accommodating to me and my arts of the wine and oil press."

"You're a god in hiding from your should-be worshippers. And it's *he's*."

"If you had to recite hieroglyphics aloud, you'd sound most artificial also."

"Agreed, partner. Speaking of 'greed,' it's time to meet the high-end Strip mouthpieces."

"These 'mouthpieces' are a variety of musician?"

"Very much so. The music of coins."

I preceded Shez through the Glass Curtain, but I fear that Grizelle and Sansouci stood to attention only when the Lord of the Slaughter stepped into the showroom.

Grizelle growled, and for a shocked microsecond shifted into her white-tiger form.

"Meet my business partner, Shezmou," I said while she corrected her impulse. "He's the genius behind the vintage wines, scents, and oils this establishment offers the Las Vegas attraction world."

Shez shook his bewigged, glass-bead-swagged, and braided mane, and growled godlike approval.

Sanscouci muttered, "Holy Seared Shitakes. This is a Clash of the Titans."

He edged my way, arms folded on his chest, while the two larger-than-life types eyed each other like enemies and lovers. "Starting your own harem with Bijou Boy there, Street?"

"Jealous, *Mr.* Souci?"

Sansouci winced. "What I do for my boss. What's with the guy's albino kilt? And I don't get this boozy beauty parlor concept."

"You haven't sampled his wines yet."

Shez's divine super-sharp hearing whipped his impressive head our way. "Mr. Souci may sample any bottle he pleases, but he should not drink the massage oils."

Sansouci's almost-emerald eyes rolled like Quicksilver's when he heard me try a ridiculous command, like "Stop."

"I do not sell beer," Shez went on, "although I could brew it. The two gold taps at the end of the bar are a special house brew, ideal for"—Shez frowned, striving to be modern and hip—"the nightclub set." He regarded me quizzically. I supposed that he'd been watching TV in his spare time at the roomy laboratory Hughes had provided atop the Karnak Hotel. "Night . . . stick. Does that not mean, ah, the police?"

I realized then that Shez had first met me wearing my used cop duty belt with the attached billy club. I'd left all that fighting gear home. Perhaps a mistake, I thought, as I eyed the three deadly paranormals in the room with little mortal unarmed me and poor Fawn Schwartz.

"The Police is a music icon," Grizelle purred to Shezmou. "You seem new to our entertainment-centered world. I could introduce you to the Seven Deadly Sins rock band at the Inferno Hotel tonight."

"Rocks I know from my native soil and sins are my specialty," Shez answered, being far more provocative than he knew.

Beside me, Sansouci growled in his turn. "I'm supposed to get his attention away from that sleek Inferno catwoman? Cicereau had no idea he had any competition."

"I'm a partner in this operation," I told him. "You can make points with *me*."

I hadn't meant to flirt, just to make Sansouci feel better. That was an Our Lady of the Lake convent school girl-graduate problem. We always wanted to make everyone feel better . . . in an abstract, selfless, spiritual way. Not a good ploy with vampires.

Sansouci was about as spiritual as a machete.

"You don't want to talk 'points' with me, Delilah, without being ready to deliver." He flashed a grin broad enough to showcase the strong white canine teeth he usually kept under lip and key. "That why Shez calls you Deliverer?"

Mistake. Another one.

Trying to distract Sansouci to give Shez and Grizelle some one-on-one time, I'd upped the sexual and homicidal tension in the shop so you could cut it with a diamond saw. I guess Shez hadn't been off a pillar for a millennium too many.

I was just a mortal wearing loose tee and shorts, the tourist uniform.

By comparison, Grizelle was prime Las Vegas Strip showgirl with a Siegfried and Roy pedigree. She was the modern equivalent of a Vegas goddess, much as I hated to admit it.

"What's off between you and Grizelle?" Sansouci whispered, standing way closer than necessary.

"We tangled."

"Seriously?" He leered at her, not me. "Girl-to-girl. I'd have liked to see that."

"Rein it in, Romeo. It was tiger-to-girl."

"You were the girl and walked away without bone-deep tracks in your face?" He stepped back to eye me as if I'd grown a unicorn horn. "Hey, Delilah. I know you have the nerve act sharp with Christophe and Cicereau, but Grizelle? Tell me another fey tale."

"It was one of my more desperate moments."

"You two hellcats were fighting over the Cadaver Kid, I bet."

I just nodded. Sansouci didn't need to know Ric had still been comatose at the time.

"Grizelle must go for the Latin lover type," he said, frowning at Shez. When I just stared, disbelieving, he added. "What? This Shez guy is Mediterranean, right?"

"Just barely." Egypt did border the southern seashore, but the ancient population came from the cradle of Africa, not Asia or Europe.

"And what's with the major eyeliner?" Sansouci asked. "He looks like the Rudolph Valentino CinSim at the Karnak."

"It worked for Johnny Depp. Re-creating his ancient beauty potions is like a religion with Shez. He isn't shy about marketing his products."

"How'd you get mixed up with him? What kind of super is he?" Sansouci asked.

"Ah . . . his job for *his* big boss was about the same as what you and Grizelle do for yours."

"So he's paranormal muscle of some kind."

"You could say that."

"And his hobby is making wine and . . . perfumes?"

"That's his physical therapy."

"For what?"

"PTS."

"Post-traumatic stress? This guy doesn't look like an army vet. You're losing me, Delilah, not that I wouldn't like to find you in a dark, deserted cul-de-sac."

"Don't you have enough women in your blood-bank harem already, Sansouci?"

"Yeah, but I can always use a fresh item on the menu."

Sansouci was a modern, civilized vamp. He sipped a little from enough adoring ladyloves to live without killing, at least just for blood.

"See those cobra-headed gold taps Shez was mentioning?" I said, eager to distract him from his favorite target, me.

"Yeah. Not beer on tap, I hope," he said. "That wouldn't be smart, given the high prices on the beauty potions. Just the bottles are worth a bundle. Malachite, lapis lazuli, tiger's-eye." His gaze had drifted to Grizelle, who was interrogating Shez without him even knowing it.

"Sterile artificial blood," I whispered in Sansouci's ear this time. "Totally legal and dependent on no living creature's circulatory system. Interested?"

"Hell, no. Would I drink near beer on a bet? Blood on tap? You've obviously never had vampire sex. Where's the seduction? Where's the danger? Where's the warmth, the beating heart, the heat? Where's the fun, Street? Huh? You like it hard, don't you? You don't like life, or death, too easy."

His eyes were on the hair covering my neck. His eyelids had almost closed as one outer upper lip lifted over his teeth in a classic Elvis-sneer, but his voice went so low and deep I felt the vibration in my veins. I also felt myself swaying toward him like a cobra to a snake charmer.

I jerked away. "Where's the profit, you should be asking."

He hissed out a sigh of frustration, and then finally gave the gilded faucets a serious survey.

"Those look like real gold," he said.

"Right."

"Okay. I give Metrosexual Boy that. Blood would look deliciously tasty flowing from those eighteen-karat snake fangs. It would appeal to the kind of upwardly mobile vamp who sniffs cocaine." His eyes narrowed to malachite-hard slits. "Your sponsor at the Inferno could market the hell out of a product like that. That might nudge your amateur cocktails off his featured drink board."

Yeah. Christophe, aka Cocaine of the Seven Deadly Sins rock band, aka Snow, knew how to market danger and death. And he'd stolen my Albino Vampire and Brimstone Kiss cocktails recipes for his bar after I'd invented them there on the spot.

But there were other rich entrepreneur hoteliers in town, and only one of them was undead for sure. And only I knew who he was for sure. Did I want to share with Sansouci?

He claimed to feel the "warmth," something Howard Hughes would never have been capable of, man or vampire. We both were at odds with his boss, Cesar Cicereau. I could use an ally on the dark side.

Cozying up to Sansouci might make Ric uneasy. Still, Sansouci, representing Cicereau, had been a major player in Ric's rescue party. So had Snow. Which one did I prefer to confide in? Sansouci was wrong about me. The answer I liked was easy. Him.

"Try the tap," I advised Sansouci. "You're a new breed of vamp. This is a fresh type of blood from an inventive new source. What can it hurt?"

He eyed my mouth while I spoke as if he wanted to eat it.

Holy Hathor! Shez's seductive ancient scents sure brought out new hormone levels in the old town.

"If I lived on brewed blood out of a golden spigot," Sansouci said, "I wouldn't need to sup on a nightly harem. I could concentrate on one lady. Would you like that, Delilah?"

"Would you?"

"You're the monogamous sort," he mused. "I might

like your type for a change of pace. I confess I find fidelity really hot, but it's not available."

Fidelity? From a vampire with a harem? I suppose the novelty would last . . . for a while. We were back to talking sex and blood, again, and a deep nagging doubt tugged at my composure.

"Look," I said. "Try the new brew. Some vamp has to be the first. Why not you?"

His grin was lethal. "Yeah. Some vamp has to be the first. Why not with you?"

"I'm taken."

"Granted." Sansouci eyed the cobra-headed spigot. "I'm taken too, indentured by Cicereau's Blood Price. I don't expect that condition to last forever. Come on and watch. I'll toast you with the first . . . what? Mug? Glass. What's this Shezmou going to serve his make-believe blood in?"

"I have no idea." I turned to our host. "Shez?"

"At your command, Deliverer." His impressive presence dwarfed even Sansouci and me. I glimpsed Grizelle scowling over his bare red-bronzed shoulder.

"We have a first customer for the house vintage," I said. "Can you pour a . . . draft?"

"With pleasure." Shez swept a gold-band-wristed arm over Sansouci's broad shoulders and muscled him to the bar. He plucked a jeweled gold cup from the shelves and filled it at the tap, jerking the cobra neck to a broken right angle with relish.

A thin ruby stream pissed into the cup.

"Nothing from here goes to the police lab, right?" Sansouci asked.

Grizelle snorted.

Sansouci took the cup from Shezmou's dark hands into his own pale ones. For the first time, I recognized Sansouci as Black Irish, like me. Just how old was he? In pre-vampire years?

He lifted the rim to his lips, threw back his head with the abandon of a howling wolf, and downed the liquid in one gulp like a shot of booze.

Three previously held breaths suddenly whooshed through the small showroom.

Sansouci lifted his cup Viking-style. "Brewer. Another round. Most satisfying," he declared, eyeing me, "but not quite up to what one finds at the Inferno Bar."

This was a reference to me, not Grizelle, who neverthe-less growled softly as she edged closer to tower over me.

"First," she told me in a hissing feline whisper, "you betray my master, Christophe. Now you hoodwink Cice-reau's security chief, who is apparently a blood addict. When will you abandon your beloved Ric? You fought me for his redemption. I predict that one day soon you will fight for his death."

When it came to Mean Girls, Grizelle was top of the heap, claws down.

"You're just annoyed at not being the center of atten-tion," I answered. "Shez is now the prize impressive super-natural on display on the Strip."

"When does he join the Chippendales show at the Rio?"

"Never. Trading on his macho appeal is beneath Shez's dignity. He's an artist of the old school, a wizard with herbs and spices and wine grapes and sometimes . . . souls."

"Soiled souls, like yours?" Grizelle asked, her contralto voice sinking to an even more sinister whispered hiss.

"I know what you owe my master for stealing his Brim-stone Kiss and sacrificing his very skin for your lover's pleasure," she told me in a low, furious growl. "Montoya's scars were old and no longer pained him physically. My master suffered the fresh and brutal physical burden of years' worth of whipping in one session. I only realized *you* had to be the source when it was far too late. Christophe is more than Cocaine or Snow. He'll call in your debt one day, believe it. I can't wait to help that happen."

Lordy! I'd been besieged by two sets of seething green eyes that wanted more than I was willing to give them this morning. Way too much excitement for a Kansas girl.

Someone loomed behind me. "If you talk of souls," Shez told Grizelle, "I don't wish to hear it. This is only my . . . day job."

I nodded encouragingly. Shez was getting the lingo fast.

"You don't wish to see me at my night job," he told both his corporate suitors. "It is too rough for the likes of you."

Sansouci's dark eyebrows peaked like Mephistopheles' with curiosity, while Grizelle merely looked haughty.

"The mighty Delilah," Shez went on, to my glee, "is my . . . mouthpiece. You must negotiate with her. I weary of deciding too much. I prefer formulating my preparations or taking swift action. This talk of business and percentages and of 'cloning the shops' is annoying. My workplace is not . . . *isn't* the place for discussing such boring things. You must deal with the mighty Delilah if you wish to bargain, or my serving girl, Fawnschwartz, if you wish to purchase."

Shez withdrew through the tinkling glass bead curtains.

"How rude," Grizelle growled.

I smiled and shrugged. "He's the creative genius."

"'Mighty Delilah,'" Grizelle spat.

"You had to have been there."

"Where?" Sansouci asked immediately.

"None of your business. Now. I'm going to be unavailable for a week or so. I suggest you two meet with your principals and each draw up a business plan I can review on my return.

"I wouldn't advise slipping back to deal directly with Shez. He looks like a big, easygoing lug, and does indeed have a softer side, but he has quite a demonic temper and I can't be responsible for your safety unless I'm present."

"*You . . .* responsible for *our* safety?" Shadows of Grizelle's white whiskers were coming and going on her dusky face as her human upper lip curled with fury, the urge to shift barely under her control. Her long red fingernails fanned in and out. "I could eat you alive, and almost did once."

Sansouci just smiled, on firm ground again, and donned his deep black sunglasses. "Looks like the mighty Delilah could use an escort to see her safely out."

I jerked my arm out of Sansouci's firm custody. No way did I want it to look like I needed male intervention in front of Grizelle.

She remained, pacing the shop, studying its wares, and terrifying the young clerk with a thoughtful, hungry look.

Sansouci led me down the street to the awning over a deserted doorway.

"What did you do to frost Grizelle's whiskers?" he asked, admiringly. "I knew you were capable of rushing into the lion's den, but she is no cat to mess with."

"We had a discussion. It ended in a draw."

"I don't believe that."

"That's all I'm going to tell you. And you gave yourself away to Grizelle as a vampire, not the presumed werewolf everyone takes you for."

"I wouldn't mind giving myself away to her, were she

a client of mine, in her human form. She's not one to gossip, Delilah. Besides, she respects vamps more than wolf boys."

"You need her respect?"

"It'll help negotiations when you return, remember? Come on, Delilah. I'm your pal. I was in Montoya's rescue party. I went into that damn fey maze under the Gehenna with you. You *will* award me the franchise, right?"

"The word is 'negotiations.' It's not prearranged, even for frenemies like you."

"I've been promoted to a frenemy? That sounds promising. Love-hate relationships can be damn stimulating."

"Cool it. I don't want phone-line chat. I only came outside with you because I want to ask you something about Ric's time with the Karnak vampires."

"Beyond nasty."

"I know that."

"He has the stones of a statue, I'll say that, to resist giving them the information they wanted despite the leeches and the vampire tsetse flies and the lords of the blood-dance siccing every vamp in the place on him."

"I *know* that. I don't need a play-by-play. I'm beginning to wonder if they *did* get what they wanted. They've been quiet since then."

"Montoya did not give them a word, I'd never believe that," Sansouci said.

"Your faith is touching," I said, my grin going crooked even as I produced it. I took a deep breath. "What if they weren't just torturing him by draining every last drop of blood?"

"Yeah, they did that. He was dead, Delilah, until you put those ruby-glossed lips of yours on his. Your CPR chest-thumps didn't revive him. Your kiss did." Sansouci's expression grew grave. "Now that I think about it, a kiss than can revive a corpse might off a vampire. Maybe you and I don't have a future, after all."

"Of course we don't! What I'm wondering, all of a sudden, is if the damn twin pharaohs got exactly what they wanted."

His forehead wrinkled under the rakish forelock of silver-streaked black hair, but his eyes remained an unread mystery behind the shades.

Then he nodded ever so slightly and slowly.

"Ric dowses for the dead. He can raise them. The dowsing and finding I get. Ordinary people can do that for water, or even gemstones and precious metals. I know that from my . . . long and inglorious past. Finding is one thing, but raising the dead as zombies? How?"

"The dowsing rod and Ric's special talent do the finding. It takes a few drops of his blood on the dowsing rod to actually raise the bodies."

Sansouci did what I wanted from him. He speculated like a predator. "And if one had pints and pints of that dead-raising blood?"

"Oh, my God! The twin pharaohs' vamp troops weren't *consuming* Ric's blood. They had their own inbred stock for that then. They were *taking* it. For use later to raise any dead they wanted resurrected."

"You're just feeling me out to confirm your own suspicions, Delilah. Flattering, but useless. I have no idea why they'd want that power, but their having it can't be good for the rest of us. "

"And Ric."

"Always Ric with you." He swept off the sunglasses in the shade, those emerald-hard eyes looking for something in me I had no desire to ever show him. "Call me green with envy," he said wryly, "but I can't deny he's a good man in a bad world. If he's still 'just' a man."

The words chilled me more than his gemstone gaze.

Sansouci, any vampire, was something of a soul-shifter as well. Once he'd been mortal and human, and he remembered that time. Now he was immortal and unhuman. He knew way more about merciless adaptation and accommodation than a fierce shape-shifter like Grizelle had ever had to learn.

That's why he scared me even more, in his fashion.

I was glad to be getting out of town this afternoon, even if it meant looking my past bogeymen in the face.

Chapter Six

Packing for Kansas had forced me to dig out one of my conservative TV reporter suits. The Enchanted Cottage's invisible "personal shopper" apparently wouldn't touch anything so contemporary and commonplace. My chrome multihanger bought from a closing dress shop remained bare.

What a wardrobe witch! She—or he—had never bothered with my growing collection of casual jeans and tops since arriving in Las Vegas, either. That made me realize my new locale had dropped the whole, mid-tier "working woman" wardrobe out of my life. But that was Vegas. You either tromped the hot streets in flip-flops, surfing shorts, and fanny packs, or you hit the hot spots in glitz and glamour.

I checked my email on the office/den computer one last time . . . in fact, it was noonish, so Ric was outside tooting Dolly's horn and Quicksilver was adding the exclamation of a sharp bark to each toot. Guys just don't want to let a girl have fun.

Only . . . I glimpsed several occasional but familiar email addys, fresh since the wee hours of this morning. Several bore the .sup extension for the hot new "supernatural" domain. I was hearing from infernobait, stonedonsnow, snowgasm224, cocainiac, snowkissedslut, all at the web address, kissedoffsnow.sup, and brimfulbabe and others from the original leading Snow fan site, snowkissedsluts.sup.

The subject lines were ominous. "It's OVER!" "Who wants JUST a FREAKING scarf except an Undead Elvis freak???" "Glad I kicked the KISS."

Ignoring the impatient outside clamor, I opened some of the messages, heart pounding.

My God, I was right. Snow was no longer closing his shows by lassoing his mosh-pit fans with a silk scarf and making them swoon from the multi-orgasms of the Brimstone Kiss.

How long had this been *not* going on?

That's what these women had been feverishly texting each other about. The emails were meant to update the older blog members. I saw my name mentioned, usually with gratitude that I'd convinced them to go "cold Kiss" and forget about hoping for a second round of bliss. It sounded like they'd all "gone electric," anyway.

I was shocked. Could *I* have been the last Brimstone Kissee? This was no time to do the math. I grabbed my duffel bag and hustled out to install it in Dolly's huge trunk.

Ric sat behind the convertible's big red-and-chrome steering wheel, clapping sarcastically. Quicksilver sat in the backseat, his big red tongue lolling out like he was getting heatstroke from waiting for me.

"All right," I said, jumping into the passenger seat. "Let's roll."

My sigh on takeoff blew off any more thought of Snow and all his works for now.

At first, I'd been surprised by how much I resisted leaving Vegas on its own for a week. Now that I'd put various bigwigs of my acquaintance into suspended animation, I felt much better about abandoning the city to its overlords for a while.

Somehow I'd become a freelance gadfly-combination-warrior maid-of-all-work for werewolf mobster Cesar Cicereau, undercover vampire entrepreneur Howard Hughes, and rock star–supernatural question mark Christophe/Cocaine/Snow. Not to mention my landlord, media boss Hector Nightwine.

Pursuing hot new attractions like Shez and his offbeat enterprise was the Vegas mogul's favorite competitive sport. They'd all be a lot less likely to get up to anything really despicable as long as negotiations over Chez Shez remained in limbo. Much as I wasn't crazy about seeing Wichita again, I was pleased at the prospect of not having to face evil on a cosmic scale for a whole week.

Quicksilver always loved to ride in Dolly, and seemed even happier than I was to be leaving the Vegas Strip behind as Ric drove us out of town.

No more hoarding Dolly's big vintage steering wheel for me. I was glad to have Ric alive and well and putting me in the passenger seat. I'd done a hell of a lot for him lately, and he needed to feel he could return the favor.

Quick dashed from one side to the other of the Caddy's wide backseat, his long tongue flopping ludicrously from side to side in his mouth. The sunglasses that protected his unusual wolfhound-blue eyes from the wind gave him a guy-movie, stunt-dog look, silly but happy-go-lucky.

As we drove up Highway 93, slowed by heavy Vegas traffic, I kept glancing in my side mirror, watching the huge profiles of the Karnak, MGM-Grand, Bellagio, Gehenna, and the Inferno hotel-casinos shrink into the distance.

"Look," I said when my eye caught a blur of black motorcycles on the freeway access road. "Isn't that the Lunatics half-were gang?"

While Ric was giving them a glance, Quicksilver was already pawing the sunglasses off his wolfish nose. He leaped out of Dolly onto the bed of a pickup truck loaded with feed sacks in the next lane and then disappeared as he leaped down to the roadway.

"Madre de Dios," Ric swore, fighting to maneuver Dolly's nineteen feet between the pickup and a roaring semi into the far right lane. "My Vette this is not."

"Dolly may not be nimble, but she has the horses and the heart," I told him. "Just keep flooring it."

Ric roared the car onto the next exit ramp, reporting on the rearview mirror action while I twisted my head to watch it.

"Those crazy bikers must be doing seventy on the access road," he shouted into considerable wind noise. "They're a public menace."

"Do you see Quick?" I pleaded.

"No. He'd be a block or more back by now at this speed," Ric yelled.

"Not necessarily," I said, as I watched the last motorcycle in the long line spin out sideways in a cloud of dust. The desert seeped everywhere. "Don't slow Dolly down to more than forty."

"The speed limit is . . ."

"Forget any law-abiding FBI guy stuff," I told him. "I'm watching. We'll need to accelerate fast to get back on the freeway on the next entrance ramp. Time it so you make the crossroad light on green."

"You want me to race the biker gang to the crossroad? Are you crazier than those half-werewolf Lunatics? Your dog on foot has fallen half a mile behind us by now."

"Nooo. That's why we have to time getting to the intersection just right. Quicksilver really doesn't like the Lunatics. They attacked me on practically my first day in Vegas."

"I remember, but . . ."

"You don't remember like Quicksilver remembers . . . *ooh,* see that? Ouch."

Ric, who'd responsibly kept his eye on the road and the speed limit, stole a sideways glance at the oncoming knot of formidable motorcycles. The salivating, fanged, hairy half-werewolf riders added a new dimension to the Hell's Angels' long-terrifying image. Another Harley spun sideways, taking out two . . . no, three bikes beside it like huge shiny black bowling pins.

"I can cross lanes and stop that gang, Del, if you think they ran down Quicksilver, but I don't want to crease Dolly on my watch. You'd be more likely to kill me than those bozos. *Hijo de puta!*"

Ric jerked Dolly's big wheel to keep her untouched as neighboring vehicles fled the oncoming action, heading into our lane while dodging the were-bunch on the rolling thunder overtaking us all.

In my side mirror, the lead biker's snarling face was growing bigger and uglier, his overreaching front wheel closing in on Dolly's pointed chrome taillight. We were verging directly into the gang's path.

The bikers maintained their bowling-alley vee formation, not about to back down from colliding with a despised "boat" like a vintage Caddy giving them a challenge.

Then a cloud of gray that reminded me of a mini-version of the creepy spectral hyena desert "fog" surmounted the leader of the pack's leather-jacketed back.

The rider's clawed, fingerless gloved hands shot up off his handlebars. His fur-eared head twisted hard to the left as he fell from the saddle. His Harley went down, striking sparks from the pavement as it drove ahead in a sideways stop and his gang plowed into it and each other in one howling, screeching, shattering, squealing cloud of metal and leather and blood and fur.

And chrome.

Dolly.

"Hang on, Del, and don't look back," Ric shouted. "I'm making that green crossroad light like you said, and I don't want to do an accident report on this one. We'll circle around and find Quicksilver on foot. Damn, I'm sorry. I don't know what to say. Don't do anything insane."

Something thumped into the backseat in a cloud of dust as police sirens converged on the intersection dwindling behind us, where small engine fires were sending up smoke signals into the settling dust.

"Go up the on ramp and back onto the freeway," I shouted.

Ric sent me a disbelieving look as Quicksilver nudged my shoulder with his dust-powdered nose. He smelled of gasoline, leather, cheap hair gel, and flea powder. *Ugh.*

"I knew the dog could fight, but you never mentioned he was a racehorse too." Ric nervously eyed the rearview mirror. "I don't think any civilians got caught in that mess."

"Nope. The gang had bullied all the accompanying traffic off the road, so Quicksilver had a clear alley all the way to take them out before the next intersection."

"You're not telling me he planned that mayhem to the last second?"

A cold wet nose brushed my cheek.

I twisted around to pat the backseat for his sunglasses until I, *oof,* found them and perched them on his nose again.

"Delilah?" Ric insisted.

"Yup. He's a yuppie puppy. A can-do puppy. Quicksilver can pace most any vehicle for a short distance, and at street speed, indefinitely, I know from experience. He knew he could get those dangerous Lunatics off the asphalt without involving any innocent victims, or he wouldn't have gone after them."

"You can't tell me a dog, any dog, would take that into consideration."

"That's just his breed instincts coming out. He's half wolfhound under that lupine package. Werewolves are the only lupines left in the Continental U.S., and these half-weres are the worst of the breed. So Quick's their law-enforcement nightmare."

I eyed Quicksilver stretched out on the long backseat, licking his toes free of dust, gasoline, and probably asphalt burns. Not to worry. Dog saliva will soothe wounds, but Quicksilver's saliva has proven to have instant healing properties for him, and, on two occasions, Ric. That's how my two mucho macho males had bonded despite initial territorial disputes over custody of me. They knew I didn't want to see either one of them hurt.

"It's the motel bathtub for you tonight, buddy," I told Quick, "for a good soak and cleaning. No arguments."

He ignored me and lapped away like a cat.

"Okay. This time we're really on the road," Ric said, letting Dolly out to high speed and settling his frame into her cushy, red-leather comfort.

"Your Vette is a railroad flatcar compared to Dolly, isn't it?"

"I like road feel. Dolly drives like an overweight rolling marshmallow to me."

I peered into the side mirror. "She didn't lose any tail-light?"

"Naw." Ric grinned and pushed the speedometer up past the speed limit. Vegas had diminished to a piece of sparkling glass winking from Dolly's mirrors. "That broken chrome you spotted was from the tinsel on all those hopped-up Harleys.

"And if you want to put *me* into the motel bathtub tonight for a good, long soak," he added, "I'm all for it. Hell, I earned it for my performance as a dog chauffeur."

"A-plus driving, partner. With a gold star."

UTAH'S SUNSET-COLORED MESAS and cliffs resembled the spectacular Valley of Fire attraction near Las Vegas, only it went on for hundreds of eye-candy miles.

To reach our first night's stop near Green River we crossed a plateau of almost eight thousand feet and came back down to earth through Spotted Wolf Canyon, where Quicksilver ran along the winding interstate. Quick resumed his rumble seat through the sheer canyons of the San Raphael Swell.

Ric was driving, so I enjoyed striking views of Devils Canyon as we ascended Ghost Rock Summit and noticed a side jaunt to Goblin Valley State Park. By twilight, we found a motel with separate cabins and a big claw-footed tub. Quicksilver dried himself by spending the chilly night outside, howling for a full moon, no doubt. Ric dried himself on the cool, scratchy motel sheets with me.

Fed and fueled, we got on the road early, all of us smelling of pine soap as we headed into Colorado and its mountain air. Even Dolly looked freshly washed and shined. Maybe the ghosts and goblins had given her a moonbeam rubdown after her rocky start out of Vegas.

My silver familiar had morphed into a New Age necklace studded with turquoise for the morning drive. Instead of curling shyly around my big toe nights, as had been its habit, now the familiar was twining itself over Ric's and my interlocked fingers and limbs, slipping like a mobile cold shiver over our overheated skin.

I didn't mention the new silent partner in our sex life. Ric had the single Silver Eye now, whatever that meant. He popped a brown contact lens over the pale reflective iris every morning, like taking a pill, to normalize his looks.

Remembering the nightmare visions from being the main course at a vampire feast under the Karnak only made him more gung-ho to get to Kansas and unearth the cause of my trauma. Part of that was his ex-lawman, good-deed mentality. I think another reason was that concentrating on my issues pushed his own back from the front line.

So . . . this was a contradiction: I was actually happy that my youthful unhappiness made such a good diversion for Ric.

Here we were, both pretending the other needed our help most.

I started out driving while Quicksilver made up doggy dreamtime in the backseat and Ric turned Dolly's radio dial left and right up and down the FM and AM ranges. All we got was static wail.

Dolly's big wheels were no joy to navigate around hairpin mountainside turns. I recalled reading a beauty tip that driving a big old wheel without power steering was great exercise for the bust support muscles. Dolly had power-everything, but, even so, my entire body was putting English into those continuous hairpin turns. I was sure to be sore tomorrow.

Still, the sun poured down sparkle on the speedy road-side creeks following the twisting mountain roads. Towns and even glimpses of habitation were rare in the mountains. Ric used his cell phone to map the highway for likely stops. I'd never adulterate Dolly's vintage integrity by adding any slick, modern gadgets, not even the threatened fuzz buster.

Light faded fast amid these impressive peaks. I yawned in the deepening shadows and checked the gas gauge. Dolly wasn't stingy with gasoline, but her tank was built for travel. The road went ever down and down until we finally hit the deserted flats again.

"I'll drive now," Ric said. "All those major curves must be exhausting to hold on to. I speak from experience."

I smiled faintly at his double entendre. I was pretty tired from the constant tension in my shoulders, and it was twilight in the shadow of the Rockies. He sped Dolly along the empty road, knowing my arm and back muscles craved a hot shower.

"A good kind of exhausting," I added. "That's real driving, not just steering."

"Yeah," Ric said. "And I was sitting, helpless, on the outside, gazing two miles down into ravines and hoping Detroit's Largest didn't plan to take us on a Thelma and Louise dive."

"Guys just so hate being not in control."

Quicksilver, who'd slept through the mountain pass, sat up and growled protest from the backseat. He was a guy too.

"Look." Ric pointed to a highway sign that was all words and no pictures.

The type was huge, but impossible to read while we were whizzing by at ninety miles an hour.

"Let's do that," he shouted into the wind whipping past Dolly's big-screen fifties windshield.

I had no idea what kind of off-road hokey attraction he was talking about. They were usually ill-kept reptile farms or fireworks shacks out here.

"The sun is setting," I pointed out, jerking my head over my shoulder to look past Quicksilver's sunglasses-free mug, all black nose and white teeth.

A spectacular, pollution-abetted sunset was setting the western mountain peaks afire, turning the dimming sky into a psychedelic painted desert of purple, orange, green, and gold.

"We should be finding a motel for the night," I said.

"This is better." Ric surprised me. I was sure he was eager for a replay of last night. His ordeal had done nothing to weaken his libido. The contrary, even.

"There's nothing out here but mileposts, Ric. I know this is the Big Nowhere, but I need a hot shower, some food, and a comfy bed *right now.*"

"It's all right back there," he said. "In a unique way." He swung Dolly into a U-ey on the deserted two-lane that her *Queen Mary* turning circumference shouldn't have been able to make without hitting the shoulder gravel.

I winced for her vintage everything, but most guys have some freaky car mojo going. Dolly spun the one-eighty in a disciplined, ladylike fashion, no squealing brakes or unseemly spray of road grit ruining the polish on her black-satin chassis.

I felt my right wrist getting heavy under the weight of a single handcuff dangling a broken chain. No, not this time. I was wearing a charm bracelet again, loaded with tooth-sharp, tiny icons I couldn't see in the dark. Even the silver familiar was going along for the ride.

"I'm getting to love this babe of a boat," Ric said, turning her up an asphalt-paved two-lane road I'd missed spotting in the rapidly descending twilight.

I still was in the dark about the meaning of the sign, especially as Dolly's headlights scanned no sign of human habitation except barbed wire fencing along the small but oddly smooth road.

"It gets really dark out here without any lights for miles," I pointed out. Again.

"So what? We're not afraid of vampires, are we?"

"Out in the heartland, vamps are not major tourist attractions, or hidden empires, or mere mob muscle, like in Vegas," I said. "They're plain and simple bloodsuckers, and always hard at it."

Ric just laughed.

Frankly, his laughter was worth as much to me as my non-vamp-perforated skin these days.

Staring into the dark for a sign of civilization, I spotted a large silvery pale expanse with faint lines forming interior squares, like a concrete wall. And we were heading right for it.

Quicksilver whined and braced his long-nailed front paws on my leather seat back. He knew that was a no-no. At least he knew enough to plant them and stop, with no overexcited canine churning that would damage the leather, but he wanted a good view of our eerie destination as much as I did.

And then I spotted . . .

"Cars. That's a parking lot in the middle of nowhere?"

"Yup." Ric sounded smug.

"I don't see any motel cabins or buildings. Or showers."

"I wasn't really looking for rain while driving a convertible with the top down."

"Food."

"See that blocky little building in the middle of the parked cars there?"

"Looks like an animal shelter in a very small town. *Ish.* Sheets?"

"Red leather *not* turn you on?"

Ric eased Dolly into a vacant area up against what looked like a parking meter. Then he buzzed up the driver's window a few inches and clamped the parking meter head onto the glass.

"Ric. Why is that thing abusing my vintage window? Those fifty-six Biarritz Caddy windows are hell to replace. I know, because Quicksilver smashed through one to defend me against the Lunatics the day that I adopted him in Sunset Park."

"Relax," Ric said as the hovering white alien ship dead ahead produced a vaguely colored glow and tinny music blared into the Cadillac.

"Are we going to be abducted, or what?" I shouted, hands over ears and body braced for instant levitation. "I've got enough 'missing time' in my personal history already."

Ric remained calm. "Guess you never had a chance to patronize a restored twentieth-century drive-in movie theater. Me neither."

He stretched his arm over my seat back.

"What do you want from the food shack, Date?"

Chapter Seven

WE HAD OUR first "discussion" while the giant screen showed inane cartoon characters and animated boxes of candy and popcorn. If I never saw another Dancing Milk Dud, it would be too soon. And the music was the sappiest I'd ever heard in my life.

"Ric, I'm not sure this whole trip is a good idea. Happiness was Wichita, Kansas, in Dolly's wide-screen rearview mirror. And this side trip is creepy. I know I wasn't really abducted by aliens as a kid, but that scenario is way too close for comfort to what might have actually happened. The closer we get to Wichita, the jumpier I get."

"Hey, Delilah." He pulled me across the bench seat to lay my head on his shoulder. "Not many restored drive-in movie screens survive in the country. I thought you were a vintage film buff. Anyway, the girl is supposed to get a little scared and snuggle up, right?"

"Drive-ins were dead before I was alive. Why are we here?"

"You love vintage, right? I just thought we could do something fun for a while, be together like a normal couple at a movie instead of chasing down IDs on buried bones and digging up ancient vampires along with lots of early Vegas history and getting exotic supernatural killers on our tails."

"Speaking of tails . . ." I glanced around for Quicksilver.

"He hopped out as soon as we were hooked up to the speaker to find a better viewing spot."

"Now Quick's gone and we're sitting in this parking lot of strangers in the wilderness."

"Cold Creek," Ric said.

"What?" I thought the phrase meant something like "tough shit," at first.

"Cold Creek, Colorado," he repeated. "That's the town just fifteen miles away. We're not in the wilderness, and Quicksilver is just off doing doggy guard duty, I bet."

"There's a hot shower and fast food just fifteen minutes away?"

"Yeah, and we'll go there after the show. Meanwhile we can do what Dolly was meant to do, take a couple of hot kids to the drive-in with her top down and the guy hoping to get the girl's top down. We can neck through a few reels, and I do mean reels, because they show old black-and-white movies here. Just neck like the normal teenagers we never were. Smear your lips with that hot new color lip gloss you're using and I'll get to work wearing it off."

I did adore the kissing part. I dug in my hobo bag on the floorboard. "You like this stuff, huh? It *is* flavored." I screwed up a bullet-shaped tube of deep raspberry color with flecks of silver glitter.

His "yeah" was one of those gruff, turned-on understatements he made during sex.

"Let me put it on you," he said, suddenly. "What's it called?"

"Midnight Cherry Shimmer," I said before he tilted up my chin and ran the smooth oily stick over my bottom lip so slowly it was like he used his tongue.

"'Cherry,'" Ric repeated. "Perfect for the tender teen mood I want you in tonight."

He slicked the gloss over my top lip as I felt a deep quiver inside.

"We're way past that stage, Ric," I said anyway.

"What's the harm in going back?"

"Going back? You never *were* at a drive-in movie. You're way too young too. Didn't you get enough thrills sneaking around dating those rich and spoiled baby socialites in Washington, D.C.? You were the exotic wild child turned bureaucrat's foster kid and high school heartthrob. Don't kid me."

"I meant going back to a more innocent time. The minute I laid eyes on Dolly I was wishing I could take you and her out on a date."

"We kinda got to the endgame of a date right there in Sunset Park over an overexcited dowsing rod before you ever laid eyes on Dolly at the curb."

"I wouldn't regret that moment for the world, Del. Look, that teenage tear of mine wasn't real, any more than those Barbie girls were. Sure, I made it with them . . . in the beach house, in the boat house, in the upstairs maid's quarters, in the gazebo in the garden, in their graduation Beamers and Porsches with bucket seats and central consoles, and upright shifts making it an instant three-way. I never made love with them."

I had nothing to say to that.

"Del, you must *know* that *I* know all the things you've been doing to spare me any aftershocks from being eaten by vampires."

I could only mutter the next sentence. "I'm supposed to laugh at that phrase, but they tortured and almost killed you."

"I know. I've got most of those memories back. I know how you bent your whole heart and soul to making sure when I came out of my coma it wasn't like waking up fresh from a nightmare, like you do so often. And it wasn't, was it?"

Now he was nibbling on my earlobe, my neck.

Necking. Just the word made me nervous now that vampires were surfing U.S.A. across the whole world. Back in Dolly's day, the term had meant lots of smooching and maybe even tongue if the guy was a J.D., a juvenile-delinquent-in-training, and lots of above-the-waist groping. I'd seen *American Graffiti* too. It was a forty-year-old antique, even though it was in color.

"I love being behind this steering wheel," Ric said.

"Ric, we're not even moving now. We're parked."

"Right. And I'm in the driver's seat and you've got both hands free. And girls just want to suck face forever."

He pulled me against him. I looked around nervously, but the tall gateway and road lights were shining in the now totally dark distance. Our car was open, but we were pretty hidden.

Ric's face bent to find mine for a passionate kiss that took my breath away, breaking it only to murmur sexy Spanish words against my lips, moving from short, soft nibbles to soul kisses that were so much searching tongue I was thinking who needed anything more and how could we keep finding new angles and different rhythms that would keep us on the brink of this insane delirium?

We never stopped lip-syncing. The vast night air and our hot-breathed body moves in a confined space and confined clothes were beyond erotic. It was sexting in the dark. Ric's mouth was everywhere, burning up my skin and moving on so fast I seemed bathed in pre-orgasmic sensation. Despite my lips' many near-collisions with his neck, I managed to avoid his bite scar, remembering that in the first heat of our relationship I'd accidentally bitten him a little and scared myself silly. I'd kill myself if I found out I had any vamp tendencies, although that would be tough. Suicidal vampires don't exist.

Ric finally broke off to let me breathe, leaving me dizzy, my fingers curled into his thigh to keep myself upright. My head lolled onto the seat back while I stared up at bright swaths of stars sowed like seeds on the wind in the black sky. Ric lowered his head to my heaving chest as if dowsing for my heartbeat, his mouth kissing a line up to my collarbone and chin.

I certainly was getting why drive-ins had been called "passion pits." Warm, wet lips suckled my earlobe; teeth pinched it. A hot, probing tongue plunged into my ear. The sudden nip and plunge sensation pushed a sexual rush from my brain down to my toes and back up again.

On that wave, sucking me beneath the waterline of sensation into utter surrender, Ric's face nuzzled behind my ear, pushing under my hair. A fiery burning sensation on my neck paralyzed me. Then I realized . . . I started to mouth the word, "No," but his fingers fanned against my lips as if to sign *shhhh*. I reined in my galloping breath.

The sudden ceasing of our motion except for Ric's mouth burning, burning, burning the skin on my neck made time freeze. I heard crickets screaming all around us for the first time, but mostly I felt a hot, surging pulse coursing through my body, sensed its echo in his. I didn't want to stop him. I didn't want to move. I wanted to let him take me, take me, take me until he could take no more.

My lips parted to draw his caressing fingers inside, but otherwise nothing in me could move but the pounding, pounding of blood and desire, until his face drew back and his fingertips caressed the stinging sweet-spot on my neck.

"Te amo," he whispered. "I won't use that word you hate, but every teenager in the world has done this in a place like this. You see now? How the kiss that seeks the hot blood that drives our love excites? Let me give this as well as take it from you. All right?"

"Will I . . . bruise?"

He stroked me there again. "That's the point, *amor*. It's the badge of our passion. That's why I put it far back on your neck, under your hair. Only you and I will know it's there. Only I can see it."

"That seems . . . possessive."

"Passion is possession. I love that you thought about stopping me. It's so hot that you didn't. I know," he said, stroking me again, bolts of desire surging through me now on every caress, "you always feared an attack here from vampires. That you overcame that to let me make my love visible; there's nothing better."

Our mutual fever still raged, so I understood what he meant, I guess, but icy tendrils of doubt still stirred my soul.

"Chica," Ric whispered, "don't you want to explore the deepest levels of our love? Don't you want sex that shakes your soul? Don't you feel safe with me no matter what?" he asked, coaxed.

Now he had me. The last thing I wanted to mess with right now was his machismo.

Only one answer, Irma butted in. *Don't blow it.*

"Yes. I trust you. Of course, I do. *Sí. Te amo, hombre.*"

I guess I'd just have to look up "suck me" in my Dirty Spanish dictionary for future use. I didn't have the nerve for the even dirtier version. Yet.

BUT I SURE didn't feel safe in the drive-in's great outdoors.

It's not like Ric did a suck and run. He held me close,

kept kissing my mouth, my face, the small damp spot near my carotid artery that throbbed and pulsed with the still-ragged beating of my heart. My head on his chest felt the echo of his own slowing rhythms. We pulled apart to let the urge to merge subside until later.

I heard a thump from the backseat and knew Quicksilver had returned as soon as the mushy stuff was safely over. Having Quick in the backseat meant we could prepare for the actual supposed point of the outing, the movie. Ric, of course, had wanted to initiate me in the proper setting all along.

Reality took over. The liquid heat at the crux of my body was major. I pulled myself together and made my first trip to the cinder-block women's "restroom." Hip boots and tongs required.

While Ric went to relieve (men have it easy) and retrieve (the menu gave fast food a bad name), I established myself back in Dolly's passenger seat. Just letting Ric drive my baby had been a good move. The whole point of this trip, I realized, was to let Ric take charge on the professional investigative turf that was his, and take care of me for a change. And did he ever.

Deep sigh. I'd grown up wary, edgy, ready to be pounced on by some vamp boy or mean girl every moment. This trip "home" was going to be a hard assignment, except for the extracurricular activities. Maybe I was being a worrywart about Ric's minor physical . . . alterations and his randy schoolboy fixation on "branding" his girl. "Won't you wear my ring around your neck?" I saw that iconic fifties' song could refer to a more intimate claim. Same symbolic point. I doubted a class ring on a chain could have me nearly stroking out the way Ric's fifteen minutes of semipublic necking had.

Looking at the charm bracelet on my wrist, I realized the silver familiar hadn't given even one defensive twitch during the entire episode. It certainly was getting with the nineteen-fifties program.

I could only hope the familiar wasn't also a one-way spy-line for Snow. Now that I was getting a lot more clued into sexual subtexts, I remembered Snow's remark when we first met near his Inferno Hotel bar that our conjoined black and white long hair would look sexy in the mirror above his bed.

I'd taken it for a not-too-subtle message that he wasn't a mirror-phobic vampire—since he *was* phobic about being taken for an albino vampire—but I hadn't discovered my own mirror-based freaky powers then and had only just met Ric and my own libido.

Maybe the remark had been a pure come-on I was still too naïve to recognize.

Maybe I can sub for you under that mirror, Irma suggested.

Maybe Lilith already had.

Good. I wanted to leave Snow as far behind as I'd recently wanted to lose Wichita. Forever.

WHILE WE WAITED for Ric's return, I shared my smaller misgivings with Quicksilver in the backseat. His ears perked and fanned forward while his eyes, glued on my every word, expressed bottomless sympathy.

"Romantic, isn't it?" I began. "I'm gonna get a cricked neck from watching a horrible, scratched film way above us. I won't hear the rotten sound over Ric's munching, and he'll probably throw you more popcorn than is good for you. We'll hear a chorus of growling tummies from ersatz snack food. And endure cramped legs from awkward petting positions. I mean ours, not yours. Oh, well. Ric's been a sick man. We have to humor him."

Quicksilver growled, leaped out of the car, and lifted a leg against the metal sound unit pillar before he vanished again for his usual nightly run.

"Right on, brother," I called after him. "I'd do that, and then make my escape if I could. You should see the women's restroom here."

Shhh, Irma warned. *Ric's coming back.*

Ric had returned bearing a tray holding four red-and-white-striped boxes of popcorn, enough to make up a dapper barbershop quartet, and huge paper cups of soda pop. I scooted far across the bench seat and leaned even farther over to open the heavy door for him.

"Not a lot of cup holders here," he muttered when we were back in our respective seats. "We'll have to drink fast."

Me, I was doing nothing that would require a second visit to what passed for a women's restroom here. "Stall" was indeed the correct expression.

Dolly was pre–center console, pre–cup holders. I opened the huge glove compartment and lined up the drink cups on the horizontal lid.

The sound unit spouted alive, producing chuckling music and a laugh track as film trailers and commercials for long-gone car models and local businesses unreeled on the screen. I could hear rustlings and heavy breathing from the cars all around. One great heaving beast of lust had materialized in the parking lot.

Meanwhile, giant numbers were counting back from ten on the screen. From the surrounding parked cars—some convertibles, all with rolled-down windows—came an echoing shout. "Four—three—two—one!"

Meanwhile, the film started flickering on the giant graph-paper-lined screen.

Meanwhile, the sound system surged into *Phantom of the Opera* shrieking organ mode. Heavy block letters as distorted as the sound covered the screen.

NIGHT OF THE LIVING DEAD.

"It's a contemporary newsreel," I said.

"It's a classic," Ric said. "You must have seen this on the TV in your group home."

"I turned off anything made after the nineteen-forties, pretty much."

"Delilah, this was released years before we were born."

"So were the film zombies! I turned off the gory stuff. Peter Lorre and Bela Lugosi and Vincent Price were scary, but elegant. And a bit too hokey to believe."

"Come here, baby," Ric coaxed. "You can do this. You've offed vampire mummies."

"But they were real. This is just freaky-scary."

Ric stroked my hair as I peeked through its strands to the screen. His arm was around my waist. My hand on his chest could feel the calm, steady thrum of his heart.

"I'm here for you," he whispered into my forehead.

Yes, he was. Guess I could sit through one gory guy movie after having risked my soul to bring him back from the dead.

And the chance to see a black-and-white film blown up to Times Square billboard size was awesome.

TOO BAD THE black-and-white people on-screen weren't my favorite CinSims, but no-name actors from the sixties. I amused myself for a while by eyeing the heroine's ultra-short skirt and long blond hair in a shoulder-brushing flip.

Ric picked up the popcorn and pop and munched and sipped, even when lumbering, glassy-eyed zombies crammed a liver into their mouths or gnawed on an obviously human bone.

Yawn. The humans took refuge in a deserted farmhouse. They broke furniture to nail breakaway boards over the doors and windows, to no avail. They cowered and screamed, the zombies walked. Very, very slowly. And walked. Relentless.

Around us the audience gasped and shrieked a little.

Me, I fell asleep, waiting for a witty line of dialogue, on Dolly's body-warmed red leather, in the embrace of my zombie movie-loving significant other. My silver familiar had become a calming, actually ticking, old-fashioned locket-watch on a neck chain, resting right where my heart slowed and disappeared into a dream.

THE SHRIEK THAT awoke me echoed on and on, nothing new in this movie.

Another voice had joined the panicked chorus and I knew it.

I sat upright.

"Some date, sleepyhead," Ric said. "Where's the fire?"

"Quicksilver's howling at the half-moon."

"How could you hear him with all this zombie growling and gnarfing and victim shrieking? This is classic. Nightwine should lease some of these zombie CinSims to guard his grounds and yours."

"Something's wrong, Ric."

"That's a line from the movie, Del. Aren't you glad I'm into classic films, like you are?"

Grrr. Arghh! The dialogue leaves a lot to be desired, I thought.

"Quicksilver?" I got on my knees in the front seat to look into the back one.

My dog lofted over the car's side, his hackles fluffed enough to masquerade as a bad dame's good fur coat in a thirties movie. *Real* classics.

"Ric!" I screamed.

He had set the nostalgia food and drink on the open glove compartment lid and was staring at the pandemonium on the giant screen.

"These zombies are marvelous," he said. "Romero, the director, got away with murder. Nude rear shots, cannibalism close up and personal, helpless humans, the living dead on a rampage. This is the forerunner of spatterpunk."

Oh, joy.

Quicksilver was panting and salivating as he stared at the screen. I followed his intent canine gaze.

Oh.

Oh.

The zombies were walking, all right.

Right off the screen.

And they all looked eight feet tall.

Chapter Eight

"THERE'RE PUTTING VINTAGE movies in three-D?" I exploded. "That craze has gotten out of hand. Some of us find what Romero did in 1968 plenty scary, not to mention icky."

"I'm no film purist like you or Hector Nightwine," Ric agreed, "but adding three-D *is* odd for restored drive-in-movie fare. It's very realistic, though."

I noticed some smaller figures actually running between the cars parked closest to the screen. Some were scrambling over car hoods and tops and trunks, heading our way.

"Those aren't the walking dead people," I yelled. "They're the fleeing audience members."

By then I'd recognized the lone figure that had run over the car silhouettes to perch on an HHR roof and brace its feet while shouting a challenge.

Actually, it braced all four feet and howled a challenge. Quicksilver.

By now, Ric and I had scrambled out of the Caddy as fleeing people on the ground and victims on-screen streamed toward us.

"Why are the zombies escaping the film?" Ric asked me.

"I'm not the zombie expert," I shouted back.

Then I blinked at his face. "Your brown contact lens is missing."

He put his fingers to his cheekbone. "I bumped into the cheesy screen door frame leaving the food stand with all the boxes in my hands. That must have jolted the contact out. I've got another dozen packed in Dolly's trunk."

"Did you—did your naked silver eye—*call* the zombies off the screen? Have you got a brand-new way to dowse for the dead?"

"These things aren't real," Ric said. "They're figments of old film."

"So are CinSims, and they're solid enough to dance cheek-to-cheek with casino customers. Where's the projection booth?"

"I've never raised anything without a dowsing rod," Ric objected, still working out the phenomenon.

"Eyes have 'rods' in them, don't they? Aren't there millions that control the black and white part of vision?"

"That's anatomy in miniature, not . . . not a piece of wood or metal from the real world." Ric's hands fisted in a balked desire to hold a physical Y-shaped implement.

"Don't rationalize. Something's going on here, and even if we didn't start it, we have to stop it."

Quicksilver's protective instincts had realized that. He was leaping into the oncoming zombies, giving them gnaw-for-gnaw. They ignored him, shrugged him off, even though his teeth gritted to tear off what little clothes and, in some cases, flesh, were left on them.

Not my fave movie monsters, and now they were coming right for us. Luckily, they were vintage zombies, very, very slow and shambling.

Dolly's trunk levitated behind me like a large shiny laptop screen opening. Ric must be going for his contact lenses . . . no, for his licensed Glock semiautomatic, our only serious weapon besides my cop duty belt.

I tossed the paper cups, closed the glove compartment, and grabbed the metal Club on the passenger side floor that locked Dolly's steering wheel in iffy locations, like near the Vegas Sinkhole. It made a better weapon than a wooden billy club.

As Ric slammed the trunk lid shut, a woman rushed past him, screaming, "He must be one of them. That glass eye gleams like solid ice."

By now we were playing dodgem cars with our bodies, slipping between the few high-riding elderly SUVs the Gas Wars had left on the road to hide from the suddenly animated horde of screen zombies.

I heard the scrabble of claws on metal. Quicksilver leaped to the ground beside us, a disgusting bone in his teeth. I had no idea if the bone belonged to friend or foe but ordered, "Quick! *Leave kitty.*"

Ric rolled his oddly colored eyes.

I think even the oncoming zombies paused to mill about in confusion at hearing that command. I'm sure they assumed a tasty tidbit to gnaw was nearby.

I saw the whites of Quick's baby blues as he reluctantly dropped the big, juicy bone that now was in living color. Was it a prop, or part of a 3-D zombie? I knew he wouldn't gnaw on a victim. He was K-9 to the core.

Come to think of it, some of the fleeing moviegoers had vivid red scratches on their faces and arms.

Oh, shoot, I thought, just as Ric shot his automatic into the air. I noticed that his pockets were stuffed with extra ammo, not candy bars from a food mission to the snack shack.

Speaking of snack shack, I heard bones cracking and splintering all around us.

"We've got to reverse this film," I shouted at Ric. "Where's the projection booth?"

"In front of the concessions building," he answered.

"And it's built like a bunker. We're going to have to mount an assault. I bet the projectionist is quaking among his reels in there."

"That's just what we have to get away from him. This movie must stop before the cast devours the audience."

"Okay. You run for the building. You see it over there?"

"The zombies have almost reached it."

"I'll follow, shooting. Beware of spraying bone chips."

"And Quicksilver will lead," I muttered, as the dog loped into the open, hurling his hundred and fifty pounds on fragile zombie shoulders and bringing these skeletal remnants down, even as they clawed their way forward on their bellies.

Shack to shack and jelly to jelly, it's a zombie jamboree.

Was that Irma jiving me, or my own mind in overdrive-in?

Since Quicksilver had committed his bone and blood to the zombie attack, I ran after him, swinging my steering wheel security device right and left. It cracked on so much moving sagging flesh and bone that I didn't have to look very hard to see what effect I was having.

I heard Ric pounding behind me, letting off single, on-target but sadly ineffective shots.

Ric and I shouldered against the projection room's locked wooden door, hearing the loosened film strip snapping like a playing card in the wire wheels of a fifties Schwinn. Why else did they call them "Bicycle" playing cards?

Ric kicked open the door.

Quick dodged inside the squat structure as Ric and I slammed the door shut just behind Quick's long wolfish tail and right on a couple of clawing arm bones aimed at joining us.

"Aiiiii," the farm boy projectionist was chattering.

I recognized those dungarees and that plaid shirt from

my previous life in Wichita and wanted to sit down beside the young guy to reassure him.

Ric brandished his sinister matte-black firearm, jerked the boy away from the old-fashioned Mickey Mouse–eared projection machine, and threw him to the dirt floor. He was a lot safer there.

Outside, the clawing sound of fleeing human and hunting zombie beat a tattoo on the crude wooden door. Soon it would be toothpicks and we would be on the zombie menu. I guess they liked to serial snack on a night out too.

As Ric and I stared through the lit square that cast the film images larger than life on the massive screen, we saw writhing human and zombie silhouettes looming large on the rural landscape.

My silver familiar, meanwhile, had lost the charms and was looping itself around and around my wrist in lengths of thin but hindering chain.

Before I could draw Ric's attention to this, the familiar leaped like an anorexic boa-constrictor-turned-bicycle-chain onto the film projector, wrapping around the shiny silver nitrate surface.

The reaction resembled a diamond saw blade mating with an oil slick.

The turning reels ground and squealed, and then the film strip came splintering off its track, glittering with a silver aura that reached the screen and set white lightning dancing across the moving black-and-white images of predator and prey.

In the projection booth, the splintered film, bleached to white, coiled around and around on the floor, an endless maggot, while the boyish projectionist sobbed with horror.

"Stop it," he gasped out. "Please stop it. I'm killing them. I'm killing the customers."

"Not you," I said, squeezing a hand on his shoulder. "They'll be all right. Every one of them. This is all just a real scary feature at the drive-in."

Ric disabled the projector with the butt of his gun, watching the young guy to make sure he'd know the demonic machine was dead and gone. Ric rolled the unreeled film into a fire-hose thickness around his forearm.

I winced at one more vintage film destroyed, even if it was from the sunset of black-and-white.

Only zombies were left ranging around the deserted cars, including Dolly.

"This bunch have escaped the film forever," I said. "We've got to . . . destroy them."

We ventured outside for a wide-screen view of the situation.

Ric set his teeth in the moonlight. "I haven't got enough ammunition, or time, to shoot all of them to writhing bits. They'll be on us in a couple minutes."

Quicksilver was still barking himself hoarse trying to round up these monsters as if they were merely feral Zobos.

"Ric." I put my hand on his arm. "I can't call him back. 'Leave kitty' won't cut it. He knows better. I won't leave Quicksilver."

"Where's your familiar?" he asked suddenly.

I lifted my arms. "I don't know. I could use a pair of silver whips right now."

Ric grabbed my left wrist. A lightning-bolt-shaped cuff bracelet twined my forearm.

"Huh? Pretty . . . but pretty useless," I complained. "'Into the valley of darkness,'" I began, pushing forward.

"No." Ric was eyeing the scene, calculating the fan of zombies ranging farther and farther from the screen. "We need to go back to the projection hut."

"The projector's broken," I protested, but he grabbed and dragged me along.

I spotted the unreeled old-fashioned film flapping on his arm. In front of the hut's pathetic little darkened window, he stopped.

"All right. We're at the last row of sound poles. Grab an end of the film and move to the nearest pole on your right. I'll take the left."

"This is not square dancing," I shouted.

The damned zombies growled, drowning out normal speech. I saw cadaverous, nauseating faces and bodies, all rotting, coming into far too sharp a focus. At least Quick was backing up toward us now, belly down and barking.

"Grab the pole, Delilah," Ric yelled.

Somewhere, very far behind me, Irma giggled insanely.

I grabbed, he grabbed, and the film between us suddenly snapped and went luminous. A coat of speeding mercury covered the aluminum-painted poles and raced among them left and right and forward and back, creating a buzzing, snapping grid of some sort of electric power the zombies walked, relentlessly and slowly, right into. They winked out like cinders at a barbecue.

By then, Quicksilver had retreated almost back to us. He took a fast look-see to make sure we were still standing, then had to dart forward to sniff each former-zombie hot spot.

"They did something like this to stop *The Thing*," I told Ric. "Now that was classic horror movie. No mindless sleepwalking and gnawing. I think it was scientific stuff, not paranormal."

"I don't know what this was," he said.

"Do you suppose some silver nitrate remained on that unreeled film?"

"Maybe. Or maybe some of your silver familiar. I just know you're not going to believe where I got this silver network idea."

"Yeah?"

He glanced at the jagged lightning bolt form of my forearm band.

"The familiar was trying to tell us something. Use conductivity—whether electric, metallic, or magic, I don't know—but it worked."

A few fading zombie ghost-images were still circling the drive-in fringes when Ric burned the film in the deserted snack shack's hot-dog turning machine and— zombie by zombie by bone by bone by blood by blood— they each went up in flames in turn.

Vehicle engines were coughing into life all over the parking lot, choking, and then turning and grinding through the maze of aisles leading from the drive-in lot. Folks had crept back to claim their cars. I saw the half-moon, its hard center line softened to a blur, reflecting off Dolly's generous dollops of chrome. She looked fine.

"Let's get out of here," Ric said.

"First, I need to wash my hands."

"You want to visit that no-woman's-land again?"

"I can't touch Dolly with these hands, much less Quick-silver."

"Delilah. Your dog is a carnivore too. He was good to go."

"I'll never understand males. I'm going to freshen my face, all right? And then we get out of this hell-forsaken retro-ghouls-gone-wild scene. Got it?"

Ric shrugged. I think Quicksilver, standing beside him with legs braced and hackles still up, shrugged too.

I just wanted to wash my hands and face and apply some

fresh Lip Venom gloss to my desert-dry lips. The familiar had morphed into a Swatch telling me it was half past the witching hour. Everything looked okay inside the women's restroom. The concrete-floored sink area was deserted; the black-spotted mirrors above the dripping sinks were blurry and misted. Nothing to fear in them.

I pulled out my Lip Venom tube, shaped like a high-octane bullet, and slicked it over my lips. Ric and I still had to get to a motel room for the night.

That's when I heard the whimpering from the stalls around the cinder-block corner.

Yes, it smelled like a urinal in here. Where a lot of the guys had also been suffering from periods, or just bleeding out. No, I was not going to leave the Cold Creek Drive-in without a civilized touch on my lips and libido and self-respect.

I turned when the whimpering and lap-dog noises got overpowering.

Quicksilver would never go into a girl's bathroom.

Oh.

Crawling out on the unspeakably wet concrete floor came terrified humans of both sexes. They'd found safety huddling in the women's bathroom.

Not even the zombies would go here.

I was so going to personally "liberate" the next male john I came across.

Or the next male, who was the usual suspect and who wasn't twenty feet away.

"Come on, Lassie," I told the familiar, "we have fifteen more miles to a motel room tonight. I hope there's only cable."

Chapter Nine

THAT NIGHT AT Cold Creek Motel did us all a lot of good.

The water was hot, the sheets were flannel, and Ric slept like a baby while Quicksilver roamed the night and I lay awake trying to figure out the connection between my silver familiar, old film, Ric's new silver iris, and the raising and rescuing and slaying of zombies, offscreen and on.

I also mused for a while on two far distant kids with bizarre backgrounds, the boy turned man by a vampire bat bite and the girl turned off on womanhood by the threat of boy-vamp bites.

I decided all these issues deserved to be interred with film-phantom zombie bones, and finally went to sleep.

DRIVING DOLLY BACK on the highways that had taken me out of Kansas to Las Vegas felt like a time trip. It had only been a couple of months but—oh, my Auntie Irma—how things had changed.

The golden daylight felt a world away from the night's dark silver-nitrate depths.

Having Ric along, commenting on windmills and shimmering fields of wheat in west Kansas and eagerly anticipating our last big town before Wichita, Dodge City, opened my eyes to scenery and history I'd always taken for granted. It seemed so normal.

"Dodge's Wyatt Earp Boulevard is no more exciting than Sunset Road in Vegas," I cautioned him. "Yes, Boot Hill is here, smack dab in the downtown area, but it's pretty touristy tame these days."

"Maybe on the way back we can stop and do all the tourist shtick," Ric suggested, eyes still glued on his phone screen as it jumped from one hokey website to another. A boy and his remote, on the road.

"Sure," I promised like a parent would, not really meaning it, but open to being bullied into something later if I had to be.

Ric was into the second week of his second life, so I tried to be tolerant.

"No more replays of the Cold Creek Drive-in zombie jamboree," I warned him. "That was gross."

"That was a little . . . weird," he conceded, "but fascinating. I don't know if your silver familiar or my sterling new iris drew or repulsed the zombie attack. Maybe my revamped eye is too powerful for supernaturals, and I'll have to wear sunglasses all the time, like your new Vegas posse, Snow and Sansouci."

"Lord, you three all in shades would make a freaky Blues Brothers trio for the new millennium. And those two guys aren't my posse. They're my . . . frenemies."

"You seem to be a fan already," Ric teased me, referring to my tales of Chez Shezmou while he was driving. "You can't deny you keep running into Christophe and Cicereau's main man."

And vice versa.

Ric had reason to bring that up. Two months ago, I leave Wichita an old maid of twenty-four with an orphaned past and an allergy to intimacy. I get to Vegas, meet my own true love in the first twenty-four hours, and then start tangling with potent paranormals who suddenly find me highly flirtable material.

I guess falling in love and becoming sexually active gives a girl a glow other dudes might want to warm their hands on. Oddly enough, we were all four on the same side, intermittently. The three guys did sometimes feel like a backup group for the female empowerment identity quest: my super-trio and me, not counting the canine member who provided the falsetto howling.

At least Shezmou regarded me as only a liberating goddess, nothing personal.

While I mulled my sudden popularity with the opposite sex and my dismal record with my own, including my elusive mirror double, Ric moved on to serious topics that he faced.

"Delilah, I've got to figure out what's happening with my offbeat eye and my dead-dowsing skills," he said, pushing his sunglasses up on his forehead.

It *was* hard to decide whether to gaze besottedly into his hot chocolate-dark brown eye or to catch tiny glimpses of myself in the iris of his new silver one.

"Your vision remains twenty-twenty in both eyes?" I asked.

"As far as I can tell. It'll be good to try some things out here in the boonies."

"Wichita isn't a small city, Ric."

"I know. I read the chamber of commerce site. Two hundred thousand 'pop.' We'll meet my local contact about fifteen miles outside of town. Place called Augusta?"

I nodded. "Famous for hiking trails. Not for Dolly to negotiate. She doesn't rough it."

"Don't worry. We're hooking up outside the park at

some fast-food restaurant named Red Ryder Ranger Station. A fellow ex-FBI agent will be our native guide."

"You and I hooked up in Sunset Park," I reminded him. "Who's our third here? Some hot wench from your unbridled yet privileged D.C. prep school romantic past, no doubt."

Ric shrugged with a disarming grin. "Can I help who my friends are?"

His answer made me even more suspicious. Ric usually slipped into Spanish when mentioning friends, but doing so now would clearly have to indicate gender. *Amigo* or *amiga*. He'd just been twitting me about rival Vegas guys. Maybe I really *was* going to meet an old FBI flame of Ric's.

I touched the silver familiar on my chest, still posing as an art-gallery-class piece of turquoise-embedded Native American jewelry.

"That silver shape-shifter sure knows how to complement your eye color," Ric said as he noticed my gesture.

Quicksilver barked in the backseat.

"Your baby blues too, Gray Shadow," Ric twisted around to tell my dog.

"This is awfully Southwest style for Kansas," I said doubtfully, fingering the familiar, which warmed to my touch. "Although Coronado did mosey this far north hundreds of years ago, searching for silver."

"Coronado? The conquistador?" Ric sounded sharply surprised.

"*Ooh*, say that again. It sounds so sexy with the proper accent."

"Coronado?" Ric repeated in an are-you-nuts tone.

I wasn't about to confess that his authentic pronunciation of the lovely rolled *r* and soft *d* of the Spanish language was quickly becoming my instant aphrodisiac.

"No. *Conquistador, hombre,*" I cooed.

"Don't flirt so hard when you're at the wheel, Delilah. Dolly might end up in the ditch."

I laughed, feeling good about going back to Wichita for the first time.

Now you're getting it, Irma said. *We've got nothing to fear here but fear itself.*

She was right. Wichita was my home, "sour" home. It housed my orphanage and group homes, my fancy private high school on scholarship, my old job, the empty lot of my destroyed rented bungalow, and my old enemies. All "former."

"Take this next exit," Ric said.

"Are we heading for the horse pasture or the cow pasture?"

"Neither. I *hope* we stay on the road. We're aiming at the state highway junction with the county road, where the 'gas' and 'grub' signs tower. I didn't know Kansas looked so Western east of Dodge City."

"Millions and millions of longhorn cattle have been herded over this earth since the mid–eighteen hundreds. We are in 'bleeding' Kansas, city boy, the Free State that started the Civil War over the slave issue."

"Then it fits that vampires should show up here early and often after the recent millennium meltdown. All that historic blood spilled."

"Interesting point. I never thought of those greaser vamp gangs that hassled me in the group homes before puberty—mine—as early adaptors."

"That's what I'm here for," Ric said, redonning his sunglasses. "To give you new insight on your unhappy childhood history. You're not the only bleeding heart in this car."

I slowed Dolly to take the exit ramp, again wondering if I wanted to know more about a past that included repeated assault attempts and some unknown event or events that had made me too paranoid to ever lie on my back again.

"Rape survivor" wasn't a convincing piece of personal history I wanted to claim. I shivered in Dolly's sun-warmed red leather interior. Usually she felt womblike, and—after I'd met Ric—sexy. Now, she just felt damn bloody. Like Kansas.

RIC AND I sat outside at a wooden picnic bench, slurping giant paper cups of root beer, soaking up early summer sun. I'd bought a corny straw cowboy hat inside the Red Ryder Ranger Station to shade my face.

"You put on your high-SPF sunscreen this morning?" Ric asked, eyeing my blazing white forearms.

"Yes, dear. Gallons of it. Isn't that citified silk-blend blazer hot without Vegas air-conditioning to duck into?" I asked in turn.

"Yes, dear. I'll dress down for the job later."

I looked around, hearing an oncoming horsy clickety-clank and then spotting a bleached-blond-maned woman in gold lamé spikes and bun-hugging capris, heading into the restaurant. She was layered in brass jewelry—on neck, wrists, and ankle.

Hardly a Fed.

Unless . . . she was a CI, a confidential informant. Maybe she was a gangster's wife in the witness protection program. In her place, I sure would want Ric for a contact agent on that detail.

Me too, would-be mob honey, Irma said.

Ric's sunglasses were not following her tail, but aimed at other ones in the adjoining pastures. Grazing cows don't do much for me, though I find a mare and foal pretty to watch.

In a bit, my eyes spotted and followed a tall, lean man with a kick-ass belt buckle holding in a faded denim shirt over a significant belly. He bent through the wooden fencing to amble his Justin boots across the road to the restaurant asphalt.

When he got to our table, Ric stood in his pale Vegas suit and held out a dark hand glinting with bleached golden hairs. "Good to see you again, *amigo*."

The man wearing the straw cowboy hat that made mine look like a kid's model nodded in my direction. "This your *amiga*?"

"Wichita girl, born and fled," Ric said. "Delilah Street."

I stood to shake hands, that not being necessary socially, since I'm a lady. Something about the man required standing.

"Leonard Tallgrass," Ric introduced him.

Tallgrass's sunburned skin was darker than Ric's. The black eyes in a seamed face with broad cheekbones told me Ric's ex-FBI buddy was pretty pure Native American–born.

Exactly what tribe would be hard to guess. The Cheyenne and Kiowa fought the Long Knives here, and almost every tribe in North America had been moved to Kansas after the Indian Wars before most of them were finally moved to Oklahoma. That left contemporary Kansas with a trio of tiny reservations of Kickapoos and such in the state's northeast corner. Most of its Native American population lived all over the lower forty-eight, and beyond.

"Mr. Tallgrass," I said.

"Miss Street. You look even better in person. That was a real interesting TV piece you did on the mutilated cows a couple months back, but there was no follow-up."

"I left the station rather unexpectedly."

He nodded, giving me that Western scout squint. Leonard Tallgrass had been living up to that cowboys-and-Indians cliché with a tongue in his seamed cheek for a long, long time.

"That anchorman did give it a lame mention later," Tallgrass said. "Reported it was found to be teenage mischief. You must have known him, the paleface with the lipstick."

I swallowed a smirk. "Undead Ted is an up-to-date media vampire. Apparently they prefer a vivid background for their bleached canine fangs on TV."

"Speaking of canines—" Tallgrass turned to squint at Dolly. "That your ride?"

"Yes, sir."

"That your dog in it?"

Quicksilver heard, of course, and sat up in the backseat to establish his presence, front paws braced on the open window rim, looking seriously protective.

"Yes, sir," I said.

"What's this dead-dowsing young *amigo* of mine doing in such fine company? And that is not a dog, Miss Street; he is Brother Wolf, and a member of my tribe. Why isn't he dining with you?"

"He guards Dolly and Ric guards me, and I guard both of them. And the food here sucks, Mr. Tallgrass."

"Then we'll all go to my place." He turned away, then turned back. "Miss Dolly is the Cadillac?"

I nodded.

"She is prime. Follow me."

LEONARD TALLGRASS'S RIDE was a new but mud-crusted hybrid black Ford 350 pickup, and his "place" was an apartment in a complex with a soaring fountain in the courtyard. Inside, an art gallery of weapons ancient, new, and unknown to me decked the walls. So much for "prairie squint."

"I like that necklace," he said when we were seated in his dining alcove digesting his walnut and blue cheese chicken salad with lemongrass and extra-virgin olive oil. "It's not an authentic native design, though."

"It's not an authentic necklace."

He slouched onto his blue-jeaned tailbone. "*Mi amigo* Ricardo has found an extremely interesting young lady. I've already made contact with a series of your social workers."

My sass went south.

"Those folks mean well," he added, "but your job clearly was to survive them, and you did. They're still here in Wichita, and you're not. You have a much better ride than any of them, and a better class of company."

"I assume my 'classy company' includes you. I don't remember any social workers."

He nodded. "They were pretty forgettable. An ungrateful job. Almost as ungrateful as ours sometimes was, eh, Ricardo?"

Ric nodded.

Tallgrass took a new tack. "That cow mutilation story of yours, Miss Street, was an important one."

"Call me Delilah. The station barely deigned to run it."

"Don't call me Leonard. Tallgrass will do. Was it the usual stupidity? Or a cover-up?"

"I didn't stick around long enough to find out."

Tallgrass eyed Ric. "We should check out the site. You a movie star now?" He directed his formidable squint at Ric's sunglasses.

There was a long, long pause. I knew enough not to say

a word. Quicksilver stood defensively, which made Tall-grass lilt a shaggy eyebrow.

Ric finally doffed his sunglasses. He hated wearing the brown contact lens and obviously hadn't anticipated an indoor meeting. So his silver eye winked like a built-in monocle.

Tallgrass observed, mulled, and finally nodded. "*You've* become an even more interesting young man. I think Miss Street—Delilah—should liberate that film she got on the messed-up cows from WTCH-TV."

I opened my mouth to unreel a string of reasons why that was unnecessary, humiliating, and impossible.

"While," Leonard Tallgrass went on, "*mi amigo* takes me to that field and Mr. Quicksilver does a thorough nose job on it."

I objected. "Quicksilver isn't a drug- or bomb-sniffing dog, and he certainly isn't a cadaver dog."

"I told you the moment we met, Miss Delilah. He isn't much dog, but he's a lot of something else."

At that point, Quicksilver went to Leonard's chair and sat, after glancing his agreement at me.

My necklace shrunk into a plain, career-woman circlet at the base of my throat that wouldn't protect me from a mosquito bite, much less a vampire fanging.

It was *The Three Amigos* (like the movie) and an animated hair against my self-respect.

Guess who won?

I programmed the cow pasture directions into Ric's GPS and revved up Dolly for our return to Wichita. At least she wouldn't be getting her undercarriage dusty on unpaved country roads.

Chapter Ten

WITH THE GUYS off in Leonard Tallgrass's pickup to examine the cow-killing ground, we girls had time for less gory expeditions of our own.

First I stopped at a centrally located, low-profile place I knew, the Thunderbird Inn (Tallgrass would approve) to book a room for Ric and me. When I called Ric with the info, we agreed to meet there when it got too dark for field explorations.

Suited me. An unloaded Dolly and I made a beeline straight for my Wichita place of employment . . . before I'd been effectively driven out of it by a lecherous vampire, a scheming weather witch, and a rogue personal tornado.

Most TV stations are modest one-story buildings attached to tall broadcast towers occupying high ground where land is cheap, far from the city center. WTCH-TV had the usual long entry driveway and suburban neighborhood.

I reflected that by now the male investigative team of two guys and a dog was sniffing and sifting through a cow-patty-laden field I'd last seen by the gleam of a flashlight illuminating mutilated cattle corpses.

Another lovely Wichita memory, but it wasn't as scary to me as all the "missing time" in my growing-up history. Right now, my major problem was to park Dolly discreetly. The aim was to avoid contact with anchorman Undead Ted Brinkman and Sheena Coleman, the station weather witch, during this hit-and-run visit.

I eased Delilah behind the far side of one of the station's mobile broadcast vans.

Wichita was having a quiet news day. Videographer "Slo-mo" Eddie Anderson had been happy to hear from my cell phone and was at the station as of ten minutes ago. One never knew when news would break out, so I slipped around the building to the back loading dock.

I'd have to scale it in my mid-heeled suit pumps and black leggings, worn under a mini-length navy shirtdress, the casual opposite of my conservative hose-and-suit-wearing on-camera self. Eddie was an ace camera guy, but the lanky, morose type who was always down on "management," so he was a born liaison for a disgruntled ex-employee.

"Delilah," he greeted me with a whisper when I'd clambered the four feet up to the loading dock and eased into the slightly open end of the steel security curtain. "Man, it's been no fun fest with only the supernaturals running the news desk. You look like being gone agrees with you."

"I'd had some bad days before Sheena sent a 'freak' tornado to take out my rental house. Sorry I didn't stick around to say good-bye."

Eddie scratched at his scrawny new mustache. "Can't blame you. They stole your paranormal news beats and then flaked out on covering them. They even rescheduled the interview we had cancelled, with the old lady at Sunset City retirement place. Then the new regime sent me back to Sunset City with Sheena, but her interview was pretty boring."

"Really? That old woman, Caressa Teagarden, moved to the Vegas Sunset City. At least I found her there after I arrived."

"Well, she must have been swept up and out in that

targeted tornado of yours, because the old dame Sheena interviewed was named Lili West and she was a total fox of forty-something, like all of those artificially preserved Sunset City senior citizen residents. Your old Caressa lady looked senior. Kinda cool to see these days."

I smiled, knowing what he meant. "She still does. Was Lili West at the same address as our aborted assignment?"

"Yeah, come to think of it. No general manager has ever done that to me, called me back from an assignment for no good reason, like a fast-food place mass shooting. Good thing he's gone too."

"Fred Fogelman is gone? Who's running the station?"

"Guy named Javier. *Hah-vee-air.* Like I said, the place has gone downhill. It's all happy 'news you can use' now."

"It'd be a wonder if the station hadn't declined with Undead Ted and Sheena taking over my beats," I said. "Ted is an empty suit and a lame pair of fangs, and Sheena is a lousy weather witch without one reporter's gene in her artificially supplemented body."

"A little competitive with our weather gal, Sheena? You had network written all over you, Delilah. Sheena sure had it in for you."

"Was it because I'd agreed to go out with Undead Ted that Friday? Didn't even happen. He acted up and I kicked him out. He must have gone sniveling back to Sheena."

"Maybe. Whatever bee got in her bonnet, it just sprung up, like a high pressure cell. While you were off for the weekend, she was in the general manager's office trashing you from that Saturday on through Monday. She tried to get our scoop footage from the cow pasture scene off the air, I know that. Then you and I were called back Monday en route to that dumb old-lady interview assignment at Sunset City the GM put you on. I think that was her doing too."

"Saddling me with that lame feature or getting us called back?"

"One, or maybe both," Eddie said. "It was just unprofessional, that's what it was. And now, Undead Ted, he just trots along on Sheena's leash like a vamp tranqued on blood thinners."

The conversation reminded me I'd spent that Saturday off taking my suddenly ailing dog to the vet, then finding he'd contracted blood poisoning and couldn't be saved. All from biting Undead Ted's ankle after the lech had tricked me into cutting a finger he wanted as an appetizer before mainlining on one of my major arteries after our dinner out.

I'd never heard of a vampire's blood being poisonous to house pets before, like some species of plant, but then, they seldom did the bleeding and the Millennium Revelation was still revealing unsuspected supernatural variations and species. A pang of anxiety about Ric hit when I wondered what losing all your blood to vampires could do.

"I don't know what went on that weekend, Eddie," I told him. "I not only wasn't scheduled to work, but I . . . lost my dog that Saturday."

"That feisty white Lhasa? Too bad, Delilah. No wonder you were kinda down that Monday. You brought him in once. Akita or something."

Eddie's mistake saved me from a total emotional rerun. Reporters live to inform and correct. "An Akita is a breed of Japanese dog. My Lhasa's *name* was Achilles."

"Oh." As if he cared. Cameramen have seen it all and are a nonchalant breed. "Like the Greek hero with something wrong with his heel."

"Like the hero with the bum heel," I agreed, beating back the memories. As a pup, Achilles had always chased my heels, so the name was appropriate. I just didn't expect that the "hero" part would get him killed.

Eddie shook his head. "I don't know what was going on that weekend, or since, but it's been hell around here after you left. I'm thinking of quitting too."

"You're a great videographer."

"But who does traditional 'news' anymore? We're a dying breed. Whatcha doing in Vegas for a living?"

"Investigative work for a television producer, among other, er, major Vegas Strip clients."

"Cool. You've landed on your girl-reporter pumps. I don't wanta get you charged up about what's over and done at the station. Besides Sheena being Bitch Witch, it's a lot of management political correctness that's been coming on for years. Hire the minorities, like the Latino brass, and the anchor vamps and the weather witches. You know the news has been going to hell since the big flare-up after the Millennium Revelation. It's like, 'Hey, the aliens have landed,' but now they're coming up out of our caves and cornfields and They R Us. Anyway, you can download your piece on the cow mutilations to your cell off my backup flash drive."

"Great." I was glad simple computerized functions didn't need hookups now, just proximity. It was like zipless sex. In a second, his info was my info too.

"Hey, Delilah." Eddie chuckled like a TV cartoon ghoul. "I added some hilarious footage of Undead Ted and Sheena screwing up on camera. I even caught 'em actually screwing in the dead storage vault. I YouTube that stuff now and then. You wanta come into the studio and say hello?"

"No, thanks. This is all I need, Eddie. Thanks for the 'added value content.'"

"It's a howl. Sheena accidentally had it hailing in the studio a couple weeks ago. Funny, we've been having a lot of freakish weather lately, but no indoor hail."

"It's the Midwest," I said. "Freakish weather is our biggest tourist attraction."

"Must be weird living in sunshine year-round in Vegas."

"Yeah, it's weird living in Vegas, but it's not all sunshine," I said in vague understatement.

"Can I help you off the loading dock?"

Fast Eddie bent to stretch out a lank arm with a helping hand on the end of it.

"Eddie, the gentleman? You must really miss me," I commented as I grabbed his hand, although I appreciated his easing me through the four-foot drop.

He straightened up to tower above me, shaking his head, even his mustache drooping morosely. "You have no idea."

WITH QUICKSILVER ABSENT and unable to play guard, I'd left Dolly locked with her top up.

So when I opened the driver's door with my old-fashioned key—direct interface, imagine—I sat in the interior shade and played Slo-mo Eddie's treasure trove of scenes.

I watched his recording of my stand-up report on the dark country road by the cattle mutilation scene earlier that spring . . . as if from years later or a planet away. It was a good story, told without glitches, but I seemed so young and polite and parochial-school girl.

I'd reeled off the bit-role lines Hector Nightwine had given me on *CSI V* in Vegas a week ago with a new edge that came naturally. The portly producer was hoping my performance would either lure my double, Lilith, back to the *CSI* fold, or establish me as her replacement. I hoped it would lure Lilith too. I wanted to know how long she'd been doing her twin act in my life before I'd spotted her on *CSI*.

The image of the old, WTCH-TV Delilah made me rerun leaving Wichita two months ago. My first fill-up stop for Dolly at a remote Colorado gas station had forced me to fend off a trio of creepy backwoods guys and burn rubber out of there.

Having to dodge booty bounty hunters going after my "*CSI*-autopsy-star" twin the moment I left Kansas had made me a lot warier and assertive. And way less polite. Not to mention that certain confidence I derived from finally getting a sex life. Knowing how the other 99 percent lived sure increased one's daily savoir faire.

Sighing as my sweet innocent self disappeared from the small screen, I soon was snickering at Undead Ted as he practiced resting his supposedly "supplemented" fang-tips on his lower lip before going "live" on camera.

When he was caught touching up his tinted lip gloss, I fast-forwarded past, my own recent passion-pit adventures with lip gloss making me blush like a schoolgirl again. Damn! Would my pale skin always make me a patsy for the unwanted flush? Probably.

I made a fierce face at the telltale screen, then slowed it to normal.

Seeing Undead Ted and Sheena lip-locking against the station blue-screen was like watching the Christmas Chipmunks with their braces in gridlock. There was enough bleach on those teeth to off Sheena. At least, I assumed, witches remained human enough to off. But then, my idea of a happy ending was Red Riding Hood or Hansel and Gretel. Or, more apropos to the current location, *The Wizard of Oz*.

While cruising the snips of my old news reports, I realized that I'd definitely grown by leaving my once-safe niche at WTCH. Eddie had ended my trip down bad-memory lane with Sheena's later interview with the Sunset City resident of the new management's choice.

Sheena was an anorexic blonde with inflated bust and lips. Unlike a lot of "weather gals" who'd forged the way for weather witches to take their places, she was more about her looks and attitude than making "dry" weather statistics fascinating and relevant to the viewers.

Weather guys and gals had always been the geeks on the highly photogenic TV news teams of my growing-up era. The viewers sensed they had a real passion for their high- and low-pressure areas, that naughty acting-out El Niño, the evil confluence of clashing hot and cold fronts that makes the perfect storm.

Lightning and thunder were still-living gods that could throw panic into human cardiac systems in the heartland, but we had our über-outlaw, our supernatural sky-dancer, our bane and our bragging point.

Here in Kansas, of course, it was that regal couple of phenomena, the Queen and King of murderously bad weather, the spinning, twirling, shimmying, livestock-sucking, clothes-stripping, tree-hurling, house-splintering, Dorothy-napping, witch-smashing . . . tornado.

I actually took a certain perverse pride in having been the worthy victim of one, even if it had been an intensely personal strike from a weather witch on my TV "team." A minor, secondary-city weather witch didn't aim a teensy-weensy sixty-foot-circumference "twister" at just . . . any-body. I had to have really pissed her off.

Why? Not just jealousy.

Sheena was becoming as much a mystery to me as Lilith.

That couldn't be allowed to continue.

I turned on Dolly's engine and checked the rearview mirror before pulling beyond the safety screen of the station news van. Dolly was idling backward when my foot stabbed the brakes.

Good girl! Dolly didn't let out so much as a squeak.

Speak of the devils you know. I recognized Undead Ted's and Sheena's profiles through the tinted side windows of an impeccably washed black Lincoln Town Car also idling in the parking lot.

A moment later the swarthy capped driver got out to open the back passenger door.

I watched a hose-sheened, long, lean leg thrust out to place a scarlet platform spike shoe on the asphalt. *Ugh.* Sheena always dressed like the head bitch on a seventies nighttime TV soap opera. The short skirt of a slim red suit followed, along with her red-taloned fingernails, swollen-sphincter crimson lips and "done" blond hair.

The same old Sheena, only much more expensively dressed.

Undead Ted crawled out after her, gazing like a love-sick puppy at the lady in bloodred.

Everybody at WTCH had known Ted took injections to resist daylight so he could do pre-sunset newscasts. A George Hamilton product pumped melatonin into his skin, giving him that golden glow. Now his vampy complexion looked just plain sallow, freckled with a carefully cultivated thirty-six-hour brown beard smudge. He was a liver-spotted puppy.

His dried-blood-color designer suit—I'd seen Lightdays pads more attractively shaded—was much more posh, but only two-thirds up to Ric level. Standing next to Sheena, Ted looked . . . drained. Who was the vampire here?

The driver had moved around to the car's opposite passenger door.

I grabbed my cell phone and twisted my head over my shoulder to film the unhandsome couple and wait for a glimpse of their obvious lunch date. At first the Lincoln's roofline just gleamed in the sun. Then I glimpsed something black rising over the hot metal horizon.

A hat. A wide black-leather brim somewhere between a flat-crowned Western hat and the razor-sharp oversize fedora affected by seventies pimps. It was almost a hat a woman might wear . . . if she were Janet Jackson onstage.

Under the sinister brim surfaced a furrowed, seamed brow the mahogany-deep color of a Greek island suntan and peaked, scowling Satanic black eyebrows. The nose was long and bulged in the middle like a digesting boa constrictor. The tip narrowed and dipped so delicately it made the nostrils into thin upward-slanted slits you might see on a serpent's face.

In contrast, the mustache had a ragged upper line and drooped down over sloppy lips almost as obscenely full as Sheena's collagen-pumped beauties.

I kept filming, thinking this moment was like watching a strike-ready royal Egyptian cobra rear its fanned head.

The man's suspicious, slitted dark eyes scanned the building and lot so intently I felt sure he'd seen me. Luckily, Ted and Sheena moving around to the car's rear stopped his gaze before it passed the parked van that concealed Dolly. Black is beautiful . . . camouflage.

I watched the three passengers wait while the driver came around to open the popped trunk. He handed out two exotic-skinned wooden briefcases, presenting the black one to Sheena, the brown to Ted.

The stranger with the bad-and-the-ugly eyes was

shorter than my ex-colleagues, maybe five-eight, like me. Despite his dark mustache and beard stubble, I guessed his age at sixty or so. His suit and shirt may have been expensive, but both seemed wilted by the intemperate intensity of his expression and stance. His business was not being telegenic. I sensed his business was about not being seen at all.

My fingertips felt cold on the cell phone now that he'd been captured inside it. The driver was already ushering him back into the rear seat, sweat beading in a salty dew line under his cap band as he came around to drive the boss away.

Undead Ted blinked in the sunlight when the driver's door slammed shut.

The big black modern luxury car glided away, a shadow of Dolly's timeless power and grace. Ted and Sheena turned and marched for the main entrance, suddenly swinging their overstated briefcases and grinning at each other.

Okay. I took my foot off Dolly's brake and I backed her out until we were clear of the van, which took several seconds. Then I wrenched her steering wheel left and spurted forward with an engine thrust no one could ignore.

I braked in front of the briefcase buddies with a deliberate squeal.

They'd turned to regard my car with dropped jaws as I lowered the passenger side window.

"Delilah . . . ?" Undead Ted began, his face turning pale saffron.

Sheena strutted toward Dolly.

"Delilah Street and her Cadillac clunker, my, my. I thought you'd hitched a ride out of town on a Kansas twister."

"No. That teensy little tornado missed me. Don't you two look sharp. Must have had a lunch date with the new management. Care to share the contents of those briefcases with a fellow reporter?"

"It's . . . it's nothing," Undead Ted spilled. Of course it was something, something they didn't want anyone to know about.

Sheena keyed his shin with her spike heel.

"Looks like payday to me," I said, watching Ted writhe in intimidated silence. What a wimp.

Sheena was advancing as if she was about to do the same damage to Dolly's shiny black side.

"Don't worry," I called, waving my hand. "Lucky for you I'm just visiting."

I accelerated before Sheena's foot could connect with anything but air.

Unfortunately, air is all around us and Sheena was a weather witch.

I hit the power button to lower the top, but that took *mucho* seconds. They had more time to waste in the fifties and less nimble technology. Dolly accelerated while I punched the side window button closed.

The shadow creeping over me was not just the descending top, but a nasty black cloud the size of a railroad car. My rearview mirror told me raindrops were falling on Dolly's trunk. We sped down the endlessly curving drive. Hailstones were moments behind.

I needed to hit the main street faster. I could hear the brittle pings on the driveway behind me. At a crosswalk near the parking lot's other end I roared Dolly onto the broad intersecting sidewalk and then cross-country on WTCH-TVs expansive green lawn, under a landscaped grove of maple trees, over the street curb—*ouch* on the springs!—down a few blocks, and under a gas station canopy.

"Cool wheels, lady," exclaimed the teenaged male store clerk who'd rushed out to ogle Dolly. He cocked an ear at the hail ping-ponging off the metal canopy above us. "That rainstorm came up quick."

"Easy come, easy go," I said. Sheena wouldn't want any inexplicable weather phenomena reported too close to WTCH. "I don't need fuel, although this is a thirsty big girl."

"What year?" he asked, following me as I circled Dolly looking for damage, as puppy-doggish as Undead Ted was these days. "Maybe fifty-eight, sixty? Biarritz! I heard Cary Grant owned one of these."

I stopped cold. "You know who Cary Grant was?"

"Sure. He was a movie star back in the last century. They owned a lot of cool cars. Can I look under the hood?"

Wouldn't you know Dolly would get a proposition in Wichita and I wouldn't?

"Sorry. I've got to get going. But you can polish her tail fins and trunk before we leave. Don't want any dust spots on that finish."

"Gollee, no."

I provided a flannel cloth from the glove compartment and he went to work.

You were really thumbing your nose at fate back there, Irma noted as I finally pulled back onto the main drag under a clear sky. *You should have had the kid check Dolly's shocks.*

I ignored her until she went away.

THE DAY WAS still young and the boys and I hadn't planned to meet back at Tallgrass's place until much later. I suspected some beer-accompanied reminiscences of mutual FBI days would occupy them after the pasture inspection.

Before my visit to Wichita delved too far into my uneasy past, I decided to do some less scary snooping on my own behalf. Dolly seemed inclined to cruise the familiar neighborhood past the station, so we veered together to the site of my rented bungalow, which a mighty specific tornado had torn off its foundation.

What a jolt to see a half-completed house already going up on the site. I'd liked my life and my little house and dog and doing a paranormal reporting TV job I thought was important, informing people about their brave newly supernatural world. . . .

Construction was idled today, but I spotted the back of a big sign on the lot. I drove past and craned my neck. Habitat for Humanity, it read. I couldn't help smiling. Somebody did me wrong, and now somebody was doing someone who needed it right. Of course, even nowadays I supposed the houses must be available to all "minorities." I doubted we'd ever see the name changed to Habitat for *Un*humanity, though.

Still smiling, I decided to wheel out to Sunset City and look for Lili West's extended-life address. I'd been a reporter, right? Maybe it was high time to "report" my own backyard.

Chapter Eleven

ALL THE SUNSET City "retirement" homes had the owners' customized look and a matching mailbox with
their name out front. Security was constant and universally
electronic, no visible gates and guards needed.

Despite the open look to the curving streets, no one
quite knew what kept these elderly residents "living" on.
Rumor was that a good part of their physical presence
was virtual and expensively maintained by only the very
wealthy, as cosmetic surgery used to be.

Caressa Teagarden, who'd either moved to the Las
Vegas Sunset City about when I'd left town, or had followed me there, was a Golden Age film actress originally
named Lilah, who'd had a twin, Lili, she was estranged
from long before I was born.

I had been an abandoned infant named after my found-
ling location. Delilah Street. Not in Wichita, Kansas,
thank you. No biblical bad ladies name streets here. I also
had a double, if not a twin. Lilith Quince was my sister
shadow, glimpsed in my mirror after I'd seen her on TV.
Lilith. Delilah. Yeah. Do the word game. Lili and Lilah all
over again.

I was curious to see if Eddie's "Lili West" really lived
here and would somehow fit into the complex crossword
puzzle of my life and times.

Caressa, formerly Lilah, was unusual for this post–
Millennium Revelation era in that she actually allowed

herself to look old. That was a choice nowadays, and I don't
know if I'd have the starch to make her decision forty years
hence. Assuming I had another forty years. After anonymous docile years in Wichita group homes and educational
institutions, I was suddenly finding the long, curved lifeline in my right palm facing serial, sudden-death over-
times. The left-hand lifeline is the one you inherit. The
right line is the one you make.

Speaking of sudden, I glimpsed an ornate wrought-
iron "Lili West" on a mailbox pillar formed from pebbled
stones in concrete.

Dolly eased to the opposite curb like a well-trained
greyhound, hardly requiring my hand on the steering
wheel. And why not? Any superior automobile would be
privileged to park outside 240 Knot Way.

When you didn't know whether you'd been born in a
house or a hospital or just next to the nearest Dumpster,
you tended to fantasize about the perfect residence. Mine
were always vintage, and this was a lovely 1920s creation,
not a squat bungalow like I'd actually rented in Wichita,
but a two-story brown stucco affair with a pine-top-high
pointed roof promising numerous lofty attic gables to
explore, and a towering brick chimney to match.

My home-longing imagination was already decorating
this giant dollhouse.

Inside would be built-in glass-fronted bookcases
flanking a tiled fireplace, cozy window seats in every
bedroom, a mirror-topped built-in buffet in the dining
room, which was big enough to seat twelve, many cozy
closets under stairs and in gables for the inventive child
to hide in.

It would be so different from the bland, one-story group
homes I'd called prison.

I got out of Dolly and slammed her front door shut, knowing that solid, secure sound would be echoed here by the big wooden front door with the giant black wrought-iron hinges.

I could almost smell warm apples and cinnamon, the Realtor's favorite lures, wafting down the curving walk as I headed for the massive front door. Every town in the country had a neighborhood of homes this vintage—except Las Vegas.

True, I lived in the Enchanted Cottage on Hector Night-wine's estate, but that was a 1940s movie set made real. This house was another twenty years older, and, although not enchanted, it mesmerized me. Caressa's Sunset City residence near Las Vegas was so lakeside cottage compared to this.

I waltzed forward until I was eye-to-eye with the big iron knocker, paused, picked up the heavy striker in the shape of a W and let it fall back with a thump like thunder. I'd grown up in Wichita hoping to be invisible, but I no longer would be unheard here, that's for sure.

Spiderweb leading supported the door's frosted glass round window. It was too high off the ground for me to see into, even on tiptoes. And I so wanted to peek. I felt like a kid again, with an actual neighborhood to explore besides suburbia.

The door opened to showcase a petite woman who only came up to my shoulder.

I searched her forever-forty features and found the symmetrical bone structure she shared with her aged twin sister. Her hair was a vibrant, almost statically fluffed ginger color, neither red nor brown. No wonder Eddie had called her "foxy." It wasn't just for her perfect figure in miniature. Caressa must have been a knockout in her day. How could she have let herself wrinkle and whiten when she could be preserved in vibrant, living amber, like her sister Lili?

I pictured Lilith and me doing the "portrait of Dorian Gray" thing, with her image in the mirror puckering and melting and me not knowing if she was my reflection or a fading life force.

"I hope you're not selling anything door-to-door, young lady," the resident warned. Her voice was sharp and scratchy, the only thing "old" about her. "That's not allowed here and the penalties are severe."

Her raw, suspicious tone startled my undercover reporter instincts into coming up with a plausible story for just being curious.

"No. Of course not. I'm . . . writing a web piece on your sister Caressa's film career. My name is Delilah Street."

Her amber-brown eyes blinked alert at mention of her sister. "You may know your name, but my sister apparently still doesn't know hers. It's Lilah West. I won't talk about 'Caressa Teagarden' and that stupid so-called film career of hers, but I will discuss Lilah. Will that do?"

"Of course."

I sensed odors of potpourri and perfume swirling inside and heard tinkling chimes. The furnishings emitted metallic and glassy winks from the room behind her. I was dying for a house tour.

"Then come in," she invited, sweeping the huge door wide as if it weighed as little as a feather.

I studied her as I passed through a tiny entry hall into a huge main room anchored by a carved gray stone fireplace tall enough for Frankenstein's monster to reach for the sky in.

This was the dramatic ambiance I'd expected for a vin-

tage movie queen like Caressa, not the cottage she inhab-
ited in the Las Vegas Sunset City.

Lili spun to face me on her dainty red high-heeled
mules. Louboutins, I'd bet. I didn't surf the discount
designer websites in vain. She was wearing an aqua microfiber top and genie-styled capris, tight at the ankle but
swagged at the hips.

"How did you find me?" she asked.

"WTCH did a recent feature on you."

"Film at ten. A minute-thirty. Hardly a feature, my
dear. I hope you're going to deal with my poor sister in
greater detail."

"The Web allows for unlimited content."

"Yes, doesn't it? Pity. Brevity is the soul of substance.
Sit."

Quicksilver wouldn't have bowed to that spat command, but I was a reporter in search of facts that could
affect my personal future. I sat.

Goodness. What was at the back of my knees was a
large blue ottoman brocaded in an Asian cloud pattern.
Every piece here was an exotic rarity, including the lady
of the house. Her ego was as large as her body was trim. It
was time to go gaga girl reporter, an easy role to slip into.

"I can't believe I'm still in Kansas," I bubbled, quite
honestly. "Your house is so fascinating and so are you."

Lili's complacent smile as she sat on a giant brown
leather wing chair confirmed my instincts.

"Actually," Lili said, "I was far more able to express
myself wherever I was than Lilah. She needed the medium
of film. I thrived on the direct effect."

"So she became a film actress and you became—?"

"A performance artist. Surely you can sense the tem-
perament in my house alone?"

Invited to ogle the interior, I did. High against the coffered ceiling, I finally spotted Plexiglas fan blades slowly turning, turning, turning. That's what made the scene swirl around and cooled the interior.

Now that my eyes were adapting to the dimness, I spotted lots of museum-style pedestals holding rare artifacts.

Like the gold and black head of Anubis. That's when my spine decided to do the paso doble.

And . . . a rare green geode bristling with rectilinear green-glass towers.

One of those freaky glass globes holding lightning in a jar that Sharper Image used to sell when it was solvent and we were still the champions of the world.

A severed tattooed arm floating in what appeared to be lime green Jell-O.

And . . . a pair of silver tap shoes from a nineteen-thirties chorus line.

"I have quite a collection," Lili said. "Perhaps I could interest a sharp young lady like you in working as my assistant. I plan a biography as well."

"Really. You'd have a lot to tell. I mean, I can tell you've lived a fascinating life."

"Unlike Lilah. She withered. Literally and figuratively. She was booted out of this Sunset City, you know."

"Booted?"

"We can't have the wrong sort of people ruining our ambiance."

"Your own sister?"

"Sisters are overrated, my dear. Live longer and you'll see that. Not trustworthy."

I nodded.

"She gave up and got old," Lili said. "I remain active. In fact, I have my own lucrative business going."

"Wonderful. What is it?"

"Ecology," she said. "Going green is quite the thing these days, and right up my alley. I was always interested in formulas and scientific effects on our world. The wind, the weather, the warming globe. I'm particularly fond of globes. You may notice that many, many decorate my home."

I'd spotted the spherical glimmer of glass everywhere.

"Snow globes," I said.

"Some. I do not limit my horizons, dear girl. Ah. I've forgotten to offer you tea and sympathy or at least scones."

"Thank you. I'm not hungry."

"Growing girls are always hungry," she growled at me.

I was beginning to feel like Alice at a mad tea party with the Red Queen.

"Just a nibble, perhaps."

"Fine. I'll go toss something tasty together."

She clipped off on her petite red spikes.

While she was gone, I got up to do a polite but thorough inspection of her main room.

I smiled and shook up a globe of downtown Wichita. Over there was Manhattan, of course. *Wait.* Manhattan, *Kansas.* Letdown.

And . . . Augusta, not in Georgia, but the nearby community with the old downtown and its restored movie palace.

They were really up-to-date . . . in Kansas City and environs, and there weren't just snow globes, but rain globes and fog globes and sleet globes. And so fanciful. One even had the Emerald City of Oz inside it, with a tiny broom-riding witch shooting fog across the sky reading: *Surrender Dorothy.*

"Oh, you've found my specialty globes," Lili said, clicking back into the room with a tray.

"Can you duplicate *The Wizard of Oz* scenes without permission?"

"Oh, my land, girl! Of course I got permission. I told you I headed a big corporation. Now sit down and drink this lovely, local tallgrass tea and have some homemade gingerbread scones."

Ah . . . no.

But I'd be willing to sit in front of them and ask some questions. I didn't have to. Lili was pleased to chatter about her sister.

"Kansas wasn't good enough for Lilah. I told her the center of the country was best for us West girls, but she had Hollywood dreams. She blew off the family business and went"—she rolled her eyes—"really west. And what did she have to show for it? A few minor roles in third-rate films. At least she changed her name so as not to embarrass us."

"What was . . . is . . . the family business?"

"Nothing glamorous like motion pictures. Heating, plumbing, air-conditioning."

"That was . . . available when you two were young?"

"Gracious, child! Of course. In fact, it was air-conditioning that seduced Lilah from Wichita to the Wild West."

I sipped a little tallgrass tea, and tried not to spit it out. It was chili-flavored!

"You're right," I said when I could speak again. "Air-conditioning doesn't sound very seductive."

"It's a fascinating field, with unlimited growth potential."

"Didn't the early movie theaters have it?"

"Exactly right. Those Roaring Twenties were also purring with Willis Carrier's rival air conditioner. He was a city slicker who sold the idea to the Rivoli movie house on Broadway in 1925. Our father, Weatherbee West, leaped into the business at the new Augusta film palace near Wichita and captured the central U.S. market. Alas, Lilah fell in love with the movie palaces and the silent films inside them, instead of the mammoth pulsing machinery cooling them. She made the oddest remark when she took the train to California against all our family's wishes, when she left the heating and air-conditioning factory for the film factory."

"What was that?" I asked, sniffing a terrific quote. Not that an investigator needed one like a reporter did. Great quotes, and recognizing them when you heard them, was a reporter's lifeblood.

She said, "The heart lies between the hand and the head."

"That *is* a great quote." I'd heard it before, but where or when I couldn't say.

"I didn't say it was great," Lili snapped. "I said it was odd."

I studied her petite curvaceous figure and momentarily frowning face.

Caressa Teagarden was a funky old lady, but at least she looked her age, unlike her so-called twin. What was really odd was how different they had become.

"Really, I must go," I said, standing. "You've given me so much insight into your sister. Thank you."

"I haven't said more than a couple paragraphs about the bitch, all you'd get in a mediocre obituary for a mediocre film career."

"So much insight," I repeated, backing toward the door. "I can't wait to do a double profile on you two, kind of like the John and Yoko famous fetal-twin photo."

The reference so·confused Lili that she stopped stalking after me on my hasty exit.

By the time I got down the sidewalk to the curb, Dolly's engine was already running. I'd been so taken by the charming house exterior, I'd left the keys in the car.

So now Dolly was taking matters into her own . . . gears? Talk about initiative; she had *ignition*.

Right on, sister, Irma chortled.

Chapter Twelve

WITHIN TWENTY MINUTES, Dolly and I were gliding into an old familiar setting, and a much more naturally scenic one.

Why does returning to your Catholic girls' high school campus make hot sessions with your road-trip lover rerun obsessively through your head as if you needed to make an accurate count of every little mortal sin for Saturday confession?

Maybe because my familiar had morphed into a hidden but taunting rainfall necklace of tiny silver beads shimmying over my breasts. Instead of wafting the scent of the motel's no-name soap, I feared I reeked with the aroma of fresh guilt.

Why should I? The co-star of my mental blue movie collection was off bonding in the boonies with Leonard Tallgrass and Quicksilver. The trio was becoming such a steady partnership I was almost jealous. . . .

Actually, I relished being on my own, since Our Lady of the Lake had sole custody of a four-year chunk of my sketchy history. Today's expedition was just Dolly and me, with Irma on standby, the way I'd left Wichita two months ago.

Dolly had never seen Our Lady of the Lake, but her whitewall tires spun up and down the gently rolling, landscaped hills. The glint of the man-made lake at the campus's heart sparkled like a blue diamond through the lush shrubbery and trees. I also glimpsed campus buildings constructed of what we students had called "mellow yellow," the native limestone mined from the state's Flint Hills scenic area.

In a few hours, I'd moved from the ugly scene at WTCH to meeting Caressa's weird sister to cruising the only natural scenery I'd ever recalled reacting to with a . . . sentimental glow.

Please. So not us, Irma commented. *I'm happy you are going to get the goods on the reason for our inner angst and that annoying supine phobia of yours—not mine, I assure you—but let's move on here.*

I'd thought I was.

Were you with me here too, way back when, Irma? I wondered.

I didn't have many vivid memories of this place, just a blur of classrooms and talking nuns in Flying Nun headdresses, and of myself bundled up to the frowning black eyebrows, wallowing across the snow-piled campus in deep winter, shivering. With tiny icicles forming on my eyelashes.

My graphic memories bestirred Irma again.

Brrr. Toss the Nanook of the North *reminiscences. You and me were on and off here, depending on which clique you ticked off and your nondating life. I mean, all girls. Duh. I gave up on you totally at that dorky state college, and then you hit the big time at WTCH. But I will agree that this place looked cool, at least. Too cool for half the year! Snow, I'm talking, and not our seriously sexy Vegas empire builder. I mean winter, and the falling white stuff that freezes your nose and toes. Not mine, of course, but I do suffer along with you, on the inside.*

Snorting, I tuned out Irma after her mention of my confounding rock-star . . . "nemesis" was not too strong a word.

Dolly slipped into a small lot carved out for gawkers as I stopped for a look-see. My conservative pump heels moved like clodhoppers over the sloping grassy hill to the lake.

Birds were shrieking.

Well, not really. I realized then that you don't hear birds chirping on the Las Vegas Strip, unless a few are bopping around the greenery in the Paris's Le Cafe Ile St. Louis restaurant.

As I neared the teardrop-shaped lake, I spotted a single tree-thick island in its center, reached by a wooden foot-bridge. I felt a creeping sensation at my neck. The silver familiar was off sex patrol and changing into an innocuous chain with a long, freshly cold pendant. The familiar ran hot and cold, depending on my whereabouts, the air temperature, and my personal emotional tenor. Now it was less "Fever" and more *The Waltons*.

Saints preserve me from so-square John-Boy, Irma wailed.

I lifted the pendant. Maybe the ambiance was more . . . Camelot. The familiar had morphed into a miniature sword with an aurora borealis crystal on its pommel.

I told you, Irma said. *Cool.*

The smile in her voice brought one to my lips. This had been a calm retreat after the group homes. Here, I had apparently ditched real memories of any trauma or abuse for occasional nightmares too unbelievable to bother anybody else with.

I studied the sun-dappled lake and tested a wetted finger to the light wind, as evening prepared to don her best gown and thought about dimming the sky. Soon the sun's rays would be slanting through the trees, and then, hours later, maybe moonlight. I searched the gentle ripples for signs of an immortal woman's naked arm.

Nope. Still no lady in the lake.

Smiling again, I climbed the hill to reclaim Dolly's driver's seat, and I didn't stop until we parked at the limestone administration building. Maybe even an orphan can go home again.

The Young Thing at the reception desk had matching "Edward" tattoos inside her wrists and wore her long uniform sleeves rolled up to her elbow like a workman's shirt, the better to flaunt her workout muscles.

Golly. They were allowing visible self-expression here now?

"Is the mother superior still Sister Regina Caeli?" I asked, pronouncing the Latin properly as "Chay-lee."

"She goes by Sister Ermangarde Wallace now. Yeah. You got it the first time. Ermangarde. You can kinda see the vocation coming there, from the baptismal certificate. Who wouldn't want to exchange that bummer name for something like Queen of Heaven? Not many new nuns now. Maybe the first names got better. You're a grad, right? I recognize the navy. Never lost the uniform, huh? The campus is crawling with all these, like, older women, coming back. Like this was fun."

"It's a beautiful campus."

"Try getting a date for the St. Lancelot's military ball on that one."

"St. Lancelot's boys' high school is still a going concern?"

"Do punks have pimples? We mostly date the guys from State College, unless there's a big St. Lancelot's formal 'do,' where we can put on the bustiers and the black lipstick shtick. Of course the nuns forbid cleavage, but they don't go to the dances. You don't look like a drag hag. I mean, like you haven't been gone that long."

"One piece of advice I'll give you—?"

"Carnaby. Horrible first name, I know. My grandparents used to be counterculture. Still not worth going into the convent over."

"Okay, Carnaby. You are going to be uncool so soon. Enjoy the hip now."

"If you say so. That *is* a sweet pendant you're wearing. You should have called for an appointment, but what the heck. Gimme your name? Mother Superior Ermangarde is still here. She never leaves."

"Delilah Street," I said, trying out the truth.

"*Ooh.* Delilah. Biblical bad girl. I'd kill for that name. Major cool. You ever done any black lipstick? With your white skin that would wring the Goth boys out and throw them away for the duration."

"I've done some radical lip gloss in my day," I purred. "What are you complaining about? Carnaby is a cute name."

"I *know,* dammit. 'Cute' is so lame today. Hold on. I'll ring the olde dame."

Somehow, the way she said "olde dame" had a Chaucer-like, uh, ring. I bet English Literature was still a required course here. Particularly the Arthurian Cycle.

Had it only been seven years? Felt like seven centuries. I hesitated before knocking at the head nun's age-darkened wooden door. It had an opaque pebbled-glass window like a noir private detective's.

"Enter," an imperiously distracted voice commanded before my knuckles hit wood. Nuns had a ninth sense.

For a moment, I longed to be back in a stinky, darkening pasture with Ric and Quicksilver and Leonard Tallgrass.

I opened the door, overcome by a scent of lemon oil.

Through the big old-fashioned sash windows behind the desk, the sun was setting, going for the gold before it turned bloodred and sank pouting into the horizon.

Sister Regina Caeli wore the same habit as always, the bulky headdress producing a decades-outdated, Matterhorn-peaked silhouette against the dusk. Its profile reminded me of the mythical Minotaur, the horned and bullish beast from ancient Crete. From what I remembered of her seven years ago, by now Sister should be about as ancient as Crete.

"Delilah Street," her firm but rasping voice greeted me. "I've been waiting for you."

Whee. Welcome someplace at last. I felt the silver familiar changing into a chain mail necklace that covered my chest and décolletage. Especially any hidden cleavage.

Ric would so want the details of this. The conversation, that is, not the familiar making an armored nun's wimple on my chest. Too kinky for a Catholic boy.

"WE ENJOYED WATCHING your reports on WTCH in the convent recreation room, Delilah," Sister said when I was seated before her. "They were most informative. And then you recently . . . disappeared."

"Pretty much fired," I said.

"Ah. Women still have an uphill fight in the media. So now you are—?"

"A PI in Las Vegas."

"We watch the *CSI Las Vegas* show religiously."

"Did you see . . . uh, me, as a corpse?"

"Oh, doing some work as an extra, are you, Delilah? Most interesting experience, I imagine. Sorry, no. We don't really watch the gruesome parts. You did wear a complete sheet?"

"Yes, Sister," I said virtuously.

I had been clothed during my recently filmed cameo, which certainly couldn't have aired yet. And all eyes here at the convent had turned away at Lilith's nude appearance. Why watch a forensics TV show, though, if you shut your eyes at the autopsies?

"Why have you been waiting for me?" I asked.

"Our Lady of the Lake was the closest thing you had to a home here in Kansas. Many of our girls do return for class reunions, but you missed yours in oh-eleven."

"That was only five years out," I said quickly. "I'll make the tenth."

Sister's cumbersomely attired head shook. "It's not that, is it, Delilah?"

So, I was going to have to admit to the mother superior and academic dean, scenic campus aside, that my four high school years were mostly forgotten and might have been as unpleasant as my group home sojourn? Naw. Better to shrug it off.

"Even the pundits can't decide if the true millennial year is the turn of two thousand," Sister Ermangarde went on, "or two thousand and one. Graduates from both of those years seem to have made themselves scarce when it comes to school spirit, including donations."

"Really?"

The reporter in me was getting interested. I'd always assumed I was the only disaffected one around as a kid, blaming it on being orphaned.

"Is the reason the Millennium Revelation or the

upheaval of the nine/eleven attack, do you think?" I asked. "They almost coincided."

She tented pale white hands, balancing her chin on their prayerful support.

"What an excellent question, Delilah. You always asked good questions in class. We hadn't considered, frankly, that the . . . ah, spiritual upheaval of the Revelation may have affected certain of our graduating students in those two years even more than the unprecedented political assault of mass murder."

I stared at Sister Regina. Ermangarde was just not a name I could stomach. Then it hit me. Ermangarde. *Irma?* Irma who is a guard? Just *when* did my internal voice show up?

Please, Irma herself interjected. *I am eternal. I don't punch time cards.*

I brushed her rude comment aside.

"When you say 'spiritual,'" I told Sister Ermangarde, "you really mean . . . 'supernatural.'"

Her hands parted and slipped over the large wooden rosary lying atop the broad white wimple. At her gesture, I felt the familiar shape-shift into something smaller and longer again, like the sword. I wondered if she'd spotted my morphing metal accessory in action.

Luckily, Sister's faded hazel eyes were fixed on mine. "Spiritual? Supernatural? Aren't they the same? Unlike your eyes."

Rats! I'd forgotten I'd been wearing my gray contact lenses in Wichita to avoid being identified.

"You always had the most dazzling morning-glory blue eyes, Delilah. I'd hate to think time and travail had faded them, like mine."

"No such bad luck. I left town under a cloud." I guess

that description honestly applied to a wildcat tornado. "I'm back here to find out who I really am and don't want any WTCH-viewer getting distracted by my former persona as a TV reporter."

"At least you haven't lost faith."

"Ah, no . . . but I don't follow you."

Her gaze darted to my chest, which started the heat wave of a blush as I recalled recent activities.

"What a splendid Celtic cross you're wearing, Delilah. The garnets are a particularly deep and limpid red, like Our Savior's blood."

I looked down, of course, to see my familiar chain wearing a heavily ornate cross studded with cabochons of the same intense color as—strike me, lightning!—Midnight Cherry Shimmer.

"No need to blush, Delilah," the mother superior said. "Always such a modest girl, the ideal Our Lady of the Lake graduate. I'm glad you're the sole member of your class to pay us a visit." Her gaze sharpened. "Not that you particularly got along with the more affluent girls."

"That's exactly why I'm here," I pounced, to distract her from my scarlet-woman-red chest, the damn cross, and the flush heating my cheeks. "I was the only scholarship student, as they constantly reminded me. What scholarship?"

"Oh. That *is* awkward. Almost as awkward as when Margaret Mary Rasmussen raised such a fuss about your driving lessons. No need to blush over that entirely innocent incident, on your part. I'm sure you were taught in Ethics the motto of the Order of the Garter, *'Honi soit qui mal y pense.'* Evil to him . . . or her . . . who evil thinks."

"My scholarship," I insisted, not allowing her to distract me.

"Not exactly a scholarship, dear. That would require the school itself awarding the money, and we had very little for that in those days."

"*I* didn't have *any* money in those days. I had to work twenty hours a week as a dorm receptionist, but everything was paid for. Classes, uniform, room, and board. There was even a 'necessities' fund at the bursar's office, which had me putting in requisitions for pens and sanitary pads."

"Please, Delilah. Too much information." Sister's pale face colored. "You were on a stringent budget, true, but that builds character. Obviously. Look at you now. A poised professional."

"If the school didn't have the academic scholarship money for me, who or what did?"

"This is awkward, as I said. We were charged to be discreet. Actually, to silence."

"I'm long gone, Sister Regina." I deliberately invoked her name at the time. "Where did I spend summers? I don't even remember."

"We have a camp. In the woods."

I recalled the long-sword glimmer of a body of water far larger than the campus pond. Trees. Shadows. Horses and hoot owls.

"A camp?"

Sister cleared her throat. "Camp Avalon in the North Woods. Very cool and bracing during the hot and humid Kansas summers."

"I was at a f-forest camp and I don't even remember?"

"Really, how much do any of us remember of our pasts, Delilah? Most of the girls who come back laugh about the oversized gym suits, the required physical education classes, the—"

"The May crowning of the Virgin with flowers," I filled

in. "The winter Snow Fest, the SATs, the crummy mixers with the local boys' high schools."

I could have been describing the photos in the high school yearbook, had I ever had the cash to buy any of them. In any Midwestern private girls' school yearbook. I finally had a generic nonhistory, I realized.

"So," I said. "Who was the benefactor?"

"Not a who, Delilah. A what."

"Something supernatural?"

"Hardly." Sister chuckled indulgently, which I doubted any Our Lady of the Lake students had ever heard. "Not a yeti from Tibet, I assure you." She laughed even more unconvincingly.

The reference had my hackles rising. Achilles, my dog who died in Wichita, was a Tibetan breed, named after the land's capital city, a Lhasa apso. Yetis, aka the Abominable Snowmen, were the mystical white hairy creatures rumored living in the mountains of Tibet.

While I rocked back on my pump heels at that link, she trebled on.

"Not, Delilah, a . . . a witch doctor from Timbuktu. Merely a nondescript corporation from Corona, California."

"Corona, California? It sounds like a Beach Boys song title."

"I wouldn't know."

"Does the corporation have a name?"

"The checks were signed La Vida Loca and always went through promptly."

That's what I needed. A paper trail to hack into. I stood, smiling.

"Thank you, Sister. It's been wonderful to visit the campus and see you again."

"Feel free to wander where you will."

Except it was getting into early evening, and I had a date with two guys and a dog.

OUTSIDE THE ADMINISTRATION building, the twilight was doing a fade to black, as the film direction goes. I'd glanced up to check for any washed-out version of the moon to gauge how far it had passed the half-moon stage . . . when my sky-gazing self crashed into a hapless pedestrian.

"Pardon me," the man's voice said, for no good reason.

"Sorry." I'd been the inattentive one.

He was a bit shorter than me, which wasn't hard for rumpled, middle-aged men if I'm wearing a shoe with any kind of heel. I needed a moment for his short-sleeved black shirt and wrinkled forehead exaggerating a receding hairline to register.

I'd almost flattened the only person on campus that I remembered vividly and really wanted to see.

"Father Black," I said, eyeing the white collar and checking the familiar to see if it retained the cross form. It was now a large shallow vee shape. *Traitor!*

Schizo, Irma hissed at it, back on board again. Sister must intimidate her much more than Father Black.

"Delilah Street," he echoed back, looking more confused than ever. "Something's very different." He gazed blinking into my eyes.

"New contact lens sunglasses," I said glibly. "You know, the kind that change shades of gray depending on the light amount? Only now they make them in contacts."

"Oh. Well, you look splendid." He turned to the curb. "Is this your . . . car?"

It's hard to deny it when you're cozying up to the front fender, keys in hand.

"Yes. Found her at a farm sale way out near Glen Rose. A steal. I mean, not literally."

"Of course not." He began strolling around Dolly, which was quite a walk. "Perfect condition. Mileage?"

"Twenty-nine thousand."

"Unbelievably low. Not that you'd lie," he added.

An awkward silence prevailed as he finished his tour and returned to my side.

Father Black had been the only person at the high school who'd realized I had no vehicle and no one to teach me to drive so I could get my license. He'd taken me out in his old donated Volvo to the empty church lot and quiet roads around Our Lady of the Lake.

One of the girls' mothers complained to Mother Superior that such tutoring was "inappropriate," and that had been that. Except the mother was instructed to finish teaching me to drive her BMW and use it for the test, which I passed on the first try because I was so mad about the gossip I didn't want to spend another moment with that witchy woman.

"You like wheeling this much steel around?" Father Black asked now.

"Big and safe, and if anybody tries to mess with me on the road, they'll be sorry."

"What about parallel parking?"

"Maybe hard here, but I don't need to do that where I live now."

"You did . . . vanish from the airwaves at WTCH rather abruptly. They never said a word. Where are you living now?"

"Las Vegas."

"Las Vegas? Delilah, that's Sin City!"

"Not news, Father Black," I said gently. Such a sincere,

mild-mannered man. I'd always felt more protective of him than of myself, even during the "incident."

"No, Delilah. I mean . . . really and truly. I'm very concerned about your safety there."

Now was not a good time to mention my pals, the parking valet demons.

"Las Vegas is not as bad as you think. Frankly, Father, some of the . . . people on the air at WTCH were not exactly nice and weren't friendly to me."

His usual mild expression hardened. "You mean the 'New and Now' supernatural news team members, especially that incompetent weather witch. The chapel on our island has been hit by lightning six times this spring, no warning on the news, out of a clear blue sky, to coin a phrase for Kansas. Fortunately, we have a most effective lightning rod. Steps may have to be taken."

"A weather witch wouldn't . . . target Our Lady of the Lake."

"None with any sense. Watch yourself in town, Delilah," he told me, his expression softening as he patted my arm farewell.

"I have friends now, Father, and some of them have big teeth."

"You . . . can't mean that vampire anchorman?"

"No, my adopted wolf-mix dog. He runs about your weight."

"Oh. *Oh.* Excellent." Father Black winked at me, a very lame wink, and walked on into the administration building.

I hopped into Dolly, revved her up, and majestically drew away from the curb and a big part of my past. On the way back down the meandering drive, I peered at the little lake and the island when I reached the scenic overlook, squinting in the dying light through my "sunglasses" contacts. Sure enough, the spire of a steeple poked through and there was a metal needle protruding from the spire, upon which perched, like a wind vane, a sculpture that looked very much like a . . . gargoyle.

Gooo-aa-l! Irma chortled.

I didn't echo her cheer. I knew already I was surely going to Hell for lying about my gray contacts to kindly Father Black.

Chapter Thirteen

"Don't cows sleep at night like everything else?" I asked, irritable about being startled by every distant *moo*.

"City-raised," Leonard Tallgrass commented to Ric as we crouched in a cornfield bordering the grazing land we were "watching."

What you can "watch" crouching in corn plants in the dark of night is zero.

"Me too," Ric said in defense of my city-girl history.

"You? City-raised? Naw." Leonard Tallgrass had spoken. "You've got an inside-the-Beltway D.C. manner and you'll never tell me what or why, but you were used to living out-of-doors young."

I knew Ric would leave Tallgrass's pronouncement unanswered, so I broke the lengthening silence.

"Say, guys. I still don't get what we're doing in a cow pasture in the dark of night, or what you've been 'looking into' on the rural scene. Or why you were so interested in the footage Slo-mo Eddie got of the cow mutilation scene here."

I'd returned Dolly to the Thunderbird Inn from Our Lady of the Lake to find Ric, Tallgrass, and Quicksilver waiting, all ravenous. After a fast-food dinner, Tallgrass wanted to eyeball my TV station tape of this very scene, then get the two-footed members of our party appropriately garbed for a nighttime "operation."

So here we were two hours later in the dead of night. At least the nighttime temps dipped to a tolerable seventy degrees and the Kansas humidity was low. I couldn't believe that my quashed TV story on cattle mutilations was of such interest now, although the enlarged clawed tracks I'd noticed at the original scene had looked mighty bear-like on my laptop.

"Now that we know their route," Tallgrass told Ric, "I figure the herd will be ambling our way in twenty minutes or less."

"Somebody's driving them hard," Ric said. "They'll probably get here in ten to twelve minutes."

"Herd?" I asked. "Nobody herds cows overland these days. Aren't we laying a trap for the rotten teenaged cow mutilators? Probably half-breed vamps who've never gone mainstream and are living off livestock."

A weed was shifting in the night wind right under my nostrils, so I gave up the knee-creaking crouch and let myself fall back on my rear. Ric's fingerless workout gloves grabbed my wrists to pull me up again.

Ric and I had outfitted our designer jeans for unexpected night surveillance with work boots and long-sleeved black cotton shirts from Western Werehouse. My size eight boots weren't broken in. The stiff leather would chaff my ankles raw if I maintained this classic crouch position any longer.

"She okay?" Tallgrass asked softly.

"'She' is fine," I whispered. "I may not be Annie Oakley, but I got you guys back to the same field I'd filmed two months ago."

"Yes, you did, scout," Ric answered. "Any pasture where several cows have been mutilated and some officious Fed shows up to kick out the local media is prime scouting material."

"That was weeks and weeks ago," I objected. "A lot of weather has been over this field since."

Tallgrass snorted. "You got that right. Especially lately. Wichita's been having excessive 'weather' for early summer. Doesn't matter. When blood is shed, the earth remembers."

I shivered a little, even though it was a perfectly temperate night. Crickets chorused their approval all around. We could occasionally hear the almost metallic rustle of birds of prey briefly silhouetted by the nearing three-quarter moon, looking like a mottled football, in the dark sky above.

The guys had their night-vision, bone-finding field binoculars glued to their sinuses. They radiated teamwork and concentration for the hunt. What exactly they were hunting other than cows, they'd been seriously tight-lipped about telling me, but all our faces wore swaths of cammo paint.

I couldn't blame them. I was along to share the cramped discomfort they reveled in only because Quicksilver was doing the real scout-work somewhere out there. Also, I'd been pursuing broken threads of my past all day on my own in Wichita and wasn't keen on spilling the unpromising details when the male contingent had been finding out serious shit.

Obviously, Ric's FBI assignments and later freelance consulting work had brought him far north of the Mexican border. And Leonard Tallgrass was about as "retired" as the Energizer Bunny. Comparing the taciturn Tallgrass to something pink relieved my boredom and all-over outdoor itches and made me smile.

"Don't show your pearly whites on point unless you're going to use them," Tallgrass grumbled in my ear.

Damn. He didn't miss a thing.

"What about those funky tracks in the field?" I whispered into Ric's ear.

"Yes," he said.

Okay, so we weren't here to share, but pounce. On someone or something.

A moment later I heard rustling in the already trampled cornstalks behind me.

Turning my body around was going to make a no-no of a ruckus, so I twisted my head over my shoulder. I could see the tassels of corn plants shifting against the lighter panorama of the moonlit, cloudy sky.

Something was crawling toward our position.

I poked Ric in the ribs and nodded behind us. He lowered the binoculars and frowned, hearing the same, steady advancing crinkle of broken foliage. I was slightly behind the crouching men, so my rear would be the thing's first appetizer.

"*Ty-ohni,*" Tallgrass whispered without turning. "Your wolf-heart returns, silver-woman."

I watched the shadowy earth move as if a giant furrow was being churned up. Did Kansas have any burrowing predators, beside possible post–Millennium Revelation ghouls?

The moon sailed free of a train of cloud to reveal Quicksilver belly-crawling to join us. Some joker had smeared his snout and paler colored lower face with sooty cammo paint.

He crawled alongside me, offering a quick lick of greeting along my unsmudged neck just below the black shirt's collar line. He knew not to remove my cammo face paint. Cleaning us all up at the Thunderbird Inn after this outing was going to be messy and awkward, like some cheesy B-movie threesome.

More than one cow lowed, much closer. I realized the critters sounded like giant mourning doves, plaintive and knowing they were meat for nature's whims and human hunger.

After seeing the royal Egyptian vampire empire "food stock" of a human herd kept for generations, I was soon converting to some form of vegetarianism.

Quick's short, coyote-style yip made Tallgrass's head nod.

"Three minutes, tops, and they'll be on us," he warned.

Oh, come on. Like Quicksilver can tell time.

I curled my fingers around the black leather collar he came with, the silver discs circling it feeling fatter and overheated, as if the sun had been out. *Ouch.*

"*Okay.* You *can* tell time," I whispered in his perked ear.

He flicked me off like a mosquito, suddenly lunging to his feet, digging claws into earthen clods and darting into the clearing made by the cow mutilation incident two months ago.

Tallgrass and Ric jumped up to follow him, carrying weapons I'd noticed and couldn't name. They were big, thick, black, pug-ugly automatic weapons somewhere between a submachine gun, an assault rifle, and a flame-thrower.

I didn't have time to watch our team members attack.

A whole freaking herd of cows—longhorn cattle—were moving forward as one boulevard-wide mass, with horn tips that could extend to the height of a very tall Texan, to hear those braggarts tell it. I was ready to become a believer. I'd never thought of cows—steers and cows, I should say—as majestic, but they sure were a vision to behold, surging toward us with thundering hooves and rumbling lows and Viking helmets like an army from the clouds above brought down to earth.

The earth, Tallgrass had said, that never forgets a drop of blood spilled on it.

And maybe that explained the vampire and werewolf resurrection in our times, bleeding Kansas, the Civil War nexus, my own moon-driven monthly agonies, the notion of cattle as human sacrifices, which would really rile the beef industry, my old TV news reporter persona realized.

I'd been taught my Kansas history. In the twenty years after the War Between the States, only the ten million head of Texas Longhorn cattle driven north on legendary trails to railheads in Kansas and beyond kept the nation fed. It was called the largest movement of animals under man's direction in world history. I couldn't help thinking of the Karnak vampires' puny human herd, but how many had they added up to over a couple thousand years?

Yet the cattle drive I was witnessing now was beyond the ordinary, eons-old business of eat and be eaten, graze and be slaughtered, be animal, vegetable, or human and be worried.

This was a herd whipped up from Hell.

These cattle drivers weren't those legendary cowboys partnered with another grazing herbivore, the conquistador-descended mustang ponies. They were shambling along on foot, dozens and dozens of them. Mexican peons and parade prima donna *hidalgos* mounted on palominos of pale aspect. A skeleton corps of horses and riders, pale horses, pale riders, pale cowherds on foot beside them. Ghosts and zombies and flesh-and-blood cattle, oh my.

I was watching a multicentury parade of the blood price between human and beast laboring by in a half-phantom form.

Quicksilver was in constant motion, flashing, fog-gray bone and blood and fang nipping at the herders' paranormal heels, driving them into a single once-and-future mass of past and present, real and supernaturally preserved life . . . and death.

And, among this supernatural Wild West Show rode and walked the real game-masters, actual men. From Ric's intent expression, these were the criminal elements from south of the border he had been tracking before.

Meanwhile the silver moon was pouring light down on whole flocks of clouds that were massing and cascading down to earth in disembodied herds. I'd never imagined the Kansas plains could host such an abundance of forgotten and now refreshed life and death. The vast scope of the prairies made the lavish neon sprawl of the Las Vegas Strip look tawdry and pinched.

Here, in the wide open spaces, the Millennium Revelation could expand and multiply, celebrating all the dead and undead life of our endlessly evolving planet. Nothing was lost. Nothing failed to survive, but everything had been reborn in some extravagant, frightening, haunting form.

I watched this gruesome, gritty, inspiring, ghostly panorama, bedazzled by the times I was living in. Anything could happen, could be real, could require dealing with.

Especially Lilith and Lili, me and Irma, all my new frenemies in Vegas and especially Ric and Quicksilver and Leonard Tallgrass beside me joined in a quest to free the future from the past.

That's when something knocked me off my feet, pointy-toed cowboy boots and my nose both digging into the earthy ground.

So much for moon-gazing at ghost longhorns in the sky.

While I spit out dirt, someone pulled me up by the elbow and jerked me several feet sideways. It was either a very annoyed friend or a very impatient foe.

"Del," Ric shouted over the major mooing, "this is the drive-in all over again, only these zombies are on fast-forward. Okay? We need to do some major mowing-down if we don't want to *be* mowed down."

I looked around. He was right. Most of the mounted men were literal ghost riders in the sky, literally "spook-ing" the cattle to move on. The zombies in ragged clothes and ragged flesh were darting at the edges of the herd, bit-ing and clawing like a pack of attacking wolves, occasion-ally clotting when they pulled a calf down, tearing it apart while it bawled and the protective long-horned mother charged, kicking and head-pronging the hell out of the zombies, but eventually falling helpless into their never-dying, gobbling midst.

Obviously, I needed to keep a lot of bad things from getting close enough to off me. The demure silver familiar, which had so far accepted a role as the metal strap adjust-ment clips on my industrial-strength sports bra, went as molten as Quicksilver's collar disc on me. It seared up my shoulders and then down my arms into its major set-to weapon of choice, twin braided solid silver whips.

When the silver familiar had ripped like mercury down my arms, filling my hands with the butt knobs of twelve-foot-long whips, Ric stepped close behind me, putting his hands over mine as he had when he'd helped me "dowse" the day we'd first met in Sunset Park and we'd together dredged up the unbeloved dead.

I felt my breath whoosh out of my body as an electric charge knocked me back even tighter against Ric, as if we'd been melded into one body. His hands vibrated with strain on mine. An electric rainbow aura played aurora borealis all around us. I remembered an image of us in the mirror when we'd first made love, when I'd gladly let him kiss my virginity good-bye.

I'd glimpsed our auras then, and only then. Mine ice-blue, like my eyes on fade. His hot and yellow, like his . . . desire. They had blended into green and purple.

Now the aura was all ice-blue, spreading from Ric's hands through mine onto the silver whips, remaking them into argent electric eels of power, snapping and sizzling as they curled around charging zombies and wrenched off undead heads and limbs.

And what they touched still moved, but shriveled and exploded into Fourth of July sparklers.

And then the night sent its own long, seeking leather tongue of fire our way. I recognized El Demonio's thirty-foot bullwhip. I saw it aim like a striking snake at the precise part of Ric my love had healed. His back.

It was now a battle of the lizards, whip tongue to whip tongue. I ripped my hands free of Ric's, made a sweeping gesture as my fisted fingers sent my hate and fury down the silver whips in a conjuror's gesture of control.

Luckily, I'd turned my face aside as the black-leather lightning strike from the past headed our way. It struck whatever force field our silver auras had cast around Ric and me, and coiled away into the air and futility like the zombie bodies.

Ric wrapped me in his arms, wrapped my arms around myself. Our conjoined powers made us into whirling dervishes, the center of an electric twister. I couldn't breathe. Think.

Outside our magic circle there danced such a demon as I have never dreamed of.

A dancing bear? It was heavy and cumbersome, all right.

So, why did foot-long spines march down its backbone and . . . tail?

I'd seen the marks of a trailing "tail" when I'd first recorded cow mutilations for WTCH-TV. Which the station had quashed, pretty much.

There was no "quashing" this beating, switching, spiny tail.

"Ric? You ever see such a critter?"

He nodded. "El Demonio and his minions didn't call me 'goat-boy' for nothing. I slept with goats. This blood-sucker needed dead prey, so I escaped it. But it was out there. Always. On the edges of things. Waiting."

"I never heard about such a thing in Kansas."

"It's a Hispanic demon who's crossed the border after the Millennium Revelation. You could say it's native to Puerto Rico, where it was first reported, the Dominican Republic, Argentina, Bolivia, Chile, Colombia, Honduras, El Salvador, Nicaragua, Panama, Peru, Brazil, Mexico, and the United States."

"Puerto Rico and the Dominican Republic are island nations," I said.

"I know south-of-the-border geography, *chica*," Ric said. "And I'm the one who went to kindergarten in herds of goats and donkeys. I've glimpsed *el chupacabra* before. It warns of its attack with a screech that turns its eyes the color of glowing coals. I was beating off his interest in goats and kids before I was five years old. It is a far, far better beast than El Demonio."

"Baby Ric, the dragon slayer," I murmured, brushing his cheek with my palm. The thrill of admiration I felt for Ric's youthful bravery was almost sexual. I could have used a champion like him when I was five.

He quickly kissed my life and heart lines before charging up out of the cornstalks to the fight, joining his battle cry to the screech of the chupacabra.

I charged up right after him, and nearly got run over by a zombie going for Tallgrass.

Run over by a zombie? These weren't your local drive-in sleepwalking zombies.

The speeding zombie turned as my twin silver whips slashed the thigh bones out from under it and threw them over my shoulder to Quicksilver, who chomped them to bits even as they jitterbugged away.

Ric and Tallgrass planted their boots, using automatic weapons fire to blast the loping zombies to pieces of dice-size dancing bones. The whole scene was like the Cold Creek zombie jamboree on fast forward.

My arms were aching from tripping zombies that never stopped charging or moving. So many skulls were skittering through the cornstalks, chattering like joke false teeth, that the entire field was scythed down as if by Death himself.

Meanwhile, the driven herd of real-life cow flesh moved on, flanks already gnawed raw by its carnivorous herders. The sight so reminded me of the Karnak vampire empire human herds under Las Vegas that my whip slashes beat with even more fury into animated undead flesh and bone.

I'd never seen myself as merciless, but I was that night, fighting to keep Ric and Tallgrass and Quicksilver whole and in action.

It became a snapping, shattering, grim reaper's Wild West Show, with the driven livestock finally passing us by, tailed by a custom convertible limousine holding a standing figure lashing the bizarre parade forward with that thirty-foot snake's tongue of braided leather. Behind the rampaging limo galloped a conquistador wearing a skull-shaped helmet and riding a weary skeletal horse.

History, pass on by.

I watched the mortal and immortal herd disappear on land and in the sky, both the physical and psychic seeming mirror mirages.

We four remained weary and standing. Alone.

"We've got what we need," Tallgrass said, panting hard. "The stragglers."

Like a prize Australian sheepdog, Quicksilver had found two fallen longhorn cows from the ground-bound Milky Way herd. The still hummocks of their bodies resembled primitive burial mounds. Tallgrass knelt by one, and something in his posture made me flinch. My whips recoiled into silver wrist cuffs, cold as ice.

"You and the dog up to dealing with reality for a while here, pard?" Tallgrass asked Ric.

He didn't look my way.

What a pity. Male investigators didn't get to see and join the circle of life and swirl of the planets. We stood alone among the sacrificed stock. Real, motionless cowhide on the trampled earth. I would maybe never eat ground beef again.

"Ugly work," Tallgrass said. "Always was. I recommend the city girl leave. Ric?"

"I need to know," he said. "Delilah?"

Sure. Call me a wimp and a bleeding heart. I turned and left.

Quicksilver followed, whimpering softly. He knew how near death always lurked for four-foots.

Ric joined me ten minutes later. "Tallgrass has field-dressed deer, which I haven't," he said by way of explanation, or apology. "We needed to understand . . . dissect . . . the cow mutilations you filmed."

"Yeah? Sadistic mischief, right?"

"A crime, right. Not mischief. The border drug-smuggling cartels have been using the herd cattle as drug 'mules.' Cows have four stomachs, don't they? All the more room for smuggled narcotics. Those you saw here a couple months ago must have dropped dead on the trek and were left behind after being gutted and stripped of the bagged drugs."

"Cows? Can you abuse a more helpless animal?"

"Yeah," Ric said. "Humans. Like us."

So, his message was . . . weep not for the four-foots. The two-foots are even more pitiable prey these post–Millennium Revelation days.

I walked away, sick of my own species.

Except nowadays, species was a relative term.

Chapter Fourteen

FORGET DRIVE-IN ZOMBIES and cow-mutilating drug lords. That was last night. Ric and I had slept in until noon. We should have been ravenous, but could only nibble on road snacks.

Today was the first day of the rest of my life, and the really scary part of my trip back to Wichita was starting *now,* this afternoon, with Ric and me sitting in Dolly's front seat wearing what could pass for our "Sunday best" anywhere, preparing to enter a bland brick three-story building to find out all about . . . me.

The place looks like a morgue, Irma warned me. *You do not want to go there, Street, in any meaning of the phrase. We do not want to go there, even with a bodyguard as professionally accomplished as Ric.*

"Hush," I said to quiet her nervous chattering.

"Huh?" Ric asked. "I didn't say a thing."

I just shook my head, unable to explain my paralysis. I was so full of dread I'd let him drive, even here in Wichita, through streets I knew like the lines on my palm. Leonard Tallgrass had provided the computer-map route past the three group homes he discovered I'd lived in until I was sprung from the system to attend Our Lady of the Lake convent school.

They were all sprawling one-story ranch-styles set in modest neighborhoods. I remember there had been uproars about having group homes in single-family communities, but I was used to being something of an outcast and that hadn't really affected me.

I didn't even recognize the exterior of the one home I'd supposedly lived in for four years. What might go on today in these five-to-six-bedroom homes gave me the willies.

Ric's hand stretched across the wide front seat to take mine.

"Your fingers are like icicles, *amor*. It'll be all right. You can stop hugging the car door. Dolly will be here when we get back."

"You're sure Quicksilver is all right with Tallgrass?"

"They hit it off like old camping buddies, you saw that. A dog wearing sunglasses waiting in a parked fifty-six Caddy convertible wouldn't be cool in Kansas, you know that. In Vegas, anything goes, but here we're undercover. Think of us as census takers. We're official. We want dates and places and details and we are a couple of mean bureaucratic badasses no one will want to mess with."

He wore a dark gray suit I'd never seen, drab and slightly shiny. I had inserted my gray contact lenses again and had clipped my hair in back so it seemed vaguely bun-like but covered my neck. I wore my TV-reporter outfit, a navy suit and matching pumps that did nothing for me but make me blend in with any background, from political press conference to neighborhood murder scene.

I'd copped an idea from lady police detectives. All my working suit jackets had deep, if discreet pockets. Carrying a bothersome purse makes a woman easier to dismiss as girly on the job. A narrow reporter's notebook and pencil, ID and money clip were all I needed on me. With my black eyebrows and lashes, I'd only needed a pot of lip gloss and a dab of concealer for the camera. Nowadays, of course, I also armed myself with Lip Venom and Midnight Cherry Shimmer. That was New Delilah, though. I was here in Kansas to meet Old Delilah's worst nightmare.

I still kept my eyes glued to a fire hydrant coated in shiny aluminum paint on the street in front of the Wichita Child Protective Services building. That seemed like a good omen.

"Will I recognize this Haliburton woman Tallgrass dug up?" I asked, needing to clear my throat first.

Ric shook my captured hand. "Doesn't matter. Lighten up, Delilah. I know a nonentity from a bad past can be even more terrifying than a monster in the present. I've been there, right? You saw me through. Now I'm seeing you through."

I nodded, opened Dolly's heavy door, and got out, checking the building's side windows. Was anyone watching the parking lot below? My gaze panned rows of uncurtained windows with flower vases, photo frames, and office knickknacks lined up on the indoor sills.

"Mrs. Haliburton," Ric said, "was in charge of group homes during the years you were in the system. Tallgrass had to do a lot of white-collar-crime type of digging to come up with someone who should know everything we want to find out. Relax. This is the simplest party we've ever crashed. Remember the Karnak."

I couldn't help smiling. Only Ric would call our life-threatening expedition to an underground empire of ancient vampires "crashing a party."

The trouble was, I'd mostly done all my derring-do to save someone else's skin. It's harder to be as brave on your own behalf, especially when confronting childhood monsters.

Toughen up, Irma advised. *The man is gonna find answers; it's his calling. His inner kid has faced night-*

mares that make ours look like Saturday morning cartoons.

Except I'd never been a morning cartoons person. I'd hid out in the group homes to watch midnight monster movies. Any cruising vamp boys found the rec room with its Ping Pong table, jigsaw puzzles, and small-screen TV too nerdy to venture near.

I was beginning to understand why my memories of living in Wichita had gaping holes. We walked through the social services building into a bland lobby, elevator, and halls so forgettable I couldn't describe them moments after passing through. Maybe that's why I couldn't remember much about my childhood; it was so forgettable. *Not* terrifying.

"We have an appointment," Ric told the ash-blond receptionist in rimless glasses.

See what I mean? Irma prodded. *Boring and bland and forgettable. No wonder we split this burg for Sin City.*

We were shown into one of the offices without a vase or any trinkets in the window.

Mrs. Haliburton was sixtyish, with permed iron-gray hair and the required rimless glasses, and she, too, wore navy blue, which suited her pinkish complexion. Navy blue made my white skin look bluish, like skim milk.

She rose to greet Ric. "Mr. Montoya." She gave me a demanding stare.

Already I hated her.

Ric was all professional interrogator. "Good to meet you, Mrs. Haliburton. This is my assistant, Miss Place."

"You're formerly with the FBI?" she asked Ric as we sat on molded blond-wood chairs while she reclaimed the squeaky black desk chair.

"Yes," he said. "The Phoenix office."

News to me. I guess if I could learn more about Ric, the trip to Wichita would be worth it.

"I don't see," Mrs. Haliburton said with a superior little laugh, "what you're doing here, making inquiries. We're up-to-date in Kansas, you know. We have our own FBI offices."

"This is a Kansas case file I'm investigating," he said, "involving a Wichita group home resident of a dozen or so years."

"No longer in our system?"

"No."

"You do understand, Mr. Montoya, that our group home clients are disabled in some way, have learning or behavioral difficulties? We must protect their privacy."

Even Irma cringed inside me.

"I have a signed and notarized paper from the individual in question," Ric said, producing a folded document from his inside jacket pocket.

"Is this related to a civil suit—?"

"Not at all, Mrs. Haliburton." Ric's smile was dazzling. "Merely a routine question of information—where, when, that kind of thing. So far," he added, without the smile.

Mrs. Haliburton's poodle-cut head reared back as she frowned at the paper. I didn't sense that she recognized my name.

She handed back the document, folded. "Well, Mr. Montoya, Miss Place. You're in luck. Everything was computerized during this girl's residence. I can look her up in an instant."

Gulp, Irma moaned.

Ric slid me a glance, his eyes a perfectly trustworthy brown with the colored contact lens in place.

Place. I smothered a nervous giggle.

To find me a fake surname, we'd worked our laughing way from Avenue to Boulevard to Circle to Drive. I'd firmly rejected Lane as being too reminiscent of Lois, before deciding that only Place, in honor of the Sundance Kid's notorious girlfriend, Etta Place, also made a convincing last name. She'd been a mysterious lady lost to history. I might be en route to becoming another one.

Mrs. Haliburton's scanty eyebrows lifted above the thick lenses of her glasses. Her keyboard clicked and her unblinking eyes scanned a series of computer pages invisible to us as we sat staring at the back of her monitor.

Then her frantic fingers stopped and her face went white.

Really. I'd never seen anyone actually do that, and she had started out a pearly pink.

"This file is sealed," she announced, anger underlying her words. "You must have suspected that."

"No," Ric said, glancing at me. "Not at all. Only juvie court documents can be sealed. This isn't one of those?"

"No," she answered, to my relief.

"Then the file can't be sealed," Ric said.

"It is. That's all I know. I can't enter it, even if I would be willing to violate the seal."

"That's crazy," I said, leaning forward in my slippery-seated chair. "She left the system at age fourteen, when she entered high school."

"Check with the high school, then," Mrs. Haliburton snapped at me. "I can refer you to the public school superintendent during that era. He would have to approve admitting someone with a record so . . . extreme it would be the only one ever sealed."

She was one of those old-time female bureaucrats who

still knuckled under to men, but gave women a bad time. I suddenly knew I'd probably run into her ilk many times before, among the social workers and group home supervisors.

"Thanks a bunch, Mrs. Haliburton," I said, "but Delilah Street didn't leave the system for a public high school. She had a scholarship to Our Lady of the Lake convent school."

"That place! I don't like your tone, Miss. I'm giving up my time to look into this matter as a courtesy to Mr. Montoya and his former affiliation. I know nothing of what yours is."

Oh, I so wanted to snap that I'd been a reporter on WTCH-TV. How could she not even recognize my face? I hadn't exactly been anonymous.

Ric put a hand on my forearm as he stood up, bringing me upright with him.

"I'll take the superintendent's information, Mrs. Haliburton," he said, his voice as smooth as milk chocolate. "We appreciate your efforts."

He held out his open hand until she huffed a sigh and scribbled something from the screen down on a memo pad. By the time she looked up and handed it over, she was simpering.

"Quite all right. Glad to oblige *you,* Mr. Montoya." Her glance flicked my way and hardened. "You'll find that Our Lady of the Lake is even stingier than the state with their records . . . to anyone."

Ric took my arm firmly in hand until we were in the hall. "Amazing," he murmured. "There's no love lost between you and female authority figures, whether you remember it or not. That's a valuable piece of information."

I tried to shrug off his "gentlemanly" custody. I was ready to explode with indignation.

"State building, Del," he murmured. "Security cameras everywhere, outside, in the elevator. Maybe even voice recording. Stifle yourself."

"You—" In a minute, he'd be telling me I looked beautiful when I was angry, just to add fuel to my fire.

I bit my lower lip, a gesture I knew he found inciting, and shut up all the way to the parking lot. There, I stopped at the driver's side and held my palm up until he tossed the keys into it.

"Where to, *mon capitaine*?" I asked.

"The motel, to regroup." He got into the passenger seat and laid his left arm along Dolly's channeled red-leather seat back.

"The Thunderbird Inn?" I wondered. "Sounds like a waste of precious time when here I got all dressed up to snow the ice queen."

I turned the key in Dolly's ignition, put her in gear, and sped her out of the parking lot fast to spin the dust of bureaucracy from her tires.

Ric's fingers stroked the nape of my neck and curled under the tendrils of my pseudo-bun until shivers slithered over my spine.

"I don't know why," he said, "this Delilah Street is such a hot potato she's got the only sealed file in the history of Wichita's Department of Child Protective Services, but I intend to take Miss Place to the Thunderbird Inn and take her apart until I discover that."

"You're not scared?" I flashed him a sizzling glance.

"Only in a good way."

The silver familiar uncoiled from its role as a sedate neck circlet and icily eeled into my concealed cleavage. As my spine shivers settled in my stomach, it wove in and out through my navy jacket's front buttonholes, leaving the top two gaping open.

"Way to dress up a dull navy suit," Ric said.

I depressed Dolly's gas pedal hard enough to slam him back in the seat.

"Jerk," I said, smiling. "If you think a little sex will make me feel better about being a bureaucratic forbidden zone . . . you may have a point."

"I was thinking . . . a lot."

"Is that why you sent Quick on a sleepover with Tallgrass last night?"

"I figured we needed downtime alone. Together."

I nodded. "It's so far past lunchtime it's dinnertime. We'd better stop for fast food. Remember, chicken or fish."

Ric consulted his cell phone screen. "Right at the second light."

I followed directions and slowed Dolly on a wide turn into a drive-through lane before I saw and read the big sign on the tall pole. Ric was not only back, body and hopefully soul, so was his sense of humor.

"Jack in the Box, dude?"

When he shrugged, I noticed that even his lowbrow suit had great shoulder tailoring. "And you are so going to get fries with that."

I did, in fact, feel a lot better.

Chapter Fifteen

A SCRATCHING SOUND, like a cat claw raking across a hard surface, awakened me from dreams of being bound to an ancient Egyptian mummy preparation table.

Not only a dream. A memory.

I'd been sleeping on my side, as usual, so in one motion I rolled out of bed and was standing on my feet in the shadowy room, my bare toes curling into nylon shag, something unlikely to carpet any ancient chamber. The silver familiar filled my right palm with a cold metal weapon of some kind.

"Del," Ric's sleep-slowed voice drawled from behind me. "Where's the fire?" He was half-sitting on the . . . yes, bed—not a stone table edged with a slim gutter for draining blood—behind me.

"I heard something," I said.

"I guess," Ric said as he turned on the bedside lamp. "What're you carrying?"

I turned my hand over in the weak light. "A humongous biker switchblade. The haft is etched with a screaming dude face wearing buffalo horns etched like a bad tattoo."

"Place-appropriate, I'd say," Ric said, yawning and checking his watch. It was so multifunction I couldn't even *find* the time display. "Ten a.m. I didn't hear any—"

The scraping sound came again, longer and louder. From the motel's metal door. I went to the curtained picture window and peeked out the side.

"Quicksilver wants in."

"That's new. Tallgrass must have dropped him off as a wake-up call."

"They've both had enough of our long, luxurious coed bedroom time," I guessed, going to undo the chain lock that was shimmying like a stripper from Quick's latest "knock." Luckily, even his big nails couldn't etch steel.

I looked around before I opened the door wide enough to admit him. Most of the parked cars that were here when we came back for the evening were gone. The motel was in the dead zone between guest shifts.

Ric had already retreated to the bathroom, so Quick gave my weaponless hand a lick in greeting and headed for the stainless food and water bowls next to my side of the bed. I hid them under the chintzy chintz dust ruffle when we were out during the day. No problem. The maids never cleaned in the closet or under the bed, and, frankly, I didn't blame them one bit. I hurried to the bedside to slide my feet into my cowboy-boot mules.

Meanwhile, I'd lost the awesome knife, replaced by a bicycle chain–style bracelet.

I put kibble in Quick's bowl and turned on my bedside lamp to use my first chance to inspect him for damage, although he'd probably licked it all away at Tallgrass's place. The big black leather collar he'd come with at the Sunset Park adoption event had a few more fang scratches between the silver circles that never dented, although they changed shape with the moon cycles and were now nicely three-quarter shaped.

"You're my Moondoggie," I told him, causing his per-petually perked wolfish ears to flatten a bit. Quicksilver wasn't one for mush. "I wonder what this collar is about?"

I gave his hackles a rough fluff with both hands and

ran them deep into the thick silvery gray hair of his back and chest. It's unusual that a big dog, a dog with both wolf and wolfhound genes, would tolerate being petted or even touched while eating. Quick continued gulping.

He'd seemed fine after the Zombie Cattle Company jamboree. Of course, he was the first of our partnership to exhibit a healing tongue, and I was not about to try mine out again on anyone but Ric. I leaned down to murmur, "Physician, heal thyself," in one big-bad-wolf-large ear. He was too busy wolfing his food to react to my little nothings.

Just then, Ric came out of the bathroom, and I turned to look. A new man, freshly showered, bare-chested and barefoot, contact lens inserted, and jaw shaved so close he must have lost half of his follicles.

"First," I suggested. "I'd get your baby-pink bottoms off that unsanitary motel carpet and into some shoes, then I'd tell me why the super-close shave. I know you had to have one *yesterday* for your new girlfriend, Mrs. Haliburton, but *today*?"

"Today, I've got to make the Wichita Mid-Continent Airport in less than an hour to pick up a big gun I had flown in." He frowned at my wrist. "Lost the switchblade. Too bad."

"Yeah, I feel naked without major edged weapons too."

Naked we were not. Quicksilver had a prudish streak for an unfixed dog, but that wasn't why both Ric and I, without consulting each other, had brought along jogging outfits for pajamas. We needed to be action-ready in case something big and bad besides Quicksilver wanted into our motel rooms along the way. Stray supernaturals of exotic ilk were still turning up all across America.

Like us.

"We need to talk about those fast-forward zombies and company," I told Ric.

"Yeah, but not until we settle Mrs. Haliburton's haughty hash. We're not leaving the Child Protective Services building today without more answers than are in your skimpy file."

He was at the tiny closet, donning his one French-cuffed silk shirt. White, that made his Latino skin gleam like a bronze god's.

"I could steam out the wrinkles over a tub of hot water."

"No time, although I'd enjoy watching you be domestic. Wrinkles will ease out with my body heat and won't show under the suit jacket. Trust me, I've traveled before."

"You tempt me with bare cheeks and references to body heat and are ready to bolt out the door. You are sure all business this morning, Montoya."

"Don't whine," he said with a grin. "You'll get yours later. You have anything to do here while I'm gone?"

I gestured at the wireless router I'd bought and installed yesterday beside the small flat-screen TV. "Going to catch up on the local news."

Ric thoughtfully pulled on his suit pants under his shirttails, whether in deference to Quicksilver or me, I wasn't sure. He grabbed his conservative diagonal-stripe tie and bureaucrat-navy jacket.

"You okay with me taking Dolly solo?"

"Now you ask? Guess I gotta be."

"Wear your on-camera suit. We'll have to grab a late lunch after the next assault on Mrs. Haliburton and her minions."

"And you're not going to tell me whom you're picking up at the airport?"

"Whom? Guess," he challenged on the way out the

door after snatching Dolly's keys from the dresser top. "I'll honk when I'm back." He flipped the Do Not Disturb sign to the outside knob as he left.

Hmm. He was looking way too polished for Mrs. Haliburton.

Quicksilver finished his loud lapping and came to where I sat on the foot of the unmade bed, remote in hand.

"You want to see where Mommy used to work?"

He made that doggy gacking sound, too conveniently for it not to be a comment on my phony tone.

"I'm looking for anything suspicious about my former newscast co-workers," I told him. "Feel free to add any of your opinions. Gacking is okay."

Actually, I was glad to be alone for this chore. It took my mind off what Ric was bound and determined to do, for my own good: uncover the source of my phobia against lying on my back.

Men can be so singled-minded. It had never occurred to him what I might most be afraid of now, even more than finding myself in my must-not-do sleeping position, a possible memory of rape. Childhood rape. I'd reported on such atrocities, and there was no way the word "survivor" could ever undo the reality of having been a "victim."

"IN OR OUT?" I asked Quicksilver when I heard Dolly's mellow Miss Piggy scream for attention, otherwise known as a horn, ninety minutes later.

He was at the door before me, so out we went, after I'd turned over the Do Not Disturb card. Actually, I was pretty disturbed when it came to the butterflies in my stomach region doing a maraca rumba.

Sure enough. Ric was watching for me with his arm thrown over Dolly's front seat and an expensively highlighted blond head of hair sitting in the passenger seat. He was either using Dolly to chauffeur a glam rock 'n' roll dude or . . . another woman.

Dog, I thought. Whoops. I'd never known I was the jealous type.

Quicksilver didn't pause in shock. He lofted over Dolly's polished black side into the backseat and *arf*ed loud and sharp right into the nape of the blonde's neck.

That turned her around pronto.

Oh. Ric's *moth-er*. Foster mother. The star psychoanalyst and Washington, D.C., professor. Georgetown University and all that jazz.

I raced to the passenger seat. "Dr. Burnside! I must apologize for my dog."

She turned around again to regard his now-grinning face. "My, what big teeth he has. But he also has his mother's eyes," she added wryly. Then she got a good look at my undercover gray contacts. "You certainly *can* hide your lying eyes, Delilah. Ric's explained the situation to me."

"He shouldn't have. I mean, he shouldn't have dragged you into this, Dr. Burnside."

"I thought I was 'Helena.' Has something changed?" Her eyes were a paler shade of blue than mine, but they narrowed with understanding into the transparency of water. "Ah. Goldilocks is sitting in your chair, Mama Bear."

She pushed the heavy door open and stepped onto the parking lot asphalt. "You sit up front. I'll take the rear."

"But . . . the dog."

Ric spoke for the first time. "I suppose he doesn't want to wait and scare the maid?"

"No," I said.

"That's fine," Helena said. "I go for younger men. What

is he, three or four? That would be the twenties in human years. Move over, bud. Ladies last. And last."

Quicksilver gave a small whimper of confusion and edged over . . . to the middle.

"Like that, is it?" Helena said. She reached into the side door pocket. "These yours, fellah?" She held up the extra-large sunglasses.

Quicksilver bowed his head so she could slip them on his long snout.

"Ric," I said warningly in a low tone as I sat in the passenger seat. Now I knew why dogs growled softly.

"Wait and watch," he said. "You clean up nice too."

So I shrugged. I'd let my hair grow from its TV-reporter neat bob since moving to Vegas, and the ends were waving a bit so I got some blue-black highlights to match my eyes. Which were now hidden, of course. Still, my clipped-back bun had some oomph and the silver familiar had made itself into a three-inch-long piece of vintage Eisenberg Ice rhinestones on my tame navy lapel.

"Where are we having that late lunch?" I asked.

"Closest decent place," he answered. "I'm starved, but on to Mrs. Haliburton first. I want to be hungry when I back her into a corner."

"She so does not deserve us," I said.

Chapter Sixteen

THREE MOLDED-WOOD CHAIRS were now lined up before Mrs. Haliburton's desk, Ric and I flanking Helena Troy Burnside, whose suit was a smashing power red, probably Prada.

Quicksilver was guarding Dolly in the parking lot, but he'd made his druthers clear. He'd rather be intimidating the bureaucrat in the office above.

Mrs. Haliburton shifted on her wheeled desk chair, which squealed like a little boy. She didn't quite glance at anything but the computer screen facing her.

"All the proper authorizations have reached your email address?" Helena inquired.

"Yes," Mrs. Haliburton murmured, her pink face turning fuchsia. She licked pale, dry lips. "From the secretary at the Department of Human Services in Washington, the assistant director of the FBI." She frowned at Ric. "And the lieutenant governor. This is most unprecedented, but I'll download the files to any device you wish, Dr. Burnside."

Helena extended a business card across the desk that Mrs. Haliburton whisked into her custody. "Both addresses?" she inquired.

"I always like a backup, don't you?" Helena replied.

Mrs. Haliburton ignored her while clicking in the e-addresses. She hit ENTER with the high-handed flare of a concert pianist, totally unlike her tightly wired self.

"I think you will find that this young woman, Delilah

Street," she spat out, still addressing her computer screen rather than our party, "will be very sorry indeed to have the contents of these files in anyone else's hands, even hands with so many highly placed connections. I know your specialty, Dr. Burnside, is severely damaged, and damaging, children, but you will have those therapeutic skills sorely tried in this case, as our social workers here in Wichita did thirteen years ago."

Gulp, Irma whispered. *And she doesn't even know about me.*

"Gulp" was right. I was sitting with the two people in the world whose respect I most wanted.

Ric laid his arm across the back of my chair, standing and drawing me up beside him.

"Thanks for your cooperation, Mrs. Haliburton, but warnings are unnecessary. I've found in my FBI work that files are sealed more often to protect the holders, not the subjects."

Helena was checking her mini-netbook. She looked up and nodded. "Mission accomplished."

Ric escorted me to the door, opened it for his foster mother, and ushered us into the hall.

"She's shaking, Helena," Ric told his onetime therapist in a furious undertone.

"Don't let that harpy frighten you, Delilah," Helena consoled me. "Little people like to make big threats." She took my other arm. "Now, Ric tells me you've invented another fascinating cocktail, the Brimstone Kiss. I know where you got the idea for that one." Helena smiled and added, "Let's find a well-stocked bar that can make it, where we can munch on a sinfully caloric bar menu."

She could make happy talk; it wasn't *her* secret file that was heating up her personal computer.

Ric knew how to calm my nerves. He let me drive again, with Helena in the passenger seat while he and Quicksilver occupied the rear.

Ric searched his phone screen. "Here's the place for us. The Petroleum Pavilion on Polo Drive. Delilah's cocktails always use exotic and expensive ingredients," he explained to Helena, about to pass me the GPS.

"Dolly and I don't need that high-tech aid," I said. "Any description of the physical neighborhood?"

"Um," Ric said, "the usual waterfront, probably a lake, near an exclusive gated community, riding stables, the ubiquitous golf course designed by the world's finest over-paid landscaper—hey!"

His recital broke off as Quicksilver whapped the cruising sunglasses off his snout and leaped out of the convertible, running ahead of Dolly on the street.

"I don't have to squint at some tiny screen in the sun like a vampire in extremis," I told my passengers. "Quick loves to find lost golf balls in Sunset Park. I'll just tail him as he follows his world-class nose."

"HOT DAMN!–BRAND CINNAMON schnapps," Helena mused over our glasses in the mahogany-paneled, crystal-lit bar.

"How," she persisted, "did you come up with such off-beat ingredients for your Brimstone Kiss, my new favorite drink, Delilah?"

Blush modestly . . . not. Helena was a psychotherapist whose already acute insights could pick up random visu-alizations from people's minds and subconscious after the Millennium Revelation. I did *not* want Ric's onetime "mother" glimpsing my forced interlude with Snow. She even knew who and what he was. Well, the albino rock star–hotelier part, anyway. Nobody really knew what brand of "super" Snow was.

"I'm self-blocked, Delilah," Helena assured me, already betraying that I was an easy read at the moment. "Believe me, I can feel the heat between you and Ric without any amplification, and I couldn't be happier for the both of you."

What luck that she couldn't tell my mental reruns right then had been about Snow.

I consigned thoughts of that bastard to the Inferno Hotel's subterranean Nine Circles of Hell attractions and explained.

"The Brimstone Kiss concept begged for a liquor brand with a 'hot' taste and name. I think Vegas pretty much twenty-four/seven these days, and it is truly Sin City now."

"I saw that on my brief visit," Helena said. "So . . . this is an ultra-Goth cocktail with a sweet undercurrent of innocence lost."

"You could write ad copy in today's Las Vegas," I agreed with a forced smile.

In the middle of our granite-topped table sprawled a platter of tomatoes and mozzarella, crab-stuffed mushrooms, and angel-winged shrimp, a post-Revelation delicacy discovered in the deep sea. Food definitely took the edge off my nerves.

Ric and I slipped into feeling triumphant and mellow, while Helena was scanning her screen between bites and sips.

"Okay," she said finally. "I've got the gist of the files."

"Should Delilah be shaking in her pump heels?" Ric wondered. "They're really not her style."

"Not," Helena said, "unless she has multiple tattoos." She turned the screen toward us.

"Me? Tattoos?" I demanded.

"Ric?" she consulted him.

He liked playing with the idea, and my skittish state. His eyes warmed as they met my startled expression.

"Tattoos? Oh, not a one, Dr. Burnside. I swear." His hand slipped under my social services' bun to caress the "love bruise" on my nape. "I don't like the idea of anybody or anything else, especially a needle, coming between my baby and me."

"I would say, 'Get a room,'" Helena commented, "except you kids already have one at that dreadful motel."

"Dolly and Quick are the reason," Ric explained. "We needed dent-free parking, which eliminated ramps, and a place that doesn't ban hybrid wolves. Don't worry. I booked you into the downtown showplace."

She nodded approvingly. "We need to go somewhere private to discuss these files. Your place or mine?"

"Yours," Ric and I answered as one.

"I'm so relieved," Helena said. "I haven't been in a motel since before the Revelation. I shudder to think what vibes I might pick up in that tacky room of yours."

So did we.

SUNSET WAS THINKING about taking a bow by the time we ambled out of the fancy bar. Fountains gushed like Old Faithful through the trees, probably installed in "water features," as they were in Las Vegas. The rich loved gushers on their property.

I was feeling calm, although edgy and curious about the tattoo remark. I'd been an overly careful girl, dodging preteen trouble from the "bad boy" half-vamps on my trail, studying and moving on, hoping not to get noticed, hiding in the midnight dens or dorm rooms where the TVs blared all night, blocking out danger and questions.

We ambled toward the parking lot, Ric and me an openly entwined couple, Helena still cruising her backlit screen with a frown I didn't like the look of, but was too happy to worry about.

The sound of a sustained, deep, threatening growl interrupted our separate reveries. We stopped and looked ahead to the isolated, distant spot where Ric had parked to avoid door nicks.

A group of six men surrounded Dolly.

Ric's hand left my waist to push his suit coat aside and reach for the firearm at the small of his back. Yep, my guy "carried concealed," thank, uh, thank my recent friend of a friend, Anubis, Egyptian god of the underworld. (My religious high school education made me take God too seriously to invoke Him for any minor life crises.)

Wait. These guys dressed like Vegas werewolf mobster Cesar Cicereau's tame "small job" muscle. They were probably dead men, and they wore plaid, all right. Green and yellow and blue plaid baggy trousers now in danger of a thorough ripping, along with said contents.

Quicksilver was standing in Dolly's backseat, his thick fur raised in a fearsome Mohawk from between his flattened ears to his seriously bushed-out tail. His snout was curled back, black-lipped to display the formidable mountain range of his wolfish fangs.

I rushed to put myself between Quick and his gentleman callers. That allowed me a glance into the backseat. Which was pretty much filled with small, dimpled white balls bearing three gilt initials on each one.

"Those are our balls," a tremolo tenor announced behind me. "Is that your . . . dog?"

"*Your* balls?" Helena intoned curiously, moving past the late-middle-aged men with a well-preserved wiggle.

She turned to confront them. "I am so sorry. What *shall* you do without them?"

They gaped, open-jawed like Quicksilver, but not nearly so formidable.

I started shoveling golf balls out of Dolly's pristine red upholstery. "Teeth okay, not claws," I instructed Quick. "This is not Sunset Park. Down. Back. *Leave kitty!*"

Men in checkered caps topped with white fuzzy balls scrambled at my last silly command to reclaim airborne presents from Christmas Past.

Ric leaned against Dolly's side, eyes buried in his hand, trying not to laugh, but utterly failing.

THIS TIME I let Ric and Helena use their high-tech toys and Ric drive.

A not-too-chastened Quicksilver ran alongside Dolly, giving chase to bad drivers in Ford 350s who cut off good drivers at every opportunity. I wondered where the motorcycle cop genes had come from. Maybe he was an escaped K-9 dog, who knows?

We reached the Old Town in no time. I sat in the backseat and consulted Ric's phone. A nineteenth-century warehouse had been gutted to house the boutique hotel, with soaring atrium and piano bar, but it was no Marriott, nor did it have Billy Joel live.

Like all hotels now, especially in Vegas, it boasted wireless access everything and all-suite rooms. The surrounding city center featured restaurants, shops, and Indian artifact museums.

The ambiance was charming, but Quicksilver was confined to the parking garage and Dolly. Downtown Wichita, no matter how restored, was not post–Millennium Revelation Las Vegas.

Good lord, I was homesick for *Vegas*.

"Very nice," Helena said, giving her foster son positive reinforcement for his choice. "We can order room service while we study the files."

My stomach started calisthenics again.

"The files" were *my* files. Were I tattooed. Which I wasn't. What was that about?

Maybe you *got all the tattoos,* Irma cooed. *And* I *got all the men.*

In Helena's room, we all doffed our hot, sticky business suit jackets and sat at a slate-topped table near a sink/small refrigerator unit.

Helena's phone buttons linked her net-comp to the room TV screen.

"Some of this is very puzzling," she warned us. "Most of it, in fact. Ric, take Delilah's hand in yours. Delilah, let him."

"What is this," Ric asked, now uneasy too, "a shotgun wedding?"

Helena's face looked a little old for the first time, shadowed by the suite's trendy spot-lighting.

"I can't say it's good, but I can say this is not the Delilah we know. And love."

She punched a tiny button on her keyboard, and scanned copies of printed pages hit the big screen.

Most were tiny-typed reports. A few photos flashed by: me looking like a deer in a police lineup spotlight, front and profile. I gasped audibly.

Helena clicked into close-up. "No panic. See the tattoo on her neck? Almost lost under the hair at her nape? A coiled snake, I think. It looks like you, but the expression is defiant and knowing. Not you, Delilah. Or the photos have been manipulated. Easy to do. Look. Here's a from-the-hip-up photo. You can see the twin cobra tattoos on her biceps. Definitely not you, even I can see that."

I eyed the loose-limbed, gaunt version of me in a raw preteen ranginess I didn't remember, wearing a Rolling Stones wife-beater tee-shirt, a chain hip-belt, and stone-washed jeans.

Young Lilith. It had to be.

I shook my head, feeling Ric's hands compulsively running over my arms and hands, circling my hips, covering—sheltering, claiming—the parts of my screen-revealed body.

"Honest, Mom-doc," he said, sounding like a defensive teenager for the first time in my hearing. "No marks on her that I haven't put there. I swear."

"TMI," Helena said, raising her palms.

She shut her eyes, revealing azure eye shadow gathering like a glittering monochromatic rainbow in a few faint age creases.

"I said this was a puzzle," she reminded us. "These images are not Delilah. Not only do my eyes and your joint testimony tell me that, but my . . . amplified insight. This might explain why Delilah had a difficult childhood. She had, at times, a supernatural shadow persona. This girl. This very disturbed girl. No girl is bad, but this one had very little good shown toward her and returned it in kind to others."

"An evil twin?" Ric put my thoughts into words.

I'd never told him about Lilith, another dirty little secret kept to ensure his peace of mind and my keen sense of privacy.

"The TV soap operas are dead, Helena," he said, dismissing his foster mother's theory. "They lost their audience years ago. Evil twins have been a hokey plot device since forever."

"Call me hokey. Few would dare, young man."

How fascinating to watch the two revert to a non-blood-kin parent/son mode. I liked Ric going hot-blood and testosterone-y in my defense, something he'd never do if we were facing real danger. I'd never had an inner teenager—except for Irma, come to think of it, who acted like an eternal teenager—but I felt like a prom queen now.

Wichita was peeling off all my hard-won defensive layers. I couldn't indulge that luxury for too long.

"I'm talking about a post–Millennium Revelation effect," Helena said. "The dates when 'Delilah' was picked up for juvenile delinquency are after January first, two thousand."

"I was never 'picked up' for anything," I protested.

"You admit you don't remember a lot about your childhood, until after high school, really," Helena pointed out.

"Who does?" Ric argued. "You remember the high and low points. I know I do, and I'm a star graduate of your methods, Helena."

She sighed. "The records show her—you, Delilah—with a history of running away from the group homes and hanging out at pool parlors, garages, tattoo and piercing shops with 'a bad crowd.'"

"No," I said, shaking my head. "I hid out in plain sight, in the group homes. I had a metal nail file for a weapon, yes, but it was against those creepy half-vamp punks who gave me a hard time. I wasn't even menstruating then, but they still came after me."

Helena's lips folded tight. Then she said, "I believe you, Delilah. I believe you had your own history in your mind, and . . . this person in the police photographs was never a conscious part of yourself."

"Or an unconscious part," Ric insisted. "She was a virtual virgin. Only it was real. She had a lot to overcome before we . . . became a 'we.'"

"Did she bleed the first time, Ric?" Helena sounded all cold-blooded physician.

He glanced at me, embarrassment a no-show in this emotionally charged conversation.

"Why should she, Helena? Did you?" he fought back for me. "Modern girls are way more active than some kind of . . . Victorian fading flower. The hymen can break in school sports, horseback riding—" He turned to me. "Does Our Lady of the Lake have riding stables?"

I nodded numbly. Some of the girls were even rich enough to keep horses stabled there; some of us just snuck in and patted them, or were occasionally invited to ride. I didn't feel these details merited breaking into this semi-mother-son debate.

"Ric." Helena's gaze turned steely. "You know and I know and Delilah knows she's got a deeply ingrained phobia against lying on her back, in bed or out of it. I can literally see the black cloud of suppressed fear hovering at the rear of her brain, and that's a formidable barrier to sexuality. You've done an admirable job of easing her around that barrier, but you can't change the underlying pathology."

"It's no 'job,'" Ric exploded. "It's a labor of love, and I can live with that black hovering ghost without knowing its name forever."

"Can Delilah, Ric? The files show an off-the-books medical 'procedure' when she was twelve. With an ob-gyn. Mrs. Haliburton can lie, but the files can't. It's against the law to destroy them, although they can be censored and blacked-out and buried in bottomless circles of bureaucratic hell. Somebody came along later and *knew* they'd be liable for something. The trouble is, whatever went so very wrong is also buried in Delilah's psyche."

"I don't care what those files blacked out," he answered. "I'll find every last blotted-out name—doctor, lawyer, Indian chief, 'bad crowd,' whatever, including supernatural stalkers. I'll track them down and I'll take that wolfhound with me to gnaw the balls off them until they squeal their guts out."

I believed every word, remembering how Ric had gone after Haskell, the rogue cop who'd roughed me up. And maybe my big dog had too.

"You have to face it," Helena said. "Revenge won't erase whatever it is Delilah confronted at a way-too-early age, likely rape."

Rape. The only four-letter word that rocked my world off its axis. I'd sensed the ugly word circling and hovering in my blacked-out history and now it was in the open, slavering for my will and soul.

"Thanks, Ric and Helena." I finally spoke for myself. "I'm perfectly capable of decoding those defaced files. I'm an ex-reporter, remember? I know Wichita history, names, and places." Then I looked only at Ric. "I'm pretty damn good at fighting impossible odds. And Quicksilver will get his teeth into any dirty work required more enthusiastically for me than for anyone else on the planet."

He stopped cold, unable to keep up the façade that I hadn't been seriously damaged, here and then. In Wichita, years ago.

"Now, let me see those files," I told Helena. "I appreciate your help, Madam Freud, but they are mine, you know. I'd like a printout to take back to the motel room. Can you manage that without letting the hotel staff get a duplicate file, or snoop? I don't trust anyone about now."

———————

"WE NEVER HAD a decent real meal today," Ric commented from Dolly's passenger seat as I drove us back to the Thunderbird motel, a sheaf of rare hard copies in a folder on the red leather seat between us.

"Takeout time," I said. "Let Quicksilver choose."

We passed a Wendy's, a McDonald's, and a Captain Kirk's before a sharp bark came from the backseat. Red Riding Hood's, wouldn't you know? We got the family basket. Brisket and cottage fries.

Leaving Quick on night duty with the bulk of the basket, we brought the remainder inside to pick at.

I fanned through the folders.

"I love you, and I don't want you hurt, now or in the past," Ric said.

"I know the feeling," I pointed out, with feeling. "That's why I was leery about coming back to Wichita."

"I was so sure you were haunted by just a natural, general fear because of the Revelation hitting when you were only a preteen."

"Maybe that's all it is. I do know if an abscessed tooth is a constant pain, you need to pull it out before it poisons you."

WHEN RIC FINALLY fell asleep, I got up and went to the cheesy medicine cabinet over the sink mirror I'd avoided seeing myself in.

I really didn't want to mirror-walk in Wichita. That disconcerting new option was a Vegas wrinkle. Helena was right that the Millennium Revelation revved up paranormal powers in ordinary people.

I suspected now that I'd never been ordinary, the thing I'd longed for most as a kid. I wasn't worried about facing

Loretta Cicereau, the vengeful ghost I'd bound. She was in mirror-suspension back in Sin City. I was beginning to see that even supernatural power depended on places as well as people.

Wichita had its own circuit box. Power could travel from node to node, but you could tap into only what mojo you had built up in various locations. Here, I was more plugged in than I wanted to be.

I took out my gray contact lenses, although they could be worn for weeks without changing. Then I leaned the heels of my hands on the cold sink surround and pushed my trademark blue eyes close to the cheap-grade mirror.

"So you had to stick me with a sealed juvie record, Lilith? You sure weren't borrowing my clothes in those days. They were all Goodwill and buttoned up to here and down to there to keep the creepy boys away. How did I get funneled into a socially and psychologically deviant population? I was just an orphan. And you did everything you could to hurt me."

The blue eyes in the mirror blazed with anger and angst. Me, or Lilith, or Memorex?

"It ever occur to you, Dee," my mirror lips curled in answer, "I was taking the pressure *off* you?"

Her glossy black head of hair shimmered like Midnight Cherry as she shook it. We really had great hair. Why I had never seen that? Because Lilith was hot, and I was not.

Now she was saying she took the . . . heat . . . off, so I could remain safe behind my defensive devices, my solitary ways, my old movies, my wounded shyness?

"So hopelessly naïve," she went on. "The times they were a-changing, but you just wanted to soldier on in your stupidly smart, safe, low-profile way."

"Your escapades gave me a record."

"Everybody wanted to pin a case file on you and forget you. I met their expectations and then they left you alone."

I could feel my fingernails trying to dig into fake stone.

"Lilith, did you get me raped?"

The blue eyes in the mirror shut.

Funny, I could see that.

Was this denial or . . .

"Lilith, did you get raped in my place?"

She tossed that superstar hair of ours, and flashed our ultrabright baby blues.

"A little."

Oh, my God.

She shrugged and sneered and went on. "But the system got you, after all, in its own way. It always does."

"I'm so sorry."

"Don't say that. Don't ever say that. I'm not. And that's why I'm in here and . . . you're not."

"You have more than a mirror existence," I told her even as I realized it. "You have powers. You didn't really kill yourself to get autopsied on *CSI V Las Vegas*?"

"TMI, Delilah Street. I can see why you wanted to disown me, though." She turned her half-profile to me. I could see the tiny blue topaz in her right nostril. "The only personal distinguishing mark you ever voluntarily went for. And you lost it fast. Because of me."

Had I lost more than a subtle piercing, because of her?

I sighed. "Lilith, I don't like where this road trip to Hell is leading."

"It's not a theme park joyride, Dee, but you have way more allies than I ever did."

"You're not one?"

"You want to claim the tattooed lady with the smokin' past?"

"Hey. I can always use chutzpah in Mirrorland."

"Yeah. But where you need it is here and now, baby. Kiss the past and my baby blues good-bye. And screw Ric for me while you can."

My fist headed for her face on that last taunt, but my knuckles stopped on cold mirror and at the brink of my own confused, angry image.

Lilith was right. The only way of going forward to the future was back to the past.

It was a paradox, and my vehicle was not a DeLorean car, but one of Detroit's nostalgia best, Dolly. Frankly, the vintage past I so loved in general had been pretty much a real-time bust in my case.

Chapter Seventeen

"TWELVE YEARS TO young people your age," Helena Troy Burnside told Ric and me with a rueful smile, "may seem like an eternity. Luckily, it's just a little over a decade for us old folks."

She flashed the printout of a Wichita map from the Web. We'd come to her hotel suite that morning to pick her up for the drive to where I'd been sent twelve years ago for a mysterious gynecological procedure at age twelve.

"We have the same cast of characters," she added. "Not encouraging to you, Delilah, as a patient, but as a reporter you know what that means."

I nodded grimly. "They know what happened to me there, and why."

I didn't add that I'd been freshly armed with several dire hints from my mirror twin. Why hadn't I ever told Ric about Lilith, the last secret I'd kept from him beside my internal invisible friend, Irma. I knew why.

Who wants to be dating *The Three Faces of Eve,* even if he's too young to have ever seen that old movie on multiple personalities?

Of course, I was firmly my own person; I just had these slightly weird add-ons. Some people called that "baggage." Before and after the Millennium Revelation, some folks called that "haunts."

Ric rubbed the nape of my neck, massaging away tension, secretly caressing a shared intimate mark, and tapping my inner "*chica*."

"We'll be with you," he promised.

Yeah. That's what made it so scary.

Leonard Tallgrass had requisitioned Quicksilver again. While Ric and I were delving the personal side of my Wichita links and past, the local ex-FBI agent was drawing a bead on the area's powerful paranormal and criminal elements.

Frankly, I couldn't wait to get my angsty stuff over with, and get back in the field with the crime fighters.

Ric drove us to another bland three-story building. I was beginning to long for the soaring hubris of Vegas with its gouts of spot-lit fire and water and neon spitting up at the cloudless sky.

The office waiting room boasted the usual upholstered chairs and magazine racks, with a huge fish tank framing a lethargic trio of clown fish.

Helena accompanied me to the reception window, leaving Ric to flip through an actual print edition of *Modern Mother and Infant* featuring Madonna and her latest adopted Third World child on the cover. Menopausal adoptions were the new "Follywood" superstar rage.

"*Hmm.*" The receptionist frowned. "I don't find a 'Delilah Street' in the records. You've been here before?" she asked, her gaze darting between Helena and me.

I looked too old to need escort to the gynecologist's office.

"It was more than a decade ago," Helena said so briskly the receptionist almost saluted. "Dr. Youmans was the physician." She nodded to the door behind us, which read YOUMANS, HORTON, AND FLIEDERBACH.

"And you are Miss Street?" she asked, her flicking glance settling on me.

She knew her patient name game. Helena didn't look young enough to carry an offbeat name like Delilah.

I nodded.

"First visit, virtually," the receptionist said. "The doctor will want to do a thorough exam."

"So will we," Helena said sweetly.

We went to sit with Ric, where his foster mother proceeded to tell him how the cow ate the cabbage. This cow was in a much better place than the zombie-driven herds moving through the dark of Kansas nights.

"They won't let you in," Helena told him. "You're not related."

Ric was cool with it. "I'll wait until I hear the doctor going into the consultation room, then get a 'family emergency' call on my cell and barge right in."

"Ric," Helena said. "This is women's business. Did it occur to you that Delilah would prefer to keep it private from you?"

"Yeah," he said, "and I hate to intrude behind those pink doors, but we don't have much private from each other, and she knows I can take it."

And he knew I'd seen his soul stripped bare. Turnabout, fair play.

Helena shook her smooth blond head. "What a different generation. Philip would sooner be waterboarded than set foot in a gynecologist's office."

Ric grinned. "You might be surprised, if it involved your well-being."

She shrugged and smiled to herself.

Then my name was called, for everybody in the waiting room to hear.

"Delilah Street."

Helena accompanied me through the door. I saw Ric station himself at the brochure rack near the receptionist's pass-through to keep an eye on the action in the hall and consulting rooms.

"Does this ever change?" Helena asked after we were shown into a room.

We'd sat on two light side chairs. I eyed the rolling stool near the sink counter, and the recliner lounge with the metal stirrups at the foot and a paper cloth down the center. It sat against one wall like a bizarre sacrificial altar.

"I wouldn't know," I said. "I've never been in such a place before."

"You mean this specific place, in your memory."

"I mean, never."

"You've never had a gynecological appointment?" She sounded shocked. "Not at college, or after?"

"My . . . phobia."

"But . . . you're in your mid-twenties. Birth control." She was looking flustered.

"I'm on the Pill for severe menstrual cramps. Have been since college."

"You had to have had a pelvic exam done then?"

"No. There are underground places where you can get all sorts of pills."

And I'd managed to avoid such routine school inspections for years. Amazing what a determined minor can do. I was newly impressed by Teen Me. I was also getting tired of apologizing for my back-lying phobia and my monthly pain and my apparently abnormal history.

"The only pelvic exams I've ever had were from your foster son."

Her face produced a raging flush I thought only my ultra-pale skin could show.

"Sorry, Delilah. I deserved that. You were indeed a 'virtual virgin,' as Ric said. How clumsy of me to ask those questions. I needed to know what to expect when the doctor comes in and wants to do that procedure."

"It won't go well," I said, "but why would we need to go that far? I just want to ask some questions. You're certain this is the doctor who saw me when I was twelve, with the result that I buried the experience deep in my subconscious?"

She nodded. "Yes. Even the nurses are the same. The doctor is in his early sixties now and president of the local medical society."

"Which doesn't know he was doing pelvic exams and who-knows-what-else on helpless twelve-year-olds?"

"I would think not. Let me ask the questions, Delilah."

"I was a reporter. I'm good at that."

"I know. I know his type too. He's of the doctor-as-God generation. He'd respond better to someone of my maturity. Don't you trust me to be your advocate?"

"I want to be my own advocate."

"I understand. But . . . this will work better. We'll surprise Dr. Youmans into frankness better if you remain quiet and in the background."

"Apparently I did that before, and it didn't turn out so well."

She lowered her head and shook it. "We have no authority here. Surprise and subtlety are the keys. I know you don't want to be s—"

"Sold down the river?"

". . . to be superseded again. Let me try first. Please?"

I folded my icy hands together and choked back a sudden tide of rage. My heart was pounding and my breath came fast and shallow. Between my fingers, the silver familiar assumed the form of curved surgical scissors.

My blood-fury surprised me. I fought for control, as I must have twelve years ago, not knowing what this place was and what they did here. I still didn't, quite.

A nurse came in and cast a glance at Helena.

"This is just an annual exam, isn't it?" she asked me. "I'll take your blood pressure, and leave the robe and sheet on the examination table. It opens to the front. Strip completely, of course. A nurse will accompany Dr. Youmans, *Mrs.* Street, but you're welcome to stay. My, BP one-forty over ninety, a bit high, Miss Street. I know seeing a new doctor can be nerve-wracking. Dr. Youmans is very gentle."

She left as I hurled Helena a betrayed look.

"I do know how to handle this, Delilah. Trust me. It would be more effective if you donned that paper robe, at least. You don't have to strip. Just give them the impression this is an ordinary visit."

"It isn't?" I asked as I struggled to put the paper robe over my clothes. It was like wrestling a crepe-paper cutout in a cartoon. Laughable.

"It isn't. Consider this a trial, Delilah," Helena told me. "I have the evidence in my possession. This doctor doesn't know it, but *he's* on trial here. Don't give any testimony until I ask you for it."

"You can't tell me beforehand?"

"I believe I know what happened here, but I need to frighten him into admitting it. Your striking looks will be the first weapon. I suspect he'll remember you quickly enough when I get him going. I'm a psychologist, Delilah. I know how to unravel this man."

"And what about *me* unraveling?"

"It's a risk," she admitted. "You're a brave woman and you must have been a very brave girl. This won't be easy, but it's the only way to get the truth into the open for the peace of mind you need."

"Does Ric know?"

"No. Listen, I can't mislead you. My suspicions are ugly, but, in case I'm wrong . . . I can't tell you them prematurely. I wouldn't do this in most cases. Hell, Delilah, only in yours. It's my professional opinion that the truth, no matter how brutal, will free you. If the facts are what I think, it would destroy most young women. But one must go to extremes for the people one loves. I think you understand that."

I stared into her eyes through a glaze of tears. Hers, not mine. Then she took a deep breath and the unemotional scientist glared through, icily controlled again.

"Well?"

"You've scared the spit out of me, Helena Troy Burnside. But I'm tired of worrying about what I might be afraid to know. You want me to sit on the end of that torture table and swing my feet while we wait for Dr. Frankenstein?"

She smiled tightly. "Yes. Exactly. Look as innocently at ease as you can manage, and let me do all the talking."

Boosting myself up onto that table with the sinister stirrups took all the gumption I could muster under the circumstances. Everything about this place was conjuring a hellish conjunction of my darkest fears, distant and recent.

I recalled the elaborate but primitive Egyptian mummification chamber with the central stone table for the dead body I'd awakened on only days earlier. I reran the TV mock documentaries I'd seen through the years about alien-abducted victims lying paralyzed with fear on examining tables.

Looking up, the big rectangular milk-glass light in the ceiling and the goosenecked high-power lamp affixed above the stirrups seemed both ancient and alien.

Would white linen–sheathed, sloe-eyed Egyptian waiting women soon file in to witness my blood-draining and sacrifice? Or would dumpy nurses wearing old-fashioned white scrubs surround the table to imprison me?

What was really going on here? Did I have an appointment with some long-uncaught pedophile doctor Helena would now expose in his turn, somehow relieving me of anxiety and guilt? Had I been some modern maiden sacrifice, turned over by the social workers, maybe because of the bad rap Lilith had overlaid on me? Was there no end to the betrayals?

I eyed Helena, so calm and competent. Did she really know what she was doing to me, what she was risking? I thought of Ric in the waiting room, where the men were always kept while unspeakable things happened to the women behind closed doors.

Where was Quicksilver? His instincts were supreme. He was my über-guardian, like poor little Achilles. Those were the only "people" whose instincts I could always trust. I was ready to jump up and run out, but a flutter of sound and murmurs outside the room's door made me freeze with fresh panic. I could hear paper files being shuffled.

Then a white-haired doctor bustled in wearing his white coat, looking just like a bushy-browed kindly old Dr. Gillespie CinSim from *Young Doctor Kildare,* 1938, except he wasn't in a wheelchair.

Man not alive! I'd been abused by my favorite CinSim doctor as played by the great Lionel Barrymore?

My hands tightened on the razor-sharp scissors between them. At least the silver familiar could never desert me.

Chapter Eighteen

"**M**ISS . . . STREET?" Dr. Youmans said, overlooking Helena in his focus on his clipboard of papers and me, the patient in a plain paper wrapper, which said a lot for his focus.

The doctor kept skimming the sheets I'd filled out in the waiting room, glancing toward me, until his glance was finally hijacked by the legendry beauty of Helena Troy Burnside sitting in the chair against the wall.

Even I stared at her. She was suddenly glowing with a Millennium Revelation–bestowed glamour, brimming with charm and confidence. A brilliant, gorgeous trap.

"Mrs. . . . Street?" the doctor said, dazed. "I see the patient is fairly young. You're not expecting anything out of the ordinary? Besides dysmenorrhea, the patient has no complaints—"

"No, Doctor," Helena said, reassuring. "We're expecting a routine physical. My daughter has been living abroad and I'm afraid she hasn't been getting regular care."

"Ah. These young women all feel immortal, especially *these* days," he said with an admonishing chuckle. "Young ladies must have their annual checkups."

His comforting smile as he turned to me slid off his face like melting snow. He glanced back at Helena.

"Your . . . daughter? But you're so gloriously fair-haired and she's so—"

"I'm afraid, Doctor, that my original, natural hair color is long forgotten by all concerned."

As he automatically moved to the foot of the exam table, it was all I could do to avoid kicking him in the crotch. I wonder how many females who'd had to "assume the supine position" here had entertained that impulse. Probably none.

Me, Irma whispered.

I ignored her. She wasn't corporeal, and I was. And . . . I'd been here before. On this table maybe, facing this old guy in a white coat. Only the first time I'd still been innocent and trusting.

"Do you recognize her?" Helena inquired. "You've seen her before."

"Ah, no. She's quite striking, of course. Rose Red to your Rose White, if you'll pardon a fairy tale reference, madam.

"But, but . . ." He pulled the rolling stool behind him under his lying white-coated ass.

I inhaled slowly, gathering.

"She was only twelve," Helena mused. "A ward of the state. That was before I *adopted* her, of course."

"Oh. Of course," Dr. Youmans murmured robotically, his parchment skin paling to match his starched white coat.

"Like any new mother," Helena reminisced, quite convincingly, "I wanted to preserve every detail of my darling's early years."

"Of course," Dr. Youmans murmured, eyeing my shod foot with a frown. Apparently my feet should be bare when placed in the icy steel stirrups.

Helena was on her own feet and flourishing an old-fashioned manila folder.

"You may not recognize me, Dr. Youmans. That's all

right. Not everyone is plugged into the internet media, even these days, especially those in your generation. Helena Troy Burnside is my name, and I'm a doctor of sorts too. Academically. I have some small international reputation for working with . . . troubled youth. Frankly, they have good reason to be troubled if they had this young woman's medical history. Why would a twelve-year-old girl sent to a gynecologist for unspecified 'procedures' not be troubled by the experience ever after?"

He swiveled on the stool seat to face her. She had him pinned between the stirrups, and me. He looked up at my face for the first time, recognition drawing his benign aging features into a mask of horror and fear. He began babbling.

"Dr. Burnside. Naturally, I've heard of your ground-breaking work. I was a volunteer for Child Protective Services for many years. Social service groups always have insufficient budgets."

"So you were a cost-cutter. On a minor?"

"Some cases were extreme. I was told this . . . child was deemed potentially . . . ah, promiscuous."

I opened my mouth, but Helena leaped into the breach, evidently expecting that.

"On what evidence?"

"It was the first year of the Millennium Revelation, for God's sake. These . . . predatory supernaturals were showing up everywhere. Some were half human and had to be housed somewhere. The group homes were festering with adolescent boys, who are ordinarily randy little beasts and now we had half-breed supernatural boys on our hands. Half-werewolf and half-vampire and all lusty, bloodthirsty, powerful young monsters. This girl . . . you've adopted, this Delilah. Yes, I remember her now.

She was underage, but that didn't stop the vampire punks from going after her like she was bait. They'd have propagated some drastic hybrid on her. The social services could hardly deal with first-generation supernaturals, much less second-generation ones. She had to be stopped . . . protected from generating. The damage to her physical system alone—"

"Of course," Helena said sardonically, while my mind struggled to understand what he had confessed to, and he *had* confessed to something. "Inflicting damage to prevent damage. How original."

Helena shook her papers. "Old records never die, Doctor, nor old sins. What did the social workers want you to do?"

"It's obvious."

"Not to Delilah. She still doesn't know what was done to her here."

He glanced at me, cringing.

Helena's District Attorney act was so fascinating I'd finally done as she'd advised: just watched and listened. It distanced me from the trauma. Also, I really liked to see the old doc cringe. No one was ever going to find me on an ob-gyn examination table again."

"So." Helena was pacing, digging her heels into the room's mushy vinyl tile. "You were paid by the state to do what to this underage young girl?

"It was for her own protection."

"So they all say."

"A very simple, safe procedure."

"A procedure utterly mystifying to a young girl who'd never even had a pelvic exam, don't you think, Doctor?"

"Yes, of course, but every young girl must face that sooner or later."

"Without any knowledge of what's about to happen to her? Without informed consent?"

"She was a minor. A ward of the state. No consent was needed."

"Exactly, Dr. Youmans. *She was a minor.*"

Damn! I couldn't help not personalizing for a moment. Perry Mason would have been proud of Helena. I was.

Meanwhile, the door had been pushed ajar as the hall outside the room started buzzing. The office staff was assembling like Howard Hughes's attendant vampire nurses in Vegas. My personal horror story had become a courtroom drama, and the theatrics of the scene gave me a strange sense of it not really being about me.

"And what did you do to her?" Helena demanded in a ringing voice.

The sound of doors being slammed against walls indicated that Ric was no longer content to eavesdrop from the waiting room.

The office door hit the wall and sprung off its hinges. The nurses flooded in after Ric.

"Sir," a nurse objected. "This is a private office."

"Not when it commits crimes against the public," Ric said in his deepest, darkest crime-busting voice. "Delilah! Take off that obscene paper sheet."

I readily complied, then hopped off that obscene table and took a place against the wall beside Helena. It was her show.

Ric came over to hook an arm around my shoulder and touched the surgeon's scissors in my grasp with a questioning look.

I couldn't answer it. The silver familiar would be what it would be. Maybe since they were armed with superior knowledge, I needed to be armed somehow. The overcrowded room finally took me back in time, to my first personal appearance here.

I was small, lost, and fearful, back in the don't-go-to place, where even Irma was silent. This was in the time before Irma, and even before Lilith. Maybe even the time when Lilith came out, dark debutante that she had been and still was.

"It's too much for her, Helena," Ric's voice rumbled against my side.

"Who *is* this man?" the head nurse demanded, coming to the defense of her doctor. "Who is this strange girl? She's never been a patient here. You lied," she accused Helena, even as her worried face betrayed uncertainty.

"Ric," Helena told him, "Delilah has to face the reasons for her fear, just as you did."

"I was a lot younger," he argued. "Still malleable. Delilah's grown past whatever it was. Look at her! You're sending her back to childhood."

"Tough love, Ric. And it'll get tougher. Stay with me. Fear is an infection worse than its cause."

She turned to the alarmed doctor again, then brushed past him to a cloth-covered tray on the sink counter, lifting it and then the cloth like a magician producing a trick.

I stared at the horrible array of instruments revealed. Again, I was jerked into a terrifying moment of my past, one just days ago, when I'd awakened paralyzed with panic on the Karnak mummification table, doomed to be forced to watch the blood slowly drained from my veins.

The wall behind me felt ice-cold, like a stone embalming table, even though I was still standing. The solid cold surface and being upright were the only things that kept me clinging to a shred of sanity.

"This," Helena said, lifting a long, thick steel tube, "was what you used on a twelve-year-old girl. She'd never even bled, until you forced this into her."

"God, Helena," Ric said, turning my head into his chest and clapping a hand over my only exposed ear. "You're putting her through worse than that old medical rapist did. Don't move an inch, you slimy bastard. I can still strangle you with one hand."

The emotions of other people's fear and anger swirled around and above my still, small center, absorbing what to me was a grotesque reality and blending it with the disguised reality that had haunted my nightmares ever since.

Lord, I was a textbook case.

Staring at the implement Helena brandished, I'd recognized the "turkey baster" wielded by the white-skinned or garbed "aliens" of my nightmares. It was my industrial-strength version of the "needle in the navel" procedure alien abductees claimed had happened to them . . . only it hadn't been anything so fine and small as a needle and it hadn't been aimed at my navel.

I could feel Ric's anger and tension, his muscles taut and strained to their breaking point. Any minute he could spring on the old man to tear him apart, like Grizelle the Inferno Hotel's shape-shifting white tiger.

"What is that thing?" Ric demanded.

"An old-fashioned speculum," Helena said. "Modern ones aren't cold steel, but warmer plastic. A woman finally had some say in how her body was examined."

"This place is medieval," Ric said.

"Men are wimps," Helena answered. "You have no idea. You have no idea of how severe a menstrual cramp can be, nearing labor even."

I wanted to say "Amen," but words were caught into a

mute ball at that icy center of my gut. I watched Helena pull open the top drawers in the sink cabinet.

"Here we are," she announced, "the next thrilling stage of the 'unspecified procedure.'"

She held up something, steel again, that looked like a fancy eight-inch-long bottle opener, something with a wing nut on one end and a long undulating Art Nouveau stem and a silly fluted bottom.

"A cervical dilator, isn't it?" she asked one of the gathered nurses.

She poked it in their directions and they retreated like Hammer Film vampires at the sight of a silver cross.

No one in this room dared leave. Helena's expertise and anger held the medical personnel at bay, and if Ric relaxed his convulsively comforting grip on me, he'd probably tackle someone. Or I would.

He had his own childhood reasons for justifiable murderous rage. Now, the still-vague wrong done me, a wrong that violated me where he was most intimately involved . . . for the first time I feared that the truth could break him as well as me.

What was Helena doing to us all? Could she put Humpty Dumpty back together again?

She was not about to stop her avenging angel act now. I knew in my soul that to intimidate the truth out of the medical staff, she had to risk damaging me, and possibly Ric, more. She must believe that the outcome would free us both, but even a Millennium Revelation–assisted shrink could be wrong, as wrong as whoever had ordered my . . . institutional rape . . . had been wrong twelve years earlier.

Helena's voice was shaking with fury now.

"Can any of you med-school robots imagine her confusion, her fading trust, her growing panic, her incredible agony? Grown women have a tough time with the pain of cervical dilation, because you can't give a patient anesthesia in a medical office. You didn't even give this twelve-year-old any ibuprofen before she came in. I see nothing to reduce pain on the chart. Nothing to make it easier, or make her suspect that something bad was coming. Can you imagine the nightmare you became in her psyche? You heard her cries and screams. Several nurses must have had to hold her down. She'd not yet been culturally trained to lie on a gynecological table and handle pain like a super-soldier."

Heads hung, but mine was among them. The humiliation was profound. I'd been a lamb to the slaughter. I *had* been trained by then. *Don't move no matter what,* they'd said. *It'll make it worse if you move.* Still, the nurses had to hold my arms, I remembered.

I remembered . . .

"I was cold and shaking afterward," I heard my own dazed monotone. "So dizzy I kept almost passing out. I remember they had me sit in an office and they gave my first cup of hot coffee to drink, because I'd been 'a big, brave girl,' and crackers."

Helena went ballistic. "She went into shock? You obviously treated her for it. That's not on the record, Doctor. How could you conspire with self-serving social workers who were afraid they'd have to answer to a juvenile pregnancy to make the innocent object of *possible* assault pay like that, and let the boy would-be rapists run rampant? Why didn't you put the males on drugs?"

The old man spoke up, his voice hollow. "You know. Prescriptions are recorded and must be justified. Putting adolescent boys on medications reserved for sex offenders . . . too many in the system would question it."

"Too many male supervising doctors and lawyers and administrators, you mean," Helena corrected. "That's why there's still no systemic male contraceptive pill, promised since the sixties. Let the women take all the risk."

Helena held up the beautiful silver instrument so like an Art Nouveau wine bottle opener. "You needed the cervical dilator to force open her immature cervix and insert an intrauterine device to prevent pregnancy. That was the 'unspecified procedure.' The social workers couldn't control the boys, so the girl had to pay, to bear the risks and pain."

"You don't understand, Dr. Burnside," trembling old Dr. Youmans said. "Delilah was an exceptionally beautiful child, like the young Elizabeth Taylor, if you remember the actress that far back. They were all after her. We had to protect her from the consequences of a juvenile pregnancy, from birthing some half-supernatural monster."

His words, sincere, but representing years of denial, stirred me to speak for my lost self at last.

"I had ways of defending myself against *them,* the vampy-boy creeps, you old fool!" I felt the shout torn out of me. "But I had no defense against *you.* Not against my group-home keepers. They could take me anywhere, order anything done."

I stepped away from the wall on trembling legs. The silver familiar had gone into hiding, as if I had to stand alone, without any of my guardians.

"You unethical cowards should never be allowed to practice medicine again," I shouted. "Look at you! Was it easy money, a contract with the social services? Yes, those creeps were threatening me. Did nobody think about really protecting me where I had to fight day after day? Were you willing to let me be gang-raped as long as no evidence showed up? As long as no 'helping' medical or social professional would be held accountable for being unable to control the group homes?"

I grabbed the goosenecked lamp and yanked it, wrenching the electrical cord out of the wall. I swung the metal lightbulb hood at the overhead light fixture, bringing huge splinters of the plastic lens and then the shattering fluorescent tubes down on the examining table, dimming the awful glare, making the table a sea of sharp shards.

"I remembered you all as aliens," I told them all, "aliens who'd abducted me, and you are. You are alien to the human race, the real *un*human ones."

I started tearing the paper covering off the wave-shaped examining table. I kicked over the foot-operated white trash can that would have held the bloody cotton. I grabbed the tray and crashed all the metal instruments to the floor. I launched myself at the table itself and somehow pushed it off center and into the wall.

When I paused for breath and brushed my hair off my face, the room was a shambles and the nurses were cowering in a sheeplike clot by the wall rack crowded with torn, years'-old magazines now out of print. One title read *Modern Contraception*.

"T-t-this is my office," Dr. Youmans said. "You've trashed it. I could s-s-sue you."

Helena stepped into the mess to put a hand on my shoulder. "You sue us? I didn't find any place in the buried records where you ever actually *removed* the IUD from your underage patient."

The silence said everything I needed to hear.

I lashed out with my boot-toe, dead center of where it hurts a guy the most.

"*And* you gave me hideous menstrual cramps for eternity? May you have phantom ball pain for the rest of your days, Dr. Malpractice."

I held back from contact, but he cringed, writhed, and cupped his privates anyway.

A nurse objected from the corner of the consulting room. "This is . . . this is a physical attack. The police—"

Ric stepped between us. "I'm a Fed. You don't want to involve the locals." He glanced to the doctor's clenched knees and protective, palsied hands.

"You're lucky she's taking it out on . . . uh, inanimate objects, Doc, and only figuratively. Me, if she wrung all your necks, I'd just call it in as self-defense. Who's to say different? The last time Delilah was here she was assaulted against her will by all of you."

Chapter Nineteen

"**S**HOCK THERAPY MAY be okay to use on an illiterate boy once enslaved in the Hell Zone between the U.S. and Mexico," Ric told his foster mother.

Angrily.

He slapped his palm on the table of her boutique hotel suite, making Helena's eyelashes flinch. "Not on Delilah. Not with me there."

Me, I was beyond flinching. I'd batted my last eyelash. My mind and emotions were churning, trying to make sense of the last half of my life. The post–Millennium Revelation part, when I'd been physically altered against my knowledge and will.

Ric was not done ranting.

"It's not something to spring on a woman who blotted out a childhood medical assault because it was too damn traumatic to remember at all." He stopped behind me, bending down, voice lowered.

"You didn't damage your hands or feet, did you, *paloma*? Butt-kicking inanimate objects can hurt you more than it will ever damage them."

I let him kneel beside me to examine and clasp my fingers. His hands were as warm as his riled temper, and my ice-cube core of dazed fear and fury was melting. I was mad enough at Helena to let him rage, which was rather mean, because I could see Ric's every accusing word flayed the foster-mother inside the scientist.

"She had to confront it, Ric." Helena's soft, controlled voice was pleading. "She had to see what had happened to her in a legal as well as a personal sense, and grasp it all at once. She needed her 'day in court,' because she won't get justice in any real sense."

"She could still bring a civil suit," he argued.

"And put her character on trial?"

"She is fucking flawless," Ric shouted.

Damned if my lips didn't try to break their grim parade formation to smile a little shakily. That kind of described our amorous adventures so far.

"Language," Helena murmured, as she must have reprimanded the teenage boy.

"You've heard—and said—it all, Helena," he returned. "You can't do your demure act on me like you do on the D.C. military brass when you want something, including Philip. I was a feral boy. You and I fought like chupacabras over a goat corpse in 'therapy.'"

"Always so colorful," she murmured, daring to glance at me. "It wasn't anything Annie Sullivan didn't have to put up with when she was domesticating the deaf and mute child Helen Keller."

"That rough?" I said, my voice cracking from not having spoken since shouting myself raw in that . . . butcher's office.

Ric flung himself into the chair next to me. "Drink some wine, Del. It'll soothe and calm you." His lips brushed my temple, doing more than any wine could.

"I need to ask Helena some questions," I said.

"So do I," he said, glaring across the table.

Helena answered mildly. "She means alone, *hijo*. Girl talk."

"About today, or about then?" he asked.

Helena shook her head gently from side to side, meaning "Yes, and this and that."

"About . . . *us*?" he asked, his voice hardening with a touch of . . . dread.

She nodded. "I'm a head shrink, not a medical doctor, Ric. I need to determine the degree of damage and how Delilah's doing with her current life issues."

"He told you," I said. "I'm fucking flawless."

"*Ouch.* Your *chica*'s claws are in fine condition," she told Ric with a gleam of humor. "Don't worry. I'll be gentle. I know you were."

I watched his dusky face flare dull red.

Wow. I'd never seen anyone or anything make ex-FBI man Ricardo Montoya, the Cadaver Kid, blush.

"Where am I supposed to go, what am I supposed to do," Ric asked. "When am I supposed to come back?"

"You've got a cell phone," Helena said. "You do know how to use it? Just pick it up when it ring-tones and put it to your ear and talk. Try the bar, Ric. It's guy country at this hotel."

He had no idea he was being given the Lauren Bacall brush-off to Humphrey Bogart, in paraphrase, but he left.

"The hotel provided me with this insanely overstocked room bar," Helena told me, pointing to a pair of louvered doors. "Whip me up a new drink before we settle down to talk. Your Vampire Sunrise is the party circuit hit of Alexandria, Virginia."

"Really?"

"Ric's right. You're a very talented girl."

"Virginia, huh?" I walked over and swept the double doors open on a mirrored wall of liquor bottles and glasses. "No minibar for Helena Troy. You figure keeping me busy will ease the angst?"

"Generally, it does. And I figure we need something stronger than this sissy wine Ric ordered. Men think we women are made of glass."

"Just bar glass," I said, pulling down a few bottles and setting up two martini glasses. "I wish there'd been more glass in that consulting room to smash."

"Do *you* have any questions?" she asked.

"Let me try something mind-bending here first."

I mixed some flavors in a set of three shot glasses, sipped and remixed, sipped more. My mind and mouth were working in concert again, as she'd intended. I wondered what poor Ric was downing in that main floor bar in the noisy, echoing atrium.

"There you are, Counselor," I said, placing something dark, tall, and bloodred before her.

"Why are you calling me that?"

"You got your client off the hot seat and into the driver's seat."

Her eyes closed a moment in relief.

"What are you calling this?" she then asked, sipping the drink and closing her eyes again, this time in relaxation. "Delish, Delilah."

"It's named in honor of my biggest Darkside Bar fan from the party state of Virginia."

"Yes?"

I sipped from my own glass. "It's a Virtual Virgin."

"I take it you're ready to talk," Helena said.

"Way too overdue. Do you like my cocktail?"

"Love it. A Virtual Virgin, wouldn't *that* be fun to dabble in again?"

Of course my dead-white skin flushed like Mrs. Haliburton's chagrined face. Helena didn't truly understand how recently that condition had been mine.

"What's in it?" she asked.

"Chilled Coca-Cola, or you could use Dr Pepper, for starters. Some black cherry vodka and then citrus mixes to cut the edge."

"Black cherry vodka," Helena mused over our tall, footed glasses.

Besides exotic ingredients, I prefer stemmed barware for my cocktails, when possible.

"How," Helena persisted, "did you come up with black cherry vodka for your Virtual Virgin, my new favorite drink, Delilah?"

"The cherry was obvious and my mood is a bit dark right now." I was *not* about to explain Ric's addiction to my Midnight Cherry Shimmer lip gloss. "You could leave out the vodka for minors and those who dislike strong spirits."

"Not us, Delilah."

"No, not us."

"What do you want to know?"

I sighed and leaned back in my chair. The numbness was wearing off. My reptile brain was curling back up to sleep after giving almost everyone around me a good tail-lashing.

I'd never had anyone to tell me these things. "This IUD?"

"A method of birth control for decades, of varying use-fulness. Not really meant for nulliparous women."

"I'm this nul*leper*ous woman?"

"Nulliparous. The word means non-child-bearing. We're both nulliparous women."

"Cheers," I said, lifting my martini glass rim to hers. "Why is the installation process so gross? Computers do it better."

"Ancient Arabs put stones into the uterus of a camel to prevent pregnancy."

"Sure don't want inconvenient pregnancies in beasts of burden," I noted. "Weird, the Rolling 'Stones' recorded a song titled 'Beast of Burden.'"

"In the last century's twenties, a German named Ernst Gräfenberg placed rings of silk—and later, silver—within the uterus of his female patients to prevent pregnancy. Too much bleeding."

"I can testify." That mention of silver unnerved me, so I sipped my Virtual Virgin and let Helena enlighten me further.

"Starting in the sixties IUDs became much more workable and popular. The trouble is the body tends to reject foreign objects unless the uterus has hosted a fetus."

"This all sounds like a biology class at Our Lady of the Lake, where they told you all the scientific stuff, just not exactly how the egg and sperm get together."

"I think we can gloss over that part too, Delilah. What's crucial is that you were not even in puberty, yet you were fitted with a birth control device without your knowledge. Your ignorance of the medical procedures made the act an assault. It was a crime, and it's a sin that it's not prosecutable in a court of law."

"If I were one of these leprous women," I started.

" 'Liparous,' " she corrected. "You'd be used to routine pelvic exams since puberty."

"And that turkey baster?"

"Would be a familiar if not favorite article once a year, when you were given a Pap test for cancer. It's criminal that you haven't had any basic female organ care."

"And the dilator?"

"Would be used briefly to obtain a scrap of uterine tissue to test for abnormal cells. It would be a necessary—possibly uncomfortable, but no more—procedure for your good health."

"So the procedure, the pain, I experienced as a kid was no worse than a woman who wanted an IUD would go through."

"Except such women are usually sexually experienced." Helena stared into her Virtual Virgin. "You weren't. You weren't accustomed to penetration, to intimate invasion. Your fear and natural resistance would make it far more painful. For a young girl of your age and history, it would be a nightmare."

"It was."

"Your highly creative subconscious converted it into an alien abduction dream. Since others went public with such claims, it gave you something 'real' to cling to after what must have been a devastatingly surreal experience. That's not so different from Ric converting his first adolescent wet dream stimulated by a vampire bat bite into an appearance of the Virgin of Guadalupe. The immature mind needs cultural coat hooks. Yours was alien abduction. I'm sorry, Delilah. You needed to know the truth, no pussyfooting around it."

I nodded.

"On the other hand, for those responsible, it was an unconscionable dereliction of duty. Which Ric realized, and which infuriated him. Essentially, the social services powers-that-be then punished you for being attractive to predators. Blame the victim."

Now that she'd put it in bald terms, the injustice of it all hit home. It wasn't even just the single invasive, controlling act. It was all the consequences, even more to my mind than my body.

"It's why I've always hated my looks," I said slowly. "I thought it was my coloring, my white skin looking even paler because of my black hair. I thought vampires went for me because I already looked like a corpse."

"They went for you because they were also teenage boys and you were a very pretty girl. Still a predator-and-prey situation, but one we call 'normal.'"

I shook that damning head of black hair.

"Now," Helena said carefully, "here's why Ric is probably drinking boilermakers down in the bar. I need to ask about your sex life together."

"You can't. You're virtually his *mother*."

"Virtually, Delilah? That's a dividing line these post–Millennium Revelation days, isn't it?"

"Except for the me-never-on-my-back-thing, it's none of your business. Now my phobia makes sense, and I feel a lot better that I wasn't hallucinating aliens. I also feel better knowing that a woman of my age would have experienced pretty much the same thing I did, minus the panic, to get a routine Pap smear."

"Is it possible you'll actually make an annual appointment now?" Helena smiled ruefully. "It's for the good of your health."

"Yeah, but I'm finding a woman doctor who will understand my issues. The twentieth century must have sucked for women."

"You should have seen the nineteenth. I read about it in grad school."

I lifted my Virtual Virgin glass—weren't we all that at one time?—and we clicked rims.

"Delilah," Helena said, "you have to realize this is devastating for Ric too. He literally didn't know what he was doing, with you."

"He owes me. I like that."

"I'm not kidding."

I shook my head. "Mama Doc, don't worry. Ric was the best thing that ever happened to me. You raised him right. We're so much better for each other than you could ever imagine."

"You don't understand the male mind. Now that your true history is revealed, he'll feel like he's been a . . . an insensitive human battering ram."

"You don't get it. He can't be insensitive and I can't deny I like what he can deliver. Are we done here? Best haul him back from that den of macho iniquity downstairs. We still have some troubling cases to solve in Kansas."

"I admire your spirit, but I know more about the damaged psyche than you're willing to admit. And there's one more revelation you need to face this millennium."

"Nothing medical? I'm not going 'annual' for a good year, at least. And it'll be on my terms."

"Nothing invasive. And very, very soon. I'll be there."

"What are you talking about?"

"Delilah, I know you've experienced a huge shock on all levels, physical and mental, but there may be a bigger one coming."

Exploring her classical Helen of Troy features, I saw faint worry lines beneath the mineral makeup and even the composure.

"What now?" I demanded.

She took a long, deep breath.

"We still need to find that IUD."

Chapter Twenty

I SAT NERVOUSLY in another examining room with one of those freaky tables wearing a paper sheath and steel stirrups. Too bad I wasn't wearing spurs. It was interesting, but not comforting, that all this "female" scenery unnerved me more than 3-D zombies streaming off the wide vista of an old drive-in movie screen.

"Women really lay themselves down on that sacrificial altar once a year?" I asked Helena in a hoarse whisper.

Yeah. My voice felt like it was being closed up in a black box in my throat.

"More often if they're pregnant," Helena said. "I understand."

"They get used to submitting to this?"

"Women have had to get used to submitting to a lot over the centuries," she said grimly. "What we're dealing with now, Delilah, is just modern gynecological practice. Thanks to the Web, I was able to find a woman doctor who's tops in her field."

"I still wouldn't mummify a killer crocodile on that torturous-looking table," I muttered.

Helena looked both confused and repelled. "Why would anyone want to mummify a crocodile?" she asked.

"You'd be surprised," I answered direly, confused to hear women laughing together outside the closed door.

I'd never remembered having much to do with doctors, but I sure didn't like it when the door burst open and a white-coated black woman strode in, her head bowed over a slim manila folder.

"Dr. Youmans refused to release any records, Dr. Burnside," the woman murmured. "And it says here Delilah Street is a juvenile."

"Do I look juvenile?" I asked, standing up from the office chair to meet this new doctor eye-to-eye.

She met my demanding glance with her own, then set the folder onto the usual sinister countertop holding a sink and a box of tissues and the array of steel implements.

"Hardly." Her smile came easy. "I'm Dr. Sabitini Torres," she told me. Then she eyed the still-seated Helena.

"You said this was an emergency when you made . . . I should say, demanded . . . an immediate appointment this afternoon."

"It is." Helena wasn't going to rise and she wasn't going to give a centimeter.

Dr. Torres eyed us both . . . tall brunette woman with attitude, clearly past twenty-one years, and seated regal blond woman, clearly past menopause. Both clearly unrelated.

I looked the doctor over, grudgingly approving the sleek fuchsia silk dress glimpsed under her lab coat and the steampunk buckled platform shoes on her feet. Her skin was a glowing negative, an undiluted black like my hair, but her tresses were braided into a cornrow pattern as intricate as a maze. She resembled an ebony version of the famous ancient Egyptian head of Nefertiti, with more Nubian features. She would outclass the ancient vampire sister-pharaoh at the Karnak Hotel in a heartbeat, had both of them been living at the same time.

Meanwhile, Helena had been digging into her over-buckled designer bag to extract a sheaf of papers.

"This is what we hacked out of Dr. Youmans' computer records."

Dr. Torres winced. "You hacked his records? The ethics—"

"Read them," Helena suggested sweetly. Sweet was obviously not her usual modus operandi.

Dr. Torres leaned against the torture table and skimmed them as rapidly as an IRS tax examiner preparing to administer a big fat fine.

Her exquisitely penciled eyebrows went up. And up.

She eyed me with narrowed, incisive black eyes. She looked at Helena, bit her full bottom lip, and nodded. "I see. I'm glad you insisted on getting right in."

"The records don't show the type of IUD used," Helena said.

"The records don't show anything they ought to. You think this . . . young woman still has this thing?"

Helena nodded.

"What?" I asked, suspicious of the knowing shorthand these two women exchanged as if they were soul sisters. Ebony and ivory. Like me.

Oooh, Irma crooned in my head. *I don't like this conversational trend, either. Cool doc, though. What the hell lipstick color is she wearing? Be sure to ask. Would look even better on us than Midnight Cherry Shimmer does.*

Will you *please,* I told Irma, *not* remind me of intimate episodes in a clinical house of horrors like this?

I bit my own lip in turn. I'd made such a huge private emotional and sexual leap with Ric these last several weeks I was having trouble regarding myself as a public plumbing problem.

"That would be . . . malpractice," Dr. Torres was saying.

"That would be . . . obscene," Helena answered, standing.

"You're her mother?" Dr. Torres.

"Here and now, yes."

I let my gaze snap to Helena. I couldn't believe what she'd said. She was . . . adopting me.

For the time being.

For a never-adopted child now an adult, that was mind-boggling.

Did even she understand how this would impact me? I veered between choking up and getting furious. Hearing the never-used phrase "her mother" for the first time at twenty-four. Thinking . . . too little too late.

This visit to Wichita's medical offices was resurrecting my insecure inner orphan and kick-starting my outer ungrateful bitch. It was giving me emotional whiplash.

"I'm *here*," I reminded them.

Jeez, it was like Kipling. "When two strong women meet . . ." They were east and west and black and white, and both damn scientists.

Helena's faded eyes turned to me. "Don't worry. We don't need more probing, Delilah." She eyed Dr. Torres. "A sonogram."

"And how," I asked, "am I to drape my chic paper sheath for *that* procedure?"

Dr. Torres's low chuckle escalated into an infectious laugh, making her the woman in the fuchsia dress first and the doctor second. She eyed me with sympathetic warmth. "Girl, my nurses and I will give you such a runway wrap you will want to wear it outa here."

I grasped at her good humor. I could tolerate only so many life-shattering moments at once.

"Do I get a . . . a free braiding?" I bargained like a kid.

I'd seen Vegas tourists getting that treatment alongside the "beachy" hotel pools. Nobody had ever done my hair for me before, as far back as I could remember.

"Absolutely."

That is how I ended up drinking an awful lot of bottled water while three nurses braided my thick, wavy Irish hair into a magnificent mass of shiny blue-black plaits. The women were so adept they manipulated a couple paper sheaths into a loose Egyptian-style linen gown.

Was I going to come out of this a Macy's Parade balloon, a taco wrap, or a fashion model? While I drank the required water, the familiar fashioned itself into an intricate basket-weave ankle bracelet in slow motion to keep me entertained.

Forty minutes later, a fairly relaxed me was shown into another consulting room, where a computer screen sat beside the examination table. Helena was installed on the visitor's chair.

"I'll be here all the time, Delilah. This is totally external. There's nothing to worry about."

"Except the results," I said, hopping up on the table before anyone could order me to do it.

Helena's eyelids fluttered shut for an instant. This still wasn't easy for her. She was being strong for me. I've never had anyone do that before but Ric.

Okay, Irma said. *Cut the surly ingrate act. We need to know why we are the way we are, or will be.*

I nodded, Helena taking the gesture for solidarity and loosing a sigh.

I was no longer a lamb to the slaughter when the nurses came in and unwrapped my torso to spread some gel on my abdomen. I told them I'd get a really naughty tattoo there before any future incidents like this. If you can't avoid 'em, surprise 'em.

The gel was warm and sticky like blood, and the radiologist, a white-coated woman named Irene, gently but firmly ran a wired paddle over me while staring at the TV screen. The pressure was uncomfortable, but at least it only lasted a few minutes. I was wiped off and told I could use the bathroom and "change back" in a small adjoining cubicle.

What would I "change back" into, I wondered.

My heart was pounding again, my fate in the hands of these two doctors, one for the reproductive organs and one for the head.

Dressed, I was led back into a consulting room. This one had no ominous equipment lurking in it, no stirrup-equipped tables or televised sneak peeks into discreetly hidden organs. Just two women doctors wearing bravely smiling faces.

Uh-oh.

"Sit down, Miss Street." Dr. Torres gestured me into the chair beside her built-in desk. "You've always had severe menstrual cramps."

"As long as I can remember, which can be . . . spotty. Could this IUD have caused that?"

"Most possibly. The body doesn't like foreign objects in it, even donated organs."

Or blood? I wondered. All of Ric's had been replaced.

Helena sat forward, impatient. "This is speculative, Dr. Torres. Delilah could have spontaneously ejected the IUD during one of her painful periods and never noticed."

"Also possible," the doctor conceded, "but not the case. The IUD is still there."

An ugly chill—or the silver familiar—climbed my spine. The familiar usually "defaulted" to a thin hip chain. Had it automatically girded the body part that was most compromised?

"If you found the device," Helena said, "you can remove it."

Dr. Torres pursed her fluorescently fuchsia lips.

We gotta get that brand and color name before we leave, Irma nagged.

Even Irma was trying to distract me from what was coming. I'd been screwed up for real, my body writhing monthly to rid itself of a parasite that had existed inside me for more than half my lifetime.

"Not necessarily," Dr. Torres said.

"You can't remove it?" Helena was disbelieving. "What type is it?"

Reaching a hand with short, unpainted fingernails inside a bottom desk drawer, Dr. Torres finally pulled out what looked like the T-shaped end of those white plastic "strings" on clothing price tags, a tiny, tamponlike string dangling from the end.

Gross, Irma moaned. *I am so glad I'm all sass and no moving parts.*

"The common form now," Dr. Torres said, "is a plastic and copper T. It can also have embedded hormones instead of copper. They are very safe and effective, although not for women who've never had children."

Helena's face had gone almost as white as mine always was. "And for *children* who've never had periods? What would one of these things do? Nothing but cause unnecessary trauma."

"I understand your anger, Dr. Burnside. It was unconscionable to use such a device. It would, though, prevent pregnancy later."

"No need," I burst out. "I had a major phobia about any of that insertion stuff." No wonder I'd fought off vamp boys so fiercely. "And I've been taking the Pill to help with cramps for years. That's double exposure for no point. I want that thing out of me. Now!"

Hold it, Irma urged. *You don't know that this IUD is the source of all your pain.*

There is periodic pain, and then there is unrelenting psychic pain. My brain rebelled at processing all this bad news.

"We can't take it out," Dr. Torres said in a soft, sad voice.

"What?" Helena and I expressed simultaneous shock.

The gynecologist stood to pull a thick, spine-worn trade paperback book from the shelf above her desk, riffling through.

"The IUD as a birth control device goes back to prehistory, practically. About sixty years ago, it was modernized and offered as an option to the Pill. They experimented with different shapes, but plastic was the 'new' material that offered so much 'promise.'"

"Delilah didn't have a T-type, did she?" Helena asked, sounding sick with worry.

"No. It was this." Dr. Torres started to hand the open pages past me to Helena, but I grabbed the book first.

And there it was, my giant, hovering alien abduction nightmare apparition, reduced in a photo to a speck of translucent white plastic on a palm, maybe an inch high and a bit wider.

Here was the huge white sting-ray-shaped mass suspended over me like a lighting fixture, down to the long thin tail stinger, the IUD's "string." The ray's angel-like "wings" were scalloped and spined like a bat wing, not a boneless manta ray's form. Each tiny "spine" ended with a sharp point.

"You'd put stickery things like that inside the uterus?" I asked, unbelieving. "How'd they get it out?"

"One quick yank," Dr. Torres said with a sigh. "Medicine is still primitive in some respects."

I was speechless. That was insane. What male doctor had thought that one up?

"Can't you do that with Delilah's?" Helena asked. "Prepping her with a sedative pill and a couple local anesthetic injections into the cervix?"

Great. Now the aliens' needle wasn't going into my navel but my cervix. Twice, yet. Who were the "aliens" here? My body tensed to run, my hands squeezing the chair arms, my calves bunching to spring me away.

"We could," Dr. Torres said, "but the IUD has . . . altered . . . with time."

Helena reached a hand out for mine, but I resisted taking it. I didn't need comfort, I needed escape before they screwed up my insides worse. Right now, I had no allies but Irma, and she had been struck speechless again too.

"It's medically impossible," the gynecologist went on. "I've never seen such a sonogram. The tiny IUD and string you see pictured is gone. Its manta shape has spread and thinned into . . . tentacles . . . like endometriosis leeching onto the very bones of her pelvis. And it's . . . not the same anymore. It's impossible, insane actually, but . . . the copper appears to have transformed into sterling silver."

Chapter Twenty-one

I SAT IN one of the motel room's two cheap armchairs wondering why the Millennium Revelation was turning me into some million-dollar silver-metal woman.

Well, maybe I was just a thousand-dollar one, given the current price of silver on the stock market.

Dr. Torres hadn't had much explanation, except to say that the new "intertwining" with the bone wouldn't have caused menstrual pain, but that she couldn't recommend I ever have children, given the pressure that puts on the pelvis. Otherwise, I was fine.

The familiar had completely disappeared, unseen and unfelt. I figured it was hiding out among the plaits of my hair the kindly nurses had made.

Quicksilver sat on the floor beside me, my palm on his thick-furred wolfish head.

Ric and Quick had been waiting in Dolly for me and Helena to leave that last doctor's office.

"Delilah, your hair," Ric had said anxiously. "The braids. What about—?"

"Home, James," Helena had cut him off. "A new hairdo can be a healthy distraction for a young woman."

Ric got the idea fast.

"Love the look," he said, and then drove us back to the Thunderbird Inn without comment, Quicksilver riding in what had become his doggy rumble seat. Leonard Tallgrass finally had found an occasion to get my dog back to me. Just in time.

I'd gotten out and, trailed by Quicksilver, unlocked the motel room door. When I turned back, I saw that the others had remained in the car.

"You relax here on your own for a while, Delilah," Helena suggested. "I'm taking Ric for a drink."

"Banished to the bar again?" he objected, his hopeful expression turning anxious.

I wanted to joke that I was the one who could stand being taken out for a drink, but Helena shut up her foster son with one tough-as-a-nail-gun look and the command "Not a word."

Off they drove while she enlightened him about the bizarre state of my insides.

No one could stop Quicksilver from looking anxious, though. I ran my hand over his head, saying, "I know, I know. Just be patient."

At least dogs didn't need to have the messy facts of female anatomy explained to them.

Helena supposedly knew what stressed people required. I wasn't so sure she did now. Was there anything worse than being stuck alone in a Wichita motel room feeling that alien spawn had set up shop in your very guts for some unholy reason? The past I'd been struggling, successfully, to put to rest had punched a literal hole in my very being.

Though this was summer, the room felt cold. I ran my hands down my chilled upper arms and over my clenched, denim-clad thighs. I rocked myself back and forth, recognizing the motion as a childish self-comforting ritual from the group homes.

Quicksilver's warm furred side pressed against my legs,

but my teeth began to chatter anyway. It wasn't the temperature in the motel room, because the summer day was ideal, offering the rare but perfect Midwestern moments between winter heat and full summer air-conditioning, between mayflies and mosquitoes.

A faint purring drew my hands to a pair of dangling silver cat earrings suspended from a wire curved like spectacle frames over my ears.

At least the silver familiar had the smarts not to pierce anything on me at the moment. I tried to count my other "at least" blessings. At least my "rape" had been medical and institutional. At least what had been done to me without consent had been done to hundreds of thousands of other women by their own request. So I was not as alone as I felt. It'd probably hurt them too, but they'd known what to expect.

Quicksilver whimpered and rested his jaw on the chair arm, producing that "hang dog" look. Gosh, I didn't want to bring anybody down with me. I was lucky I had people—and a dog—who cared to stand by me during this.

I thought about all the things I'd survived here in Wichita, and in spades in Las Vegas lately. Feeling sorry for myself had never worked. It was time to think, not feel.

What if, over the years . . . my body had turned the intrusive bit of plastic into something more useful? Something I *really* needed. Maybe it was a pre–Millennium Revelation "gift." Maybe it was the source of my current silver talents: my ability to see things in mirrors and walk through them and reflective surfaces. Maybe it had even "grabbed" and created the silver familiar from Snow's lock of hair as an external extension of itself. Maybe it had become my inner armor, my protector.

I had no idea how long I sat there in the demi-dark with the window curtains drawn, but eventually a knock came on the door.

I looked around. The perky patterned comforter was installed on the bed, so the maid had come and gone. Still shivering, I went to the door peephole.

I spotted a baseball cap with embroidered script and a rose on it, seen through enough gaudy coleus leaves and tiger lilies for a New Orleans funeral. Undoing the chain lock, I confronted a gawky delivery boy obscured by baskets of tissue and greenery.

I could now read the fancy script on the cap: *Flowers 'n' Bowers*.

"Kin I put some of this stuff down, ma'am?" he asked. "It's the whole Spa for a Day Super Package."

I swept the door wide and stepped back.

He quickstepped to the table by the window and relieved his forearms of basket handles and his hands of the ambushing greenery and a tall bottle of champagne.

While he was setting everything upright so it wouldn't fall over, he played eyeball-tennis with the occupants of the room. Since that consisted of the usual motel furnishings and Quicksilver and me, it didn't take long.

"You just need to sign that you got this stuff, uh, ma'am. The charge is taken care of."

He produced a receipt pad and a pen. An overbearing odor of roses was rising like swamp miasma. I hesitated to take custody of the lot.

"You, ah, alone here, ma'am?" he asked nervously.

"I'm not scared, if that's what you mean," I said, surprised.

"The champagne can be tough to pop. I kin jest get that, ah, started for you, if you want."

I realized his roaming gypsy eyes were now concentrating on my figure.

"I can handle a champagne cork by myself," I said. "Also, the dog is great at extracting things that are in my way."

He nodded and gulped simultaneously, backing toward the door.

"Jest our friendly Flowers 'n' Bowers super-service, ma'am. You take care now."

I intended to, turning the dead bolt and restoring the chain lock as soon as his skinny ass was out of the way.

Meanwhile, Quicksilver was using his supersensitive nose on the array of baskets and audibly sniffing. I joined him in exploring our bounty.

The champagne was a no-name brand. I twisted the bottle's wire basket open and managed to maneuver the cork out with a pop that made Quicksilver jump and growl.

Two stemmed plastic glasses hid among some potted bachelor's buttons.

Everything was beyond cheesy, but whoever had sent this knew that any kind of bubbly right now would unravel the knots in my neck and shoulders as if they were made of satin instead of steel.

I gulped the first chintzy glassful of slightly sour champagne and poured another.

The showy flowers surrounding the potent posy of tea roses weren't scented, so I set them on the dresser in front of the mirror. I didn't linger to probe any images in it, including mine.

There was another bottle of bubbly, this one full of pink powder.

I imported it into the bathroom and took a long, foamy, pink bath.

By the time I got out, wrapped in a towel with my braids clipped atop my head, the safety chain was off its slide. I didn't want to know who and how, but Quicksilver was obviously out on patrol and Ric was waiting on one of the plastic chairs. He'd taken off the visiting-social-services tie, and I liked the view through his top three open shirt buttons. Also his smile.

"Sometimes," he said, "Mom-shrink gets way too lost in her head . . . and yours and mine. I owe her respect, but I don't buy that my absence will make you feel better than my presence tonight."

I was speechless. "She thought I needed to be alone here all night?"

"She thought you needed to be *left* alone," he said. "*Dios,* Del. I came back to say you're safe with me. We're camping partners tonight, no more. I just want to be with you, *mi virgen.*"

"Virtual Virgin," I corrected. "That's . . . really noble, Ric." I went to sit on his lap, my thick plaits tumbling to my shoulders as the savvy familiar slithered down into position as a slender ankle bracelet. "You responsible for the homey spa package, *hombre*?"

"Cheesy," he admitted, "but—"

"Sweet," I said, giving him a peck on the lips.

"And I do like the braids. *Muy exótico.*" He diplomatically neglected to mention that they evoked an ancient Egyptian wig and our second most dangerous, latest adventure.

"*Mmm.*" He nuzzled my neck. "You're so warm and soft and scented."

"You're so warm and hard and drenched with virtuous lust."

"I just want to comfort you, Del. Nothing more. I swear."

"It's not like you to fall short in the romance department, Montoya," I drawled.

He seemed surprised, but my mood had peaked the moment he entered the room. All the nightmares of the last two days had shot into the distance like a fey maze. Mama Helena had been wrong and Ric right. I'd needed some pampering to ease my stress and now I was buzzed on cheap champagne and a fierce willfulness to be taken extreme advantage of.

"Look, Ric. What I was put through years ago was inexcusable, painful, and traumatic, but now I know the truth. I'd imagined a lot worse than an insensitive bureaucracy resorting to the sexual double standard."

"Delilah, are you sure you're all right with it?"

"Not . . . yet, but it has nothing to do with us. I'm supposed to be unfairly punished again? No sack time with you? I'm feeling like a new woman. Have you got the moxie to get me over on my back for the first time and crush me into the mattress with your manly needs?" I challenged before his lips hushed mine.

I could say he groaned, he growled, he rasped, he husked, but what he did was say nothing, just moved his lips to the sweet spot on my nape he'd made his signature start and stop of our erotic journeys. The moment they touched my damp skin I folded like a bad poker hand onto the trinket-laden bed. He was already there, and rolled me over on top of him.

"You taste so sugary, so salty, so sharp," he murmured into my neck, "just sleeping partners for now, I swear."

"With benefits," I said, laughing softly until we were silent but not still, my lips glued to his neck scar, until he came and I fell asleep from emotional exhaustion and, my current BFF, cheap champagne, satisfied. There was noth-

ing anybody had done to me in the past to stop me from
being what I wanted to be in the future.

I AWOKE SLOWLY, still habitually lying on my right side,
aware of dim light illuminating the bed. Ric was awake,
watching me, his head braced on his elbow and hand, the
soft light from the parking lot caressing the sharp lines
of his forehead, nose, and cheekbones. He belonged on a
twenty-foot-high pillar in my particular temple.

I looked down to see his other hand resting on my hip.
My legs had scissored open while I slept and he'd pushed a
leg between them. The sight of his face and our entwined
bare legs set my pulse throbbing.

"Morning?" I asked.

"The middle of the night. Now *shhh*. I'm busy."

He swept my left arm over my head, torquing my torso,
lifting my breasts, almost pushing me onto my back on the
pillows, but not quite.

The slight frisson of panic I felt at the position was . . .
fleeting.

"Busy?" I asked, looking down as he caressed me.

I'd finally got past considering my white skin as
drained, lifeless, helpless vampire bait. Ric loved seeing it
on his so-sleazy but right black satin sheets. I loved seeing
his darker hands in stark relief on my pale skin, so visible
wherever they roamed.

Him not still "only" a man after his near-death experience, as Snow, and now Sansouci, had warned me? Forget it.

"You're ravishing me again?" I asked.

"What else?" His hand stroked my inner thigh. "Slick."

"Your fault."

"Then I should pay for it."

His hand moved on, disappeared. I gasped with frustration, breathing hard now while his dark eyes watched my every breath. All black pupil, his eyes, with only a wire-thin band of silver around the left one. The irises of his eyes had always been so deeply brown I never could tell when his black pupils swelled with arousal. Now, the silver was a dead giveaway.

I gave away a little mew-purr of satisfaction myself.

But I wasn't the stage director here. Ric was watching more than my face. I felt a featherweight touch over my chest and breasts, then a circling at their center. Repeated.

Ready. So ready. My hips swayed. "I'm ready."

"I'm not."

Was he kidding? My navel flamed as though freshly pierced when the dowsing rod between his hips brushed my belly.

His eyes were downcast, his fingers circling as I arched my back.

"What are you doing, *hombre*?" I prodded him. "I'm going crazy. *Loco*."

His fingers moved to my mouth, tracing my lips, sliding over their sensitive inner slick. I tried to consume his fingertips, but one stiff forefinger pressed down on them, urged silence, stillness.

The room echoed with the sound of a panting trapped wild animal. Me.

He was being so damn slow the wanting had boiled down to a painfully tight, aching ring at the fork of my body.

Ric finally extended his bracing elbow and ran his free hand into the hair at my temple, bringing my face into the light as his finger stroked my lips again. Something deep crimson, thick and shiny coated his forefinger tip. It looked like blood.

"Ric?"

He read my suspicion and let me taste the fingertip.

I licked my lips. "Sweet."

"Very sweet," his voice corrected.

"Fruity. Ric, what the hell—?"

"Smooth. Slick. Sweet."

"What is it?"

"The label's so tiny it's hard to read in the semidark, but I'd say it was our old friend Midnight Cherry Shimmer."

"Midnight. That it is. Cherry. You got mine weeks ago, bloodless as it was. Shimmer? No moonlight here. *Lip gloss?* You've been . . . into my purse?"

"You don't want me delving in your purse for interesting things?"

"Uh."

His hand was back on my inner thigh. So close to that taut, throbbing hot spot . . . my thoughts sounded like they belonged in a book with half-naked men on the cover. Nothing wrong with that, but I craved a less clichéd vocabulary to express this wild, maddening overdose of desire. All I could get out of my throat was . . .

"Finish it!" I would not add "for God's sake." I didn't want any deities peeking in on this action.

He laughed. Fondly. "Not even halfway there, Delilah. You do seem to be addicted to that naughty Lip Venom."

"Lip Venom? That tingle? There? You put Lip Venom on—?"

"I put it on your lips, *amor*. And on your lips." His hand caressed my thigh, the thumb stroking deliciously near the source of my budding agony (the wait) and ecstasy (the forthcoming climax), but not nearly close enough.

"And my navel," I guessed.

"Always so fast with a deduction, but a little slow tonight."

"I am *not* slow tonight. I don't need more foreplay. I want . . . closure."

The answer to my demands was his lips sliding over mine, inside, outside, but nothing yet in my lady's chamber. I was so glad I gagged Irma during these sessions. Just my own voice in my head was aggravation enough.

He kissed me from here to eternity. His face and mouth focused every erotic thought and feeling on my candy-tipped breasts as Midnight Cherry Shimmer passed from my flesh to his mouth and back to me again in fascinating rhythms that had me in their spell.

Enough body paint and tease. I needed the main act . . . *now*. So . . .

I let my sensually torqued torso roll me flat on my back for the first time in my remembered life, for the first time during our erotic encounters.

Instead of clenching with the usual panic, I was amazed to feel the fearless confidence of a big cat luxuriating in a belly-exposing stretch. I angled my head back, exposing my throat, then arched my spine from my hips to my shoulders, offering Ric a full frontal self he'd never seen from me before. This should snap his so-called control like a twig.

Ric's hands slipped under my back, supporting me. He leaned away to study my body as if it was an Old Master painting. He ran one hand up my arms and fixed my wrists in position.

"You're my bow," he finally said, lowering his torso over mine, his voice thick. "I'm your arrow. Always."

Then the Spanish words came tumbling out between kisses he pressed on my flesh from my wrists to my forehead and lips, pausing for a long passionate minute to burn a bruise into a dangerously near-visible spot above one collarbone. His restless mouth suckled my tinted and flavored nipples until they caught fire, too, and then blazed a further trail down from navel to tilted pubic bone.

Yes. Home at last. Finally. He slid deep inside me, his weight flattening me into the mushy motel mattress. I now had the luxury of seeing his eyes, his mouth, his expression both dreamy and excited. The mere act of our breathing hard with his pelvis so compressed on mine brought me the shuddering, screaming-into-his-mouth tsunami I'd sensed surging up from my tropical zone.

My banshee howl threatened to raise the dead and lasted long enough to send a bunch of them straight to Hell for evil thoughts, but Ric laughed into my neck after his own echoing orgasm ebbed away and tapped my thigh with a "we're done" pat as he rolled away.

Whoo.

"You can fool around with my purse any time," I said when able to manage a whole sentence.

We were sweat-slick, streaked with tracks of shimmering black cherry gloss, and satisfied as hell.

"Better shower," he said. "I'll come along in a minute."

"You came along for a minute just now. *Uhh.* Do I have to get up, I'm so . . ."

"Sticky," he finished. "Shower. Motel sheets. We don't want to leave a trail of Midnight Cherry Shimmer for the maids to giggle at."

I rolled out of the bed and went, gingerly, to the bathroom, shutting the door and turning on the lights.

Okay. Karaoke queen at a nude rock rave, thoroughly had, agreed with me. This is what Ric had finally seen with me on my back. My cherry-shiny nipples matched my passion-swollen lip-glossed mouth.

Some of the glinting lip gloss had even slicked the new bruise already darkening my white skin. I touched the spot, only sexual excitement tingling in the deepest depths where I'd once been most pain-violated. Keep the creative pelvic examinations coming, *mi hombre*, I thought without Irma's help. My body is your bow and you are my arrow.

I rubbed my fingertips to disperse the dark crimson shimmer, but . . . the color was bright red. Bloodred. Ric's suction kiss had broken the skin. Ouch. A bit alarming in this day and age, but that could happen when the love was deep and the sex was hot. I knew that now.

My fingers returned to my throat, feeling a salty sting. The skin there was thinner, more sensitive. It was just a small break, not like he'd . . . bitten me. And if he had, that wasn't anything unheard of. I'd bitten him accidentally first.

I smiled, exploring the fact of feeling both satisfied and freed.

Our previous back-avoiding positions deserved reruns but—so call me unliberated—I'd loved being finally able to lie under Ric, watching him love me, being his bow and welcoming his arrow. Taking his weight and making it work for us. For the first time, I felt that Ric had been able to do with me what he was born to do . . . dowse the depths of my heart, body, and soul.

HOT WATER WAS sluicing like tears down my body.

Now that the romantic interlude was over, Irma joined me in the shower.

Whoo-ee. Guy on top rocks. And all that juicy red lip gloss our boy was laying on your touch-me-not zones. Sexy new wrinkle. I wish someone would rouge my nipples with, say, Chambord raspberry liqueur from an Albino Vampire. I bet that would drive Sansouci and ole Shez wild.

TMI. No improper names, please, I told her. Glad you approve, but why wouldn't you? You're my self-appointed inner slut, Irma.

Recognition at last. Listen. Don't overthink the wild thing. There are guys who like women in spike heels to walk all over them. The S and M parlors are full of mock and real blood and thunder. This was a little harmless purse-diving with benefits. Like you didn't go ballistic? You love the guy, bottom line.

That's why I worry. Bottom line: neck sucking still troubles me. A last, lingering hang-up.

What do you know? You had a bizarre, isolated upbringing and the sexual experience of a cantaloupe before you met Ric . . . at age twenty-four. I take that back. Who knows what cantaloupes can get up to?

I laughed.

See. You should be more realistic and worldly by now. It's like if it feels too good, it's gotta be a problem for you. That is so twentieth century.

I sighed. I just don't want Ric to see I'm worried, I thought at last.

Simple. You gotta be a little less Deliverer and a lot more Delilah with him. Relax and enjoy. I do so need the girl talk afterward. Take it from me. Celibacy sucks. And so does great sex.

I rinsed well to ensure no Midnight Cherry Shimmer would stain my clothes and shivered with good memories. Irma was right. Midnight Cherry Shimmer and Lip Venom could work both ways and maybe even better in reverse . . . on *Señor La Vida Loca.*

Chapter Twenty-two

"**D**ON'T WORRY, MOM-SHRINK," a mischievous Ric told Helena Troy Burnside as we escorted her and her chic Chanel carry-on bag to the airport waiting area the next day. "It makes you look your age."

He leaned in to kiss her cheek and drew quickly back, to duck her reaction.

"You cactus-tongued young devil." Helena's mock annoyance ended with a smile.

Then she eyed me. "I don't get it. Yesterday was all revelation and darkness and angst, and now you two crazy kids are acting like"—she suddenly did get it—". . . honey . . . moon . . . ers."

"We're working it out in private therapy," Ric told her. "Hard."

She shook her head. "Just don't go off and do anything foolish without sending me and Philip an invitation."

"Nothing rash," I assured her, "or requiring dyed-to-match satin sandals."

"I'm always an email or phone call away," she reassured us in turn.

I leaned in, feeling awkward. I smelled an old-lady-type perfume like Estée Lauder White Linen (a name too evocative of ancient Egypt for me) and maybe a lingering whiff of psychic shell shock.

I imitated Ric in laying light hands on her silk-suited sleeves and kissed her smooth cheek.

Eek, Irma caroled. *I kissed a girl.*

"Delilah, dear—" Helena embraced me back to cover the sudden tears in her eyes. "It's been a privilege to be with you at . . . this watershed time in your life."

She turned almost blindly to click off on her kicky Stuart Weitzman pumps to check in at the gate.

"Kiss-ass," Ric whispered mockingly in my ear. "I always thought Helena secretly would have liked a daughter."

I couldn't meet his eyes as fast as I wanted to. "She's a cool lady. We both owe her."

We walked away from the gate, not looking back. Ric slung an arm over my shoulders. "You did that like a pro, *chica. Bueno.* Brava."

"So, favorite son," I asked, overdue in moving on from my Hallmark moment with his foster mother, "why'd you need to get Helena out of town so fast?"

Our pace had picked up and Ric moved on the conversation too. "Tallgrass and I have haven't been just spying on cows and zombie trail riders while you've been pursuing sentimental journeys to Old Wichita landmarks," he said softly. "We've been looking for a nexus."

"A new brand of car?"

"A Nexus. GM would love that. Not bad marketing, but no. We now know the *what* and *why* of weird events that have been going on in Wichita lately, but not the *who* and *where.* So, it's time we all get back on the same investigative track and take these suckers down. Okay by you?"

"Very okay."

"That doesn't preclude nocturnal time-outs," he added, grinning until I elbowed him in the Dos Equis six-pack.

BY THE TIME we reached a demure, top-up Dolly in the parking lot, Leonard Tallgrass's big-wheel black pickup was parked alongside her, with Quicksilver on guard in its high empty bed.

"I saw you three heading into the terminal," Tallgrass told Ric through his rolled-down window. "That your foster mother?"

Ric nodded.

"She married?"

Ric nodded.

Leonard Tallgrass shook his head and reinstalled his straw Stetson. "Always knew there wasn't any justice in the universe." He nodded at the high-riding pickup's rear. "No dogs risk their lives to ride in my truck bed, not even your whip-smart Quicksilver, Miss Delilah. So get down your Dolly Parton's top, and I'll lead you three to the most amazing sight Wichita has ever seen."

"TALLGRASS IS A character," I told Ric as he drove Dolly two tailpipe-lengths behind the black pickup.

"He plays on that, yeah. Since he's Native American, people underestimate him. Not even the Millennium Revelation changed that."

"And you're wearing your silky, pale Vegas suit today, dude," I pointed out. "That for seeing off 'Mom'?"

"That's on Tallgrass's orders. And, except for those fashionista hair plaits, you look ultra-reporterly, as *I* requested, in those closed-toed pumps and that navy Catholic girls' school suit."

"Was that a personal or professional request?" I asked.

I may have triggers of my own, but I was beginning to target his. Ric liked me either very buttoned up or very stripped and unzipped, although he'd put up with in-between if he had to.

"Professional," he answered promptly. "We might be going into the devil's den today."

"And you won't tell me any more?"

He shook his head. "You work better as an investigator on instinct."

"Really? That could be a put-down."

"Really, Del. And it's a compliment. Tallgrass and I have an agenda where we're going, but if you want to strike out on your own, do it. You have those sterling-silver instincts. Where is that little devil now, anyway?"

I had to think about it, finally dredging up a thin silver chain from the modest vee opening of my jacket.

"Would you believe," I told him, "I've got an Our Lady of the Lake class ring on a chain around my neck? I couldn't afford to buy a class ring when I graduated on scholarship."

"I'm sure they can be ordered retroactively," Ric said, following Tallgrass on a left turn and then gawking up at the sky. "Wow. Would you believe *that*?"

I was still clinging to the promise of a class ring when I looked up past Dolly's red visor to an endless blue summer Kansas sky pierced by a seventy-story Hollywood sound-stage icon made real. We'd been exploring the wrong, west side of town. Obviously, the big-time action was all on the east side, where the sun rose.

Well, using my new "at least" philosophy, I at least had a watchdog and a couple of ex-FBI guys to accompany my triumphal entrance to the Emerald City of Wichita.

Hah! Even Quicksilver looked a tad worried about driving right under the Emerald City. Once Ric and Tallgrass had parked our bulky vehicles beside each other in the lot, we paused to gaze up and up at the slick towers so like a cluster of giant sparkling water bottles, green and shiny.

"Fits the prairie setting. They look like plastic silos," I commented.

Tallgrass chuckled, looking down through his high driver's seat window.

"Don't tell my pal Ben Hassard that. He's fought like a cornered wolverine to get this opportunity for our tribes."

"This is a Native American project?" Ric asked.

"Yup. First one outside reservation land. Whole new world, *amigo*." Tallgrass collapsed a couple sticks of Black Jack gum in his mouth and chewed it like a wad of Red Man. "I did my best to discourage Ben, but he's got this far and is in there dealing with the white man even now."

My eyes and ears were panoramic webcams, record-ing, recording. This was a Big Story, right here in Wichita, where the unending march of gambling money that funded state operating needs met the reinterpretation of what was owed the decimated Native populations. Entertainment entities from *CSI* to Emerald City were taking over the heartland's minds and landscapes.

Too bad *I* didn't have a venue to report anymore.

Quicksilver nudged his head under the loosely curled hand at my side and whimpered. He either agreed with me about the sad decline of professional news reporting in the post–Millennium Revelation world, or he wanted a puppy biscuit.

RIC WAS COUNTING on me to be a quick study, so I did my Wizard of Aahs fan-girl bit and filled them in.

First I had to go through the "dazzle" phase.

The Wizard of Oz, known for its spectacular Tech-nicolor, was on my list of key black-and-white movies because it started with the classic Kansas farm and tornado scenes. Color technology was literally being expanded that very year, 1939, to become *the* forever-future format.

All black-and-white photo and film freaks felt nothing had the impact of a stark yet incredibly nuanced noncolor palette. Black resulted from all colors of the rainbow put together. White was the absence of all color. These perfect partners produced a new rainbow in shades of gray.

Like all near-Millennium babies, though, in real life I jonesed on opulent color in reel life. So the first glimpse of the Emerald City finally sold me on *Oz,* the motion picture. The studio artists, beset more by a tight schedule than the MGM budget, had blended a Disney cartoon castle with the blown-glass bubbles of futuristic space communities and had shown it all through green-colored lenses.

Add the nitrous-oxide, high-pitched voices of trilling Munchkins to the sound track, and I was in heaven.

Today, I gazed in real life at a double rainbow halo arching over seventy-some stories of gleaming gemstone-green glass towers. Then the genius of it hit me. The Emerald City was the quintessential *green* project. It was fantasy-futuristic for our times.

So cruising around the stunning structure again to park in the mostly deserted lot, we considered what to do.

"I don't get," Ric told Tallgrass, "why we're here to snoop. Anybody who'd use domestic cows as drug mules and souped-up zombies on speed as herders wouldn't be involved in an airy-fairy project like this Cloud Cuckoo-land extending umpteen stories above us."

"Two big little words," Tallgrass answered. "Money laundering. Fantasyland always comes down to profit, and don't we Native Americans know it."

————

We all piled into Tallgrass's extended-cab pickup for a strategy session, me and Quicksilver all ears, Tallgrass laying it out on the dashboard computer.

He flashed a promo photo of the immense Emerald City.

"They haven't even thought of gambling palaces this spectacular in Dubai or Macao," Ric said.

"And it's 'native' to the region legendry," Tallgrass said with irony. "Also much glitzier than the usual Indian casino with Powwow Bars and teepee men's rooms."

"Wait," I interrupted. "When I was first reporting there was a huge civic fight against opening an Indian casino in Wichita. The civic powers wanted gambling operations and all the negatives that go with them to stay in Oklahoma."

"The 'powers that were' decades ago wanted all the Indians relocated to Oklahoma," Tallgrass said, "and that's where all the oil happened to turn up later. We up-prairie tribes lost out. Several U.S. tribes have sued for the right to establish casinos on land off the tiny reservations left to them. And won. After all, it was all ours once."

"Borders make for murderous neighbors," Ric said.

"I'll give you the last say on that, *amigo*," Tallgrass told him. "Your forebears, though, still have a nation despite the drug cartels. We Indians don't." He eyed me over his shoulder. "But we will have a nice Native American casino on the fringe of this new Wichita 'megalopolis' east. Kind of a sideshow like the *Oz* movie's Professor Marvel is in."

Ric and I exchanged glances. The western part of the state could barely support a dilapidated drive-in revival. How was the eastern side of Wichita supposed to draw a steady tourist influx?

"Who are the underwriters?" I asked.

"Megacorporations," Tallgrass said. "They come in and things happen. When they're through with us, you won't be able to fly over Kansas without seeing a new neon galaxy spread over our waving fields of grain. Hell, we're going to get our own *CSI* TV show too. Bet you could write up an episode about the serial cow murders, Miss Delilah, and make a pretty penny." Tallgrass chuckled.

"TV scripts don't pay that much," I said. "You're sure about this *CSI* thing?"

"It's been previewed on the local station, WTCH."

I was still frowning with unhappiness at the idea of Hector Nightwine Productions invading my former hometown while Tallgrass continued to bemoan—and brag about—the high-profile new enterprises coming to Kansas in general and Wichita in particular.

"This is way beyond the government having to lay out tax money to get business hiring. The international arms of your Vegas conglomerates are involved. Gonna call the concept 'Wicked Wild West.'"

"Ah." I got it. "A little Dodge City and a lotta Dorothy Gale."

"Yup. Emerald City under glass is built where all the fertilizer plants used to be and stink up the air for miles around."

"That is kind of genius," I said. "Oz under the Ozone Dome. Everything would have to be licensed, though."

"These hotel-casino outfits have billions to burn." Tallgrass was cruising his Favorites menu for visuals. "Munchkins, flying monkeys, talking scarecrows and tin men, witches and wizards. They all fit in with the times. Sort of a metaphor for who we've got representing us in Congress these days."

"Still the same old cynic," Ric said, laughing. "Why hasn't there been national news on this new gambling Mecca on the prairie? I can see there's not much between Vegas and the Gulf Coast and Atlantic City, but aren't you Wichita folks right on top of Branson, Missouri, and all the established country music theme parks?"

"One word," Tallgrass said. "It almost sounds Native American. Old theme parks are 'hokey,' *amigo*. This new stuff that's going up is big, slick, costly, and tapping into the American Dream."

"What dream?" I asked.

Tallgrass winked at me. "About little country girls making it in the big city."

"Like Dorothy Gale in the Emerald City. I get it," I said. "What's your involvement with this project?" I asked, sniffing a story.

"Me?" he said, spreading palms so dark and seamed I couldn't even detect the major head, heart, and life lines scribed on them. They had to be there. Didn't they?

I wouldn't let his pseudo-innocence and time-inscribed palms distract me.

"Like you said, Tallgrass," I went on, "the Kansas tribes are reduced and scattered, and the reservations are handkerchief-size. What's left of the Kickapoo and Kiowa would need someone they could trust, but sophisticated to the ways of the white man's chicanery. Someone with native blood—and FBI experience—to investigate the big boys so their fringe casino project doesn't get taken or fail to pay off the tribe."

Ric was eyeing our negotiation-cum-mutual interrogation, and enjoying it. Watching allies from his past and present interact, even spar with each other, said a lot about each of us.

I was not about to let him down by looking gullible.

"Yeah," Tallgrass conceded. "I looked more than any-one expected into the major backers. And you."

That had both Ric and me taking deep breaths.

Tallgrass picked up his remote control. "Ricky here told me he was bringing you back."

Ricky?

I knew I looked offended, and I felt offended. My spine stiffened as I sat up straighter in the cramped backseat. Ric had been telling *other* people about *me,* and not me about them? He didn't trust me, after I'd beaten down the gates of mortality and thrown the dice on my soul with Snow to save his life?

Tallgrass's red-brown eyes on my face drove as deep as rusty railroad spikes.

"You understand," he said softly, "we all have blood family, and some of us have foster family, but the wisest of us have chosen family. I have no children but one, and now maybe two, and possibly three."

Wow. I was feeling adopted again. Was he saying Ric— and me and Quick—had a foster father?

"And now," Tallgrass said, looking only at me, "I'll show you what's been running on WTCH-TV in the week before you two showed up here."

Ric reached for my hand over the seat back. Stiffly, I extended it. It had been a rough couple of days. Holding hands like rapt teen lovers at a drive-in, we watched the tape Leonard Tallgrass had recorded from local TV.

A discordant synthesizer caught the ear. A streak of camera pan teased the eye.

"The mystery woman was first seen as an anonymous corpse on a Las Vegas autopsy table," a deep male voice-over announced.

The camera panned over a naked Lilith from black hair to Glitz Blitz Red–polished toenails, pausing on her nostril pierced by that damn tiny blue topaz stud I used to wear. I flinched to see those staring blue eyes identical to mine. Tattoos would have added some visual interest and helped cover all that dead-white motionless flesh. Where had that adolescent ink gone? Body makeup? Or had it been removed?

I was cringing at Lilith's exposure, which was my own.

Then the ad spot featured reflections of a faint face seen through a plastic visor. Mine, filmed far more recently. Hector Nightwine wasted no time, or no wine before its time. I could see the fat-cat bastard sipping a rare vintage as he previewed this totally unauthorized footage in his office.

"But . . ." his voice-over announced, "the drama continues on *CSI Madame X,* as this bewitching mystery woman lures a crack forensics team into deciphering the enigma of her life . . . or death, and finding that every turn of every criminal case on their books leads to the limpid corpse and possible reincarnation of . . . Lilith. Premiering in Wichita and worldwide for the fall season."

"That bastard!" I was hopping in my seat, hitting my head on the headliner. "He's *using* my attempt to use a bit part in his seriously sick show as a lure."

"Naked?" Ric asked. "You filmed a bit for Nightwine as a corpse?"

"No! Not exactly. This is not the time to go into it, Ric, other than that when I get back to Vegas I'll take the Cin-Sim King, Hector Nightwine, apart from cravat to spats. I'll liberate his CinSims and set up shop for my own show." I sounded like the Cowardly Lion on a tear.

"What's your definition of a bastard?" Tallgrass asked.

"You try to use him because he's such a slimeball and find out he's used you first."

"Agreed," he said. "I know a few of those. In fact, one such creep may have used the local man behind Wichita's costly side trip to theme-park Oz."

"It sounds like your local investigations on my behalf have borne unexpected fruit for your concerns," Ric said.

Tallgrass's lips twisted. "Underhanded dealings thrive where big money is involved. Sometimes too close to home. How about we soak the fuse on this particular would-be entrepreneur's dynamite show concept in cold water?"

"We?" I asked.

"*Mi hijo* is a man of endurance and integrity. I am the long-tried soul of patience and power. Your dog is a creature of two times and one spirit. Your former city and talents are the intersection for us all, Delilah Street. Shall we go see what we can kick in the area of big crooked butt?"

Chapter Twenty-three

Honest to God, when you opened the glass doors to enter Emerald City's first-floor, business-operation office, your toes encountered a yellow brick road painted on the recycled glass floor tile.

"Cute," Ric said, tight-lipped and suspicious.

"It's a homegrown operation," Tallgrass noted, "but don't kid yourself. Millions are at stake here. Ben has been nervous as hell about the final costs, so nervous that he spilled something to me about 'outside pressures' on the project."

Tallgrass flicked me a stern look.

"So you and your oversize Toto here give us Kansas rubes a break, Miss Ex-reporter. Just because we're 'country' doesn't mean major crime isn't trying to mop up the cornfields with us. I think Ben is finally scared enough to let us in on what's happening."

I nodded, glad I was wearing my serious navy suit and pumps and not checked gingham, pigtails, and ankle socks.

I started down the yellow brick road. Quicksilver sniffed and studiously avoided putting one furry foot down on the design.

A small sign outside the main office read WICKED WITCHES NEED NOT APPLY.

Tallgrass knocked, and then entered, the three of us following. A plump receptionist with long, skinny fingernails nodded Tallgrass through to the inner office.

The place was unadorned business vanilla, not trying to broadcast the usual developer ego.

The man behind the desk jumped up to greet us. "Leonard Tallgrass, you old Cayuse! You see what a mighty fine hot spot on the prairie we've raised here? Way bigger than barns. All we need to install is a few more showstopping features and this hotel-casino is gonna make Wichita and Wicked Wild West the new destination vacation."

He stepped around the desk. "These are your FBI friends, with a K-9 dog, yet? Don't think we need that, but you never know. Sit down, folks."

You had to like Ben Hassard. He ran close to three hundred pounds. He wore his Sears white dress-shirt sleeves rolled up to the elbows and his tie knot down toward the first flush of curly gray hairs on his chest.

"Pardon my informal air, folks. I've just finished some scary negotiations with a big shot from Vegas. Very showy fella. I woulda sworn he was going to sweat deal-killing concessions outa me, but I bought him off with a taste of Emerald City hospitality, a sweet bit of luck, and a bottle of Old Crow."

He came around the desk for introductory handshakes with Tallgrass's crew.

"Ric, eh. Nice suit for an FBI type. Almost as good as that Vegas bigwig's. Miss Street. Glad Tallgrass brought some class along."

He hesitated, then held out a hand to Quicksilver.

Quicksilver didn't do doggy tricks. I held my breath as Quick's intelligent, almost-human blue eyes studied the plump, lined palm, then looked in Ben's eyes. He slapped a clawed paw into the hand. Ben had the sense to give it one, firm shake and retreat behind the desk.

"Old Crow?" he asked.

Tallgrass nodded, so Ben pulled four water-spotted lowball glasses and a half-empty bottle of whiskey from a desk drawer. I couldn't imagine which "Vegas bigwig" would negotiate in person in these modest circumstances. Or for what. Except maybe Hector.

"You seem in a better mood, Ben," Tallgrass noted, sipping the amber alcohol.

"Yup. Drink up. I got the special features Emerald City needed to open. At an unbelievably good price, which is lucky, because construction overrun costs were killing me and the backers. Really, I kinda think I took the guy, Las Vegas or not."

"What kind of construction overruns, Mr. Hassard?" Ric asked, setting down his homely glass after a polite sip.

"Oh, the usual." He waved away Ric's question to eye Tallgrass. "Leonard, I overreacted on the phone with you earlier. Things aren't that bad. We just have to open fast to start recouping investment, and now the last, best pieces are in place. Wanta see?"

Tallgrass sat there with his black pupils lost in his most skeptical scout squint, but Ben pressed a button on his desktop intercom.

"Geraldine, send in the CinSims." He winked at us. "We never had any of these in Kansas before. This is the jackpot, trust me. Fresh from the download."

Mystified, Ric and I exchanged a glance. I deigned to drink some cheap whiskey neat. *Ugh.* Tepid, strong as rubbing alcohol, and throat-stinging. I'd never met a spirit that needed a cocktail recipe more.

Let's see . . . we were at Emerald City. How about . . . an Old Scarecrow Old-fashioned?

Quicksilver's claws scrambled as he rushed to his feet behind me.

I heard what sounded like a high-pitched crosscut saw belaboring a twig. Quick growled warning.

I turned to see a small creature with enough spiked hair to serve as a toupee for a male *American Idol* contestant dance down the middle of the painted yellow brick road into the office. I bent to pat the dog.

"Toto," a light, worried voice called, "stay away from that witch!"

I straightened and jumped back just as a sextet of black-and-white CinSims trouped in, fresh from the film and the farm. I knew them instantly, even though they were bathed in a soft yellow light.

The original black-and-white film of the movie's prologue was later "colored" to make it sepia-toned. That was a "fan fact" most people wouldn't know. Only characters filmed on the silver nitrate of black-and-white film could be bonded with zombie bodies to create the signature Vegas Cinema Simulacrums, familiarly known as CinSims. So Ben's Vegas CinSim-supplying bigwig was a vintage film expert. Who? Smelling more and more like Hector.

I must say my hackles rose to match Quicksilver's. Was nothing sacred from exploitation, even the sepia-colored prologue to *The Wizard of Oz*?

Dorothy Gale, with her earnest face and curled—not braided—pigtails, was still calling her little terrier, but frowning at someone behind me.

I turned, and nearly jumped out of my plaits and navy pumps to see the scowling Almira Gulch, as thin and mean as a barbed-wire hangman's noose, chasing the agile little dog around my intervening body.

I bent to scoop up Toto, so the dog could "arf" and snap at the squinty-eyed woman's face. Like my own Achilles, Toto was a spot-on judge of character.

Dorothy's Auntie Em, sweet and worried, came up behind her niece, along with kindly Uncle Henry and the trio of fedora-hatted oddball farmworkers, Hunk, Hickory, and Zeke.

Oh, had the descriptive connotations of the word "hunk" changed since 1939. The prologue's Hunk became the sweet-natured but weak-kneed Scarecrow searching for a brain in Oz. The carnival huckster who'd doubled as the wizard himself, Professor Marvel, brought up the rear.

"Look at them CinSims go!" Ben Hassard crowed. "I feel like the brave little tailor. 'Eight at one blow.'"

I reluctantly handed a warm, soft, wriggling Toto back to Dorothy Gale, a bit unnerved. I'd never seriously touched a CinSim, and couldn't believe they felt so . . . lifelike.

Ric and Tallgrass edged nearer to inspect the flock of CinSims while Almira Gulch kept a vindictive eye on Toto in Dorothy's arms and Quicksilver shadowed her every move.

These CinSims reminded me of Ric's Zobos, disoriented and not in touch with their surroundings, interacting only with themselves. They hadn't had enough exposure to the paying public yet. The Vegas CinSims I knew were firmly themselves and adapted to their fates. These newly hatched celluloid "chicks" made me feel sorry for them . . . except for Almira Gulch.

I slipped back to Hassard's side.

"Are you planning to build a special attraction around them, like the MGM Grand did before it dumped the Oz theme?"

"I don't know what those Las Vegas hotels did. All I know is I got these very Kansas characters in exchange for one old movie just found in the restored Augusta film palace basement down the road." He shook his head. "Vegas moguls. One night in the penthouse suite and he was all hot to deal. I do have some classy 'amenities' in that suite." He winked. "And a*wom*enities too."

I stepped back, hoping Hassard wasn't referring to imported party girls.

It was becoming clear who the visiting Vegas bigwig was, and the thought of Hector Nightwine cavorting with hired heartland hostesses was too ugly to bear.

I could see him parting with the *Oz* CinSims. They were far too homey and wholesome for the producer of the *CSI V* forensics TV franchise. I wondered what he'd got in exchange. Some notorious X-rated early foreign film, no doubt, like Hedy Lamarr's *Ecstasy* with the first feature-film nude scene. Hector mentioned she and Dorothy Lamour had been guests at the Enchanted Cottage decades ago.

That reminded me that Howard Hughes in his heyday had dated both of those black-and-white film bombshells and he'd be chasing after classic girlie movies too.

"No," Hassard was saying in answer to my question. I can't afford to put all my eggs in one basket. I'm going to let these CinSims make themselves at home throughout the hotel-casino. That way, customers will keep running into them in different areas and think we've got more than we do."

"You might keep Almira Gulch microchipped and confined to one location," I suggested. "She *is* the villain of the piece."

"That old gal in the battle-axe hat?" Hassard squinted her way and was met with a withering stare. "I see what you're getting at. Yeah. Maybe I'll station her at a casino cashier's cage. She's ugly enough to scare folks off from bothering to collect their winnings. I'll have my tech person handle that in the morning. Meanwhile . . ."

Hassard stepped up to the milling group. "Okay, you

CinSim people. I need you to scatter throughout the building. Check it out. Find some casino spots that appeal to you. And you, miss. Yes, the girl in the checked jumper. Make sure to get your little dog outside for enough 'walks,' if you know what I mean."

For the first time I considered the embarrassing issue of CinSim elimination. I hoped the zombie element of the combo ruled there, although feral film zombies certainly . . . ate.

"Okay, gang." Hassard clapped his hands and shooed the CinSims out of his office like a flock of farm chickens, Quicksilver escorting Almira Gulch and giving her a last warning growl.

Ric, who'd been conferring with Tallgrass all the while the CinSims had offered comic relief, approached Ben and me.

"Old friend," Tallgrass said to Hassard. "We four"— Quicksilver nosed his hand—"ah, five, need to sit and powwow, as they say in the cowboy movies."

"Waal, sure," Ben said. "Pull up your chairs again. Here's one for the little lady."

I'm taller than he, but I accepted the chair Ben Hassard scooted under my navy-skirted rear.

"Another round of Old Crow, gentlemen and lady? Big doggy? Maybe you need to walk the dog, Miss Street?"

Quick and I gave him such a tandem look of disdain that he hastily sat behind the desk and began pouring more of the Old Crow into glasses.

"None for me," I said, fanning my fingers over the glass. Ric followed suit, but Tallgrass nodded, then drank it all in one go.

"Ben, my friend," he said. "We gotta have a frank talk here."

Ben gulped from his glass, and then added Ric's and my portions to what was left.

"You saw it, Tallgrass," Ben said. "I've got the final piece of the hotel-casino in place. Those silly CinSims haven't their like in a thousand-mile circumference. I know they're kinda corny, but—"

"Corny?" I exploded. "You have an iconic CinSim coup here."

"Sorry, miss. Of course I know that. I just don't know what to do with them. Yet. The tribal casinos have been hit harder than Las Vegas with this Millennium Revelation thing and the economic crash. I got a lot of Indian money riding on this. Not your Native American charity stuff. This is our investment for the new century."

"We see that," Tallgrass said. "This is a major and impressive construction, Ben. And it's Kansas grown and bred. But you haven't been honest with us, and that's a bad start."

"Honest?" Beads of sweat appeared on Ben's brow as if dowsed up by an invisible crown of thorns. "Tallgrass, you're the consortium's ally. If you—"

"Consortium, Ben?" Tallgrass sounded angrier than I'd ever like to confront. "You had the dream and the tribes gave you the money. Now we want an accounting. Who's been blackmailing you and who have you paid off and how much?"

"That's what you've been doing?" Ben asked bitterly. "Sniffing around with your slick FBI friend and this woman and that dog?"

"Look the dog in the eyes when you ask that," Tallgrass said.

Hey, what about Ric and my totally righteous histories? Quicksilver lifted his clawed paws onto the desk edge and thrust his big, fur-aureoled head nose to nose with Hassard.

Ben Hassard wiped the back of his hand across the sweat streaming down his forehead.

"Every contractor pays extra here and there," he said. "If not to the union, then to what's left of the mob or to meet some government regulation a crooked congressman put in for his local lobbyist. We know that. That's the way things run."

"That is not the Indian way," Tallgrass said. "We dealt with honor."

"Honor was a European myth and our stupidity, Tallgrass. You know that. I had to pay off some people. That's all."

Ric and I exchanged a glance. We were the "White Eyes" in an old argument.

I realized it was best we keep our mouths shut and our ears open. Quicksilver and his wolfish heritage had more cred here than we did. We could say the Irish and the Mexicans had as many bones to pick with history as Native Americans, including genocide, but this was not our personal risk or our showdown.

"Who did you pay off?" Tallgrass wasn't leaving here without an answer.

Hassard just looked scared.

"Wait," I said.

Both men glared at me. Ric shook his head slightly, warning me to back off. This was an all-male, all Native American powwow.

Quicksilver pulled his paws from the desk to my knees and regarded me intently.

I wrapped my hands around his collar and went, like Tallgrass, with the dog.

"Mr. Hassard, I filmed something the other day at my old workplace, WTCH-TV."

Hassard froze like an ice sculpture. For some reason, that TV station was not only familiar, but an object of fear.

"Let me dig out my phone. Ric, while you, Tallgrass, and Quicksilver were off on rural investigations, I was delving into my history here in Wichita . . . which included this bitchy local weather witch, Sheena Coleman and . . . the station's vampire anchorman I call Undead Ted."

By then I'd got the film on-screen. The familiar had become a wrist bangle etched with an Egyptian Eye of Horus symbol, all the better to peek.

"A contact of mine at the station downloaded some . . . personal film to me, including the footage we got at the first cow mutilation site a few months ago. Before I left, I filmed Sheena and Ted returning from what looked like a payoff lunch meeting. They were chauffeured with a likely suspect, aka an ugly customer. I've never seen, not even since the Millennium Revelation, a man who walked more like a snake. Anybody recognize Mr. Rattlesnake-skin Briefcase?"

I ran the first part of the sequence by Ric and Tallgrass and, finally, Hassard.

"That's her," Hassard finally admitted. "That blasted local TV weather witch has been hitting our construction site with out-of-season rainstorms and hail and threatening lightning strikes to bring the entire structure down unless we pay up big. We're at the breaking point, Tallgrass. I don't dare stop paying or all the tribes' money is kaput."

He put his head in his hands and shook it. "We're so close to launch time and to EC making enough to get these blackmailers off our back."

"You'll never get blackmailers off your back unless you become the worst bucking bronco around," Tallgrass said.

"And here's the money man," I said.

Tallgrass and Hassard shook their heads at the paused scene.

Ric got my phone screen last and stared in silence. He kept so uncharacteristically still I began to feel like I'd goofed.

"I should have uploaded this to all your cell phones right away," I said. "I was distracted by Sheena's parting weather volleys and . . . visiting some sentimental spots in town."

"Not what's bothering me," Ric said.

He licked his lips, maybe nervous or maybe getting ready to confess.

"I recognize the man with the money. The less he's on our radar the better for us. He might have some way of tracking his presence on neighborhood networks, and he's the kind of bastard you really need to get the jump on."

"Ric?" I asked.

He looked me hard in the eyes. "It's the drug cartel kingpin, El Demonio. Torbellino is his surname."

"Your scumball kidnapper and zombie smuggler from years ago in Mexico? A kingpin now? Here in Kansas? Why? No . . . it can't be."

"Think I'd ever forget his inhuman face, Delilah? If El Demonio has expanded his foul drug smuggling and zombie-running operations from the crime cesspool of the border up into Kansas heartland, where he's allied with weather witches, we have to grab the chance to take him and his cartel down before the whole country is fouled."

" 'We'?" I asked incredulously. "Without backup or state troopers or the Reserves? He must have a ton of really fast zombies, not to mention his usual crime-lord army of gunmen."

Tallgrass objected in his low-key way. "We must find Torbellino's base of operations first."

"We didn't have the bastard's stink before," Ric said. "We'll start tracking at the WTCH-TV parking lot. When El Demonio made the mistake of setting shoe sole on asphalt, he made himself Quicksilver meat."

Quick had already leaped up to view the film. Now he was lunging for the office exit, ready to track and tackle.

"Delilah." Ric turned to me. "Stay with Ben in case he gets fresh contact from the blackmailers."

I was about to object to being left out of the track-down my minifilm had made possible, but I knew I'd blown it by regarding Sheena and Ted's unsavory connections as part of my personal history instead of something bigger.

So I nodded.

Ben lifted the Old Crow bottle to me with a questioning look as a peace offering. We'd both failed to recognize and report something important to our best friends.

I watched Quicksilver's thick, plumy tail flash out the office door, Tallgrass and Ric right behind him.

After a moment of mentally bemoaning being left behind, I pulled my chair up to the desk just as Ben, his hand shaking, poured amber whiskey into the water-spotted glass that had been mine.

"Miss Street prefers a smoother and costlier blend of poison," a beautifully resonant but all too recognizable voice said behind me.

My silver familiar turned tail and slipped down my clothes to wrap itself around my right upper thigh like a garter as I gulped down two fingers of Old Crow straight anyway.

Then I turned to confront the unexpected newcomer.

Chapter Twenty-four

BEN HASSARD WAS on his feet, nodding and bowing like a bobble-headed doll.

"I hope you continue to enjoy the accommodations, Mr. Christopher," he told the white man in white, "and that our . . . discussions down here didn't disturb you in the penthouse."

"Your CinSims fanning through the hotel disturbed me. You do understand that the farmyard chickens and pigs and horses are part of the package, as well as Miss Gulch's bicycle?"

"Horses and pigs and chickens? Oh, my." Ben cast me a helpless look. "Miss Street was right. I'll need some sort of unifying attraction . . . perhaps around a theme of Kansas, the Barnyard State."

Their byplay gave me mental time to insert Vegas's one and only albino rock star into this place and time and enterprise. I wasn't surprised that Hassard hadn't recognized the stage persona of Cocaine, lead singer of the Seven Deadly Sins rock group. Snow in white-suit civvies looked like a taller, younger, sexier . . . oh, Mark Twain.

"*You're* the Vegas bigwig who's been so generous with CinSims leases?" I asked, none too smoothly.

Shock does that to even a professional objective observer, and I was in no way objective about Snow.

His Western-style suit was not that different from the

white Italian designer ones he wore offstage, but his river-boat gambler hat seemed so like the ghost of El Demonio's black one it gave me shivers. Snow's long white hair was tied back into a very passé mob-style ponytail that suddenly looked back again, big-time. And, of course, he wore the eternal dark sunglasses.

"Me, generous?" he replied.

I could tell his hidden eyes were taking in my plain navy suit. Some men's looks could be said to undress a woman. His summation seemed to be burying my outfit under a chador.

"Hardly generous," Snow addressed me again. "This was a business deal. Ben and I are both well satisfied, and now I have the unexpected bonus of . . . requisitioning Miss Street's presence in my suite."

"Ah," Ben said. "Miss Street is not a potential, er, hostess, Mr. Christopher. Her presence is not a matter of acquisition. In a month, Emerald City will be fully staffed instead of running with a skeleton crew."

"Mr. Christopher," I put in, mispronouncing his name with glee, "knows perfectly well, from long experience, that I am not biddable. Is there a reason why I should accompany you upstairs?"

"The view," Snow said, drawing it out like a slow sip of an Albino Vampire cocktail, "is spectacular."

And . . . I'd get some private time to pump him on the what, how, and why of his astounding personal visit to the hinterlands.

I thanked Mr. Hassard, gave him my cell phone number, and asked him to alert me instantly if "my party" returned.

Snow waited beside the door the CinSims had just trooped through on a yellow brick road.

THE EMERALD CITY offered green glass elevators that shot riders atop each of the needle towers through an aquatic funnel of green gelatin, with a laser show of chartreuse lights lancing the emerald haze.

"I'm only here for the ride and the view," I mentioned.

"Of course. Why do you care about any impression a sleazy operator like Ben Hassard has of you?"

Nah, we get a classy *operator,* Irma noted, happy to back me up with the Big Bad Wolf. She loved these set-tos of ours. *That riverboat gambler suit fits Snow's frame just a tad looser than his rock show catsuit . . . and did you catch those albino ostrich-skin cowboy boots with the ebony heels and platinum ankle chains? If I could get me a pair I would die right here and happily go to Hell.*

Snow did resemble the quintessential Western dude, down to the white string tie with a platinum longhorn skull slide. I'm sure he impressed the local yokels no end.

"It's not about me," I told Snow. "It's about the truth. Why did you wait to make your appearance until Ric and Leonard Tallgrass left? Did you want to separate me from them?"

"Just cutting you out from the common crime-chasing herd. You're a devout Our Lady of the Lake graduate, I hear. I wanted to show you the Holy Grail."

"Oh, come on."

"You don't believe the cup Christ sipped from at the Last Supper still exists in this world, somewhere?"

"Possibly, but that's not my obsession."

"Then you'll be pleased that I'm going to . . . satisfy what *is* your obsession."

Now that was a veiled threat if I'd ever heard one.

APPARENTLY PROGRAMMED, OUR elevator had reached the top. The faceted emerald doors split open on another vista so green it seemed to be underwater.

Gosh, Irma whispered. *We've got a few of those obsession thingies. Wonder which one our sexy host is so bound and determined to cater to? He does owe you at least a spanking for transferring the physical pain and marks of Ric's bullwhipped childhood slavery to his own truly porcelain albino body. I'll watch.*

Shut up, I told Irma. I was already jumpy, knowing we were dealing here with Christophe, the billionaire casino king. I was all too aware of his slick Oklahoma oilman wardrobe and the draw of the white silken shirt and suit jacket across the Snow-white skin of his back with every move. Yet he seemed all business, all entrepreneur now. Nothing of the raunchy rock star remained. And certainly nothing of the victim of a paranormal pain transfer.

The room beyond the private elevator sported a sprawling conversation pit upholstered in so many shades of green velvet I thought I was in mossy Ireland. I noted that the suite had his and her powder rooms off the entry hall, like the layout at werewolf warlord Cesar Cicereau's Gehenna Hotel penthouse. Effete Vegas luxuries were infecting even Wichita.

Snow went ahead into the massive main room to open the verdigris-lacquered doors of a green-mirror-backed bar.

"I have absinthe and Albino Vampires and crème de menthe cocktails," he offered. "Any preference?"

I stared at a trio of green glass bottles. "Wait a minute. You've *bottled* my Albino Vampire recipe?"

"Just add the vodka of your choice, from Grey Goose to lighter fluid. Much more economical than by the martini glass at the Inferno Bar. And of course, also much more profitable to me in the larger mass market."

I shook my head. "I'm stunned that I'm allowed into this temple of greed wearing just my plain navy interview suit."

"My mistake. You're quite right. I'm violating the hospitality of the Emerald City Hotel and Casino. I should have directed you to the suite Green Room first thing. It's a must for every occupant. You *do* want to taste what this theme-park gambling joint will offer the paying customers?"

He gestured to a pair of zebrawood doors striped in pale and vivid green.

"I'll have the absinthe," I said over my shoulder, stepping through.

Whoa. I was in some kind of New Age subway tunnel, with nowhere to go but forward.

The setup, despite its relentless laser-green glow, immediately reminded me of the detoxifying entrance tunnel to germ-phobic Howard Hughes's 1001 Knights getaway on the low-rent end of the Strip.

Green laser lights buzzed and swiveled as they rose and fell on either side of me, etching my form as if I were a jigsaw puzzle piece. I walked through an emerald-green mist, feeling warm and then cool. Unseen air vents lifted my heavy plaits to writhe and untwine around my face and shoulders like Medusa's serpents—not Kelly green, I hoped.

I came though the opposite doors feeling I'd enjoyed a steam room, sauna, and massage. In fact, I felt absolutely wonderful.

Snow was waiting with two tall, thin glasses of opaque, chartreuse-tinted absinthe. The drink had been a nineteenth-century fad with a bad rep because an herbal ingredient called wormwood had a marijuana-like effect.

"'A great star fell from Heaven,'" he recited as he handed me one glass, "'burning like a torch, and . . . the name of the star is wormwood.'"

"'And Kansas, she said, is the name of the star,'" I sang like the Good Witch Glinda.

If Snow wanted to quote the Book of Revelation to an Our Lady of the Lake girl, I could quote *The Wizard of Oz* right back.

"Nice pipes," he said, the sunglasses dipping to eye my legs.

I was shocked to view a thigh-high slit in a long green satin skirt that showcased the familiar as a silver "garter" snake.

"Passing through the Green Room has a stunning effect, doesn't it?" Snow commented. "Like going through a glamorizing car wash for humans. They call it the 'Emerald City Dorothy spa option.' The lasers take your measurements and melt off your everyday wear, 'painting' the bedazzled client with more formal clothes. I see the females get a gown fit for a movie queen, so the obsessed gambler has his lady distracted from the moment they enter their suite."

"I suppose the gaming man only gets a fistful of green casino cards."

"Oh, no. They offer a spa experience for gentlemen clients too." He held out his suited arms. "They need the money man relaxed and ready to rock and roll the dice and roulette wheel all night long. You don't think I'd dress like a riverboat gambler on purpose? My only . . . successful resistance to the process was to reject the bilious green color." He eyed me from top to toe. "Well, you *are* black

Irish, and the plaits didn't suit you as well as having your hair loose."

"I *hate* wearing green," I muttered to dismiss his compliment.

Green was for jigging, red-haired, freckled Irish lassies, not a dark and deep depressive diva like me. Okay, I dramatize. Shut up, Irma.

However, I was determined to avoid any and all of the green mirrors in the suite in case they skewed my mirror affinity, so I found his comments a mystery, except for the hair, which I'd felt unwinding. He led me through another set of doors, and down a dim aisle of shallow stairs.

A giant movie screen faced us, but it was matte black and mirrored nothing.

Looking around, I spotted glassy green reflections bouncing from multiple surfaces, all too fractured to add up to a mirror. That was comforting. I didn't want to display any mirror-walking tricks in front of Snow.

I could only glimpse a tiny reflection of myself in his sunglasses' lenses. Although my hair was still black, I was wrapped in shiny shades of green, like a Christmas present.

"If I were a talking mirror," Snow said, the sunglasses moving up and down me like the laser lights, "I could report that you'd whip that slinky green vintage gown you're wearing off a black-and-white movie screen in a Wichita minute."

"If it's green, I doubt it. The latest antiterrorist technology and clothes manufacturing trends could account for much of the makeover wizardry," I speculated. "Nothing was that 'magical.' The laser measurements. The melting outer garments. Even the clothes spun like webs onto living mannequin forms."

"True," Snow said. "Millennium Revelations may come and go, but if you sell entertainment to the public, you always have to have a gimmick."

He led me down the plush-carpeted stairs to a row of pistachio-colored leather theater seats. I noticed that my navy pumps were as plain and simple as ever, but now dyed teal-green. I wondered how my blue eyes had fared in the Emerald Tunnel.

Snow continued playing tour guide.

"You must be dying to know what I'm doing here. Please sit, Delilah, and prepare to observe the wonder of the century."

I placed my long-stemmed glass in the chair's built-in beverage holder and arranged myself. My satin gown seemed to be made of green linguini, it draped so easily over me and the chair, but when I leaned back I felt a chill. The leather was room temperature and cool. My back was bare from tailbone up as the leather accepted the pressure of my skin. My naturally pale, unblemished skin.

If I'd been asked to lie on a reclining chair of thorns I couldn't have been more pained.

Seeing Snow again had focused my mind on the whip strikes I'd transferred to him from Ric. Were they still raw? In an ordinary human being, they surely would be.

No matter how luxe and silken the surroundings, that unspoken fear rubbed my expectations raw. The cushy ambiance prickled me all the more as I pictured that supernaturally white skin beneath the silk shirt festered and scabbing and feverish, no matter how much Snow always mastered cool.

Or . . . not. That was the bed of nails he had me on, constructed from my too-vivid imagination and my guilt.

"I don't understand why you're here," I blurted.

He'd taken his own chair, sitting forward as taller men will, leaning his forearms on his knees, pure white hands loosely laced together, not putting his back flat against the leather back. Was he *trying* to make me think the worst?

A reporter knows only to push. I eyed my wristwatch, squinting at a hard-to-read greenish abalone-shell dial now encrusted with green garnets. I assumed emeralds would not be bestowed on the wives of even gambling whales.

"What," I asked, "is Vegas impresario Christophe doing at a remote casino operation like Emerald City in Wichita? Not even you can jet back to Vegas in time for your seven p.m. show," I pointed out. "Unless you have dragon wings."

His pale lips split in a smile that revealed yet whiter teeth. "Can you have caught me out in a trade secret, Delilah?"

"You're a shape-shifting dragon?"

I dearly hoped so. That would make him a major new supernatural on the Millennium Revelation map and way too inhuman—and huge—for me to worry about having hurt.

That was the crazy part. *I* was worried I'd hurt the impervious Snow when he probably had the power to destroy me six times over with a wave of his little finger. I looked closely. That milk-white digit now flaunted a peridot-set green-gold ring.

Apparently he hadn't escaped the Emerald City Green Room's do-over as thoroughly as he'd thought.

Snow set his white riverboat gambler's hat on the empty chair seat next to him. He tilted back his profile and throat and ran his fingers through his tied-back hair, releasing it to his shoulders, smiling at the blank screen straight ahead.

I charged ahead. "You can't convince me you'd be

interested in investing in some over-the-rainbow casino property in Wichita, Kansas."

"Oh, but I am." He finally sat back and directed the sunglasses' blind gaze my way. "And, since you've turned up at this opportune moment, I'm here to show you a movie."

What is it with these guys? Irma crabbed. *First Ric and now Snow. We're lounging around here like blond bombshell Jean Harlow and Mr. Rock Star Hottie wants to* watch a movie *with us? Your chances of even copping us another hickey here are zero, baby.*

I sipped the slightly bitter taste of green anise in the absinthe, glad Irma was right. This was a rare retro moment in La-la Land. Private screening. Major Red Carpet slinky gown. Retro cocktail. I glanced again at Snow. Irma was right again. That bleached Southern Comfort, Rhett Butler outfit didn't do him a disservice.

Tomorrow is another day, baby, I told Irma.

Then "Rhett" hit the twentieth century's greatest contribution to humanity, the remote control. The minute he did, reels of a silent black-and-white film began flickering on the screen, and my pulse started doing the jitterbug.

I sat forward, no longer worried about exposing my uneasily naked back to Snow, Rhett, or whoever. The scenes and figures I watched were pretty jitterbuggy too. That's the way silent films were seen in the early days, like 1927, in that herky-jerky motion.

Immediately, I recognized the astonishing, luminous images of an imagined ultramodern city combining the space opera scenery of Flash Gordon with the despair of a union movement for robotic workers.

Some would say this was the most classic film ever done by the German expressionist director, Fritz Lang.

The studio and censors had hacked the film apart even before it was exported to the larger world. The Nazis would embrace the mechanized super-city as their own, making Lang loathe the product of his own genius. No complete authorized edition existed to this day. A rumored one found a few years ago in Rio had proved fraudulent.

"Snow," I breathed, "what do you have here? Not the complete lost footage? That would be . . . priceless."

His sunglassed gaze remained fixed on the screen. "I didn't say 'Holy Grail' for nothing. Yes. Somehow the foot of the *Oz* rainbow pointed to the archives of a restored Wichita-area Art Deco movie palace, the Augusta, and this lost, rare, impossible footage. That's what I want here. That's what I'll take back to the Inferno Hotel, an entire new wing built around this vintage futuristic vision. I'll call it the *New Metropolis* Towers and Condominiums and maybe, if you treat me right, you'll have visiting privileges."

I was so freaking sold. "Imagine guests *living* in this vintage film city of the future. So the subterranean Nine Circles of Hell aren't playground enough for you? You're reconstructing the film world's Art Deco Tower of Babel in Vegas? You realize those biblical Babel builders blasphemed?"

"You realize," Snow said, "that 'blaspheme' is a pretty archaic concept? Especially in Vegas? Just tune in to your film fanatic mode, Delilah. I must say having you sitting here in that seriously anti-Code evening gown much enhances my viewing pleasure."

"I would wear a green clown suit for the privilege of seeing *Metropolis* uncut."

Snow chuckled, returning his hidden gaze from the screen. "I knew you'd appreciate this."

It's hard to overstate how rare this film was. The Holy Grail of vintage films indeed. Remembering it was *twelve* years from the grim but luminous black-and-white futuristic robotic fable of *Metropolis* to the hypercolorized, deceptively happy fable of *The Wizard of Oz* shows how fast the art of film developed—by leaps and bounds—and so had its audience.

I rapidly scanned my all-things-vintage memory bank.

Metropolis was a dark antitechnology tale of Maria, a sweet, loving girl who became the movie's model for the ultimate roboticized worker-drone. The "manufactured" robot queen bee built on Maria in *Metropolis* had inspired George Lucas to create the shiny gold C-3PO robot in the *Star Wars* film saga, but a more recent descendent was Seven of Nine, that sexy mechanical Borg female "construct" of nineties *Star Trek* television.

Now I stared at the moments of heroine Maria's onscreen re-creation, a human woman being made into a silver-metal superwoman, perhaps the most powerful image of feminine power since the Neolithic fertility goddesses. Only this dame wore body armor.

She stood on platform soles of solid metal. She packed it at the hips like a gunslinger, and don't we all, a little? I was reminded of the secondhand cop duty belt I wore for action expeditions. Her metal-gloved hands curved out from the sides of her thighs. Like a gunslinger's.

Her torso was covered by a stiff metal "stomacher" bodice Queen Elizabeth I (no monarch to mess with anywhere, anytime) would wear.

Her breastplate was topped off by steel cannonballs, size 36C. Her shoulders stood up high and rounded too, and her neck sinews combined something of the swan with something of the suspension bridge.

Her face was sculpted in perfect symmetry, but blank of eye, taut of lip, and dominated by a nose that soared into a delicate pillar to the top of her head, which wore a smooth metal bonnet. She looked like she'd never had a bad hair day, having no visible hair. She also looked like she could kick *Alien* ass or take down Billy the Kid. Or both at the same time. She was eternal. And she was awesome.

So was the visionary film world that had created her.

I watched, mesmerized, aware that Snow alone had the chutzpah to reconstruct this vanished apocalyptic vision of *Metropolis* in Las Vegas. Of course, in the film, the robotic superwoman had been destroyed. That would not happen again, from the rapt way Snow's sunglasses fixed on the screen. She would escape pre-WWII Germany and get her full second round in post–Millennium Revelation Las Vegas.

"Why are you showing this to me?" I asked, hardly noticing the time until the 153-minute film had burst like a bubble on the dark screen and vanished. But my absinthe glass was empty.

"You always want answers, Delilah Street," Snow said, stretching out his white ostrich-skin boots and lacing his hands behind his neck in a way that showcased his long, dramatic frame. "The mysteries Wichita holds for you are far more serious than my being here. But . . . the film I've just acquired is a lost treasure few would appreciate. I simply wanted to show it to somebody."

Unsaid was the fact he wanted to show it to somebody who understood what a rarity it was, that he needed my mind and companionship. For an instant, I actually felt sorry for him. It must be lonely at the pinnacle.

And then I got one of my intuitive glimmers. "How

did you find this here in Wichita? Through the Augusta
Theater restoration, but only you knew what it was, didn't
you?"

His long, white, lazy fingers reached out to touch the
silver bracelet I hadn't realized had made a green circle
of thorns on my wrist. The familiar morphed again into
a green-enameled silver garter snake, reared a tiny scaled
head, and hissed at him.

He laughed, but withdrew his hand.

"Yes," he said. "I've hired what the antique dealers call
'pickers' to look for it for decades. The Augusta is a 1935
movie theater on the National Register of Historic Places.
It was never a huge urban film palace, but it *is* pure Art
Deco, rather similar to how you're looking now, Delilah,
all green and silver and black, like your sterling serpent.
It's been restored on a shoestring by devoted locals, and no
one was more surprised than I to find that an uncut version
of *Metropolis* numbered among their souvenirs. Of course,
they had no idea what they had."

"Of course," I told him. "I just didn't understand why
you'd share the find of several lifetimes with me."

"Is that all you want to know after seeing *Metropolis*?
Come on, Delilah, you can be cheekier than this."

I studied my host, an enigma who was as ancient as
a same-named medieval Christophe . . . as modern and
deadly as Cocaine . . . as cozy-familiar and icy as Snow.

I held my breath while Irma bit her tongue. My tongue
wasn't so easy to harness.

"Why aren't you giving the Brimstone Kiss after your
shows anymore?" I asked, not having planned to go there.

He braced his elbows on the theater seat arms and again
ran his albino fingers into the hair at his temples as if he
had a nagging headache. Me, I hope.

"Why?" I demanded. "The fabled Brimstone Kiss was your signature. Did I . . . use it up?"

I was thinking that maybe he . . . *it* had only one life to give . . .

Jeez, that sounded like the title of a long-gone soap opera.

He turned to face me, the unreadable sunglasses burning like coal into my anxious regard.

"Nothing to do with you, Delilah. Sorry." A slight smile lifted his lips. "I can't be tied down to a concert schedule anymore, you see. That's why I moved the Seven Deadly Sins to Vegas."

He stood and opened his arms like a showman, an albino Buffalo Bill doffing his hat and taking a bow. "A CinSim, of course, is doing my show tonight."

I stood too.

"A CinSim of yourself? How?"

"Simplicity itself." Snow shot his cuffs, enjoying his Green Room showman's suit, revealing the new Technicolor emeralds in his white-gold cuff links. "I had myself recorded on vintage black-and-white film, then ordered the CinSim from the Immortality Mob."

"One can do that?"

"They're the mob. They fill orders for anything from anyone with the money."

"And your . . . zombie CinSim can't bestow the Brimstone Kiss?" I asked to be certain.

"Why would it? The Brimstone Kiss is extremely personal." He moved closer, his voice softer. "Hadn't you noticed? Oh, that's right. You never got the multiorgasmic effect. You were too busy, as usual, Delilah, detesting the easy O and sacrificing yourself to a Judas kiss to save your own true love. You're much like Maria, the worker's champion who was made into the emotionless über-robot in *Metropolis*. You, too, believe 'the heart must mediate between the head and the hands.' But the heart harbors all the seven deadly sins, Delilah. Anger, Greed, Sloth, Envy, Gluttony, Lust. . . ." He listed all the members of his Seven Deadly Sins rock band but himself.

His cool right hand slid around to the small of my back and my entire spine tingled. I was right. It was naked. My back. So was his palm.

I froze in shock and defense.

"Have I forgotten one?" he asked.

"Pride, I believe."

"And Pride." He named his own role in the band so softly that I turned my head to hear it even as he stepped closer.

Pride made me hold my ground.

By turning my head aside, I'd put us into a perfect tango position, tightly together but facing in opposite directions.

I tried to insert my hands between us, between his chest and mine, to push him off.

Who are you kidding, kid? Irma was nattering nervously in my head. *This guy's got the ripped body of that giant white marble statue of David at Caesar's Palace. That Michelangelo sure knew how to do guys. Wink. Who knew an Old Testament sheep boy could be so hunky? What else here of interest do you think might be giant?*

Shut up, I ordered her. I can't think.

That's the point, baby. . . . Irma's voice faded.

I really did need to think, to put all sorts of incidents and innuendos in my life together. Item: the lightning-strike scars I'd seen on Snow's chest in his performance catsuit. Item: the new star-shaped scar on Ric's neck that so needed my attention.

This wasn't just about sex, but life and death, which made sense. Risk. Love. Hate. Hope. I was beginning to put all the mysteries within an enigma together and started to say it aloud, step by step, to Snow, of all people.

"The Brimstone Kiss became the Resurrection Kiss in the Hell underneath the Karnak," I told him, my voice more breathless than I liked, catching the frantic rhythm of Irma's heated running internal commentary.

"I was there," he reminded me. "I warned you."

"It became something else in the hotel bridal suite you so ironically donated as Ric's recovery room."

"When I became your proxy whipping boy, you mean?"

I wet my lips, nervous and ashamed. I instantly knew the moment he'd seen that gesture of weakness, because he pulled me closer, forcing contact, forcing confession.

"I didn't want you as a whipping boy," I told him hotly. "I never would have tolerated owing you for that. I was simply healing Ric."

My self-defense sounded lame.

"So Grizelle reported," Snow said, "when her fury permitted her human speech after it was all over."

"Did you call her off me?"

"Why would I do that?"

"You wanted to save your revenge for yourself?"

"Or I just wanted to save *you* . . . for myself."

I was *not* going there. "Grizelle didn't tell you *how* I healed Ric?"

In the extended silence, I saw there was something I knew and he didn't.

Finally!

My hands stopped fighting his custody. Now I knew what buttons to push where. His Brimstone Kiss had affected me and mine beyond belief. For good or ill? I didn't know yet. Could I return the "favor"? Did remnants of his Brimstone Kiss still linger on my lips? Was he as vulnerable to me as I was to him? Would he hate that as much as I had? A coward wouldn't want to know.

I did.

"Here's how I heal, and in your case, hurt," I said, feeling breathlessly bold.

My rogue fingers slipped the middle mother-of-pearl buttons on his shirt open. So easy with silk. Almost an "easy O." No big surprise, except I could feel a tiny tremor of shock as my warm fingers touched Snow's supercool flesh. His or my shock, I didn't know. Or care.

I leaned away to—why the hell not?—*wrench* the shirt open. Snow's strong hands at my back kept me from over-balancing, accommodating my attack. He would.

"Delilah, do you know what you're doing?" he asked. Softly.

"Yes. Do you? I don't think so."

Having bared the center of his albino chest, I stared at the lightning bolt scar tissue, shiny and *silver,* meeting from all four corners of his torso at the breastbone above those abs of stone and below those pecs of marble.

His white leather performance catsuits cut to the navel flaunted these anti-ink tattoos onstage for all and anyone to see. Who or what had inflicted them. Real lightning? A fire? Torture, even? Fiery torture?

"A great star fell from heaven, burning like a torch." He had just quoted an ancient mystic to me. Was the great star not just Cocaine of the Seven Deadly Sins rock band, but a true falling angel? Even Lucifer himself, which means "light"? And the "wormwood" was regret for all that was lost? Heaven exchanged for the Inferno Hotel and the Nine Circles of Dante's Hell beneath it?

I knew what I needed to do. I brushed my parted lips over the solid center where the lightning-strike scars met, over his heart, if he had one, and then repeated the gesture with my tongue. It was like licking frost from a steel pole in a Wichita winter—an icy, tingling shock.

Well, he wasn't a vampire. That was a dead issue. I felt his heart stumble and then jackrabbit under my palm.

Did *he* feel the pleasure effect, though? Or just shock?

"Second Circle of Hell, woman," he muttered, his voice soft but so deep in his chest that my hands sensed its breath-catching vibration.

Oh, he did feel it. I had what every woman in Vegas and beyond wanted. I had Snow in the palms of my hands.

My heart was beating pretty wildly by then. Triumph almost felt like erotic excitement. I was the puppet master here.

I ran my lips and tongue diagonally across his chest from rib to opposite nipple. His audible intake of breath tautened his pec for my attack. His hands were digging into my shoulder blades, pulling me closer.

That was ballsy, Irma gasped.

She was right. The scars made a giant X on his torso, but the nipples weren't part of the zone. I just couldn't resist payback for how he'd pulled my gown down to my waist so unnecessarily during the Brimstone Kiss.

This really was rather fun, salving my conscience while driving a sex symbol crazy. Any way you want it . . .

I opened the one button on his blazer and unclasped some way-too-Texan silver belt buckle courtesy of the Emerald City makeover attraction.

I was expecting his knees to buckle at any moment, but no such luck.

"Pleasure," I pointed out rather redundantly, "for pain. I

can offer it in equal parts. Have I made up for one whiplash yet?"

He was breathing hard, but still able to speak. "Oh, Delilah," he said putting his mouth on the hair covering my ear. "Do you think I'd be crazy enough to let you cut my hair, or tell you that?"

I'd heard that rumble with my cheek and ear pressed against his chest.

"Do you feel like this onstage?" I asked.

"Like what?"

"Like they're all in the palm of your hand?"

His soft laughter stopped when I applied my tongue again and ran it down to his navel.

"How far do these lightning scars go?" I asked, parting the zipper on his pants.

"From Heaven to Hell and back again. How far are you going to go?"

He sounded amused now, and more in control than I wanted, but his breath was coming quick and shallow.

I took stock. My cheeks burned and my lips tingled. It was either go down, to Hell, or up, to Heaven. Low road or high road.

I'd proved my theory. The silvered tissue of scarred skin was subject to my healing, soothing, and even surreal sexual influence. So I'd also proved that I could undo Snow as much as he had undone me. We were tied at the moment. His hands shifted to the top of my shoulders, ready to assist me in sinking to a new level of competitive sensuality.

Instead, I surprised us both and went up, my fingers ripping open his top shirt buttons and pulling the string tie loose and his collar agape to tilt my face sideways and suck vampire-hard at the hollow of his throat.

Who was helpless and exposed now? I wanted to ask as

his head reared back. He would have spoken, maybe even objected, but I breathed—or hissed—*shhhh* without missing a beat. So he let me have my way with him.

Only . . . his hands fanned on my bare lower back and tilted my strong, silver-laced, satin-clad pelvic bones against his.

To feel every throb of his climax.

That forced me to break my punishing kiss and stumble back to establish my balance in every way. I kept my head tilted at an inquisitive angle. "One? Maybe two lashes paid for now, would you grant me that?"

Snow had let himself sink onto the narrow hard arm of a theater chair, his clothes still split open a provocative smidge down the middle, from the pulse visibly galloping in his throat to Gehenna. Not a bad look. I'd have been a killer *GQ* advertising director too.

So.

Delilah, the small and meek, had just had a very personal peek behind the façade.

The Great and Powerful Snow was just another man behind the curtain in need of a really good blow job.

Chapter Twenty-five

Aᴄ FTER THIS PIECE of impromptu performance "art," I was more than ready to retreat behind the closed door of the suite's powder room off the entry hall.

The last time I'd made a pit stop on the way out of a major hotel-casino's penthouse suite, it had been to wash off blood spatter after ridding werewolf mobster Cesar Cicereau of a reanimated victim at the Gehenna Hotel in Vegas.

Now, I just wanted to avoid Snow for a while.

When I entered, I discovered this was a kiss-off point for the ladies.

Here I'd been hopelessly Midwestern again, thinking vacationing married couples used this suite. *Duh.* It was for big spenders and their hired ladies of the night. No wonder it offered the high-tech fantasy makeover. I began to suspect the guest programmed his fantasy tart into the process. The lights in here should have been tinted red, but they, too, were green, as was anything reflected by the mirror.

I twisted to view the back of my gown . . . gorgeous bias-cut green satin folds, tight through the torso and flaring into a mermaid skirt with a train. Yup, cut down to rear cleavage, which was accented with a rhinestone pin in a peacock tail design. How ironic that Snow fixated on bare white backs when his own was now hash, thanks to me. If he indeed bore no marks, the only way I'd find out would be with a rematch.

Speaking of marks . . . I lifted the heavy waves of unbraided hair off my neck, but no matter which way I turned and twisted, I could just barely glimpse Ric's love bruise.

Well, look at you wearing a fairly fresh new skank tattoo yourself.

Dry up, Irma, I thought.

And then I turned to face myself in the mirror. I hadn't heard Irma. "Lilith" stared back at me.

I knew her because she wasn't a mirror image. She wore low-rise jeans that underlined an "outie" belly button, pierced by a familiar blue topaz stud, whereas mine was an "innie."

That kind of summed up our opposing personalities, but we actually differed in this minor way? I'd assumed we were identical in everything physical, for some reason.

"Here you are," Lilith went on, "back in Wichita, living it up in the 'whale' suite. Watching boring old movies. Riding our old friend Snow hard and putting him up wet. I love it."

"That's between him and me," I said. "Or maybe you are."

"Nope, I never got even one orgasmic shiver out of Ice Prick. I guess he likes using you better."

"Why are you here again? Oh. Maybe it's the current theme. Wicked Witch green. A little envy going on, Lilith?"

"What you don't know, Delilah, would fill a chasm."

"You know I saw your Wichita police mug shots. You got me in trouble here years ago. You were acting out and showing up on *my* record."

"I freaked out after that gross incident you know about now. I guess subconsciously I was trying to make Wichita too hot to hold me so I had to leave eventually. You sure weren't going to bust out."

She made a face. "I didn't know we were, like, the Corsican twins until that happened."

My mind did another rapid vintage movie rerun. *The Corsican Brothers* were guys, obviously, separated at birth, but they found each again because they felt each other's pain.

"Home run, kid," Lilith said, as the reference registered on my face. "I couldn't stick around and wait for you to turn bean-grinder and smell the Starbucks." Lilith sounded guilty anyway. "That ugly doctor stuff drove me to act out . . . and finally move on. I hitched all the way to the Sunshine State to find Mother Dearest, though it turns out she didn't want either of us."

"We have a mother?"

"Most people do, even us."

"Where is she? Oh." I remembered the *La Vida Loca* checks sent to Our Lady of the Lake. "*Corona,* California?"

Lilith shrugged tattooed shoulders. The designs weren't pretty, just blots of dark ink. She looked hollow-eyed and gaunt and too indifferent to really be that way.

"Lil . . . are you all right?"

"Right as acid rain," she answered bitterly, looking toward the ceiling and rolling heavenly blue-green eyes emphasized by seriously smoked-out eyeliner. "Watch your back, Dee. There's more than Snow with a hard-on for it. Some very bad supers are on our tails and in our future. Okay?"

She winked out like a night-light with a dead battery.

MY STREET CLOTHES, the unexciting navy suit, hung from a hook. On the malachite sink counter lay a set of mint-hued French underwear and a Red Carpet–level emerald-green metallic gift bag I couldn't resist exploring.

Immediately, a sinuous chill whipped up my spine and down my arm to cuff my right wrist in a circle of "eyes" from the peacock tail pin. It was so heavy it slipped down my hand a little and into the top of the bag. Apparently the familiar was as curious as I was.

I pulled out green crystal bottles of beauty potions, even some old-time Emeraude perfume, green silk designer scarves, and emerald baubles inset in thick wrist cuffs.

I left all that heavy stuff out on the counter, but slipped out of the gown and let it coil into the empty bag. No way was I leaving another evening dress behind for Snow to send me later with an enclosed lock of his insidious silken white hair. I did *not* need twin familiars.

My underwear had melted off, so I donned the skimpy French stuff and my suit skirt and jacket as fast as I could. Only then did I glance down to the green carpet and spot the only red thing in the room.

The ruby slippers.

I bent to elevate them into the light from the overhead absinthe-colored chandelier bulbs. Up too close the combined red and green made them look black, reminding me of a nightmare, me standing on the yellow brick road in glittering funeral-black pumps.

At least these weren't modern, rhinestone-slathered, strappy hooker spikes.

They were the real Oz, sweet, kitten-heeled, closed-toe pumps glittering with sequins, with a plump formal bow tie on the toes. I clutched them to my chest and closed my eyes. Maybe the makeover machinery, possibly a blend of technology and magic like CinSims, had tapped my subconscious too.

If only I'd had the power to click my heels and bow out of all my early years in Wichita. Or maybe they'd made me what I'd become, for better as well as worse. I sat on the closed commode and did an examination of conscience. I hadn't been to confession in years, but old school habits linger.

What had just happened here? How had I gone from a defensively fierce virgin to playing groupie to a rock star? I dredged up the usual mixed bag of motives, outside influences, and fears.

Guilt led the parade, of course. And pride.

When I'd accepted Snow's Brimstone Kiss under duress to save Ric's life, I'd expected to "suffer" the multiple orgasms that had sent his mosh-pit groupies on fruitless quests for another kiss that would never come. My emotions were in overdrive. I was frantic about wasting time in rushing to Ric's rescue, infuriated about being blackmailed into a sexual situation, loathing Snow and myself, terrified I would lose my free will and become a mindless sex addict. And, face it, Lilith would tell me if she hadn't split: I'd always felt his sexual charisma as much as the most deluded groupie.

Afterward, for all those reasons, I couldn't bear to think of the incident, but maybe I should have. I was a trained observer, after all. Maybe in all the drama, I'd missed something vital. My mind had resisted going back there, but when I did, I realized I'd been a pretty inattentive witness, what with expecting to lose my soul and freedom and all.

Snow had prolonged that "one only" Brimstone Kiss into seductive minutes of a sensual battle of wills. To my eternal relief, I didn't experience even one orgasm, but I was so keyed up about what *might* happen that his sexual force did put me into a dreamy, erotic fog. Wincing, I recalled enough body contact to have a referee blow the whistle on it.

I knew Snow had expected something from the whole charade, for me either to succumb or totally resist, but I'd done neither. I *had* been so languidly out of it for a time that he'd been able to brush my mouth across his erotic zones like I was a blow-up doll.

I pressed the tops of my hands to cheeks flaming with fever at the returning memory picture and my self-disgust. Talk about zombies. I'd almost gone down on the world's sexiest rock star. Missed it by *that much*.

Usually, my mind fast-forwarded past humiliating moments. Now I slowed down the scene. He'd upheld me as I'd been sinking down to the floor in a swoon, letting my ebbing mouth slide against his body in a long, semi-conscious kiss, holding me almost . . . tenderly. As if *he* needed my kiss far more than I'd needed his.

I'd berated Snow once for not having the decency to ever sleep with his groupies even while he addicted them to an impossibly rewarding kiss. I'd found that sadistic, but maybe he was celibate, *had* to be celibate, for a long, long time, as I was beginning to suspect. And I was the only one . . .

Down with the ego, girl, Irma objected. *He's no Sleeping Beauty, just a lech who kissed you semiconscious and copped a serial feel.*

And I was just an impulsive idiot who'd thought I could duel superstar charisma and win.

So . . . HOPING TO slink out of the suite, I grabbed the bag holding the gown and shoes and reentered the hall, eyes on the dead-ahead double exit doors.

Curses! Snow appeared, string tie gone and shirt collar open to reveal and even frame the scarlet oval my mouth had burned into his albino throat. Instant contrition. I wanted that undone.

"Ice would bring the redness down," I suggested.

An onstage-style head-toss made his ice-white hair shimmer as Snow smiled down at me. Those Western boot heels made him even more larger-than-life.

"Why would you think I'd want to bring the redness down, Delilah? It amps up my rock-star image to flaunt the evidence that some hot skank has just been at me."

"Snow, you kill me. Everything I come up with— Albino Vampire cocktails, sensual tattoos—you turn them to your commercial advantage."

"Why not? You're not a scared, damaged little girl anymore. You're a serious and seriously sexy woman. And you've amped up the stakes on that too, Delilah, now that you're living up to your name. You *liked* taunting me by planting a passion bruise dead center on my throat. You *like* seeing it there now. You *like* secretly knowing you're the one who put that bold brand on rock-star me."

"The one?" I asked, suspicious again that he, at least, believed in fate.

His hand cupped my head to bring my lips to his throat once more. That resonant stage voice whispered into the hair above my ear, but I could feel his words vibrate on my lips as his other hand swept the rippling hair up from my neck.

He knew just how to cast his erotic spell on me. I felt I was in his protective custody, cherished and challenged, terrified and thrilled.

"I doubt you care to look too much in a mirror probably

crowded with ghosts right now, Delilah," he whispered, "but if you could see, I've bared the lovely white nape of your neck to reveal a ripe purple passion bruise like the one you laid on me just now."

His cold white lips brushed the spot and I felt the touch as an electric jolt at the pit of my womb. His lips continued moving around my neck to my jawline, murmuring all the while.

"You'll be surprised to know I think Montoya is a damn good influence, maybe the last positive force left in Vegas. He's a first-class crime fighter and, obviously, a hot-blooded but discreet lover. I know you two share true love and our little tangos are just an entertaining power play between what's left of the guilty girl in you and . . ."

His lips were almost on mine. Could the Brimstone Kiss still exist?

". . . whatever you think I am.

"But we liked it, Delilah, and will again," he said, releasing me gently. "And that you can't change. Grizelle tells me I've taken three hundred and twenty-two separate lash welts on my back because of you. Now that I've seen what you can do for my front, I look forward to your healing every stripe on my back."

I fell back on my old friend, sass.

"This was a one-off, Snow. Maybe you can *hope* for a freebie, *if* you give me the information in future I need to do my job. Tit for tat."

"Which will be my pleasure."

And it had been.

I stared at him, trying to clear my head and emotions. Grizelle had charged me with "stealing" the Brimstone Kiss from Snow, and maybe I had, in a way. Snow's pre-existing chest scar tissue certainly was sensitive to the aphrodisiac effect of my healing kisses. I didn't know if I could heal the three-hundred-some new scars he claimed because of me, but I knew now I couldn't do it without giving him three-hundred-some orgasms.

Once had been "bad" enough and could be called "prideful penitence." Any more would be outright infidelity and too much "Hollywood Madam" to stomach. Yet it had soothed my outraged soul to take as complete sexual control of him as he had of me.

You crazy, mixed-up minx, Irma lectured. *Who knew you had it in you? I gotta admit that parting touch on the throat, over his very voice box, was genius. You won this one. So publicly intimate. Yum. His groupies will swoon and they'll be dying to know Who.*

I don't approve of that sort of thing, I told her stiffly. And thank you for not using "the word." He can hide the mark with that pink-diamond-studded collar he wears onstage. Any trace will fade soon anyway.

Yeah, but we *know. And* he *knows.*

I'm in love with Ric.

Yeah, me too. But you can't help that you had unfinished business with Snow the minute you met him. That's karma, kid. It's not like Ric waited around twenty-four years for you. And, as the politicians say over and over again for the stupid media who never seem to get it . . . foreplay doesn't count, just like the calories in chocolate don't. Free pass.

I didn't believe in free passes. I guess *that* was my religion.

"A word of warning before you leave," Snow said in the all-too-uncomfortable present now.

He turned me to face the bathroom mirror through the open door, despite the possibility of ghosts. My usually colorless cheeks were as flushed as the intensifying bruise on his throat. I looked guilty. He just looked hotter.

"The Brimstone Kiss is more powerful than even I knew," Snow said. "Be careful whom you kiss from now on, Delilah Street, how hard and where. Be careful whom you let kiss you, how hard and where.

"Bruise, but don't bite or be bitten. That's not a bad motto for handling whatever the whole damn Millennium Revelation throws your way."

Chapter Twenty-six

GOING DOWN IN the speeding elevator, I pondered the fact that I'd grown up twenty to fifty miles from The Most Wanted Vintage Film in the World.

I'd expected it to be found, if ever, in someplace exotic like Rio, but Augusta, just outside Wichita, Kansas?

Umhmm, Irma agreed. *I wouldn't expect you to practically lay Snow in Wichita, either. You sure got hyper once you resolved your supine position issues.*

We have some kind of weird power struggle going, I told her. Seeing *Metropolis* was a teensy overexciting, and so was seeing that silver metal superwoman, even if the plot destroyed her at the end. They always do that to independent women.

I hugged the glitzy green bag to my navy chest. Snow obviously couldn't be trusted around me when I was wearing vintage evening gowns. His problem. And then . . . getting my very own ruby red slippers.

You are so typical of the modern female's bad media image, Irma huffed. *You want it all. Sex, power, rock 'n' roll, and girly accessories.*

Even as I savored the recent, unexpected triumphs, reality was starting to drop over me like a gray wool cloak of conscience, a descending storm cloud of regret. I'd been up in La-la Munchkinland, carried away by the Emerald City makeover.

This was not an episode I could explain to Ric. Or

mention to Ric, although Snow had given him some major compliments. I let myself bask in those positives. Even Snow had called Ric my "true love." Why, then, had he let me . . . goaded me . . . seduced me . . . into, ah, behaving badly? And, what was worse, predicted more of the same?

Time to stow the self-reflection and get back to what was happening on ground level. Were the boys having any luck tracking El Demonio from WTCH? Did I want them to? He was the Boss of Bosses now and mucho bad medicine.

The elevator opened on the ground floor and I strode out, the green foil bag swinging from my hand.

Somebody grabbed that wrist and swung me around by it.

"Not so fast, *puta*."

Puta? Maybe a bit misguided sometimes, but hardly a prostitute.

As my attacker swung, I swung. My free hand, now accessorized at the wrist by a sawtooth silver cuff, slashed open his cheekbone.

The man dropped my wrist to stanch the flood of blood, so I skittered down the yellow brick road for the safety of Ben Hassard's office, only realizing as I crashed through the slightly open door that it was Siege Central.

By the look of the unwelcome guests, I was back at the Cold Creek Drive-in Midnight Horror Show.

A metal-collared chupacabra on a chain dragged its spined tail back and forth over the floor in one corner, its red eyes gleaming in defiance of the Emerald City's all-green ambiance.

Ben Hassard slumped in his desk chair, his limbs bound to it by silver duct tape, a beaten, bloody parody of himself.

Meanwhile, a group of squat, amphibian-faced men with pitted skin and totally black eyes prowled his office, every knuckle on their pudgy hands scraped bloody, their mustachioed upper lips lifting in almost a communal hiss as they spied me.

Certainly they weren't zombies or any other unhumans, but they were even worse. I'd seen this subhuman type on TV and internet news sites being taken away by small armies of international law enforcement. These were the terrifying drug cartel musclemen, the men who prefaced hits with unimaginable tortures, offed whole innocent families, and killed by gruesome beheadings and acid baths.

They were all looking at me now.

Freshhhhh meat, Irma echoed my fears.

I immediately adapted my modestly high heels to a useless bimbo-spike stutter and ran into the danger instead of away. Time to embrace Dumb Blonde Gringa mode.

"Oh, gosh, Ben," I breathed. "Am I interrupting an important business meeting? So sorry."

All he could do was cough up blood, which I appeared to be too ditsy to see.

"Say, Ben. Got a minute? Here are some goodies from upstairs. Everything looks good to go for the hotel opening." I gazed around, blinking vacantly. "So these guys here are the new security crew masquerading as bellboys and parking valets? Wow. They really set the tone. Speaking of 'tone,' I left my phone with all my listed shopping destinations in here."

I scooped up my cell phone from the desk.

On I babbled. "And, Bensy, you *promised, promised, promised* to have this phone covered in Austrian crystals at the hotel shopping promenade by now." Stamp of klutzy pump heel as I dumped the bag under a guest chair. I cradled the phone to my cheek and eyed the screen. "I'm so disappointed."

A text message from Ric read "W. Goose chase. Back ASAP."

"Look, this stupid phone won't even work," I whined, punching my fingernails against the phone screen's keyboard like a demented typist. I managed to get off "Prisoners at EC" before one of the Reptilian Guard smacked the cell phone out of my hand to the floor.

I blinked at them, mainly because they didn't seem able to.

"Twist-tie the stupid bitch," my abrupt personal phone operator barked.

Two of the poisonous toads jumped me. I resisted taking a bow before I was smashed to the floor with my wrists and ankles bound by wire cable.

"Now," said one of the thugs, circling Ben. "You're gonna tell us who got the Augusta Theater goods the boss wanted."

The film? *Metropolis?* These bozos were after the film? Why?

Ben's unresponsive eyes had rolled up in his head like a saint's ascending to Heaven. I hoped he was just unconscious, not dead.

Half of me wanted to sic these creeps on the penthouse suite, where Snow was alone and rapt in his landmark film and maybe the . . . aftermath of me. Serve him right. I also suspected Snow could unleash some nasty containment spell on them. My other half knew that my quota of guilt over Snow was full up for the moment.

So, only I could get Ben and me out of this murderous

mess. To do that, I had to unravel why Torbellino wanted or needed the *Metropolis* film more than Snow.

What would link Ric and his ancient enemy, El Demonio, to a rare film now bound to become an unbeatable attraction for Snow's Vegas empire?

Besides me?

UNFORTUNATELY, A FEMALE presence did not encourage the drug cartel thugs to restrain themselves.

Their flaunted lighters and straight razors, though, could only produce bloody gurgles from Ben Hassard. These minions were too stupidly brutal to get any answers that would satisfy their absent boss. So, they were primed to commit mass slaughter to take their minds off El Demonio's reaction to their failure. I didn't want Ben to die.

I had few options, but at least I was being ignored. I'd be safe until they decided to off witnesses, or play games with the helpless girl. I really had nothing to lose here but time to act.

So, I baaed softly. *Baaaa-maaa.*

Call me goat-girl.

The chained chupacabra in the corner perked up.

My, what a multibreed beastie it was seen close-up, a little like Barney the purple dinosaur if one wanted to put a soft and cuddly spin on it. The leathery gray-green skin and the quills defining its spine and tail gave it a lizard-like quality, and its blunt-snouted and fanged face flaunted a black forked tongue. Every exhalation broadcast the reek of sulfur. Too many bean burritos for lunch? Or was "dragon" a part of its pedigree? I gathered it would eat me rather than fry me long-distance. Chupacabras were notorious for draining the blood of goats, and I was certainly tied up like a Judas one.

I'm a versatile chick. I puckered my lips and made sucking noises. Snow one hour, a chupacabra the next. Dolly and I have dual exhausts and aim to please. *Come on, Chupie,* come to *maaa-maaa.*

I saw the creature make a mighty lunge forward, straining the chain.

Behind me, Ben Hassard was groaning unintelligibly.

Bastards!

My low-key *baas* only spoke Chupacabra and I repeated them mindlessly, until the creature broke loose with a snap of its chain and a weird baying sound.

That's when I rolled under the knee hole in Hassard's desk, pushing his chair toward the back wall, hearing the unleashed monster behind me pinning the first responders in his path and sucking their blood with mucho gusto . . . *a Dios,* El Demonio's henchmen. . . .

My silver familiar shifted into a workman's switchblade—an X-Acto knife. In my fingers the heavy blade sawed through my wire wrist and ankle bindings.

Still curled in the shelter of the desk's knee hole, I managed to grab the star-shaped rays of Ben's desk chair base and spin it like a lazy Susan until his duct-taped ankles came my way. An X-Acto knife would mangle the rubbery tape. The familiar morphed into heavy pinking shears and snapped its edged jaws right through.

By the time I dragged myself up to look over the desk, the once-captive chupacabra was ranging free and dining on drug cartel muscle. Literally. Its fangs pierced major arteries in their fat-solidified bodies as its black tongue sucked up the pooling blood like a straw.

The familiar was just chomping off the bonds on Hassard's wrists when the outside glass window shattered. Quicksilver leaped through to knock down the last retreating thug and run to me, leaving the downed man for the oncoming chupacabra.

I grabbed Quick's collar.

An instant later, Ric waded through the shards of broken glass to sweep us both to the back wall while Tallgrass edged around chupacabra and victim to pull Ben Hassard's rolling desk chair back to our defensive position.

The chupacabra celebrated its freedom by draining every last drop it could from the last downed thug. With loud, impolite slurping sounds.

The three conscious men, dog, and I panted in exhaustion against a wall.

Chupie straightened to scan red carnivore eyes in our direction. And burped. Full. Slowly, it waddled to the broken glass panel to make its way into the night.

"I'm glad El Chupacabra drank its fill of El Demonio leavings," Tallgrass said.

He was bending over his friend, stanching the mass of bloody wounds with strips from Ben's tattered white shirt.

"We need to get him to Emergency," Tallgrass said.

Meanwhile, Quicksilver had thrust his big wet black nose between Tallgrass's hands and Ben's bloodied chest.

"Away!" Tallgrass's angry frown turned ferocious.

Quicksilver returned a deep, rumbling growl and burrowed his nose even closer to Ben.

"Woman, get your dog off me," Tallgrass ordered.

"Get your hands off Ben," I ordered back. "He doesn't need EMTs. Don't you sense it? He needs Quicksilver."

Tallgrass lifted an elbow to shove Quicksilver away. I instinctively moved to protect the dog. Laughable, yes, but no one raised a hand to Quicksilver while I was around.

Ric's forearm slashed out of nowhere to meet and stop Tallgrass's blow. The gaze he directed at the older man was even more powerful. I saw the night's events had jolted out the contact lens and Ric's silver eye was fully obvious . . . and fully potent.

"Let the dog do his work, *amigo*," Ric said. "He knows what he's doing."

Whether he responded to Ric's authoritative look, sound, and action . . . or the gaze of his altered eye, Tallgrass visibly lassoed his rampaging emotions. He pulled back, holding up a leathery palm, a gesture calming himself as much as Ric, me, and Quicksilver.

Quick had not waited for human resolution. He was hunched over Hassard in chupacabra-over-a-victim fashion, licking the bloody shirt fabric like it was a tasty vanilla wafer atop a scoop of after-dinner ice cream.

Hassard moaned and turned his pulpy features out of a horror movie toward Quicksilver's busy muzzle. The dog's tongue swiped the man's face, leaving swaths of clean, unmutilated skin behind.

A deep breath relaxed Tallgrass's bunched shoulder muscles. "Oh, *Ty-ohni*, forgive me," he whispered.

"They tortured Ben for information," I explained. "Superficial wounds were the most hurtful. They didn't want to kill him."

"I knew that, Miss Delilah," Tallgrass said, "and I saw the noble Wolf in your Quicksilver. I just didn't know that your 'dog' had a shaman's healing power."

"He had no way to tell you," I answered.

"Shamans are not used to explaining themselves," Tallgrass said. "It is up to us humans to be humble and trust. My fear for Ben overcame my instincts. I apologize." He looked at me. "You have a healing power as well, don't you? But it is"—his stone-faced expression crumbled—"tied to things this old Indian has no business inquiring into. As for my *amigo,* Ricardo . . . I don't know what to make of you at all."

Ric slapped the man on the forearm.

"Forget the mystical stuff, Tallgrass. That made for tales around campfires on our stakeouts, but we have dead cartel muscle here and the attack at the Augusta Theater to figure out. Also, where that damned El Demonio is and what he wants so badly he'll expose the long-reaching tendrils of his drug operation."

"What about the Augusta?" I asked.

"Quicksilver tracked El Demonio's car to the theater parking lot," Ric explained. "Tallgrass and I went in to question the staff, and they were acting like . . . zombies."

"Real zombies?"

"That came later. No, they were just intimidated people who'd been roughly interrogated. Turned out some invading mob types were after certain old movie reels one of their sponsors found in the debris in the theater basement and took away to examine on his own."

"One of their 'sponsors,' " I repeated.

Ric's grimace confirmed my guess. "Right. Tallgrass's pal Ben Hassard. We decided to come back here to figure out what was so damn precious in those old film reels, but when we tried to leave, we discovered the parking lot was being watched."

"El Demonio's men."

"We should have been so lucky." Ric eyed the carnage on the office floor. "No, his henchmen were all here already 'interrogating' Hassard. El Demonio had left some other forces at the theater."

"Zombies," I guessed. "How'd you get away?"

"This is crazy, but with the practice Quicksilver and I got repulsing zombies at the Cold Creek Drive-in, we did okay." Ric lowered his voice. "I lost my contact lens, deliberately, and found I could, ah, use it to polish up the silver discs on Quicksilver's collar. I could focus and then bounce the . . . effect. It's the weirdest thing, Del. It's like I can dowse for the dead with my silver eye now. I can find them, raise them, or—since we've encountered some really rapacious ones—suck the undead life out of them. Don't tell Tallgrass. He thinks we just fought hard and got lucky and had a dog with a mystical amount of wolf in him on our side."

I didn't know what to make of Ric's account any more than Tallgrass had.

Mulling it all over, I watched as Quicksilver stepped back to lick his big paws and start swabbing his nose and mouth blood-free. Ben struggled to a sitting position, his hands wiping his unhurt face and running over his equally sound arms and chest.

"It's a miracle," he said. "I dreamed I was in the hands of devils with their hellfire pitchforks and then I was touched by an angel with the most beautiful blue eyes in all of heaven." He gazed at me like a freshman nerd meeting a prom queen.

I was not about to tell Ben his real "angel" needed a major shave and a claw-cut.

"What did those devils want?" Ric asked, using the dazed man's terms of reference.

"Some old film cans that were found in the basement of the Augusta Theater during renovation."

"Why would you know right away about what was found there?" I asked.

"I underwrote most of the Augusta Theater restoration. Having another tourist attraction nearby would enhance the Wicked Wild West concept. My backers and I planned to rope in Dodge City's tourist exhibitions too, make it into an auto-tour ending at Emerald City. You know, from fantastic Kansas history to extraordinary Kansas fantasy. Saloon shoot-outs to a genuine restored movie palace to the biggest Kansas-set move of all time."

"Ben," I said, sort of gently, but not too. "I know what was found in the Augusta's basement, and that you realized its value and skedaddled with it to someone who could get you the CinSims you so desperately needed for the Emerald City."

Tallgrass watched his friend like an outraged hawk. "You stole something from the civic restoration project? Something valuable?"

Ben shrugged unhappily, still rubbing his restored arms and shoulders. "It was just an old film, Tallgrass. I needed something new for the Emerald City, something modern like the bigwigs in Vegas have. CinSims."

"Those animated celebrities?" Tallgrass asked with disdain. "We could do that with a wax museum and animatronics."

Ben shook his head. "Last century, Tallgrass."

"So you found a big-time buyer?" Ric asked.

"No. That was the beauty of it. He found me. The bigwig was a cinema freak. Showed up. Knew about the old film being found somehow. Already had the perfect CinSims, the *only* ones available for Emerald City. We made the deal and everyone was happy as clams. Hundreds of thousands of clams."

"You were cheating the theater restoration project of the proceeds of its property," Tallgrass said.

"I donated plenty to them," Ben said, quivering at his friend's anger. "More than they know what to do with. I tell you, everyone was happy."

A moment later, a sizzling bolt of lightning shivered down from high above Emerald City.

"Somebody up there sure isn't," I said.

Outside the complex, thunder cracked its muscles, strained its sinews to the breaking point, and strode the sky to break its back again and again.

Earth below buckled.

Emerald City towers above trembled.

Inside the massive construction, we mere humans were gripped by the oldest gods, caught tight in the fists of thunder and fixed in the fierce eyes of the lightning.

Ric's arm clasped me tight. He whispered in my ear. "El Demonio has failed to find this film on two fronts, at the Augusta Theater and in breaking down Ben Hassard. He's not done. I'm afraid he's loosed his local accomplices, the weather witches, on Emerald City and us. I think they're a bigger force here than we guessed. I'm sorry, Del."

"I'm sorrier," I was able to shout back into the wind. "Weather witches? Like Sheena at WTCH?"

"More than one TV weather girl is behind effects like this," Tallgrass huffed in a basso fury. "Wichita has had an entire secret coven of weather witches going back long before the Millennium Revelation, which only empowered them more. They can blackmail and they can be bought. They've provided weather cover for El Demonio's drug drives. Now that his thugs are chupacabra meat and Ric and Quicksilver scorched a crew of his zombies to ashes, he's bought or forced the weather witches to bring us to our knees until he has what he wants. I can't believe this is all for a few thousand feet of old film footage."

Neither could I. Something much bigger must be at stake.

"I'm sorry," I murmured, knowing no one could hear me.

Snow's Fortress of Solitude was about to be shattered anyway, by . . . weather witches and . . . me.

Chapter Twenty-seven

BEFORE I COULD corral my scattered thoughts or solve the whole mess or say a word, another crisis invaded the blood-and-body-strewn office.

"Chickens?" Ric demanded as a black-and-white flock flooded the floor with panicked clucking and fluttering wings. "This is insane."

By then the *Wizard of Oz* CinSims were all homing on Ben Hassard's office like pigeons caught flying in the midst of a Manhattan ticker-tape parade.

"We've got to get to a storm cellar," Hunk, the future Straw Man, said, appearing at my side to grab my arm. "Come along, Dorothy. Forget the dog."

What I'd forgotten was that my hair, after the Emerald City makeover treatment, flowed in black waves to my shoulders, as Dorothy Gale's had after the film's EC makeover scene. I'd also forgotten that my hair was so dark and my skin so white I looked like a ready-made CinSim with colorized blue eyes.

The CinSim Toto skittered past my ankles and I chased him, wishing for a basket.

"Storm cellar?" Tallgrass speculated to Ric. "The hotel must have lower levels."

"I spotted a service door on the way in from the parking lot," Ric answered. "Just outside this office wing."

"There must be one inside as well," Tallgrass said. *"Ty-ohni,"* he ordered. "Hunt."

"Wait!" I cried, appalled to see Quicksilver bound away into the earth-shaking chaos outside the office area on another person's orders. *"Leave kitty!"* I screamed.

"Leave the dog, Dorothy!"

Strong, callused hands held my forearms prisoner. The hands of . . . farmworkers. The other two Gale farm workmen were not about to let "Dorothy" run out into the storm. Hickory, the Tin Man, and Zeke, the Cowardly Lion, had already shooed Uncle Henry and Auntie Em toward Ric and Tallgrass.

"Come on," Ric said, pulling Hickory and Zeke off me. "I'll take care of Dorothy. You boys get the old folks."

When Quicksilver barked from just down the hall, we herded the party to the door marked MECHANICS he'd found.

Those *Wizard of Oz* CinSims were a loyal and determined bunch, but after a small taste of running around at large in Emerald City they weren't too pleased to be jammed back in the basement.

Hickory tried to grab me again and take me with the CinSims, but I slipped from his custody as Tallgrass pushed him into the stairwell and slammed the metal security door with its exterior lock shut.

I breathed a sigh the strength of a snow-globe tornado. *The Wizard of Oz* was as much about hands, head, and heart as *Metropolis*. My hands, head, and heart were happy to have all the Kansas farmyard folk and critter CinSims tucked away in the Emerald City's high-tech sub-basements. They'd have lots of room to roam, although the chickens and pigs and horses could be seen ranging through the outer offices in confusion.

Then my panicked Scarecrow brain got ticking again.

Where was Dorothy? And Toto? And Professor Marvel?

And, most of all, where the hell was Almira Gulch?

"Is everybody unreal we can get our hands on stowed safely below?" Tallgrass asked.

"Some major players are still out and about," I admitted, "but the same thing happened to them in the opening scenes of the movie, so we can't expect to totally override their conditioning."

Tallgrass frowned at me. "You Vegas people live in a fantasy world, don't you?"

I nodded.

"So do we Plains people," his confidential rasp whispered. "Millennium Revelation," he pronounced with a Quicksilver-worthy snort. "Not new to us. My people and your people may yet save Wichita, and all our asses.

"All right, 'Dorothy.' You're the white man's lucky charm, but clearly also the key to the entire puzzle we're all facing now, filmed and real, past and present.

"You take us on that corny yellow brick road to the heart of Wichita, Emerald City edition. Got it? How are you going to do that?"

How could I ever explain Snow to Leonard Tallgrass? Maybe as a . . . wizard. Or a shaman. How would I ever explain to Snow why everyone in our ragtag party and everything evil in Wichita seemed to have a serious stake in his prize vintage movie? I sure didn't know.

"Well?" Tallgrass prodded me.

"I'm going to come clean and take us all to the top of Emerald City to see a man about a movie."

RIC AND TALLGRASS, Quicksilver and I, stepped out of the shuddering elevator shaft and onto the penthouse floor to feel the tower itself shimmy and the very height make us shiver like wind chimes.

Snow was there to greet us, a commanding figure reminiscent of a CinSim ghost.

"What took you so long?" he asked our survival party. "The view here is spectacular, not to mention strategic. Let me show you."

Tallgrass looked him up and down . . . and up and down again. "You are Ben's Las Vegas bigwig."

"It's not a wig," Snow said. "I wear my hair long."

"A noble tradition, if a trifle old-fashioned," Tallgrass said. "Ric? What do you know of this person Ben calls Christopher?"

"Christophe. It's French. He's a Vegas bigwig, all right, and a man of many names," Ric replied. "I don't know if he can be trusted for the long run, but if he has interests at stake that mirror ours, he'll be prepared to indulge in mutual using."

"I don't renege on deals," Snow said. "And nobody takes what's mine."

"Ah." Tallgrass nodded. "My people have heard that first lie from the white man, but we endorse the second claim. You'll have to prove your honorable intentions."

Thank goodness no one had asked *me* to recommend Snow.

At my side, Quicksilver whined. I believe the major position he meant to convey was impatience.

Snow led our party onto the open-air balcony that surrounded the highest residence Emerald City had to offer. The evening air had that heavy, sullen stillness that promised a major storm was about to break loose. A fully three-quarter moon hung like a leaky football in an unclouded bit of night sky.

We all adopted Tallgrass's signature squint as we stared out over green and gold rolling Kansas fields shivering in the rising wind. Everything was colored the sick char-treuse color the landscape took on before a major storm. It was like looking through a glass of absinthe.

An out-of-season blue-black front of storm clouds was rolling in from the northwest. Kansans knew that cloud cover for a raging monster spawned on the flanks of the Colorado Rockies, whose howling high winds would lash the land with icy cold and snow. They called it a "blue norther."

Snow held out a pointing forefinger, his long white hair flowing back in the wind, making him resemble the monu-mental Crazy Horse statue carved from the Black Hills of South Dakota.

"There are three attack positions," Snow said. "To the south, west, and north."

I leaned over the balcony to watch heat lightning flirt with a familiar broadcast tower.

"WTCH is to the west," I pointed out.

Ric held me to anchor us against the driving wind. "The drug cartel's cattle-drive path runs south to north."

"And that unholy traffic that destroys the earth and its beings has roused the gods of my people," Tallgrass said. "From the north comes the Wendigo. That's where the zombies drive the drug-laden cattle for slaughter. Wen-digo is a giant evil spirit, a starving cannibal who dines on the greedy and devours them all. El Demonio's enter-prise is a desecration deserving of death, and that res-titution will come, no matter if we stand in its path, no matter what we do."

A monstrous conjunction of elements was assembling on the verdant stage of Kansas that night, no doubt. I stud-ied the scene.

Lightning was building around three towers. Emerald

City was the highest, and the most obvious target. Next highest was the broadcast tower to the west, WTCH-TV. Alma mater.

Speaking of my actual alma mater, I looked to the unmentioned east. The spire of a church was catching jagged lightning bolts. Was the lightning rod atop it cast in the figure of a gargoyle? Or a dragon?

"We have enemies converging from all four points of the compass?" Ric asked, noticing the direction of my gaze.

"Not really," I said. "The east is an ally under fire, Our Lady of the Lake."

"Why?" Ric asked. "What did we do?"

"Got what somebody else wants first," Snow answered.

Ric stared at him for a long, hard moment. I feared he would take Snow's comment personally, or Snow would mention Ric's new silver eye.

Neither spoke.

Tallgrass broke the silence. "What *more* does El Demonio want? His band of bad men and their dead minions have been invading Wichita for years, like a blood tide seeping up from the Mexican border killings. Now everything evil is drawn to these fantastical towers on which we stand."

"I'm no military historian," Ric said, "but if you're the center of a three-pronged attack, you need to snap one leg out from under the triad."

"Quicksilver and I will take out the west," I volunteered.

"No, Delilah." Ric tightened his grip on me. "It's insane to go out into the teeth of that oncoming physical and mystical storm. Stay."

I looked over the lurid green-lit landscape that still

resembled a Fanny Farmer deluxe box of mint and chocolate squares, with caramel drizzles on top. Wheat and corn
and molasses and apple pie. Kansas farmland, as it had
always been. I measured the blue-black tornado twisting
Emerald City way and the lightning bolts flash-dancing
around Our Lady of the Lake's spire and the WTCH
broadcast tower.

I saw the snarling face of Tallgrass's terrifying Wendigo in the oncoming blue norther.

And I was supposed to be scared of Sheena Coleman?

Weather witches were the weakest link in the forces
arrayed against us, but one of them controlled the highest
tower. Besides, it'd be a pleasure to take out the witch that
blew down my house.

Who's a storm chaser?

Ace reporter, that's who.

"I have an issue with the station's lousy weather witch,
and Dolly's horses know the way," I told everyone and no
one in particular. I didn't want to cross any glance that
could stop me. "We'll shut down that broadcast tower and
be back in no time. Quicksilver! Time to do your job."

I slipped Ric a crooked smile and didn't look back,
although I heard him being forcibly restrained, probably
by Leonard Tallgrass.

Quick and I zipped into the open elevator and hit "M"
as in "Main." We had sixty-some stories to plummet down
and a bunch of flatland to cross.

You can't take me out into this monster storm with you,
Irma objected. *It's murder.*

Eh. Murder-suicide, technically, I told her. I'm not
being heroic and I'm not being stupid. Do the math.

I'd figured out the best use of personnel. Tallgrass had
to remain at Emerald City to protect his tribe's investment

and deal with its oncoming cannibal vengeance god. The
Wendigo sounded like another Lord of the Slaughter, a
Shezmou with bear teeth, the power of all the earth's winds
at his back, and really bad breath. Nasty.

Snow had led the rescue party for Ric and produced a
dragon to do it. I was pretty sure he'd come up with something spectacular to save the newest lynchpin of his Vegas
empire, not to his mention his albino skin and the ordinary
hides of everyone around him. And me, probably. Now that
he knew what I could do for him, he'd want the satisfaction
of forcing or tricking me into healing those whip welts I'd
accidentally bequeathed to him in my uniquely soothing
way.

What about our beloved Ric? Irma wailed.

Snow saved him before and he will again, I told her.
Ric's too vital to some part of this puzzle. Snow will save
Ric and me . . . us, just for my future crawling potential.

What about El Demonio and his zombie army?

That I don't know. Ric may have to settle that score all
by himself.

Irma went silent as the elevator reached the main
floor. Quicksilver and I picked our way through the fallen
corpses of El Demonio's thugs. True, I had tricked the chupacabra into becoming my hit man, but in the ghoul-eat-
ghoul world of the Millennium Revelation, it wasn't how
you got things done, but *that* you did.

Outside, litter skidded across the deserted Emerald
City parking lot like skeletal fingers playing the "Devil's
Waltz" on an asphalt keyboard. The temperature outside at
ground level, including wind chill, had dropped to a blood-
freezing forty degrees.

There was no point in putting Dolly's top up.

The wind would just rip it off.

Quicksilver leaped in the front passenger seat with a shit-eating grin.

"You have been just *waiting* to ride shotgun again," I accused.

He showed fang.

"Riding shotgun is good for you," I told Quicksilver. "Save your footpads for later."

Dolly's engine choked for a moment, but revved high and hard when I peeled out of the lot into the dark and stormy night.

"You never knew these WTCH folk," I commented.

Quicksilver remained mum and curled his claws into the front seat upholstery. I cringed, but kept silent. My mind started toting up losses to motivate my righteous anger. Achilles. My job. My house. My history.

The streets were eerily deserted, so I ran about a dozen red lights, feeling like a ghost.

"We've got to take whoever's there down," I told Quicksilver. "They would put orphans like us up for adoption in a cage," I added, in terms he would relate to.

He growled.

"They are so wrong." I kept up a running dialogue as I pushed Dolly up to seventy-five on the abandoned city streets. Ric would be proud. "They sold out the serious profession of The News, of informing the community, for impure greed. Sheena just wanted blackmail money for giving bad weather to good people and good weather to bad people. Undead Ted was a lame tool. Literally. El Demonio could plant his shills in management and hide the fact that Wichita was becoming a drug-smuggling hub.

"Now the broadcast capabilities of WTCH-TV can multiply the powers of all the southeast Kansas weather witches. We have to cut the power to the tower. Any ideas?"

Quicksilver lifted his furred throat and howled at the three-quarter moon peeking between the gathering storm clouds.

"I'm glad we see eye-to-eye on the storm," I said. "It generates a lot of power that's not answerable to anybody but Mother Nature. Let's hope we can tap that."

By the time I cruised Dolly through the WTCH parking lot, the cloud bank had sped to meet us so fast that I could see only darkness above the tree line, and hear only the wind hissing and the lightning spitting.

Most of the cars and vans were gone. Storm-chasing, I hoped. That's what real news people would do. I was after unreal news people. Only Undead Ted's Prius and Sheena's vintage iridescent pink Geo Storm were still there.

Dolly's headlights spotted someone hunched at the driver's side of Sheena's Storm, trying to break in.

"Undead Ted." I hailed him as I pulled Dolly alongside, sandwiching his body between her hefty black side and the Storm.

"Don't call me that," he responded. "And your car is creasing my best suit."

"Where's Sheena?"

"You don't want to go in there, Delilah. Some kind of crazy feminist rave is going down. I had no idea Sheena was so invested in 'career at any price.' She's got all her gal pals doing the Macarena around a Crock-Pot in the station kitchen. When I heard their chant was calling for 'eye of Newt Gingrich' and a 'samp of vamp,' I got the hell out. I think that crazy Slo-mo Eddie is hunkered down filming it all."

Go, Eddie, go. He'd win the YouTube viral sweepstakes of the week with that footage. That would out Sheena's secret coven.

"Sheena alone has power to skew the weather," I told Undead Ted, "but not to brew up a megastorm like this."

He joined me in looking up at the roiling blue-black sky.

"I'm sorry, Delilah," he said. "For what it's worth, I really did have the hots for your blood type. And I was right that you'd taste like clarified blue blood. Awesomely rare."

A gourmand vampire? *Euww.*

"What do you want in Sheena's car?" I asked.

He nodded at two briefcases on the floor mat. "My share."

"Forget it," I said. "I'm shutting Sheena down. You don't want to ever show your sorry face in Kansas again."

He scrambled into his Prius and lurched away at top speed.

As he left, I spotted a sudden hailstorm heading for us through the lot. Sheena was still watching the exterior. No way was that witch going to ice-blast the pristine finish on my vintage car. Taking my job and my rental house was one thing, but Dolly was *family.*

Also pretty much Detroit tank.

I gunned her over the curb and the lawn, cutting across to the concrete canopy sheltering the station's main entrance. The hailstorm passed over, tinkling down a few stray ice crystals.

Now that Dolly was safely parked out of the elements, Quick and I headed into the eerily rainless storm for the broadcast tower.

I'd always taken this five-hundred-foot Eiffelesque structure at the station's side for granted. Now, it was scary. A fan of lightning bolts as tall as the tower itself grew from its top, glowing so white-hot the tendrils looked pink against the night sky.

The tower sat on a concrete pad next to a shack unsavory enough to house an illegal still. Dozens of thin guy wires anchored the mass for hundreds of feet around. Toppling the tower would be impossible. Cutting off the dark artery of cable that ran up it would not, but this electrical storm could ground itself through me, a process called electrocution. I so wished I had paid more attention in those required science classes. Luckily, it wasn't raining. Yet.

Maybe that was why the silver familiar wasn't morphing into something handy like a hedge trimmer or hatchet or a hacksaw; using it would kill me. Or it just didn't do yard work.

Quick's sharp bark drew me around the shack's side to where the metal conduit housing the cable met ground to run into the shack. Simple. Cut the power to the tower by hacking the conduit and interior cable in half. I needed a real tool. . . .

The shack's exterior toolbox was filled with goodies I pawed through by lightning flash. If I had a hammer. . . . I picked up one with a rubberized handle. It wasn't suitable for cutting a coax but reminded me that tools around here would need insulated handles. I finally lifted up an awesome little Tin Man hatchet with a wooden haft.

Hoping that the nonmetal handle would interrupt a lethal electrical shock, in seconds I was hacking at the conduit like a demented ax murderer. I'd cut through the outer metal and was denting the rubber insulation when Quicksilver growled and rushed something behind me.

Sheena stood screaming beside me, her blond hair flaring in the wind to show her brunet roots. "Stop that, Street! That hacking is giving me a throbbing headache."

I ignored her and kept slinging my hatchet, counting on Quicksilver to keep her at bay.

Suddenly a hurricane gust of wind lifted me off my feet while Sheena yanked me back by my windblown hair. The hatchet flew from my hand into the dark as Sheena and I fell struggling on the concrete. Another lightning flash showed Quicksilver nosing at the half-cut-through cable.

No! He could electrocute himself. I kneed Sheena in the stomach and swung her off me by her hair, struggling to my feet in the straight skirt and heels. I'd never wear a business suit anywhere again.

"Quicksilver," I screamed. *"Leave kitty!"*

Everything happened in jerky slow motion, as if lit by a nightclub strobe light.

Quicksilver regarded me with calm, stubborn doggy inaction.

By the next flash, Quicksilver had lifted a leg.

A rear leg.

I shut my eyes.

"Quick, no!" Water would short out the cable, of course, but Quicksilver would be fried.

Sheena was clawing at my skirt to pull me back down, but I back-kicked her away and charged for Quicksilver . . .

Just as lightning flashed and showed his hair snapping with static into a gorgeous electric-blue halo, leaping toward me . . .

As the tower-top lightning streaked to ground with the sound of berserk electrical snapping. The wet cable shorted out the tower, making it a dazzling firecracker flaring, and then fading to disappear against the night sky.

Sheena was moaning behind me. "You witch! My coven's been grounded. You've broken my perfect storm."

Quicksilver, still looking twice his normal size, regarded me with calm, stubborn doggy inaction. I reached my fingers to his punk-rock coat, and got a nasty little shock.

That's all. He'd been smart enough to piss and run before the current could connect. We turned to bustle back to Emerald City.

Halfway to the parking lot, Sheena caught up to us. She must have been planning a quick getaway too.

"Street!" she shouted. "Wait. What have you done to my car?" she screamed. "Where is my Storm?"

I looked at the parking lot. Lightning had struck the small car into a twisted mass of blackened metal with a burnt pile in the middle.

"My money!" Sheena wailed, running to the wreckage to claw at the remains.

"Will *she* ruin her perfect manicure clawing for those burnt bills?" I said to Quicksilver. "Money is the root of all evil."

I ran to the station portico to jump behind Dolly's steering wheel as Quicksilver took the passenger side, having done his business and being ready to leave. I tried to call Ric, but my cell phone had been fried. Better it than me or Quicksilver.

"And I think your whole perfect storm is going south," I yelled to Sheena as we sped down the exit road.

Chapter Twenty-eight

I HAD TO watch for the broken glass in the station drive-way, so it wasn't until we were almost at the street that I looked up at the sky again. I glimpsed Emerald City's towers coated in heat lightning, the highest point practically touching the threatening storm clouds.

Without the weather witches adding harassing phenomena to the storm, it had boiled down to a fixed, churning vortex spinning fog and lightning and darkness around the Emerald City towers, which were being swarmed by climbing hordes of El Demonio's zombies, swinging like disintegrating apes up the glittering slick green sides on thin steel guy wires. Talk about flying monkeys.

When had El Demonio and his crew besieged Emerald City?

I may have disabled the broadcast tower, but Emerald City *was* WTCH-TV now, threatened by an evil new power, and there was no longer any coaxial cable to fall victim to Quicksilver's bladder magic.

By going to the ground to take out the WTCH-TV tower, I'd put an unbridgeable gulf between myself and my stranded allies in the Emerald City towers.

I drove up to the deserted parking lot with despair in my soul.

The storm was so ferocious and high.

I was so isolated below.

There were so many fierce, hungry zombies in the many stories between.

I needed to rejoin Ric in Snow's suite. I had a lobby to cross and an elevator to get into, with dog. I parked Dolly away from any trees that could fall on her, in a dark part of the Emerald City lot.

Slipping around the side of the building, I noticed that the storm-green light distorted colors, making what was dark blacker, what was sickly yellow-green paler. So I was glad for the dark navy shoes and suit I wore and only wished I had pants. Even Quicksilver's crisp gray and cream coat looked jaundiced, like a . . . an absinthe-toned CinSim.

I peeked in the first lobby window. Had the chupacabra come back?

No, it was El Demonio himself lounging on a visitor's chair, sending tremors down his thirty-foot bullwhip so it twitched like an impatient tail. The light gave his clothing and skin a greenish reptilian cast. His squinty black eyes were bloodshot enough to match the chupacabra's. I wondered if the man who'd been surnamed Torbellino had disappeared entirely into El Demonio over the past twenty years, if the Millennium Revelation had brought out a true demon in him.

The lobby bodies had been piled in a corner, where a few limbless zombies chewed frantically on the remains. I suspected they had fallen during the assault on the towers and had broken off too much to keep going at anything but devouring, so they'd been relegated to the "clean-up" crew.

Other thugs sat around with the head man, drinking from liquor bottles. An empty one of Old Crow rolled back and forth on the floor as the storm shook the building.

Toto came skittering through the ruins, sniffing for the

yellow brick road. A thug pulled out a semiautomatic, but although the bullet sprayed green splinters from the recycled glass floor, the small black flash disappeared behind another chair.

"Where is that vicious little dog?" a woman's shrill voice demanded. "I'll show that Dorothy." Almira Gulch came stomping through in her old-maid dress and ridiculous crushed black straw stovepipe hat, a basket over her arm. "That dog needs to be put away."

"You got it, lady," drawled one of Torbellino's men.

She turned on the boss man after stepping daintily over his bull-hide tail. "You, sir, look like a man of authority. I want you to put that dog in a cage and that stupid girl Dorothy who let it bite me in jail."

The thug who'd shot at Toto lifted the gun, but Torbellino raised a lazy hand.

"Don't waste your ammunition. These things aren't real."

"They're real nuisances," the guy answered, taking a bead on Miss Almira Gulch's hat.

"I said, don't," Torbellino ordered through gritted teeth. "This isn't a carnival shooting gallery. This is our Armageddon, ass. Either grow or die, and those snoops on our Kansas drug-drives are threatening my operation going international. We'd be outa here with our prize if some damned necromancer hadn't turned all the elevator wires to silver."

"But, boss, you *want* this silver thingamajiggy."

"I want the *power* of the ultimate Silver Zombie. I've had these cheap Mexican models for the digging up, sure, for decades. But the Silver Zombie would be able to find and dig up whole armies of new undead meth-heads. I'd be King of the Zombies. I could run this continent. Hell, I could run this hemisphere with that one heavy-metal piece on the crime game board."

"I still don't get it."

"You don't need to. If the weather witches' storm doesn't knock those holdouts out of their pretty glass tower, our zombie cattle-drivers will finally reach the top and throw them off. It's just bad luck some rich guy made off with the Silver Zombie before we did."

"Won't all this throwing off and knocking off lose you the Silver Zombie?"

"Nope. No more than your bullet can kill these kinky CinSims running around here. They're zombies too and already dead."

"But they . . . look normal and talk and wear clothes and don't eat anybody's brains. That one there acts just like my Aunt Clara and I'd really like to clean her clock. One shot, boss, please?"

Almira was heading through again, like the clockwork CinSim she was and would be until she became a full-fledged hotel-casino attraction and some of the actress underneath her, Margaret Hamilton, a perfectly nice lady, came out to soften the film persona.

"Shut up," El Demonio shouted, "or you'll end up in my local body farm and get raised to run with the cattle, like these stupid zombies. Don't push me. I really need a better grade of zombie."

Thanks to the broken door, I'd heard everything. I parted my Green Room–permed hair and pulled it forward into two pigtails. The silver familiar obligingly split and clipped each tail into place.

I played director and gave Quicksilver a short but key nonspeaking role.

The moment Miss Gulch vanished, I nodded at my dog.

Quick padded silently through the broken door and slunk around the furniture so he could appear right behind El Demonio's chair.

Toto zipped out again, thanks to Miss Gulch's absence. While the men's eyes were automatically drawn to the streaking little dog, I eased on down the lobby's trashed yellow brick road and into the armed thugs' view.

Interacting with them at just the right level was the biggest difficulty.

"Where has my little dog gone?" I said sadly. "That awful witch in the even more awful hat wants to take him away to be killed."

"Say, are you Dorothy?" one guy asked. "You came through here before. You should be in the storm shelter."

"Oh, dear, I've got to find my dog first. And then I'll go."

By now I had edged over and past Torbellino's whip and was even with his chair.

Quick whisked out from behind the chair and ran into the hall.

"There he is," I cried, dashing after him.

"Hey, boss," the dazed thug was saying. "This whole scene looks more like that Alice down the rabbit hole thing, only with dogs."

I heard the real Toto following our trail, *arf*ing all the way.

"Say I can shoot this one, please."

No one or no thing guarded the elevator bank. I pressed a button and hoped.

"You, there. Dorothy. I want that dog!"

Miss Gulch didn't seem to notice Toto had added a hundred and forty-six pounds. Or that Dorothy had added a bust and a business suit. Like feral zombies, feral CinSims seemed to degrade. I was getting a whole new insight on CinSims, but probably wouldn't live long enough to come to any conclusions but my own.

"Shaddup in the hall," came from the office area. This order was followed by a sharp crack of a whip.

"I'm not Dorothy," I told Almira, "and your hat is horrible."

"Well, of all the nerve, you young whippersnapper. You'll be sorry."

The elevator doors opened . . . on another CinSim, garbed in checked pants, brocaded vest, and black hat.

"Almira Gulch," he said, "you're a mean, wicked woman. I'll see Dorothy home before the big storm turns into a tornado. You'd better find your bicycle and ride like Hell for home yourself. Come on, Dorothy, and your big dog too. There's no time to be lost."

Professor Marvel grabbed my arm to hustle me into the elevator car, with Quick behind me turning to snap at Almira Gulch to stay behind.

"This is very kind of you," I told my CinSim escort, "but I hear the elevator cables don't work."

"Not for *their* kind. I'll have you know, young lady, I have been to Kansas City in my travels, where everything is up-to-date, and have ridden in these new-fangled things called elevators for years. Oh my, I have ridden in even more exciting aerial transportation, my dear. Now. Up, up, and away."

We did indeed whoosh upward in a working elevator.

Chapter Twenty-nine

A PERFECTLY SOUND Ben Hassard awaited us in the penthouse suite entry hall, although he wore a roomy Asian robe over his trousers.

"I'm so relieved that you and the dog made it past those vicious criminals, Miss Street," Hassard said. "Who's this guy?"

"No one to worry about at all," said Professor Marvel, sketching a bow. "I must leave now. I'm expected in a storm cellar. Or was it a storm?"

The doors automatically closed on him. The future Wizard of Oz was running out on me, just as he had on Dorothy, at the end.

"Another CinSim," Ben, er, marveled. "I must say they do put on a show, popping up here and there. Glad you look hale and hearty. Tallgrass and the other FBI man and Mr. Christopher are conferring in the screening room."

"Screening room? What are they doing there?"

After my impulsive exit, I'd expected a warmer welcome back.

I followed Quicksilver into the main room and saw the storm churning like the contents of a giant blender outside the glass doors to the balcony. It sounded as loud up here too.

Ben Hassard followed, apologizing. "There's something wrong about the film I sold Mr. Christopher. I'm afraid it's the source of all my troubles. That demonic mobster wants something on it. Perhaps some hidden material that's incriminating."

I had no time to disabuse Hassard of his relatively safe and normal worldview as I headed for the home theater, opening the double doors so all three could enter at once, Hassard, Quicksilver, and I.

The movie was unreeling, but standing silhouettes obscured most of the screen.

"So I get it's a priceless piece of film history," Ric was arguing. "Am I supposed to believe you just wanted it as a collector? A little something the Mexican drug cartels were so hot to have they'd torture and kill for it?"

Snow's powerful stage voice sounded weary, as if Ric had been grilling him for a long time.

"I've told you, Montoya. I'm planning to model the centerpiece of my billion-dollar Inferno Hotel and Casino expansion on the look of this film. It cost almost three million dollars to produce in 1927, a phenomenal amount for the time, and I plan to *re*produce the sets in reality at a phenomenal amount for our time. The film is a guide, but also the crown jewel of my new multientertainment facility. I have no idea why an international thug like Torbellino would want a cultural icon such as *Metropolis*."

I could hear Ric's exasperated sigh from the doorway as he turned back to view the silent film. "There must be something *in* the film that will make El Demonio richer and more powerful. Nothing else motivates him." I saw his profile turn toward Snow's. "Or Vegas moguls like you."

Snow's silhouetted shoulders shrugged. I recognized the lines of his jacket, but wondered if Ric had seen his albino throat bearing the telltale bruise—in his case—of an angrily returned paranormal kiss.

Oh, gosh. Did lips leave recognizable prints too? I'd left

enough Midnight Cherry Shimmer on Ric during this trip for him to recognize the pattern, if so.

Tallgrass was sitting in one of the aisle seats actually watching the film, so Quicksilver trotted down the shallow stairs to sit beside him.

Ric turned back in a flash. "Delilah? You're safe and back."

He strode to the doors to embrace me. "We saw the lightning fizzle out, so I figured you and Quick were all right even though we couldn't reach your cell phone. The WTCH tower is down?"

"Still standing but shorted out. Dead. The tornado the broken coven summoned is still threatening Emerald City and so is the Wendigo. And Tallgrass, you might want to look into Lili West at the local Sunset City, when this is all done. I think she's the head weather witch around here."

Ric laughed and pulled me closer as Tallgrass looked on, shocked.

"You did some A-one detecting on your solo day in town, Del. And El Demonio and his men in the lobby? How'd you get past them?"

"By being born Black Irish and passing for a CinSim. They're not too tuned into the vintage motion-picture world. They mistook Quick and me for Dorothy and Toto, who are still running loose down there."

Snow's brief bark of laughter startled us.

"What's funny about Delilah being trapped between a supernatural storm and a horde of zombies, Christophe?" Ric demanded.

"This 'Demon' of yours, like all brutal and greedy humans, is also stupid. What would he do with a piece of rare film like *Metropolis*? He'd be too ignorant to even exploit its characters as CinSims, and the only truly valuable one, the only commercially sexy one, so to speak, is the woman-made-robot."

I resented Snow making light of the monster who'd controlled Ric's childhood. I had to say something.

"El Demonio lives to torture and kill, with drugs and drug money and with his own hand. I think you can imagine what more than three hundred strokes of his bullwhip would feel like."

"Ah." Snow left the shadows to come and face me. "You make that experience so very vivid, Miss Street. Thanks for educating me."

Sunglasses don't offer much eye contact, so I stared at his throat. A white silk aviator scarf, like those he gave away at the end of his rock concerts, concealed the place my mouth had bruised.

Oh, this was awkward.

That's what you get for confusing sex with revenge, Irma twitted me. *You owe him again. That look is so dashing young Howard Hughes on him, don't you think?*

She couldn't have repulsed me more, which got my brain in gear.

"Snow's right, though," I said, walking past him and Ric to face the movie screen. "I can see that Torbellino would like the same things the Nazis did about this film. The jerky, robotlike workers slaving away belowground like zombies twelve hours a day. The masters lording it in their gleaming towers like Vegas moguls. It's El Demonio's hidden zombie empire, in a way."

"He didn't covet this film for sentimental reasons, Miss Street," Snow said. "It isn't as if he'd need an Oscar award for Best Exploitation of Humankind he could display on a shelf."

Oscar. Hollywood's prized golden statuette.

The movie screen even now was revealing the passionate young girl and worker's salvation, Maria, being "processed" by the masters into a gleaming, unemotional robot, the triumph of scientific method over humanity, losing her life and her heroic young lover. Speaking of which . . .

"Ric."

"Here, Delilah." He stepped to my side. "What is it?"

"Did . . . you turn the elevator cables silver so the zombies couldn't climb them inside the Emerald City towers?"

"Silver has much mojo," Tallgrass said, his voice definitive in the darkness as the unwinding film flickered over all our faces. "Dog has silver on his collar. Delilah Street wears silver. *Mi amigo* has been reborn with the Silver Eye."

"I think silver controls zombies," Ric said. "At least it seems to since I've acquired the vision."

"Silver killed vampires in the old lore, as well as werewolves," Snow mused, as if contributing to the campfire ghost stories.

I was feeling as weary as he sounded. "And black-and-white film used enough silver nitrate that many classic movies were destroyed to strip the silver from them. Is there any way El Demonio could—"

I noticed, in the meantime, that Ric had begun moving slowly down the shallow stairs toward the movie screen, as if in a trance.

"This is one of the most luminous films I've ever seen," he said. "No wonder no complete versions could be found. They would have yielded too much silver to save. And the robot, she's a moon goddess for a technological age. Look at her. She's all silver, an armored Joan of Arc. Think of the concentrated aura her image would have on the black film strip. She'd be blinding. An angel of light."

He walked right up to the screen as if hypnotized, or hypnotizing.

And the silver robot moved to meet him where pixel or plasma met flesh and blood. Ric reached out a hand and a robotic arm lifted to touch a silver gauntlet to his fingers.

The theme of the film was what Lilah West had said about work and art and passion: "The heart lies between the hand and the head."

Ric's hand guided the silver robot as if leading her in a gavotte as she stepped out of the film and into the room, jerkily glancing around like Frankenstein's suddenly alive bride. Life-size, like a real girl.

We all watched, stricken to stone by Silver Screen lightning.

I knew Ric had found and raised zombies since he was a toddler.

Now he'd raised the first CinSim never touched by the Immortality Mob, or bonded to any imported human corpse. One only and wholly itself. Herself. The Eve of zombies. The Silver Zombie supreme. The supernaturally scientific creature El Demonio must have wanted to conjure himself, that he could somehow use to raise and control and master a worldwide zombie empire.

"Master?" she said in a flat, dead tone viewers of the silent film had never heard.

To Ric.

Oooh, Irma bemoaned in my ear. *We have got one hot little Roomba robot vacuum cleaner on our hands. Master? I wonder if she does dudes. Kiss your romantic aspirations good-bye.*

Chapter Thirty

"Now," said Snow, "that we know what Torbellino wants, we have the key to a battle plan. Mr. Tallgrass."

We had adjourned to the living room.

"Yes?" Tallgrass advanced, Quicksilver by his side.

Snow said, "I can project the image of the Silver Zombie face ten stories high on the black storm clouds."

"That'll be just a shadow of the real thing," I objected. "Will it project any silver power on its own?"

"Some," Ric thought.

"It doesn't matter," Snow decreed. "It'll have the power to amaze and distract the drug lord's forces. If I banish the weather witches' circling tornado," Snow asked Tallgrass, "can you turn back the Wendigo?"

"Possibly. With Quicksilver's help."

"Montoya?" Snow asked.

Ric shook himself back into sober reality and stepped forward, shadowed by his glitzy robot handmaiden.

Snow posed a second question. "You called the Silver Zombie to life. Do you have the power to banish El Demonio from the lobby and his Alpine zombies from the Emerald City walls?"

"My pleasure to try," Ric said.

"What about me?" I asked, feeling a very selfish Dorothy confronting a contrary wizard.

"Your choice," Snow said. "You can soar in the storm

clouds with me or fight in the basement barricades with Montoya and friend."

"Delilah's coming with me," Ric said.

I couldn't argue. We had the silver mojo, no matter how iffy it was at the moment. And I still had to figure out exactly what the robot Ric had seduced off the screen was.

Quicksilver had padded over to lick my wrist. I hadn't noticed until then that I'd scraped the skin raw in the battle to cut the WTCH coax cable. It healed as I watched.

"Good dog. I hope our efforts to get Kansas skies back to the clear blue color of your eyes work," I told him. "Is Tallgrass shaman enough to keep you safe?"

Quicksilver shifted from foot to foot like the Cowardly Lion being bashful. I realized he wanted to convey, modestly, that he was accompanying Tallgrass to protect him, as I intended to protect Ric.

Who, I wondered, would ever dare to protect Snow?

THERE WAS NO question that Ric's silver elevator cables worked for our party, if not zombies. Escorting the robot was like moving an automated department store mannequin to another floor.

When we didn't move, she didn't move. When we did, she marched in our wake.

What I found Mister-Spock "fascinating" was that I could see the climbing zombies loosen their grips on the guy wires and plummet to the ground as our see-through glass elevator car on the inside came even with them on the outside.

Maybe that's why Marriott Hotels favored glass lobby elevators and open atria. To keep the zombies down.

By the time we reached the lobby, the attacking

zombies, or what was left of them, were converging with us on Torbellino and his occupying minions.

Maria might be a zombie lord's magnet, but now she was a zombie repellent.

They circled the lower floor and the yellow brick road still speckled with blood. Their skeletal jaws shivered and chattered with anticipation, but either Ric or Maria broadcast a vibe that kept them outside an invisible circle of sorts.

Unfortunately, El Demonio was inside it. He wore the same black leather hat that had shaded his sinister features in the WTCH parking lot sunshine. Here, the unblinking narrowed black eyes and slit vertical nostrils over mercilessly thin lips accentuated his resemblance to a snake despite his solid, stocky body in an expensive, but sleazy shiny suit.

He was smoking a long, fat cigar and the air reeked.

He uncoiled from his cushy lobby chair, standing and drawing the whip butt to his right side.

Ric stepped forward to confront him.

I waited for the familiar to fill my hands with the twin whip butts it had produced on occasion, but it was . . . AWOL. Maria and I and all our silver mojo were suddenly no more than witnesses to the gunfight at the OK Corral.

Men! That's why they drive us nuts.

Torbellino lifted his right arm and the great long whip arched up to strike. The thing seemed as long as the Loch Ness monster, loops of braided leather that a rippling tidal wave of motion could propel until its distant, delicate tongue struck and seared flesh like a razor's edge.

Ric stared at the stirring serpent that seemed an extension of El Demonio's arm and hand. Under Ric's gaze, the dark braided leather so like scales lightened in color to shining silver. As the color lightened, the long whip grew heavy. El Demonio's arm started trembling while the whip's increasing weight dragged it down along his leg to the floor. He'd become a Midas whose gift was his curse.

A thirty-foot silver whip is far too heavy to wield.

Ric had no trouble walking up to his panting, disbelieving enemy and wresting the whip butt from his palsied grasp.

He cracked the whip against his leg, not lifting the ponderous silver train, but sending a psychic shiver that reached the end to lick out like a tongue and slash the huddled zombie bodies devouring each other into smaller and smaller pieces of bone and leathery skin and shreds of hair and lacerated eyeball.

El Demonio curled into himself like a cobra in a basket, all passive body and lethal, poisonous black eyes.

"You're done here in Kansas," Ric told him. "You've lost. You've lost the bulk of your zombies and your most murderous human underlings. Taking over the weather witches has exposed their petty crimes of abusing the weather for financial gain. Their national council and the local law will shut them down. The U.S.-Mexican drug cartel task force will track and bust all your smuggling operations from here to whatever hell you run home to in the southern hemisphere."

"They've been trying that for years, *hijo,*" Torbellino answered. "Law enforcement will never shut down the drug and zombie traffic. People want that. I'll have another zombie army in no time. I don't need just you to raise them, as when I started out. El Demonio is King of the Zombies."

"You don't understand," Ric said. "I'm taking your

title, and your zombies. I've raised the Silver Zombie to help me do it."

"That shiny wind-up toy?" He pointed behind me to Maria. "Once again you work for me, goat-boy. You raised her without my having to pay the Immortality Mob for it. I always knew you'd be useful someday; that's why I let you live. She has quite a silver suit of armor, but beware the demon within. Only I can bring it to proper life, and when I do . . . The Millennium Revelation has taught me a few more tricks since I brought you up, *hijo,* and I can bring you down again."

"Same here," Ric said calmly.

El Demonio seemed to turn purple with impotent rage and puff up like some venomous variety of snake. "I will kill you now."

"I'm not sure you can. That anyone can. I've been to death and back."

"I *am* death. Kill me, then," he ordered. "See if you can."

"Maybe. Sometime. When you've lost everything and it suits the world to be rid of you. For now I'll let you live. You may be useful someday. And you taught me that waiting is worse than death."

"Then wait some more, *hijo.*"

He took a last puff on the cigar, the exhaled smoke swirling around and around him, magnifying into a stifling cloud of fumes.

For a moment the smoke lifted to reveal a sated, red-eyed chupacabra puffing on El Demonio's cigar.

And then even the smoke was gone, leaving behind the sulfurous stench of a chupacabra.

I held my breath and darted to retrieve my frivolous bag of precious cargo from under the chair. The monster had been sitting right over it. Maybe the ruby slippers weakened his mojo.

Ric eyed it.

"Emerald City souvenir," I explained. "Girly stuff."

I gazed at the reeking spot still wreathed in smoke wisps.

"Magician or shape-shifter?" I asked.

"Or demon, finally living up to his name," Ric said with a shrug. "I'm more interested in stopping his operations than catching him. I could use some pure Kansas air."

Ric turned and went into the dark and, okay, stormy night.

I followed. And that damn Silver Zombie came tagging along right after us.

THE BATTLE FOR Bloody Kansas, 2013-style, was a good ole Fourth of July fireworks show in the sky over Wichita. Ric and I heard it heating up and looked overhead as if we were viewing a predicted eclipse of the moon, only we witnessed the clash of myths and monsters.

"Is that Christophe out on the balcony?" Ric asked. "Or Tallgrass?"

From this distance it was hard to tell who or what the wind-whipped figure was. I saw the figure's arm scatter something on the wind, a golden dust that blew away in expanding circles, like a whirlwind growing shape and form and gilt scales until the winged dragon Gargouille from a Paris distant in time and space was born again as a bright gold spiraling sunrise against the dark clouds.

Of course. I'd seen Snow strew these same ashes into the air beneath the Karnak Hotel to raise the French river dragon to aid in Ric's rescue. A mote of white reflected lightning near the dragon's great, lashing, metal-scaled head. Guess I'd missed a hell of a bucking dragon ride.

The dragon breathed fire against ice, warmth into cold and the Wendigo's scowling cloud-face. A vee of smaller bright-winged forces also shot through the blue-black darkness. Could it be? Gargoyles in formation from Our Lady of the Lake? And down the dark and twisting clouds came a foggy stream of running wolves with luminous eyes, Quicksilver at their forefront, snapping at the head of the Wendigo, biting it away in airy fangfuls.

And there? Did I see Almira Gulch and Lili West caught up in the twister, riding a tandem bicycle, and a longhorn steer spinning over and over with a chupacabra? My old bungalow tumbling like a die on a gambling table, and the huge glass bubble of a snow globe falling with a Wicked Queen in its icy heart?

Or was my subconscious just putting forms on phantasms of the mist?

The storm clouds dissipated into smoky tendrils as we watched and the moon shone through the fading shreds of storm, as silver and serene and blank as the face of Maria's robot.

RIC AND I strolled out to the far edge of the empty lot, where I checked to see that Dolly was still safely parked.

"Christophe owns this thing, doesn't he?" I asked Ric as Maria shadowed us. "I'm sure he'll be happy to take her off our hands."

"I don't know if that's possible," Ric said. "I called her into 3-D being."

"So she's just another Zobo you have to take responsibility for?"

He put an arm around me. "Not personally. It'll take an army to keep her out of the hands of the Immortality Mob, or your CinSim-obsessed landlord, Hector Nightwine, or El Demonio when he gets over losing Kansas and comes for Nevada."

"You had the bastard cornered."

"Not enough. The Silver Zombie holds some powerful potential for him we don't know about. I didn't kill him."

"Why couldn't you?" I asked.

"Is death good enough for *your* betrayers?"

"Maybe not, but it will come for them, with or without me."

"Exactly," he said.

"We've done enough this trip," I said.

"This trip," he agreed, "but the journey never ends."

Chapter Thirty-one

I TURNED FROM the green-mirrored penthouse suite bar, pleased to have seen only my reflection.

My gown's emerald-satin bias-cut skirt swirled around my legs as it wafted to display my ankles and the demure ruby red slippers I wore. So I was a bit Merry Christmas-y for summer, so sue me. This was my last personal appearance at Emerald City and I wanted to make it an occasion.

I craned my neck to see who had just committed a wolf whistle when my admittedly bare back was turned.

I faced a full house of suspects, so to speak.

The penthouse suite's long green leather sofa now seated three men, Ric, Leonard Tallgrass, and Ben Hassard.

Snow lounged in an emerald-velvet club chair and I was even less sure now that either he or Ric qualified simply as a man.

Quicksilver lounged in front of Tallgrass on the grass-green carpeting in his "Sphinx" position, belly down and forelegs extended. I knew he wasn't simply a dog.

The row of human male eyes were still dazzled from eyeing my gownless back with the silver familiar forming a long supple diamond dividing line down my spine. Even the familiar was putting on the dog tonight. Usually it was content to morph into rhinestones or Austrian crystals, since I was no jewelry snob.

Snow, of course, was seeing everything through very dark sunglasses.

I held up a tall, stemmed glass.

Finally. A little male attention that wasn't focused on the Silver Zombie standing at robotic attention behind a seated Ric. She sure did shine.

Normally, I'm not a show-off, but my new cocktail creation deserved a dramatic introduction. It flouted the Emerald City color scheme, being an opaque, faintly blue silver color, whereas absinthe was opaque green. A dash of vivid blue curaçao at the bottom made it something of a Tequila Sunrise in a blue mood and reflected a circle of electric blue at the cocktail's top rim.

"Gentlemen, and lady," I said. "Introducing the latest entry in *Delilah's Darkside Bar Book of Paranormally Phenomenal Cocktails,* I give you . . . the Silver Zombie."

The applause and whistles still didn't give away the lone wolf among them.

Snow wouldn't whistle even onstage. Ric had a mischievous streak but had been acting too possessive lately to draw other men's attention to me.

Leonard Tallgrass cultivated a poker face, but just might be up to it. Ben Hassard, patched up and very grateful to me, might have been unable to quell his enthusiasm.

Quicksilver had a lot of wolf in him, but was a howler by nature. And Maria, the *Metropolis* robot, lacked the necessary moving mouth parts.

We really must get this metal maiden a jazzier name, Irma said. *"I've Just Met a Robot Named Maria" won't burn out any lights on Broadway.*

Irma was right. She needed an updated name. Maybe Brigitte, for the teenage German actress who'd played both human and robot roles. Darn, sounded too sexy.

"What's in the drink?" Ben Hassard wanted to know.

"Three chilled ounces each of Fuse blueberry raspberry water champagne. An ounce of José Cuervo Silver tequila, an ounce and a half of lime vodka, an ounce of Alizé Bleu brandy, fruit and vodka mix, and a dash of blue curaçao dribbled down the inside of the glass so it sinks to the bottom."

"That sounds like enough goodies to make a zombie out of me," Ben said. "I'll drink to that."

So I gestured to the line of four Silver Zombies on the malachite bar top behind me.

Maria surprised me by being the first to approach, eerily noiseless for a silver metal woman. Actually, the film robot's likeness had been constructed from a new material, plastic wood, painted silver and bronze. Brigitte had to act as her own body double and wear the modern suit of armor even during nonspeaking camera shots, although it cut and bruised her body. How ironic it was, but not unlikely, that a film about abused workers would abuse its lead actress.

And that's when I realized that Maria was already a true CinSim. She *had* a built-in zombie body, that of the dead actress, Brigitte Helm. That is what—who—Ric had raised. How mind-bending was that? I thought I'd keep that insight to myself for a while.

Maria turned and, doing her C-3PO routine, brought a glass to . . . Ric.

The poor futuristic thing still thought like an Old World body servant. I was probably the only one in this room who knew that CinSims could "grow" beyond their original film personas, so I hoped this one got wise to the imprisoned superstar future Snow had in mind for her sooner rather than later.

Did the Inferno Hotel honcho somehow read or guess my rebellious wish?

Snow stood abruptly to claim two glasses from the bar and present them to Tallgrass and Hassard, now rising from their seats to accept them.

Snow stepped back to the bar, leaned against it, and took the last glass. Of course, from that strategic position he could better view his favorite part of my anatomy and simultaneously remind me of what I owed him. Three hundred and twenty-two bottles of beer on the wall . . . the paraphrased drinking song ran through my head. I'd never dreamed that stupid verse would have an erotic connection.

Heck, honey, Irma pointed out, *they all can eyeball your naked back with that mirror behind the bar.* She giggled. *Except your skin looks almost Wicked Witch of the West green. It matches your gown, but it's your least favorite color, and you're even wearing her shoes. Remember, Dorothy got the ruby slippers from the WWW's dead body through the Good Witch Glinda's intervention. Any message for the future in those facts?*

Maybe for Lilah West back in Vegas's Sunset City, I told Irma. She'd always wanted to play Glinda. Perhaps she finally did somehow, seeing to her wicked sister's coven of weather witches fall from grace here.

"A toast," Ben Hassard announced to those present, which did not include Irma.

He lifted his Silver Zombie. "To Emerald City's booming future, to the destruction of all my immortal enemies, and to the good fortune of all my unsuspected friends."

"To unsuspected friends."

The end of the phrase was murmured around the room as Ric moved beside me. His arm slipped around my bare waist, caressing me as he and I chimed glass rims. I felt my world had snapped back into place after a few moments of temporary insanity.

"Amor," he murmured against the glass rims that separated us.

"Amor," I repeated the toast, under my breath.

Meanwhile, the public self-congratulations continued.

"To unsuspected enemies and immortal friends," Snow rephrased Ben's toast, his sonorous voice wafting from behind my back. "May we always be able to tell them apart."

Quicksilver added a canine *arf* of agreement to that, and of course we all laughed, as the cast so often did at the end of so many movies.

Maria, the universally sought CinSim robot from *Metropolis,* did not laugh. She just stood there in aloof metal majesty and shone like the once and future star she was and would be.

Forever and ever.

Amen.

I was betting she was a virgin, poor thing.

Delilah's Darkside Inferno Bar Cocktail Menu

Silver Zombie
Invented in *Silver Zombie*

We have got one hot little Roomba robot vacuum cleaner on our hands. Master? I wonder if she does dudes.
—Irma, Delilah's alter ego, in *Silver Zombie*

    3 ounces chilled Fuse blueberry raspberry bottled water
    3 ounces chilled lemon-lime sparkling bottled water or
      champagne
    1 ounce José Cuervo Silver tequila
    1½ ounces lime vodka
    1 ounce Alizé Bleu with vodka, cognac, and tropical fruit

Combine all ingredients, then dribble a dash of blue curaçao down the inside of the glass to sink to the bottom. Be careful that *you* don't sink to the bottom in the snaré of the real Silver Zombie.

Vampire Sunrise
Invented in *Vampire Sunrise*

"Umm. Subtle yet spicy . . . for modern women like us."
—Psychic psychologist Helena Troy Burnside in *Vampire Sunrise*

6 ice cubes
1½ ounces pepper vodka
½ ounce DeKuyper "Hot Damn!" hot cinnamon schnapps
4–7 ounces orange juice, well shaken
1 ounce Alizé Gold Passion orange cognac
½ to 1 ounce grenadine

Put ice cubes in 12-ounce highball glass. Pour in pepper vodka and cinnamon schnapps, add orange juice to fill to desired level. Add Alizé. Last, pour in grenadine, which will settle to the bottom. Keep adding ice to this classic brunch eye-opener and daytime drink as it melts . . . for a longer, more sensual experience to the very last drop.

Brimstone Kiss
Invented in *Brimstone Kiss*

> *"Sounds like something you'd sip on all night long*
> *and I'd knock back in a couple slugs."*
> —Rick Blaine/Humphrey Bogart CinSim in *Brimstone Kiss*

2 jiggers Inferno Pepper Pot vodka
1 jigger DeKuyper "Hot Damn!" hot cinnamon schnapps
2 jiggers Alizé Red Passion
Jalapeño pepper slice (optional)
2 ounces champagne (for Version 2)

Version 1: Pour all ingredients into a martini shaker with ice. Shake gently. Pour into a martini glass garnished with jalapeño pepper slice. A hell of a drink!

Version 2: Pour all ingredients into a tall footed glass filled with ice. Stir well. Top off with champagne. A frothy but potent libation that might lead to pleasant damnation.

Albino Vampire

Invented in *Dancing with Werewolves*

"A sweet, seductive girly drink, but with unsuspected kick."
   —Werewolf mob enforcer Sansouci, in *Brimstone Kiss*

   1 ounce white crème de cacao
   1½ ounces vanilla Stolichnaya
   1 ounce Lady Godiva white chocolate liqueur
   ½ ounce Chambord raspberry liqueur
   (Other brands may be substituted)

Pour vodka and liqueurs except the raspberry in the order given and stir gently. Drizzle in the raspberry liqueur. Don't mix or stir. The raspberry liqueur will slowly sink to the bottom, so the white cocktail has a bloodred base (for a final taste sensation with bite).

Visit with Bogie and Bacall on *Key Largo*

For a click-on list of entertaining vintage film, actor, and Las Vegas sites, and film trailers, including for *Night of the Living Dead,* see the Delilah Street page at www.carolenelsondouglas.com.